THE GRAND VEESHALI

Praise for *The Grand Veeshali*

"Agent Leilani Falconi . . . always finds a way . . . usually with a touch of sarcastic wit, the right amount of disregard for authority, and the willingness to complete the mission at great personal sacrifice . . . No character is simply who, or what, they appear to be at first glance, and the human condition is woven into each character, allowing both the good and bad personality traits to add to the complexity of the story . . . Her reality aperture is widened to a massive extent as she discovers secrets kept from all but a select few in both universes . . . From one impossible situation to another, she and her team outpace and outwit antagonist after antagonist in a race to preserve the known galaxy."

—Bert Marley, USN—Master Chief (ret)
Explosive Ordnance Disposal

"Perception is reality. [Coffman-Porter's] attention to detail makes the characters believable and the story line captivating. [*The Grand Veeshali*] is a great way to step out of your own 'reality' and get lost in someone else's. #asrealasitgets."

—Justin Davis, Consolidated Training Group

THE GRAND VEESHALI

WENDI COFFMAN-PORTER

BROWN BOOKS
PUBLISHING GROUP

This is a work of fiction. Any similarity to real persons, living or dead, is coincidental and not intended by the author.

The Grand Veeshali

Brown Books Publishing Group
Dallas, TX/New York, NY
www.BrownBooks.com
(972) 381-0009

A New Era in Publishing®

Publisher's Cataloging-In-Publication Data
Names: Coffman-Porter, Wendi, author.
Title: The grand veeshali / Wendy Coffman-Porter.
Description: Dallas, TX ; New York, NY : Brown Books Publishing Group, 2022 | Series: Eldrilin
chronicles
Identifiers: ISBN: 9781612545875 (paperback) | LCCN: 2022938141
Subjects: LCSH: Assassination--Fiction. | Bounties--Fiction. | Women detectives--Fiction. |
Murder--Investigation--Fiction. | LCGFT: Detective and mystery fiction. | Action and adventure fiction. | BISAC: FICTION / Science Fiction / Action & Adventure. | FICTION / Science Fiction / Crime & Mystery.
Classification: LCC: PS3603.O322 G73 2022 | DDC: 813/.6--dc23

ISBN 978-1-61254-587-5
LCCN 2022938141

Printed in Canada
10 9 8 7 6 5 4 3 2 1

For more information or to contact the author, please go to www.WendiCoffmanPorter.com.

Freedom has become a four-letter word since I published my last book.

Therefore, I dedicate this book to the soldiers and first responders that risk everything for our freedom. Know that there are those of us who appreciate your sacrifice. And even though we can't be with you in person, we are beside you in spirit each time you step out your door to defend our right to be free.

PROLOGUE

"We have not paid you for over a hundred years just so you can ignore our orders," a tall female in ripped jeans, worn combat boots, and a thinning shirt that was four sizes too small for her snapped. Her bright blue hair and piercing black eyes flawlessly matched the chain jewelry and full body tattoos. She was at least six feet tall, but the man with his back to her was easily a head taller.

His broad shoulders were clad in a perfectly tailored Fadeeri silk suit. His long white hair was straight and flowed perfectly with his slow breathing. He leisurely turned to face the angry human female. His dark blue suit and bright blue-green tie contrasted spectacularly with his crystal blue eyes that flickered somewhat as he locked eyes with the woman.

High cheekbones and pointed ears marked him as an elari, but not just any mix-breed. The combination of height, features, build, and slightly shifting eye color marked him as one of the extremely rare Tre'dalmor—a long since abandoned caste of nobles that used to rule the elari species. Yet now they were nothing more than a random sighting here and there, much like the Mae'lacan and Fae'ana castes.

"Are you threatening me, Guest121?" His deep melodic voice carried easily across the plush office, even with the roar of the music from the nightclub bleeding through the walls.

The woman's fist balled at her side briefly before she leaned forward and slammed her fist down on the glass desk. "Mr. Reede, this is not a fucking game." When it didn't shatter, she arched both eyebrows and glanced down at it quickly before looking back up to meet his narrowing gaze.

The handsome elar's head tilted to the side as the irritation faded from his expression. He unclasped his hands from behind his back and lifted a hand into the air in front of him.

The woman gradually lifted off the ground, and her hands snapped to her throat as she clawed at the air around her neck. Her eyes widened in shock as she gasped, "How . . . ?"

"How dare you come into my world and threaten me! I don't care who you work for, Guest121, or should I say Imperial Marshall Dana Gainfield?" His face twisted into a sadistic grin.

Her body rotated in the air in front of him.

"You came to me, remember? Your emperor requested my help, not the other way around. It fascinates me how arrogant you people are. You think you are safe from my kind just because you put a firewall between us. It takes a hacker to defend against a hacker. Who do you think builds those firewalls? If we want access to you, we take it." He allowed his hand to fall to his side before moving it back behind his back and clasping it casually with the other hand.

The woman fell to the floor in a heap. She gasped for air for several silent moments before she turned an angry glare up at him. "I am not in a full-immersion suite. How did you do that?"

"And now you want intelligence from me? Very well, I will give it to you. But only because it will be funny when I do this to you again, after you install the upgrades." He reached forward and tapped his glass desktop.

A holographic three-dimensional image of a woman in a black suit with gloves and virtual reality goggles appeared above the desk and began to slowly rotate. Like the woman sitting on the ground in his office, both women were rubbing their necks in unison.

"All agents of the Kassian Empire are modified with cybernetic technology. They are told on recruitment that the cyberware will enhance their natural abilities. Such as making them faster, smarter, stronger, and so on. But in reality, it's to maintain control of you." He paused for dramatic effect, and his sadistic grin deepened as the woman's face paled somewhat. "So long as you have his hardware in your body, people like me will be able to make you do whatever we want."

A voice in the distance drew the elar's attention briefly as he looked off to his left at a digital display that only he could see. Returning his attention to the marshall, he arched a single eyebrow. "Do we understand each other now, Ms. Gainfield?"

"We do, but that doesn't change my orders." Pushing herself upright, she nodded.

The elar sighed. "I understand that Sargeras needs his report, but I am in the middle of something. Can it wait twenty-four hours?"

"Does it have anything to do with Dorthy and Falconi?"

The elar nodded. "Yes, as well as the aether intelligence he requested."

"Fine, Agent Reede. We will give you another twenty-four hours, but we will want results this time, not empty promises."

The elar rolled his eyes and shook his head. "Get the fuck out of my club, Dana."

The woman vanished just as the voice yelled again, "Damnit, BB! Where are you? We're getting overwhelmed!"

The elar waved his left hand in front of him in a wide arc, and the room shifted to a full situation room. The walls and air filled with data as more than a dozen displays fed him information on the current situation. To his right, a trid—or three dimensional holographic display—popped into reality with thousands of red dots and a little over two dozen green ones. The handsome elar smirked and made a complicated gesture in the air with his left hand, triggering a pre-programmed piece of homegrown software. Thousands of blue dots suddenly appeared on the display. The red dots shifted toward the new targets, giving the green dots some much-needed breathing room.

"Finally!" the first voice barked over the chorus of cheers. "Shut up and focus, people!"

In the digi-net, BB was king. Well, not really. No one is *king* in the digital space, but he was as close as any single individual could get. It was in the net that he found answers to secrets that most people would prefer didn't exist. Especially secrets of the differences between Kuldain and Aether. Digi-space was the only place where kuldain tech and aether tech operated in unison without clashing in a catastrophic event.

Kuldain tech was the home of the mundane: computers, spaceships, and every other technology imaginable ran off the typical anti-matter or hydrogen-based power systems. The aether, however, was different. There, everything powered by eldrich. Aethers referred to their computer systems as oracles and had no need of spaceships, since interplanetary travel was a tram system which utilized the massive rivers of eldrich that ran between the various astral bodies. These rivers created a massive web of eldrich, which tied together all living things.

BB turned his back on the trid and strolled across to a console in the room that looked utterly foreign to the rest of the technology in the room. There, above a board with several keys marked with letters and numbers, spun three crystals. Around the crystals, a web of purple and blue eldrich slowly ebbed and flowed. The resonant hum emitted by the crystals created an invisible harness that contained the energy, preventing it from arcing out and striking nearby people, but not completely sealing it.

In the beginning, BB was attracted to the beautiful patterns inherent in the energy, but when he touched it, the jolt had been far worse than anything he'd felt before. It was so powerful that it knocked his immersion tank offline for two days.

The crystal-based system was one of the first oracle designs. It operated much like a kuldain computer, but was almost three hundred times more powerful than a kuldain computer of the same size. He'd purchased it on the black market over fifty years ago for his research project—a project that was finally nearing completion. He was so close to the secret of eldrich tech that he could almost taste it. If he could just break that barrier, everything would change forever.

In the last few years, BB had the unique experience of seeing the aether in person. When Admiral Brigetta Gremm and the mysterious stranger attempted to overthrow the Kassian Emperor, BB found himself swept up in a thrilling roller coaster ride of intrigue, death, and life-altering sobriety. It gave him the additional push he needed to accelerate his research in a manner he'd never expected.

And if Leilani ever found out, she'd likely kill him for real, rather than let him figure it out. He cared for her like a little sister, but she was far too loyal to her emperor to let him complete this research. Although that wasn't the only secret he kept from Leilani. Ever since the government snatched her up when she was five years old, BB had been tasked with tracking Lei and reporting her progress to them. And apparently, her recent disappearance had agitated them enough to seek him out and demand that he tell them where she was and what she was doing. Though this time he wasn't sure he wanted to tell them the truth because the truth was bigger than anyone realized. Even Leilani herself.

He typed a key sequence into the pad, and a holographic image of a short, stocky dwarf with a beard filled with beads woven into the hair appeared and folded his arms across his broad chest.

"What do you want now?" the image barked at him.

"Status report."

"How many times do I have to tell you, I will let you know if I . . ." The image turned to the side as if it were looking at something that BB couldn't see. "Well, I'll be a troll's uncle. Scan complete. I have a lock on your file."

BB stood a little straighter as he resisted the urge to jump up and down in excitement. "That means it's here like I thought."

"Yes." The dwarf furrowed his bushy brows and pursed his lips in annoyance.

"Which means you owe me."

The hologram closed his eyes and remained silent.

"Fine," BB replied. "Join the others in the fight. Keep them all occupied while I grab the file. No one can know what we are really here for. When I am done, torch the place. Don't leave even one digital pixel standing."

"I won't harm the users and you know it. I am forbidden to harm sentient life forms." A massive battle-axe appeared on the hologram's shoulder, and he rocked it back and forth slightly as he spoke.

BB rolled his eyes. "What's the point of having an AI if it can't do the job?"

The dwarf tightened the grip on his axe and glared at the hacker.

"Fine. But leave nothing else standing. When you're done, meet me at the rendezvous. We have more work to do."

The holo slammed his fist into his chest with a deep thud. "Aye, sir. I will not fail."

"I know you won't. That's why we work well together." BB winked at the dwarf as they both vanished.

1

SECURITY THROUGH OBSCURITY

The soft jingle of the bell over the door drifted across the quiet pub. Ex-Agent Leilani Falconi looked up from the amber liquid in her hand and focused her soft brown eyes on the orange dots that appeared in the air in front of her. Orange meant armed and dangerous, something which wasn't typical for this world. She slid the glass of liquid away from her and pushed her long black braid over her shoulder. The taut muscles across her back flexed, then relaxed as she waited, without turning, for the newcomers to act.

She'd come to Mordin Prime to meet a contact who might have more information on her missing brother—the same brother that had agreed to help Leilani track down the real mastermind behind the Imperial assassination attempt, rather than Admiral Brigetta Gremm. Leilani had to give Gremm some of the credit. The woman had a vicious streak that made her a deserving scapegoat; however, she didn't have the intellect needed to pull off a crime of that magnitude. The Kassian government may have declared the case closed, but too many things still didn't add up.

The hairs on the back of her neck stood on end, warning her of the danger. In her internal Heads up Display, or HuD, the orange icons passed through the threshold into the pub and spread out around her.

Rotating on the stool to face them, Leilani furrowed her brow, resisting the urge to ball her fists in her lap. There were nine individuals in street clothes. Much like Leilani, they'd gone to great lengths to match the dirty, thin, and shoddily made attire found on the lower levels of Mordin Prime. Each of them carried, in plain sight, various firearms. These were professionals, and they were clearly looking for her.

It was early at the Thane's End Brewery; only the regulars were present. Some of them were employees, and others were just drunkards that called the pub home.

The last person to file into the pub was a tall, thin elar, with long silver hair and lavender-blue eyes. Her bone structure was finer than typical for humans, and her elongated ears ended at a fine point. Like the others, she wore attire that allowed her to fit in with the lower-class citizen on the lower levels of the planet.

Elari were a race from aether space, another realm, much like kuldain, but there, the technology evolved through the use of eldrich, rather than electromagnetic energy. It was common to find mythical creatures—such as elari, crodoc, trolls, and even giants—in the aether, which was why the Kassian emperor created the Imperial Investigative Service. Its job was to police the existence of aethers in kuldain space, but that was all over now. The senate disbanded the IIS after Admiral Gremm's failed coup attempt.

Now, the few agents that were left scattered to the corners of the empire—most of them in hiding. They blamed her for losing their livelihoods, and, in many cases, their freedom. The aether blamed her for the ongoing civil war in the aether city-states, and the Kassian government claimed she was a key witness in the case of *The Empire vs. Admiral Jason Dorthy*—something she refused to be.

This left Leilani feeling as if her universe were upside down, causing her to question everything and everyone she knew. To top it off, she was a pariah everywhere she went. Even her usual allies and informants refused to touch her, claiming that she was too hot to handle. And as more and more of the people associated with the coup vanished from existence, she'd found herself digging deeper and deeper into the dark crevices of her existence, looking for any information on what was happening and hiding from everyone . . . even the people she used to call friends.

This particular elar had developed a rather strained relationship with Leilani because of the Kamorian Incident on Dalori Eight several years earlier. Hundreds of thousands of innocent people died, and the two agents had taken the rap. Miraculously, neither of them ended up in prison.

Aleka lost her position as a field agent, and command demoted her to door duty. There, she passed the days as a glorified security guard at an aether-to-kuldain entry point.

Leilani, however, they banished to geloran space, under the guise of cross governmental training with a Kassian ally. She enjoyed the training, but she couldn't help but feel like a child banished from home for breaking something.

Glancing over her shoulder at the bartender, Leilani pointed her index finger toward the regular patrons. "Jon, you need to get them out of here."

The bartender was human. He almost always wore a button-up shirt with a vest—unusual attire for the locale, but it was also one of the many reasons she liked it here. He was over six feet tall and wide enough to play professional grav-ball. He reminded her of the common joke about a walking wall. His arms alone were as large as her thighs, and Leilani wasn't a small woman. He had no visible tattoos, but every once in a while, she saw the hint of one under his rolled-up sleeves.

The dark-haired bartender arched a single eyebrow but otherwise kept his face neutral as he wiped his hands on a towel and glanced toward the four human males sitting at a booth behind Leilani. They sat in the same booth every day, in front of the large window that displayed the pub's name.

Jon bobbed his head toward them before walking down to take Leilani's glass from the bar top without a word. He then turned his back on her and the new guests and strolled down the bar.

Shifting on her stool so she could see him out of the edge of her vision, Leilani arched a single eyebrow as the embossed mirror behind the top-shelf liquors lowered into the wall. Behind it was a rather impressive selection of weaponry, ammunition, and even a few small incendiary devices. They were all kuldain in make but nonetheless lethal.

Pulling a mark-twelve, high-velocity railgun free from its mount, Jon expertly checked the chamber and flicked off the safety. A normal person trying to fire that kind of weapon would shatter the bones in their shoulder, but something told Leilani he could handle it.

The assailants lifted their weapons toward her.

"Jon, that's overkill. I don't think our neighbors five floors down need to be involved in this." She returned her full attention to the newcomers as she chastised the bartender.

She heard him replace the weapon and withdraw something else. The loud clack, as he chambered a live round, told her that the smaller weapon was the Horton Legionnaire assault weapon. It was still too much for the situation, but at least it would only go through one building before stopping.

When several other similar sounds echoed behind her, she shifted on her stool to see the other regular patrons holding their own assault rifles. They slid out of their booths and took up defensive positions.

Her mind flashed back to that morning. The *Imperial Times Review* displayed an image of the courtroom where the investigation into treason allegations against Admiral Jason Dorthy was being held. The trial had been going on for months now, and this wasn't the first time it had made the cover of the various news outlets. But this image wasn't like the others. This time, a blotchy red mist covered the witness stand and the wall behind it. The title read:

Admiral Jason Dorthy Assassinated!
Killer at large!

Leilani turned her attention to the elar standing just inside the closed door.

"Aleka?"

"You have no idea how long I've been waiting for an excuse to do this!" The beautiful lilt that was typically present in her ex-partner's voice was absent. Instead, her words dripped with hatred.

"I understand that you may have a problem with me, but we don't need to do this where people can get hurt."

In Leilani's HuD, her artificially intelligent oracle, Sarah, continued to track the nine combatants.

"You bitch!" The elar's fists balled at her sides. "How dare you give me permission to be angry with you!" Taking several steps forward, into the middle of the room, the elar pulled her weapon. "My life has been nothing but hell since I met you! And now, you've killed Dorthy!"

Leilani blinked several times. That was new information. Why would anyone think she killed her own commanding officer?

Aleka continued her tirade. "The one man that was constantly protecting you from your own fuck-ups! You should have thought of the consequences when you murdered him in cold blood! These people's blood will be on your hands! Not mine."

"I didn't kill anyone." Leilani grimaced; that was the wrong phase to say to this particular woman.

Based on tactics and weapon handling alone, it was likely that all nine of the assailants were ex-IIS officers, even though their standard-issue internal oracles weren't answering Sarah's queries.

Leilani lifted her hands, palms toward the hit team. "That may not be entirely accurate, I'll admit. But I didn't kill Dorthy. I have no reason to."

After the dismantling of IIS a year ago, Leilani spent a lot of personal time with Dorthy. Against all expectations, the two grew close. Too close, considering that he was being investigated for treason against the crown. She was there when the military burst into his home with a warrant for his arrest. No one was more hurt by his death than her.

She went to ground after the arrest, making it impossible for them to find her. Dorthy and Leilani both knew the game—politicians needed a scapegoat. The senate had pardoned Leilani for her actions in defending the crown, which left Dorthy to take the fall, but she had no intentions of allowing them to use her against her own commanding officer. That was nine months ago.

The elar's sidearm snapped up and leveled at Leilani's head. As Aleka's rage overrode her training, she took one too many steps toward her target.

"*Permission to raise shields, ma'am?*" Sarah's casual tone didn't entirely match the intense situation.

Leilani's internal oracle was much like a kuldain neural processor, but based on eldrich technology, rather than electromagnetic. So instead of the typical kuldain radio communications, the system used a different band to transmit on, one which only required thought to transmit, meaning that powerful emotions could periodically bleed through.

"*Negative,*" Leilani replied.

Deploying her shields would only ensure a firefight. She needed to at least try to save the elar from her own blind hatred. It was the least she could do for a woman she once considered a friend.

"He was testifying about how you'd become uncontrollable when you shot him, and you know it!" The almost unintelligible words came out as more of a screeching sound than actual speech.

Leilani grimaced. Maybe she didn't have a choice after all. Her friend had snapped.

Leilani cocked her head to the side as she considered Aleka's words. The only way anyone could have shot Dorthy while he was testifying in a secured room would have been with a portal generator, or PG, as the IIS labeled them in the top-secret reports . . . which made everything far more complicated.

"Aleka, I didn't shoot him. I swear." Leilani held her hands out, palms up. Energy swelled and crackled through her synapses as her combat systems spun up, boosting her speed and cognitive perceptions. She leaned to the side as Aleka squeezed the trigger, and a standard kuldain bullet leapt from the barrel pointed at her face. As it whizzed past, a sharp sting tore through her earlobe. In her HuD, a small percentage number flashed into existence: 99 percent.

Reaching forward with blinding speed, Leilani snatched Aleka's left wrist and, with a loud snap, forced the elar to drop the weapon.

Leilani ignored the pistol as it fell to the floor. It may only be a kuldain weapon, but no self-respecting IIS agent would even consider using a firearm without at least the basic biometric safety, and without Aleka's DNA, it wouldn't work.

Throwing herself to the floor, she swept her leg toward Aleka to get her out of the crossfire as bullets ripped through the air overhead in a deafening cacophony.

The spray of blood that splattered across Leilani caused her heart to sink, but she knew better than to check on the elar. If Aleka were alive, a gunshot wound wouldn't be enough to stop her from continuing her attack.

"*Analysis complete.*" Sarah's calm voice seemed oddly out of sync with the combat. "*Of the fourteen firearms in use, only one registers as aether in make. Shields will hold against the kuldain weaponry.*"

Leilani smirked as she leapt toward a nearby booth at the end of the bar and rolled into cover.

"Deploy armor!"

A bluish sheen snapped into place around her body and faded into her clothing. It was still there, but it was less noticeable once the deployment was complete.

"Armor deployed."

A round bounced off her shoulder, and a small part of her sighed in relief. Lei poked her head up to assess the scene. No one seemed to pay much attention to her. But then, she was unarmed and not trying to kill anyone . . . yet.

In the middle of the room, the beautiful elar lay covered in blood, unmoving. Forcing her attention past the body, Leilani scanned the rest of the room.

The rest of the combatants, however, were tucked behind upturned tables or booths that seemed unusually resistant to the bullets flying around the room.

"What the hell is this place?" she mumbled out loud to no one in particular.

Turning her attention to the padded booth in front of her, she poked the material with her finger. Sure enough, it was a fascinating mix of plastic and steel, made in a thin, somewhat flexible synth-weave. Typically, this technique was found in civilian body armor, but apparently it could also be used in armored furniture.

Above her, the sound of metal sliding across the lacquered wood caught her attention. She glanced upward as a pistol slid off the bar and into the air. The smooth arc shifted as gravity kicked in and it fell in her direction.

"Forward shields to maximum!"

"Shields at 200 percent."

Leilani snatched the pistol from midair as she stood. The weapon fired as fast as she pulled the trigger, each bullet hitting its mark with deadly precision. The lack of shields or defensive boosts struck her as odd. If these were IIS agents, they should have had something—armor, at the very least—but each round blew through their bodies and into the armored furniture behind them. The assailants crumpled to the floor and remained unmoving.

After the fourth body dropped to the ground, she spun to find only the pale-yellow dots in her HuD that identified the pub's regulars, whom, she now realized, were not typical Gerthali workers.

"Easy there, Leilani." Jon's voice was soft, as he lowered his own weapon and lifted his hands, palm out, toward her.

The regulars, however, kept their weapons trained on her as they waited to see what she would do next. Lei turned her attention to the bartender. The gun hanging from his harness was an aether weapon modified to look like a typical kuldain assault rifle. She hadn't noticed the telltales when he'd first picked it up, but then, her attention had been on Aleka.

Pivoting her stance, she pointed the barrel of the gun at the bartender. "Who are you?"

The regulars shifted their grips on their weapons, adjusting their weight to move quickly.

Beaming with a bright smile, Jon patted the aether weapon in his hand. "A friend of a friend. Same friend that sold me Francesca here."

Leilani lowered the weapon and furrowed her brow. "That's a geloran model. You know Jornis."

The bartender nodded. "He asked us to keep an eye on you while you waited for him."

"I'd say you fulfilled your end, then." She waved the pistol in her hand toward the bodies around the now bloody pub. "Did he say why he's late?"

"Nope. Sorry." The bartender shrugged and reached up to the weapon case behind the liquors. He replaced the rifle on its rack and triggered the mirror back into place.

The others slid their weapons into similar locations—under the tables and even inside hidden pockets under the booth seats. Then, as if nothing were out of the ordinary, two of them began dragging bodies into the back while the others righted tables and swept up shell casings.

"Want another drink?" Jon called from behind the bar.

Leilani sighed before bobbing her head and cautiously picking her way through the blood and mess until she found a stool that wasn't sprayed with a slick red mist.

As she slid onto it, she set the pistol on the bar top and looked down at her faded, and now bloodied, sweatshirt. Without a word, she pulled it over her head, careful not to let the blood make more of a mess than it already had.

Two men walked past her with the deceased elar carried between them, and Leilani frowned deeply. "Rest well, my friend. I'm sorry it ended this way."

A glass filled with amber liquid thumped onto the wooden bar next to her. Without looking up, she took a long swig and wiped the foam from her mouth. She stared deep into the liquid.

So much had happened in the last two years. Her last mission, while successful, had repercussions that would affect the Kassian Empire and everyone she knew for decades. It wasn't the first time she'd dealt with fallout after a mission, but that didn't mean it was any less traumatic. She was beginning to wonder if she was cursed or something. No matter where she went, people died. Half the time, she was the one that killed them, and now, she was on a backwater planet in the middle of nowhere, looking for someone who clearly didn't want to be found.

Mordin Prime was the largest planet in Gerthali System. It no longer had local flora or fauna. The entire planet was a single, massive city, its buildings reaching high into the atmosphere. Some were so tall that they employed space elevators to link into the network of space stations in orbit.

Most people that lived on Mordin Prime worked for the corporate mining company, Redmond Conglomerate, and almost all of them were trying to earn enough money to climb up to the next level. The most common dream of the locals was to eventually afford a ticket off-world, but even the most valuable employees rarely managed that miraculous feat.

Thane's End Brewery was out of sync with the rest of Mordin Prime, but it wasn't just because of the wood which had to be imported from another solar system, nor was it the antique brass fittings, armored furniture, or actual glass windows. Typically, anything that allowed someone to look outside was a prosee window—a digital representation that showed a visual recording of the outside, rather than actually being transparent.

The brewery, however, believed in the age-old adage of security through obscurity. The perfect example of which was the manual door that kept most would-be patrons out simply by existing. It was hilarious to watch groups of young patrons try to figure out why the door wasn't opening when they approached it. They even had one incompetent moron run at the door so hard that he left a bloody smear when his face slammed into the glass. That stunt won the uproarious patrons a free round of beers that night.

Leilani's main reason for frequenting this establishment every night for three months, however, was the microbrewery in the back. By the gods, she loved a wonderful homemade ale or beer.

The bell above the door jingled, and everyone in the room turned their attention to the newcomer. A tall, thin human with a long coat, greasy hair, and slightly widened eyes stepped into the pub and glanced around at the mess.

The bartender pointed to the door and shook his head, grimacing. "Someone lock that till we get this cleaned up."

The newcomer glanced furtively around the room, then settled his eyes on Leilani. A regular strode past the man and flipped a toggle, sliding the bolt into place and locking the door behind him.

Bobbing his head in understanding, the stranger took the cue and carefully picked his way through the mess to stand next to Leilani. "Money?"

"Info?" Leilani retorted.

He narrowed his eyes at her for several long seconds before finally reaching into his pocket to pull up a data-stick. "It's all here, but you won't like the result."

"Is he alive?"

The tall, greasy-haired human, with bony shoulders, reminded her of her brother. Then again, hackers often lived in virtual spaces, tucked safely away from the real world in makeshift rigs which, if they were lucky, gave them just enough intravenous nutrition to keep their brains alive, but not enough to sustain their bodies. The community called this man a "face." For whatever reason, he split his time between the real world and the virtual one. This allowed him to act as the physical representation for the collective of hackers known as the Black Dragon.

He shrugged and tossed his hands in the air, letting them fall to his sides with a soft, slapping noise. "We ain't got a clue. He was working with our people on a black site infiltration when he suddenly shouted something we couldn't understand and disappeared. We tried every trace we had—there's no sign of him. He literally vanished."

Leilani reached into the pocket at the front of her sweatshirt and pulled out a bundle of physical credits.

His hand snapped up and closed on the money, but as he tugged on it, she held on.

"What did he shout?"

"*Shoth mathail aethmansa.*" The man butchered the words, but she got the gist.

Leilani let go of the cash, and he tossed the stick on the bar before swiftly making his way to the door.

The largest of the regular patrons flicked the lock open as the hacker fled the bar. He then closed the door behind him and locked it before any of the people passing by outside noticed the gory mess inside.

Leilani returned her attention to her beer and took a long drink before slamming the heavy glass down on top of the data-stick. The cheap materials gave way to the heavy glass with a loud crunch.

"Great," she mumbled. "BB gets his greatest wish, leaving me stuck here with no useful intel. Typical." And now, apparently ex-IIS agents were willing to risk capture just to kill her for allegedly murdering a man over thirty solar systems away. Something about this wasn't right. If they stopped the coup, then why were the murders continuing? And why Dorthy? He was only the admiral in charge of her team. He knew little more than the politicians. They all received the same reports. She was the actual lead investigator.

"Alright, Sarah." Leilani triggered her internal oracle. *"Why Dorthy instead of me?"*

Operators, both in kuldain and aether space, had internal computer systems, or the aether equivalent called an oracle. The systems acted as tactical systems and analysts when the operator needed an infield advantage. The less direct connection to command the operator had, the more autonomous the system was.

"You didn't exactly stick around for them to kill you," Sarah chimed into her thoughts.

"Maybe, but it still feels wrong. I'm missing something, and I know it. Why is no one talking about the person who was giving Gremm orders?"

Her internal oracle remained silent as Leilani took another drink.

A touch on her elbow drew her out of her thoughts. Jon pointed to the display at the end of the bar.

The words "Breaking News" scrolled in large letters above the speaking reporter. Leilani stopped mid-drink as her picture flashed on the screen in her IIS uniform.

"Connecting for sound," Sarah said without prompting.

"We are getting the report now that the crown has officially issued a warrant for ex-Imperial Investigative Service Agent Leilani Falconi. She is wanted for the brutal assassination of Admiral Jason Dorthy. Dorthy was shot via the same technology used in the attempted assassination of Emperor Steven Sargeras, while in the middle of his testimony in front of the senate oversight committee."

The subtle air of excitement that she read in his eyes belied the reporter's somber demeanor. Reporters always loved a good manhunt; it was great for ratings.

She allowed her glass to drop to the bar with a loud clatter, spilling some of the amber liquid onto her hand and the counter.

"Seriously! Again?" Leilani slapped her palms down on the bar loudly.

Jon chuckled as he wiped off the bar under her cup. "We should get you out of sight. We may be secure, but we can't stop all the cameras walking by outside. Eventually one of them will pick you up."

Leilani's nostrils flared as her eyes narrowed. "No. I'm tired of fucking running."

The bartender folded his arms across his broad chest.

"Oh relax! I'm not saying I'm going to walk out into the crowd or anything, but if the local government wants to look for me, they'll find me. It won't matter where I hide." She picked up the glass and noticed that it was almost entirely empty. Downing the last gulp, she handed it back to him. "I just wish my damn ride would show up already," she grumbled.

Jon took the glass and slid it under the tap that held this week's experimental ale. "He just sent word that he's ten hours out."

Leilani took a deep breath and tugged lightly on the back of her neck, trying to relax her shoulders.

"If you don't want to go hang out in the office, how about a card game?"

Leilani smirked at him. "Gambling is illegal on Gerthali."

"And you're wanted for murder. What's your point? You want in or not?" He set the filled glass down in front of her.

Snatching it up, she took a long swig. "That sounds like the perfect end to the perfect day!"

2

LOST IN HIDING

Several hours later found Leilani aboard the long range geloran scout vessel *Hadu*, in the same private quarters she'd used when Dorthy assigned her to cross-train with the gelorans several years earlier. The typical crew complement of a scout ship this size was five or six, but government agents or spies like Jornis and Leilani typically preferred a solitary life.

"Good afternoon, Leilani." A warmhearted, melodic voice echoed throughout the room from speakers that weren't visible. The language was geloran, but it didn't matter—Leilani understood him.

"Hello, Hadu!" she beamed happily.

"It is wonderful to have you aboard again! The captain would be furious at me for saying this, but he's missed you."

Leilani sniggered. Unlike her own internal oracle system, Hadu, the ship's computer system, was a fully sentient system with citizen rights within geloran space. "Your secret is safe with me, Hadu."

"Well, technically it's *his* secret, not mine," the computer system teased.

She laughed. "Does the council know?"

"Of course not." The system sounded almost offended.

"That's probably a good thing."

She stripped off the disgusting clothes she'd bought off a homeless woman near her apartment and threw them into the recycler. She then stepped into the shower and tried to scrub the smell of Gerthali off her.

Aboard the typical spaceship, a hydro-shower was impractical. Generally, a spaceship deployed with the more energy—and space efficient—sonic-shower. But Leilani used the decadent geloran culture to her advantage, allowing the warm water to cascade down her back as she contemplated the history of the geloran people. At ELU—Eldrich Line University—the general education included the history of the various aether races, as well as cultural norms and physiology.

Gelorans were a race of entities that originated on the planet Ithanu, which in the language of the Elements meant "home" or "origin." It was once believed that all life began on Ithanu, which included aether and kuldain races. But as it typically happens when education expanded and understanding of the universe evolved, the various races that evolved on Ithanu realized they weren't alone in the universe like they originally believed. Life loves to live, and it was everywhere.

As the various races explored the galaxy, they left Ithanu behind. Eventually, it vanished into myth and rumor. If it ever existed for real, no one knows. The various races scattered throughout the galaxy. Then thousands of years later the cataclysm tore the aether realm from the kuldain. Mirroring each world in both realms and destroying almost everything in the process. The few that survived the event found themselves thrust into a dark age that is still hotly debated to this day. Gelorans, avoiding the chaos, opted to gather up their numbers and take to the stars in massive colony ships.

They colonized a world, far away from the humans, in kuldain space.

There was no documentation on the events that led up to the Geloran and Kassian war, but the treaty of Ka'vani is well documented . . . for those with the security clearance to see it, anyway.

As Lielani climbed out of the shower and dressed, she wondered what was next. She needed to find the cloaked man pulling Gremm's strings, but she was running out of sources and her partners were vanishing one by one. BB was off on his own projects, and she wasn't entirely sure when she'd see him again. Dorthy was dead. Even Rothar was gone, and no matter how hard she tried, she couldn't even get word into the aether, let alone go there in person. That was why she'd contacted Jornis. He had the only ship that she still had access to that could get here there.

As she considered the next steps, her mind recalled the last time she'd seen Dorthy alive.

"You can't have expected him to stay, Lei. Not with everything going on in the aether." Admiral Jason Dorthy poured a dark red liquid into two beautiful crystal glasses.

He may have been an older human, but his athleticism was unmistakable in the way he carried himself and the rippling muscles beneath his well-tailored clothing. He could easily stand toe-to-toe with a human in their twenties. If it weren't for the few extra wrinkles around his steel-blue eyes and pure white hair, there would be no indication that he wasn't a man in his prime.

The two of them stood in his library, like they'd done many times in the last few months. It was a decent-sized room with fifteen-foot ceilings and walls lined from floor to ceiling with books, except where Leilani stood near the enormous stone fireplace.

In a society so reliant on technology for everything, just being in the presence of so many books was inspiring. She'd often teased that he should require admission to enter his home—the entire thing was like a museum.

Dorthy picked up both glasses and strolled to where she was leaning against the fireplace mantel, slowly warming her side by the flickering flames.

"No, I suppose not." She took the drink and smelled it. It was strong, but oddly sweet. "What is this?"

"Something from home." He took a sip and sat in one of the overly padded chairs.

"Rothar was an excellent partner. I just didn't expect them to deport the aethers en masse like that." As she tasted the wonderful smelling liqueur, a wave of warmth rolled over her.

Wow. That is seriously strong.

Dorthy stared at his glass as he slowly swirled the liquid. "I'm not sure what to say."

Lei turned toward him and furrowed her brow.

When the senate officially disbanded the IIS, Dorthy changed. He seemed relieved. He'd relaxed immensely, and they'd spent a lot of time together. In the beginning, they got together as friends just to talk, but their relationship slowly evolved. The casual dinners grew into nights on the town, drinking, dancing, and just enjoying the freedom. Until finally, one night, they ended up back at his place for much more.

In the nine months that the government investigated Admiral Brigetta Gremm, Dorthy, and the IIS, the two of them never fought. Not even once.

She wasn't about to tell him, but she'd liked the new Dorthy.

"Why are they utterly ignoring the testimony of the hooded man giving Gremm orders?" Leilani asked.

Dorthy kept watching his drink as it slowly spun in his glass, his thoughts clearly elsewhere today.

"Jason?"

The use of his first name drew him back to the conversation. They locked eyes briefly. There was sadness there, and Leilani frowned.

"What's wrong?"

"Lei . . ." He stood and strode toward her, his brow furrowed deeply.

But before he could reach her, the doors to the library burst open, and Kassian marines in powered armor, with fully charged energy weapons, flooded into the room.

Dorthy kept his eyes locked with hers as he exhaled. "Lei, I'm so sorry."

"Admiral Jason Dorthy, you are hereby under arrest for treason!" a male voice called into the room over a loudspeaker built into the armor.

"Don't believe everything you see or hear," he whispered, his eyes still locked with hers. Lifting his glass to his lips, he downed the drink and strode to the small table next to his chair.

"On your knees!" the marine demanded. "Lace your fingers behind your head!"

"No need, gentlemen. I'll come quietly," Dorthy replied calmly, setting his glass on the table.

"Knees!"

The whine of several weapons warned of imminent fire.

Leilani set her drink on the mantel and raised a hand. "How about I cuff him for you? No need to humiliate him."

There was a brief pause before the man speaking finally reached to his belt and tossed her a pair of sealbands. An overreaction to be sure, but they were clearly not willing to argue the point.

She stepped up next to him and pursed her lips together. They'd both known this was coming, but that didn't make it any easier. No one survived a treason charge in Kass.

Dorthy held out both arms to her without a word.

As she touched the bands to his hands, the metal became liquid and grew, encasing his hands in a solid piece of metal. The metallic liquid continued up his arms to the elbows before finally stopping.

"Don't worry. You'll be out soon enough." She tried to smile, but it never reached her eyes, and she knew it.

"No, I won't. But don't worry about me. Get as far away from here as possible and find the missing piece of the puzzle."

Two marines strode forward and jerked him away from her.

The suit that had been barking orders turned its faceplate toward her. "Leilani Falconi, you are to remain on Coreward, or in Core System, until the trial of Admiral Jason Dorthy is complete."

"Of course." She smiled warmly at the officer.

The helmet nodded curtly as it marched off to join the others.

She'd left Coreward early the next morning before she could officially get summoned. It was simple work to ditch the Kassian marines that were monitoring her. The military was utterly unqualified to match skill with an IIS officer, especially an undercover agent. It was likely the reason the government had placed a standing warrant for all IIS officers. They claimed it was for debriefing, but afterward, the IIS agents vanished, never to be heard from again.

Leilani's pardon had given her a thin blanket of protection, but it wouldn't last forever.

That had been a little over fourteen months ago. Since then, Leilani received word that Melissa, the genius-kid on Leilani's team, along with several dozen other IIS agents, were killed on their way to decommission the IIS flag vessel, *IKS Eldrich Sun*. The official report stated catastrophic engine failure killed everyone aboard, but Leilani knew that the official reports were likely faked. Where the agents actually were? Leilani could only venture a guess. Like many other missing IIS agents, they'd likely gone deep underground.

Leilani, however, was constantly on the move, avoiding detection wherever possible, living among the dregs of society, and looking for a clue as to why someone would throw the aether and Kass into chaos. Something far deeper was happening here, and for the first time since joining the IIS, she was feeling helpless and alone.

She rubbed her face roughly and tried to ignore the nagging suspicion in the back of her mind that Dorthy's rather public execution was a new piece of the puzzle. With him dead, the government wouldn't be able to get their pound of flesh to feed to the masses. They would have to look deeper, or so she hoped.

Either that or they could decide she was the new target. It wouldn't be the first time they threw her under the tram, but she had no intentions of being caught. At least not until she found the mystery man.

"Pardon me, Leilani." Hadu's masculine voice chimed into her shower, drawing her attention back to the present.

"Yes, Hadu?"

"We are en route, and the captain is requesting your presence in the galley."

"Roger."

"Ma'am, we have just transitioned to aether space," said Sarah, marking the change in engine tone and the now active eldrich power matrix.

"Go figure. Do you know where we're headed?"

"No, ma'am. I am locked out of Hadu's systems, and he is not directly communicating with me."

Leilani groaned and rubbed her face. Apparently, Jornis was all business this time around.

As she strolled into the galley, the man across the room stood with his back to her. He was over ten feet tall, with broad shoulders which rippled with taught muscles under a tight t-shirt. The typical geloran stood between nine and thirteen feet tall and was generally thin and pale-skinned. Their skintone ranged between blue and purple, though finding one with an aqua green hue was unheard of.

Jornis wore his pitch-black hair at shoulder length when he wasn't in his human disguise, which he had been in when he picked her up a few hours ago. He poured himself a large mug of black coffee. The black drink, common among many races, was one of the many vices he'd developed during Leilani's time training under him.

On the table, in the middle of the room, was a large security case with an aether lock on the top of it. It was akin to the IIS design, but it had no IIS markings or digital indicators.

He turned toward her and leaned back against the counter as he waved his coffee mug toward the case.

"Me?" Leilani furrowed her brow and locked eyes with the geloran. "From whom?"

He held her gaze but didn't respond. His posture and facial expression remained blank as he watched her. He was annoyingly good at the spy thing. The only answers she was going to get were from the case itself.

Rubbing her hands on her pants, she turned her attention to the case. Jornis and Leilani didn't know too many of the same people. They were both agents from different governments, which had a tenuous relationship at best, making the list of possible senders fairly short.

A smaller, human-sized coffee cup appeared in her vision, and she took it from him without taking her eyes off the case. Setting the cup on the table next to the case, she examined the top.

In the center of the lid was a large circle that could easily fit a large, human palm with fingers spread wide. Around the outside edge of the circle was writing in the language of magic, which most scholars called arcane. While aether scholars rarely practiced true magic anymore, its language was still commonly used among historians, linguists, government cryptographers, and conspiracy theorists.

Luckily, Leilani fell into three of the four categories. The arcane simply read, "Place hand in the circle for identity verification."

Above the writing was a set of three symbols, evenly spaced. They almost reminded her of a corporate logo or possibly some form of semiotics. Something about them felt familiar, but she wasn't sure why.

Lifting her hand, she placed it in the center of the circle with her fingers splayed. The area under her hand flashed a bright green, followed immediately by a series of audible clicks as the locks released. Finally, a soft hiss emanated from the case, alerting her to the depressurization of the contents.

Leilani waited until the case settled and stopped making a noise before she laid the lid back on the table. Inside was a black foam tightly adhered to both the lid and the bottom of the case. On each edge was a small loop of silk, suggesting that there were multiple layers.

Nestled perfectly into the foam were two utterly unique pistols. They were an unfamiliar design, but she had seen enough weapons in her long career to be awed by the detail. These were beautiful weapons. The sleek black metal had her name intricately engraved on the handle and a beautiful vine filled with jasmine flowers climbed along the barrel. There weren't many people who knew she even liked jasmine, let alone that it was her favorite flower.

The weapons didn't appear to have spare ammunition clips, but as Leilani lifted one of the pistols from the case, she could literally feel the eldrich power course through the weapon. It reeked of both magic and technology, neatly intertwined to work seamlessly.

"Ma'am, the case is requesting a link to establish identity."

"Is it IIS?"

"No, but I recognize the language of the query. It's similar to the code we encountered when the aether-net came online in the Alpha Dorini system. Yet it does not have the same . . ." Sarah paused as she seemed to search for the right adjective, *"scattered feel. It is the same coding language, but this far more stable, more organized. Interesting. I think I understand."*

"Understand what?"

"Fendrick appears to be a hacker of sorts. Like BB, his code is effective, but scattered and not well-documented. This, on the other hand, is professional code, possibly even governmental."

Leilani furrowed her brow. *"Security risk?"*

"Minimal."

Lei was positive she heard a slight smugness to Sarah's assessment. *"Go ahead."*

"*Vah shnat asereer,*" a male voice chimed across the link. It was oddly monotonous—a very machine-like sound. "*Fathnalu. Identity verified. Authorized user detected. Greetings, Leilani Falconi. Uploading targeting software.*"

"*Sarah?*"

"*It's uploading the software for the new weapons and gear. I am analyzing it now.*" There was a momentary pause. "*It is clear of back doors. And, might I add, far superior to anything we've used before.*"

"*Manufacturer?*"

"*Unknown.*"

Leilani bit her lip. "*I don't like the sound of that.*"

"*Neither do I.*"

The male voice interjected. "*Upload complete. Permission to play video memo?*"

"*Granted.*" Lei hoped the memo would shed some light on the mysterious sender.

A holo image appeared over the open case. It was Jason Dorthy, but he appeared younger, and his facial features were slightly more angular.

"Hello, Leilani. I suppose I should start by saying that everything in this case is yours. I had it made for you a long time ago. I've been holding on to it for a while now, hoping it would never be necessary." He shrugged his shoulders casually. "Though, I'd be lying if I said I wasn't at least a little happy that you're finally getting to use it. It is, in small part, an apology for throwing you under the tram like I did."

The hologram image of him rubbed his arm slightly as he frowned. "This will give you a leg up when they come for you. I wish I could have given it to you in person, but if I'd given it to you sooner, it may have tipped my hand. But the wheels are already in motion, and the players are all back on the field. So, it doesn't matter anymore."

His image grew as he came closer to the camera.

"The last few months before my arrest were wonderful. Thank you. Because of you, I will finally be able to make my arrest and return home. I just have one loose end to tie up first. I want you to know that you were the most intelligent, frustrating, and creative person I've ever worked with. I hope that in the future you will consider working with me again. For now, though, keep your head low, and use this gift to stay safe. I will find you again before I leave."

A hand lifted into the camera's view as he waved to her. He then pressed his fingers to his lips and blew her a kiss as the image vanished.

Leilani rolled her eyes. "Arrogant ass."

Looking back down at the weapon in her hand, she examined the Heads-up interface. The resolution was phenomenal, and the number of functions was easily ten times more advanced than the IIS weaponry she was used to. Like her other weapons, it had several modes, ranging between less lethal to highly lethal, the latter of which was enough firepower to punch a hole in most Kassian warships.

She moved the pistol around, testing the weight. It was slightly heavier but had a more reactive gravity stabilizer.

She spent time carefully pouring through the case. It was much like a typical IIS load out for combat, but was all the same new technology as the pistols. An hour later, she stood and stepped away from the table in the full rig.

"*Armor enhanced by 500 percent,*" Sarah cooed.

Lei smiled. It rapidly faded as she realized she might feel more like herself now, but she was still utterly alone and unsure of where to go or what to do next.

3

MEMORY LANE

"We have reached our destination." Hadu's warm voice echoed throughout the room.

"And where is that?" Leilani slid the pistols into the holsters under her arms and carefully adjusted her jacket to hide them.

"ELU."

Jornis appeared in the doorway and leaned his shoulder against the doorframe.

"Why ELU?" She turned to face him, folding her arms across her chest.

"Seemed appropriate." He mimicked the movement and shrugged his free shoulder.

"Wow, a flat out lie. I'm honored." She narrowed her eyes as she locked eyes with him.

His thin, dark blue lips crept into a subtle grin. "We both have our orders."

Leilani shook her head and turned to close the weapon case. "I don't get orders anymore. I'm a fugitive, remember?"

When he chuckled, she felt a sense of relief. The sound was comforting, despite the tense situation.

"That seems to be a trend with you."

She took a deep breath and let her hand fall with a loud thump into the circle on the box. It flashed red, effectively locking the case. She recalled Jason's words to her: *"Don't believe everything you see."*

"The council does not recognize the murder of Admiral Jason Dorthy, and therefore, we don't recognize the warrant for your arrest for such an action."

Leilani kept her hand resting on the case as she stared deep into his eyes. "So when I called for a personal favor, you didn't feel obligated to report it to anyone."

"Something like that." He stood up straight and beckoned for her to follow him. "I packed some of your belongings."

As they wound through the ship, Lei got lost in her thoughts.

When Jornis suddenly stopped moving, Leilani stepped to the side so she wouldn't run into the back of him. They were standing in the gate-room. Much like IIS vessels, gelorans equipped their ships with transport devices that could move crew from place to place without the need of a shuttle. But where IIS ships could only transfer crew from gate to gate, the geloran version could place her wherever Jornis told it to.

She shook her head to clear it. He'd led her through the ship, and she didn't even remember the walk. If she didn't stop obsessing over this, she was going to get herself killed.

On the deck, next to the transport platform, was a large military-style duffel bag.

"Whom should I be talking to while I'm here?" She strolled over to the bag and skimmed the contents.

Jornis leaned his elbows on the control console and watched her go through the bag. "It's my understanding that Professor Eagleton is waiting for you."

Leilani set the weapon case and the duffel on the transport platform and strode up to the console. The way he was bent over the panel brought his face much closer to her level. She kissed him on the cheek and touched her forehead to his. His face was so large compared to hers that it was comical, and she resisted the urge to laugh. Typically, when they spent time together, he used geloran technology to appear human—a technology that was not typically allowed in Kassian space.

"*Tahn mathalu.*" She thanked him in his native tongue and winked at him.

His soft reply was in elari.

"I understand you are feeling off-balance, Lei. As an operator, I know how hard it can be to operate completely independent of any authority, but we can only control so much. Even the gods have their limits. Albeit their limits are far more expansive than our own."

"Perhaps, but the chaos in the aether and in Kass is my fault."

"Is it really? Or were you just the person who uncovered it? The proverbial messenger, as it were."

Leilani reached up and scratched behind her ear as she considered his point of view. "Everyone always wants to kill the messenger."

Jornis tapped the edge of the console several times before pointing to her. "Precisely. So instead of worrying about what you have *no* control over, focus on what you *do*."

"Like finding the person behind it all."

He smiled at her.

"And ELU is where the next piece of the puzzle is?" She shifted her weight and tapped her foot on the ground.

"I am simply delivering you to Eagleton. I have no idea why."

"Liar."

"We've established that. What's your point?"

She chuckled and touched his cheek as she met his calm gaze.

"You're always welcome in my life, Leilani Falconi. I'd never abandon you, no matter what the council demands."

She ran her fingertips down his firm jaw and lifted her hand for just a moment, then slapped it lightly back onto his cheek. “That just makes you a sucker for a good piece of ass.” She chuckled and strode back to her gear.

“Nope.” He grinned and straightened himself back upright. Running his expert fingers over the console, he set the destination. “It makes me a sucker for a magnificent piece of ass!”

She shouldered the bag and picked up the gear case. “You’re a sappy idiot.”

“Maybe so.” He shrugged. “Good luck, Lei. Don’t die on me.”

The surrounding air charged with eldrich energy as the transport began its sequence.

“I don’t plan on it.”

The world around her morphed into the enormous University Transportation Hub.

A university guard shimmered into view. “Ms. Falconi, whom are you here to see?”

She furrowed her brow in confusion. After a quick scan of the platform, she realized armed security surrounded her. ELU wasn’t exactly a place crawling with security, and the ELU transport hub was the last place she’d expected to see this level of weaponry.

The platform typically managed hundreds of gates at once, but today, there were only two active. ELU security had each gate clearly separated and secured. In the distance, the enormous multi-track tram system was utterly devoid of power. Even the eldrich line itself appeared dead.

“Professor Eagleton is expecting me, I believe.”

The officer looked down at the pad in his hand and nodded. “You are free to proceed. However, university security is aware of your status as wanted for murder in Kassian space. If you cause any trouble here, we will eject you and revoke your access to the university grounds. Alumni or not. Do you understand?”

Her eyebrows rose in shock, but she nodded her understanding. "What's going on?"

"The campus is on alert. ELU is holding some classes, but only enrolled students are allowed on campus. All other access to the campus is by invitation only."

"Is it that bad out there?" Lei jerked her thumb toward the nearby tram lines.

"No idea." The guard shrugged and pointed to the stairs leading off the pad as he recited a heavily rehearsed speech. "The University is maintaining its neutral status. The administration has clarified that they do not intend to involve themselves in the political squabbles between the aether city-states. Now please, move on."

Lei frowned and ambled down the stairs toward the main university grounds. What had once been a bright campus packed with students of all races and sizes was now a ghost town. The sight reminded her of many holidays spent here. Unlike most of the other students, she never had a family to visit, so she usually spent her holidays alone in her dorm room or the library.

"Sarah, do you have Eagleton's location?"

"According to the University oracle net, he's in his home."

"Wow, that's a long walk." Leilani took a deep breath and grimaced as she let it out through her nose slowly. *"Are the buses running at least?"*

"Yes, ma'am."

The mood, as she strolled across the main campus toward the bus stations, was subdued. Even the few students she saw seemed wary and clustered in small groups away from the primary thoroughfare. Typically, the buses were full during the day, as they ran students back and forth from the various buildings across the massive campus. Yet when she climbed aboard the bus headed toward faculty housing, it was empty except for one other passenger.

She knew the elar as a professor of elari literature, but she didn't remember the woman's name. Not that it mattered. She kept her nose pressed firmly in her book, refusing to look up at Leilani.

Lei sat near the door and quietly watched the campus slide by outside. It was peaceful and neatly manicured by the hundreds of thousands of magical drones and creatures that maintained it, but otherwise, it was devoid of life.

When the bus paused at one of the many stops in faculty housing, the professor in the rear quickly closed her book and darted out the door closest to her.

Lei furrowed her brow and bit the inside of her cheek as she considered what could cause this level of fear and suspicion in both the faculty and the student body. She couldn't help but wonder if her last visit here had anything to do with it.

"Sarah, check on the status of the librarian."

"He is currently in the library doing a reading hour."

"A what?"

"His itinerary shows that he keeps story hours where he reads to children."

Leilani brought up her interactive Heads up Display and swiped through it until she came to the main network page for the library. Sure enough, the old man now held storytelling hours for children of the staff and students. She'd always known the university had facilities for students and faculty with children, but the librarian had shown no interest in the kids before. She thought back to when she was a freshman at the school.

A small, dark blue, winged creature smiled brightly at a tall, thin elari woman. He'd worn his tiny teeth down over time—from the usual sharp fangs to dull nubs.

"Of course, my dear. You'll find that book in aisle 3954a. It's about halfway up the aisle on the left."

Leilani waited until the small creature finished before jogging up to him. "Excuse me. Are you librarian Krelor?"

The small creature glanced in her direction before turning to stroll away from her. "I am. How may I help you today, Ms. Falconi?"

Lei paused as she stared at his back. "Um, how? Er, how do you know my name?"

Jogging to catch up, she found herself amazed at the speed this tiny creature was capable of.

"How did you know *my* name?" He waved the back of his hand toward her.

"I didn't. I asked if you *were* him."

The tiny creature stopped in his tracks and spun, his hands on his hips as he narrowed his black eyes to barely larger than slits. "What makes you think I am male?"

Lei froze. Her heart beat faster as fear gripped her mind. *Oh no.* Professor Eagleton had told her not to upset the librarian, or her entire college career might become impossible.

"I . . . Um . . ."

She felt her future slipping through her fingertips. Condemned to live on the street forever. Constantly having to commit petty crimes to scrounge up enough food for a meal.

Suddenly, the tiny librarian burst into laughter. Bending at the waist, he slapped a knee with one hand as the other grasped his waist.

Leilani blinked several times until finally her eyes darted from side to side as she looked to see if anyone around them was staring.

There was no one to be seen except for the strange, fluffy creatures high overhead. They drifted in open air above the fifty-foot bookshelves, like dandelion seeds in the breeze. When she'd first come into the library, the enormous vaulted ceilings were awe-inspiring. They were so high it was hard to see the details in the brightly colored stained glass.

In front of her, the small creature's legs gave out, and he fell to the ground with a small thump. Above her, though, the lazy patterns grew erratic as the tiny librarian writhed on the ground, the pitch of his laughter climbing even as the volume dropped. Overhead, two of the fluffy creatures crashed into each other and fell to the ground in the distance followed by a scream of surprise from one of the library guests.

A nearby dwarf looked up from the pile of books spread out in front of him. He glanced toward her, then up at the shrieking creatures overhead. His face contorted into wide-eyed panic. Slamming the books closed in front of him, he scooped them up and stuffed them into his bag before bolting toward the nearest door.

A screeching sound echoed through the library, followed by another, and then another, until the cacophony became overwhelming. The sound was something akin to a cross between a bird and a small rodent. It grew to a crescendo that was so loud, Leilani grimaced in pain as she covered her ears with her hands.

At her feet, the small, blue-winged imp rolled on the ground, still laughing hysterically, but he now seemed to be having trouble breathing.

Her fear faded into anger, and her fists balled at her sides.

Two more people bolted past her, running for the closest door. One of them was so panicked that when they dropped the books cradled in their arms, they didn't even consider stopping to go back for them.

The surrounding air slowly twisted and picked up speed as her anger grew into seething rage. A piece of paper pulled loose from the stack on a nearby table and fluttered in the breeze. Then suddenly the accelerating breeze ripped a second and a third piece free from their resting places as the breeze grew to a full wind.

"You . . ." The creature pointed at her, but his gasping for breath kept him from getting the thought out.

As she lost control of her temper, the wind's velocity climbed. Finally, a book nearby fell open, and the pages flipped violently. The tiny tornado swelled, and a smaller book launched into the air and spun around her until it slammed into a nearby bookshelf, knocking several other books free.

Below her, the laughing quieted as the tiny imp's eyes widened, his humor now firmly replaced with shock.

But it was too late for Leilani. Her rage overwhelmed her, and she could no longer think about anything else. She only vaguely remembered what happened next. The wind rose into a full-forced hurricane in the massive library. Books and papers flew around her, slamming into anything in their path. The slap across her face she remembered clearly. It was hard enough to spin her head to the side. The wind vanished, and the books and papers fell in a thundering crash.

Floating directly in front of her, his eyes level with hers, was the small, blue librarian. His wings weren't moving—he wasn't flying—he simply hung in the air. Even to this day, she had no explanation of how he'd managed that. She'd told herself many lies trying to rationalize it, but eventually she just accepted it as a figment of her imagination.

"Rude!" He folded his arms across his chest and tapped his foot as if he were still standing on the ground.

Leilani locked eyes with the creature, her eyes narrowing slightly as she refused to back down.

A small grin spread across his mouth as he bowed his head. "You show promise. Very well, I accept."

The strange non sequitur threw Lei off, and she furrowed her brow. "Excuse me?"

He nodded again, as if he were talking to someone she couldn't see. "Very well, I suppose you are correct. We will need her."

His eyes seemed to focus on her again. "I apologize, Ms. Falconi. No, that is too formal. How about Leilei? Yes, I like that. Very well, Leilei, I apologize for my joke at your expense. I suppose we were both rude."

He pointed to a pile of books nearby. "I, however, did not make this mess. Therefore, you will be the one to clean it up. By hand. No magic. Is that understood?"

Lei turned and looked the library over. Far overhead, frozen in midair, hundreds of tiny eyes stared unblinking at her. Spindly arms, which they apparently hid in their fluff, folded across their bodies, much like the small floating librarian.

They were a myriad of colors, and they currently looked like an angry abstract painting hanging in the air. The rest of the library, however, she had destroyed. There were enormous piles of books and loose papers. At least the shelves still stood. Apparently, even her mini hurricane couldn't budge them. They were, however, almost completely empty.

It had taken her a month to put everything away where it belonged. All the while, the small, blue librarian followed her around, telling her stories, bringing her food and drinks, and even giving her a room to sleep in. He teased her relentlessly, but he always stopped before she truly got angry.

For the entire month, the library remained sealed. No one came or went. When the door did finally open again, campus security swarmed Leilani like the Henvari shooter. They hauled her away in cuffs, and eventually she ended up in front of the president of the University.

She knew her school career was over; instead, the president simply gave her a formal reprimand and demanded she make up all of her classwork for the month she missed. She had one week.

She lost her dorm room because her roommates refused to live with her. Professors and students all across the campus shunned her for the next two years. Despite everything, she enjoyed school. She ended up basically living in the library for the first year and having a dorm room to herself by year two. She was the first person to ever get a job as the librarian's assistant in the entire history of the University, starting a long, and highly sought after, tradition.

The bus stopped, jarring her from her memories. Lei shouldered her bag and stood. Snatching up her case, she marched off the bus and began the long walk down the oak tree-lined road that led to the enormous house at the very end.

Of course, saying that anything attached to a greduna was enormous was like saying fire was hot. It was just a given.

As she strolled down the road, she pondered the librarian, Krelor, and his best friend, Professor Eagleton. In her last investigation as an IIS agent, she'd learned far more about these two than she ever thought possible. Rather than explaining them and their odd behaviors, her new knowledge simply made them even more confusing.

They called themselves weavers, and they were tied to the loom. What the loom was, or what their roles actually were, she hadn't the foggiest.

It had left her second-guessing her existence. It was as if reality itself was warping in front of her eyes, and she was having trouble discerning what was real and what was her imagination. All the things she knew to be facts ended up being bold-faced lies, and the people she thought she knew were growing more and more a mystery.

Her mind flashed briefly to the massive aether serpent residing in Kassian space on Mathias Moon. Something that should have been impossible to hide, especially from her and IIS. Yet she never knew he existed, let alone existed outside of aether space, and she still didn't know why.

"Leilei!" The deep, bellowing sound startled her out of her thoughts, and her hands came up to defend herself, but it was too late. The eleven-and-a-half-foot giant barreling toward her snatched her up into a painful embrace.

From behind the professor, a beautiful woman, easily seven feet in height, stepped through the doorway of the professor's home and locked eyes with Leilani as she strolled past. For a human, she was enormous, but in the professor's fifteen foot doorway, she appeared almost diminutive. She had long, dark brown hair with several large white streaks in it—a typical side effect of the misuse of magic, but this woman had easily over a dozen such streaks. That many should have drawn the attention of the authorities by now.

She wore a long-sleeved shirt, but Lei could see the tattoos on the backs of her hands that disappeared under the cuff and reappeared at her collar, which meant she was likely covered in the silvery blue marks. Her athletic build meant she was in a profession that was physically demanding. If it weren't for her size, the woman could be a greduna, but even the smallest greduna was at least nine feet tall. They were often mistaken for giants, which were a whole different category of humanoid.

As the bone-crunching hug finally caused her vision to blacken, she couldn't help but wonder who the woman was and why she was here.

I really have to stop this brooding. It's going to get me killed.

4

FOOTSTEPS OF A GIANT

A deep, male voice slipped into the darkness, gradually increasing in volume until she could hear it completely. " . . . Professor . . . remember some . . . not greduna. We can't take your greetings."

As the voice coalesced completely, a warmth drifted across her like a warm blanket on a wintry day. She'd missed that voice.

"Anthony?"

Lei blinked away the darkness and found a familiar face looming over her with a gentle smile that reached deep into those handsome, brown eyes. She took a deep breath, instantly regretting it as a stabbing pain ripped through her side.

"I have already deployed nanites. Estimated time to full recovery: three minutes." Her oracle's voice was soft, and the usual flashing display of damage percentage was mysteriously absent.

Lei fought to calm her mind and body as she balanced out her breathing and waited for the nanites to repair her broken ribs. There was a loud popping noise as they forced one rib back into place. Leilani flinched, but otherwise remained still. If she tried to move during the repairs, they would take longer and hurt more—something she knew from experience.

"Hello, Agent." Deep brown eyes set in a well-worn human face watched her intently. His handsome brow and strong jaw bore far more worry wrinkles than had existed last time she saw him, and his hair was greying at the temples. His mouth stretched into a warm smile as his shoulders relaxed. "Apparently Professor Eagleton was excited to see you."

"Leilani." She waved her hand meekly. "I wish it was the only time his greetings had rendered me unconscious. He's always added new meaning to the phrase 'bear hug'."

His grin broadened.

"Very well, Leilani. I have to admit that I'm quite pleased to see you again myself."

"Thanks. After the year I've had, it's nice to be among friends."

She coughed lightly and tasted blood, but at least the pain was subsiding. When she tried to sit up, General Anthony Marshall took her hand and supported her back.

She smiled a thank you and balanced herself carefully. "What are you doing here?"

"I got it!" a large greduna with a beaded and braided white beard and long white hair bellowed from across the room. He beamed proudly across the room at them. Like many greduna, his skin was a pale-ash color, and he had brilliant blue eyes that shone with a slight silvery hue. Much like the tattoos on the woman she'd seen out front.

"Checkmate!" Professor Eagleton roared and slammed a white marble horse down onto the marble chessboard with a loud crack.

Anthony, still holding her upright, looked back at her and chuckled. Leaning in close, he whispered, "Finally. I thought he'd never figure it out."

Leilani smirked, resisting the urge to chuckle. "Now the prof has you playing chess with him too?"

"No. I'm just playing go-between for Sitharus." Anthony helped her all the way up onto her feet, then finally let go.

Sitharus was a massive serpent that existed outside time and space and was so enormously powerful that he could alter the weather and move an entire fleet of spaceships on a whim. On her last mission for IIS, she'd introduced Anthony to the serpent in an effort to calm the creature's mood, which was affecting the moon's weather patterns. His mere existence in kuldain space was a highly guarded Kassian secret. Typically the Kassian Empire wouldn't allow such a creature to remain, but since he was bound to one specific location, they let him be.

When she'd first met the creature, he was playing chess with Professor Eagleton and apparently the games continued, even after the professor went home.

"They demoted you to delivery boy?" Leilani glanced around at the immense room.

The average greduna was between nine and twelve feet tall, which meant everything around them was enormous, making the two humans appear smaller than they really were. She'd been in the home hundreds of times, but it always had a way of making her feel seriously out of place. To top it off, the professor was also a technophobe, so everything inside the enormous, two-story home was manual. There was no technology at all, eldrich or otherwise. Everything was either enchanted by the professor himself or completely primitive.

"I hate how the giant races always make me feel like a child."

Anthony chuckled and patted her on the shoulder gently. "Now you know how a dwarf feels."

Leilani grimaced and waved her hands in a slow arc around the room. "Could you see a dwarf in here?"

She followed Anthony over to the ramp that led up to the edge of the table so they could both see the board.

Across the table, the professor was tugging on his braided beard, grinning like a child.

"Nicely done, Professor. I'll carry your move back to Sitharus, but he is not due to be awake for three more weeks. So it may be a while before I return with the first move for the next game."

"Good, good." The greduna bobbed his head absently as he locked his gaze with Leilani. "And Leilei, I am happy to see you up and around. You really need to grow stronger. You're frailer than a child."

"Of course, Professor."

He meant well, but after more than a hundred years of the exact same treatment, she knew he was unlikely to change.

"Well, I must be off."

Anthony turned to her, and they shook hands.

"I still owe you dinner, Leilani. When you get the chance, come by. We have things to discuss."

Clearly, the years had taken their toll; but then again, he had a lot on his plate. After the coup attempt against the Kassian Emperor, Anthony and his soldiers ended up replacing the royal guards while they rebuilt the order. All the while maintaining a watchful eye on the massive serpent, guarding the galactic loom.

Either job alone would tax any general's skills and resources, but tackling both simultaneously was likely overwhelming. Even for Anthony.

"When I'm no longer wanted in Kassian space, I'll do that."

He arched an eyebrow. "Wanted? Again?"

She tossed her hands in the air and shrugged.

"No offense, Leilani, but you really need to do something with those cross-hairs that keep landing square on your forehead. What happened this time?"

"Apparently, I shot and killed Dorthy in the middle of his testimony."

Across the table, Eagleton burst into uproarious laughter.

Anthony patted her on the shoulder and grinned broadly. "Indeed. Well, I bet that was entertaining to watch."

She frowned. “I’m not sure why everyone seems to find this so funny.”

Anthony squeezed her shoulder. “You will. Don’t worry. You may not find it funny, but you’ll at least understand why others might think so. I need to get back. Especially if there’s a manhunt for Agent Leilani Falconi going on. I’m sure someone will end up at my doorstep looking for her.”

“And?”

“And what? Oh, have I seen her? Of course, I have.” He folded his arms across his chest and grinned. “I saw her saving the life of our emperor. And I highly doubt she would have anything to do with the murder of her good friend and colleague. Perhaps they should investigate what really happened rather than looking for another easy scapegoat.”

Leilani laughed and tossed Anthony a thumbs-up. Across the table, the professor got up and strode happily into the kitchen.

“Until next time, Leilani.” The general bowed at the waist and faded from view.

Leilani blinked several times. That wasn’t a teleport. There were no telltale signs. It was almost as if he just willed himself away.

“What the hell?” she blurted out into the empty room.

A deep voice echoed from the kitchen. “Would you like some tea, Leilei?”

“Do you have coffee?”

“Of course!”

She made her way toward the noise and wondered if the prof still had human-sized mugs. There was a table set up in the kitchen with a teapot and a large, greduna-sized mug with thick, steamy tendrils wafting off of it.

Like the chess board out in the living room, there was a ramp built up to a platform along the edge of the square table. On the ramp sat a human-sized chair and a smaller mug.

“How long was Anthony here?” She sat in the chair and pulled herself to the edge of the table.

"A couple of weeks, I think." The greduna walked over and sat a small, steeping coffee press in front of her. "He also prefers coffee."

After moving to his own chair and sitting down gingerly, he smiled at Leilani. "It's been lonely here lately, so I take my time deciding on moves so he can keep me company."

She frowned as she poured herself some of the coffee. "What happened here?"

"After I returned, the university was in disarray. The president was dead, along with almost a hundred faculty members. Many of the students had fled, and those that hadn't were hiding in their dorms, too terrified to leave."

Eagleton chewed on a section of his white beard as he recalled the events.

"Krelor lost it. He demanded that anyone with a political affiliation of any kind would either leave or die. After that came the soldiers, wave after wave. Each wave claimed that the university belonged to them."

He contorted his face into a fearful grimace as he met Leilani's gaze. "I didn't know the aether had that many factions! Eventually, a single Seef'aini representative came to talk to him. She went into the library and two days later came back out. The attacks stopped, and so did Krelor's temper. Of course, the trams ceased, and only two doors remained active. But at least classes started up again. Well, sort of. The professors that were left offered classes to the few remaining students, but it's been difficult. Most of us have nothing to do."

"Wow. That sounds awful."

Leilani took a sip of her coffee and pondered the events that set Admiral Gremm into motion. When she tried to seize the throne, the resulting wake of chaos rippled through both aether and Kassian space. And even though the woman admitted to killing her father because the man in black told her to, it was as if no one heard the confession but Leilani. The media ignored it completely, not even a small blurb buried on the back page. And the senate opted not to investigate the matter further, letting her confession of a puppet master vanish into the dark abyss of forgotten politics.

"Professor, Jornis said you wanted to talk to me?"

"He did?" Eagleton tugged on his beard. As his fingers settled on one particularly worn bead, his eyes widened. "Ahh, yes. I remember now!"

He stood suddenly and marched out of the kitchen. Several minutes later, he came back with a small, velvet sack and dropped it on the table in front of her.

"After you came to me at the loom with that portal generator, I found some of my journals from around 5990. I wasn't all that surprised to find several discrepancies. So I started doing some research. After all, I had nothing else to do."

He shrugged his massive shoulders and settled back into his seat before picking up his steaming hot tea and sipping it gingerly.

Lei leaned across the table and pulled the pouch toward her. When she dumped the contents onto the table, three human-sized books fell out, one on top of the other. When she shook the bag to be sure it was empty, two stasis vials fell out and bounced off the leather binding of the top book. When they landed on the table with a soft clatter, she lifted her gaze to the giant across the table.

"These are the older ones?" She pointed to the vials.

He bobbed his head up and down.

One book had a bookmark in it, and she pulled it from the middle of the pile and opened it to the page. There she saw a detailed sketch of the original portal generator. It was similar to the ones that Gremm used in her coup attempt, but this design had different markings.

Her mind flashed back to the first time she'd asked the professor to identify them. He'd said there were two different makers: one from several hundred years ago, and the other made more recently by Markes and Schoomer.

"I came by those a while ago. I kept them because they're fascinating, but you can have them. I hope they'll be of more use to you."

"Why does 5990 asound familiar?" She picked up one vial and peered through the clear casing to the PG inside. Her eyes flicked to the drawing of the device, and the markings caught her attention. She realized where she'd seen them before. She snatched up the book and jogged down the ramp back to where she'd woken up in the living room.

Snatching up the weapons case, she flipped it over to see the markings over the top of the ring. As she compared the images to the book, she realized they were all similar in design.

"It's the same language!"

Her mind reeled. Had Dorthy made these? Then she remembered what the holo had said. He'd ordered this for her, but from whom?

A greduna-sized book sat on the ground next to her. She glanced over at it and read the title, *A Brief History of the Kuldain–Aether Wars.*

"Holy shit!" Her history thesis popped into her mind. "The Kassian Ambassador was shot in 5990!"

Her undergrad degree suddenly paid for itself as she scoured the timeline in her head.

In the middle of a private meeting with the president of Seef'aini, someone shot the Kassian Ambassador, Theodore Gainsfield, which led everyone to believe that the president had lost his temper and shot the ambassador, thereby launching both realms into an all-out war.

Then Mai Lenali ran for Seef'aini president on the platform that she'd bring peace between the two realms. The people elected her into office by a landslide. But before she could act on her campaign promise, Fendrick overloaded the aether net and blew up Gami Thorain—the planet where President Mai Lenali and Ambassador Gerald Thornwright were meeting with Hodair for peace talks—catapulting everything in the Shamdi system into kuldain space, where it created the Grelashi mining belt.

Both sides presumed everyone dead until two years ago during Leilani's investigation into Admiral Gremm's attempted coup.

"Where did you get that?" He pointed at the case on the ground in front of her.

"Dorthy."

"Ahh." He nodded as if it now made sense to him. "How about some dinner?"

Leilani clenched her jaw as the large professor strode back toward the kitchen. She'd learned long ago that any outburst of temper caused Eagleton to utterly shut down. Depending on the level of outburst, he could go hours or even days without speaking to her. Early in her postgraduate work, one outburst cost her an entire semester, causing her to utterly fail his class and forcing her to take it again the next semester.

Instead of following him, she sat on the floor and began skimming through the journals.

The fourth of Fordal, 5990

Meeshani came to see me today. She was furious, throwing things around my office like a lunatic. Apparently, she got fired . . . again. I wish I could say I'm surprised. But it's not the first time her temper got her into trouble. When she finally calmed down, she pulled a stasis vial from her pocket, claimed that someone had murdered the Kassian ambassador, threw the vial at me, and stormed out.

The fourteenth of Fordal, 5990

It took a grad student four days to find the stupid vial. It had rolled between a stack of ungraded papers and a book on delonian to elari translations—something I found ironic a few days later. Law of large numbers and all that. It took me a week to fully analyze the tiny device. It is a ring, three-quarters of an inch in diameter, with heavily encrypted Delonian enchantments.

It is one-half of a quantum tunneling device. It can operate in both aether and kuldain space. It only has a one parsec range, but the design is ingenious. The portal has a rather spectacular dilation range, allowing something as tiny as a quark up to a squad of greduna marching side-by-side. Whoever built this thing is nothing short of a genius. I must meet this person. Oh, side note: ask Meeshani why we only have the destination end.

The twentieth of Farune, 5992

I went to the capital today and saw the oddest thing while I was there: a delonian royal guard. I mean, he wore the sword and everything! He was strutting around out in the open, acting like he owned the place. Why in the universe would one of them be here? They are never on this side of the galaxy anymore. I, of course, pretended I had no idea who or what he was—which caused its own problems. Apparently, he is someone important, and since I refused to move out of his way when he strutted by, he called me a moron and had security escort me from the premises. When I see Meeshani, I'll have to ask her who the little delonian was.

I can't help but wonder if he's the source of the portal generator. Only one of his kind could have created it. Though if there is one here, the law of large numbers says there might be more. Should I tell Krelor?

The tenth of Goruna, 6005

A government agent came by today. He had questions about Meeshani and the portal generator she brought me. Then there was something about some missing ships that I really didn't understand. I told him I hadn't seen Meeshani in several years, but when I had nothing else to tell him, he grew angry. He began threatening to arrest me for obstructing justice. I simply reminded him he was on university grounds, and if he had a problem, he should go talk to the president of the university. That seemed to spin him up, and he stormed out, cussing at me in crodoc. He likely assumed I didn't understand him.

Right after he left, Keelie, one of my many pets, brought me her newest "shiny." Apparently, the good investigator had the other end of Meeshani's PG. I reprimanded her for stealing, and then fed her a huge steak. She waddled around like a duck for most of the evening. It was very entertaining. They are both tucked away in my dirty sock drawer. I can't wait to run some tests on them!

Leilani's nose wrinkled, and her face contorted into a grimace. "Why in the verse would anyone have a dirty sock drawer?"

5

WARNING! DEAD END!

"Dinner!"

The sound echoed from the kitchen, down the hall, and into the sitting room. Leilani gathered up all the books littering the floor and stacked them neatly on top of the massive history book built for the professor's enormous hands.

As she waddled into the kitchen and up the ramp with her heavy load, the professor pointed to the books.

"Find anything useful?"

"Yes. Who's Meeshani?" Settling into her human-sized chair, she leaned forward and sniffed the steaming bowl of stew. It smelled amazing, which surprised her, though she wasn't sure why.

"My granddaughter."

Leilani's eye snapped up to stare at him. Her eyebrows arched high on her forehead, but the greduna simply lifted another spoonful of stew to his mouth.

"Did you ever find her?" Shifting her own attention to the bowl in front of her, she took a cautious sip. It was hot, but utterly mouthwatering.

"No."

Leilani questioned a lot of families in her years as an agent for the Imperial Investigative Service. It was rare that there was no sadness or remorse regarding a missing person. Unless the family knew something they weren't saying.

When she looked up from her bowl, she found the greduna smiling at her.

"Something you care to tell me about her disappearance, Professor?"

He slid his hand across the table and pushed the smaller journals off the larger book. He then picked up the tiny vial between his fingers and the journal covering 5988. He held them both up in the air briefly, and set them on top of the larger history book. With his hand resting on all three, he grinned, showing aged yellow teeth underneath his pure white beard.

"It is easy to miss at first glance, but they are all tied together, and you, Leilani Falconi, will find the answer."

Lei dropped her gaze to the stew in her spoon and blinked several times. When she looked back up at the greduna, she took a deep breath and narrowed her eyes slightly as she contemplated his statement. Shifting her weight back and forth in the chair, she stuffed a spoonful of stew into her mouth and chewed slowly. She barely noticed the delicious flavor as her mind wandered through the dark hallways of her memories.

Suddenly, her mind flashed to the mine on Grelashi. The man they called the heart wore a rather strange-looking sword with the oddest-looking markings on it. Markings that she suddenly realized matched her case and the PG currently sitting on the history book in front of her.

"Fendrick."

Across the table, the greduna smirked and took another bite of his stew.

"So, what do Fendrick, Dorthy, and the PGs all have in common besides the language?"

"Besides you?"

"Technically, Fendrick has nothing to do with me. That was happenstance, and he removed me as soon as he realized that someone had altered your code to not be his anymore."

Her brow deepened as she continued to search her memory. Then her eyes popped wide open.

"Dorthy altered your code! Sarah, when were the IIS agents given internal oracles?"

"My records show sometime around 6607, just after the treaty of Ka'va."

"Isn't that just after Dorthy joined IIS?"

"According to his records, which I store locally, yes."

"You store his personnel records locally?"

"Correct. By order two-nine-five-gamma. I store the records of two agents locally to ensure no tampering from command. I report any discrepancy from the official records stored in the IIS database to Admiral Jason Dorthy immediately."

"By two records, I assume you mean his and mine?"

"Yes."

Lei cocked her head to the side. *"And you don't find that odd?"*

"I find everything that has happened since being implanted in you, 'odd.' So, in comparison, I suppose, no, I do not."

Leilani grimaced and began tapping her foot. *"I wasn't even born till long after Fendrick disappeared."*

She continued eating, utterly unaware of the food going into her mouth. Her mind was so focused on the problem that she was missing a wonderful meal.

After the abolishment of IIS, Dorthy and Lei had stayed in touch and saw each other almost every day. Yet, he saw no other member of IIS. Why? They were close, but she wasn't the only member of IIS he was close to.

Dorthy kidnapped her from the orphanage and BB, but in all reality, they didn't even see each other again until university. And while they'd operated together as protégée and mentor in the beginning of her career, when he took a command position, their relationship had dramatically altered to be one of constant aggravation on both sides.

She assumed that when everything fell apart, she'd never see him again. Her chest tightened at the thought, and she curled her upper lip. It could have just been that they felt strongly attached to each other, but that didn't fit. They were both consummate professionals. Even if there were feelings there, they were both perfectly capable of sending the other to their death if need be. So why her? What was different about her? Was it as simple as him wanting access to her oracle? After all, a good spy hides things where no one will find them. Odds were that the personnel records weren't all he was storing in Sarah.

"Screw it."

Leilani took a deep breath and pushed the thoughts aside as she returned her focus to the delicious stew. As she set her spoon down for another taste, the metal clinked against the ceramic. The bowl was empty. She glanced up and found that not only was her bowl empty, but so was the kitchen.

Picking up her dishes, she turned toward the sink to find that there was no ramp. Any attempt to get the dishes in the sink would require some degree of throwing. Odds were they wouldn't survive the toss.

Rolling her eyes, she opted to just leave the dirty dishes on the table. She'd apologize for not cleaning up later. Instead, she strolled through the giant's home, listening for any sound of him. When she finally heard a slow and even snoring sound, she turned toward the noise, grinning.

She found him in his office library, reclined in an overstuffed chair, sound asleep in front of a roaring fire. She stood next to him, watching him sleep for several moments. On his chest was an open book—*Missing Worlds: Gateways to Abyssal Points*. Gradually, she lifted the book from his chest and carried it to a nearby chair, using the seat as a table. Keeping her thumb on the page he was reading, she scanned the first few chapters. It was mostly basic textbook stuff that was taught in grade school.

Everything in the aether was inherently tied to eldrich. Planets, solar bodies, and solar systems were linked by a dizzying array of eldrich lines creating a web of life that was not only awe-inspiring, but immensely lethal if unstable. In the aether, these lines were used for inter-planetary travel via trains called eldrilin trams. They also used eldrich to power their technology and even life itself. This link to the eldrich was why the trillions of aether citizens preferred to live in aether space rather than kuldain space, where no such link existed.

The eldrich lines that linked the planets to one another generated so much raw energy that any break or large wave in the line would generate a catastrophic result. Typically when this happened, the closest planet shattered into a cloud of debris and wild energy, rendering the solar system uninhabitable in an instant. These uninhabitable points were referred to as abyssal points.

Abyssal points were not a common occurrence, but they happened often enough that researchers made their entire careers trying to document, predict, and reduce the risk of creating more in the future.

She scanned the page he'd fallen asleep reading. It was a timeline of abyssal point creation or discovery. As she skimmed the years that ranged all the way back to the great cataclysm, one date caught her attention: a solar system, or node as the book referred to them, went dark on the third of Yemel 5998. She flipped pages back to the number next to the date.

On the top of the page, she found the words "Severious Prime." The entry below read:

> *Severious Prime does not fit the pattern. For over a thousand years, we have been able to predict which planets were in danger of becoming unstable during the next wave and falling to the abyss. Severious was not unstable; in fact, it was the reverse. Among the remaining nodes, Severious was by far the most stable. Even with the Shamdi event, which rippled throughout the aether web of*

eldrilins, Severious was not at risk. Yet there is clearly a break in the line, since none of our research drones have returned. Severious is the first, and only, example of losing two nodes at once. Whether this is from the mortal nature of the Shamdi event or from something else, we cannot determine.

In the chaos following the Shamdi event, Doctor Hendral was in a unique position to retrieve a copy of the logs from tram GNT-two-four-nine-eight-five, bound for Severious Prime. Exactly three minutes before the ripple from Shamdi reached Severious Prime, the tram oracle sent an emergency broadcast before going offline. It simply read: Warning! Dead end!

Leilani drummed her fingers on the book as she considered the implications. Closing it with a soft thud, she carried the book to the professor's desk and pushed it up over her head, out of sight.

As she marched out of the library, she knew where she needed to go next. There was no way anyone took a node offline without creating a break in the line. Was there? If it wasn't an abyss point, then what was it? To find that out, she'd need to do some research into eldrilins. Ironically, she was in the one place that specialized in that kind of research.

The moment she stepped outside of the professor's house, the hairs went up on the back of her neck. She couldn't see the future. She wasn't a precog, but it never failed. If she got the feeling that she was in danger, she'd learned to listen to it. So instead of riding the buses that ran all night and all day, she opted to walk.

It took her three hours to walk all the way across the campus to the massive central building. The public relations hype led people to believe the library was the only building here originally, and the rest of the university built up around it as people flocked to learn at the seemingly endless fountain of knowledge.

It was peaceful on the campus at night. The only sound was that of the bugs and frogs chattering with each other. There weren't any truly dangerous animals on the campus grounds, except for the occasional student looking for trouble.

ELU was an unusual place. It was not uncommon for the typical realities associated with even an aether world to be different here. The black sky overhead was the perfect example. ELU wasn't a world, per se. It was simply ELU.

There was forest around the outer edge of the campus that was heavily enchanted. Anyone who wandered into the forest ended up back on the campus grounds an hour later, usually in a random location. Even if they took the same path, they would come out someplace different. It was often a sorority test for new initiates, and all too often the students used it in their secret gambling rings.

ELU also had no seasons, no sun, stars, or even severe weather. Day and night were on a rotation, which mimicked rotations of a planet, but it was always precisely the same time every day. Even the rain was on a schedule.

At the end of each semester, the various science departments had finals which often included some kind of weather machine. That was the only time the weather was erratic, which, in and of itself, made it on a schedule.

The students and faculty knew, along with the bizarre reality that was ELU, there were also other strange events, such as the library's tendency to become . . . testy.

When Leilani reached the center of the campus, she stood, leaning up against her favorite oak tree, her arms folded across her chest, watching the magnificent building. At the base of the front steps, a group of Seef'aini marines milled about. They seemed uncertain about getting close to the entrance.

Students were far more likely to vandalize or pull pranks at night on any college campus. ELU was no exception, but any troublesome student learned swiftly that the library was not a safe place at night if you had ill intent. A lesson the marines were likely learning firsthand.

Leilani chuckled as a group that had approached the front door suddenly turned and ran to the base of the stairs. She took advantage of the commotion and slinked across the dark grass toward the faculty entrance at the rear of the building.

6

STRENGTH

Leilani slipped inside the library without a sound and scanned the dark hallway. A sudden overwhelming desire to hide washed over her, and she spun into the room closest to her. She deftly slipped the door closed and released the handle. Luckily, everything in the library, like in Eagleton's home, was archaic. She slid the dead bolt into place and took a step back from the door. She found a dark corner and stuffed her bags and the case out of sight. Drawing a weapon, she clicked off the safety and scanned the storage closet for the best place to hide.

Testing new hardware in live combat wasn't smart, but she wouldn't have a choice if a fight broke out. When IIS disbanded, the navy ordered her to surrender her IIS gear.

The handle jiggled on the door, and a muffled male voice said, "Where is the key to this door?"

She heard a garbled response that was too far away to understand.

"Yeah, this isn't stuck. It's locked."

Lei slid behind a shelf filled with rags and cleaning supplies. Drawing her second weapon, she took a deep breath and slowed her heart rate. She really wished she had a time-stop grenade right now.

There was a loud crash as the door slammed into the wall, showering the room with slivers of wood.

"Young man, you are seriously beginning to raise my ire." The familiar voice of the tiny librarian filtered into the room.

"What the fuck is an ire?"

The gruff male voice laughed. "It's an empty cleaning closet, sir."

Lei waited, unmoving, as the person searched through the small room. She knew what would happen if she began discharging her weapon inside the library. She planned to avoid it if possible.

The sound of her case sliding across the floor caused her to tilt her head to the side.

Shit.

"Sir! I found something."

"What is it?" A third male voice echoed into the room.

Leilani narrowed her eyes. The voice sounded familiar. Shifting her weight gradually, she moved her head until she could barely see between two cleaning jugs. She could see only the bottom half of the two men. A dark silk suit with an emerald green shirt stepped into the doorway.

The Seef'aini marine lifted her duffel into view.

"*Sne fash'kali nathu.*" The language had a similar cadence to elari, but had a much harsher inflection.

"What?" the marine asked.

"Nothing." The man in the suit waved his hand. "I was right. She *is* here. I can practically taste that damn oracle of hers. She's on the campus somewhere. Tear it apart until you find her!"

The soldier snapped to attention. "Yes, sir. Unit four, meet me outside."

The soldier turned and marched out, taking her bag with him.

Well shit. There went her clothes, and the journals.

The person in the suit turned toward the door, and she could see the tip of what appeared to be a large blade strapped to his back.

"*Fendrick.*" She tried to trigger her oracle, but Sarah appeared to be in stealth mode. She must have sensed his presence and immediately silenced herself.

"And you!"

"Don't even think it." Krelor was closer to the door now.

She could hear the faint crackle of power as he spoke. That was a telltale sign that someone was growing dangerously close to angering the quiet, little librarian. Something she'd thankfully only witnessed once or twice before.

"If I find out you're harboring her—"

"You'll do nothing, child. You and I both know what happens if you cross me."

A screeching noise crawled painfully across Leilani's skin as the blade on Fendrick's back swung out of sight. She was familiar with the sound of the strange blade slicing through the air. The last time she'd heard it, she was its target. The closest analogy would be the screams of thousands of people dying a slow death all at once. Something she'd also heard before.

Her grip tightened on her weapons as every nerve in her body told her to shoot him, but she remained still and focused on bringing her heart rate back down to slightly above normal.

"Don't threaten me, Krelor."

The sound of the tiny blue imp's laughter caused Leilani's heart rate to leap back into overdrive.

Krelor laughed regularly, usually at someone, but this guttural maleficence was something new. It was somewhere between the sound of a villain in a horror tri-D, and a demon with centuries of built-up hatred for mortals. "Do you honestly think I am even remotely concerned with you or your ill-fated oracle?"

Far down the hall, in the main library, the shrieking began. Leilani was intimately familiar with the furry, little floaters, but like with Krelor, this shriek of fury was a new sound.

"Your entire race is arrogant, bloodthirsty, and utterly flawed," the small librarian continued.

A loud crack echoed through the small storeroom, charging the air with power. She could feel her hair lift off her shoulders. The unique sound of eldrich striking metal chased the echoes of the original crack through the room. Eldrich and metal created a unique song, with each type of metal having its own notes to play. The sound grew to a deafening cacophony in a brief second, then slowly faded.

The tip of the blade swung back into view. However, the bright silver with a red hue was now a smoky black, which was far more than simple charring.

"Your kind is nothing but a broken shell without your little toy there."

Leilani didn't need to see the librarian to know that he was grinning. The sound of sheer pleasure was unmistakable.

Fendrick stumbled backward, falling to his knees with one hand firmly on the blackened sword and the other on the floor. She could see his face now, and instead of his usual smug grin, she could see fear and a rather impressive measure of anger.

"It feels like having your soul ripped from your body, doesn't it?"

A dark cackling sound caused Lei's skin to crawl as it warned her of the imminent danger. "But then, that was my point."

Fendrick pushed himself back up into a standing position, his legs sprawled slightly as he fought to retain his balance. She didn't like the guy, but she admired him at this exact moment. She knew from experience how much strength it took to stand up to the tiny librarian.

"Why anyone would do that to themselves on purpose, I will never understand. It makes you inherently weak. Now get out of my library and never threaten me again. Or next time . . ."

Lei could see only Fendrick's legs as he slowly backed out of view.

"Remember old one, we know each other's secrets." The seething anger in the delonian's voice was unmistakable.

"Which is precisely why you are walking away, rather than being carried."

There was a brief pause before Leilani heard the outer door open and close.

An eyeball appeared in the small hole she'd been peering through.

Leilani leapt backward, jarring the shelf and knocking over several bottles of cleaner. She heard laughter from the other side.

"Jumpy, are we, young Leilei?"

"Has anyone ever told you that you're an insane, old imp?" She unfolded herself carefully, trying not to knock over any more of the cleaning solutions as she shuffled out from behind the shelf.

"It does seem to be a common theme, yes." He folded his hands neatly in front of him. He was wearing his typical slacks, vest, cardigan, and smile. Despite everything that happened only moments before, he was his usual, effervescent self.

Lei slid past the imp and scanned the hallway, both weapons still drawn.

"You know how I feel about weapons in my library." The small creature strode past her into the hallway toward the central library, where the screeching was fading into silence.

"Yeah, well, there is a unit of soldiers outside looking for me right now."

"Little Leilei in trouble?" He heaved an exaggerated gasp. "When is that not the case?"

She didn't bother to look at him. "Gee, thanks."

"Honesty is rarely mistaken for kindness." His hands lifted into the air as he shrugged.

When they stepped out into the main hall, the fluffy floating creatures that resembled vibrantly colored miniature clouds were still swirling rapidly overhead. But the noise was tolerable now.

"I really wish you'd tell me what those are. They are seriously fascinating creatures." She tore her gaze away from the intricate pattern and scanned the library.

When Krelor didn't answer, she turned toward him. He was staring at her, his brow furrowed in confusion.

"Krelor? You okay?"

He blinked several times and took a deep breath in, letting it out slowly. "Is it really that time already?"

"Excuse me?"

"You are here looking for the door, are you not?"

"The door? Um . . ." She frowned and shook her head slowly. "No, I'm here looking for any books you might have on Severious Prime."

His wings sagged as his usual soft smile melted into what appeared to be a deep frown. "I had hoped that this wrinkle in the fabric was further away."

His voice held sadness, and Lei couldn't help but grow concerned. In her 120 years of knowing this small creature, she'd never once seen him sad.

"Very well. We all have our parts to play." He turned and waved for her to follow him. "I can only hope that you choose the path which allows me to stay here. I like it here. I enjoy the company of the students."

She thought she heard him add under his breath, "I'm not ready to leave yet."

Lei opted not to play with fate and instead changed the topic. "What did you do to Fendrick's sword?"

"I shut it off."

Lei paused mid-stride. "You shut a sword off?"

"No. I shut off the link to his soul, which is carried in the sword."

She shook her head and jogged to catch up to the tiny librarian.

"But you said something about a toy oracle . . ." Her voice trailed off as the realization struck her so hard, it was as if she had the wind knocked out of her. "Holy crap! They put their soul in an oracle? That's insane!"

"There are many who agree with you."

Looking past the librarian, she saw his private quarters at the center of the library. She'd never been in his quarters. No one had. As far as she knew, anyway.

The large double doors to his quarters swung open as they approached, and she saw a room no larger than twelve feet in each direction. In the center was a miniature padded chair facing a free-standing stone fireplace. Like outside, books lined the walls of the room, but these books seemed older, and they were all sized for the librarian's tiny hands. On the far side of the room, nestled into the wall, was a kitchenette.

As the doors swung closed behind them, she sheathed her weapons and looked around the miniature apartment. "Where do you sleep?"

"I *am* asleep."

"What?"

He winked at her as the walls started sliding upward and away from them. After a quick scan of the room, she realized the walls weren't moving—the floor was.

The fireplace roared to life. The soft, warm glow flickered across the imp, casting eerie shadows, but it was at least enough light to see the edge of the floor. Above her, the walls vanished into the darkness, leaving only the floor they stood on and the surrounding blackness. The cool air of the library shifted to a thick, moist warmth.

The lack of walls made her feel as if she were outside in a vast, empty field. The faint breeze moving upward told her that the platform was still descending into the darkness, but the sheer black expanse told her nothing else. She had no idea where they were going or even how fast they were moving.

Lei moved closer to the chair and the fireplace, resisting the urge to draw her weapons. She may not have understood what was happening, but she highly doubted there were enemies ahead.

They fell silent for what felt like an eternity, but the chronometer in her HuD read twenty minutes. Thankfully, the floor of the room had some kind of gravity compensation, which meant the sensation of falling was likely just in her mind. When the light from the fireplace began illuminating a ground below them, she scanned the area.

As the floor of Krelor's private quarters finally slowed to a stop, the only thing visible—other than flat marshy-looking ground, which disappeared in the dark edges of the firelight—was an old-model gravimetric car designed to move via gravity plates rather than wheels. It was definitely not archaic, like everything else in the library, though she *could* argue that it was an antique.

He pointed at the car. "You drive. I'm not sure I remember how."

Without a word, they both climbed into the vehicle, and Lei pushed the power button. Nothing happened.

Next to her, the blue-winged librarian chuckled. "Apparently, it doesn't remember either."

He reached a single clawed finger toward the dash, and a spark of eldrich arced into the vehicle. The engine roared to life, and Krelor grinned, folding his hands in his lap.

"It's been a while since I've been down here."

Lei stretched her neck briefly before asking, "Where to?"

He tilted his head as if he were trying to remember. Finally, he pointed to her left. "That way, I think."

She lifted the vehicle to hover about three feet off the ground and rotated the car toward the left, giving it some forward thrust. The grav-car had lights and an older style sensor system that used sound-based radar, but the display showed nothing in the hundred-mile range except the flat marsh below.

She kept their speed low, just in case the sensors were malfunctioning. Something about this didn't feel right. If there were caverns of this size under the university, someone should have found them by now.

Krelor lifted his hand and splayed his fingers, waving the hand in a large circle. "It's somewhere in that general area."

Lei glanced down at the radar and grimaced. "What are we looking for?"

Her Heads up Display suddenly flickered back to life as Sarah came online.

"*Welcome back.*"

"*My apologies, ma'am.*"

"*No need.*"

"*Where are we?*"

"*I don't have the foggiest.*"

"*This vehicle does not have an aether link. Odd.*"

"*Everything about today has been odd. But I have some very interesting information that we might use to our advantage in the future.*"

"*What's that?*"

"*Did you know Fendrick bound his soul, his power, to an oracle that he keeps in his sword?*"

"*That's absurd. But I see where you're going with that. I'll get to work on it right away.*"

"*Perfect.*"

7

PEARLS OF WISDOM

Five hours later, there was a soft ping from the radar as something finally came into range. According to the image on the display, it looked like a massive cliff face. It was so large that the monitor couldn't display the top or the bottom.

As they approached the cliffs, Leilani touched the sleeping imp's shoulder.

When he snorted himself awake, she chuckled. "Do you think you can tell me what we are looking for now?"

"Hmm?" He stretched his arms and wings to their fullest and released the restraints. Standing in the seat so he could see out the windows, he placed his hands on the dash and examined the surrounding darkness. "Oh, what are we doing *here*?"

Lei narrowed her eyes at the ancient creature. "Krelor?"

She couldn't see his face, but his shaking shoulders told her all she needed to know.

"Relax, Leilei." He chuckled softly. "I'm kidding."

She rolled her eyes.

Krelor climbed across the front seats and into her lap as he peered out her window. "Yes, this is good. Let's get a little closer."

"Closer to what?"

He tapped the windshield with a dull claw. The vehicle's lights were barely illuminating a sheer cliff face that went far out of sight in all directions. This mountain range was the largest she'd ever seen.

"Down." He patted her shoulder as he clamored back in the passenger seat.

"Roger." She began the descent back toward the cavern floor. Leilani had increased altitude while the imp slept so she could increase the speed without fear of running into anything that might be sticking up out of the ground.

Despite its antiquated controls and interfaces, the vehicle was amazingly responsive. It took another five minutes to get the radar in range of the ground. As they approached the marshy floor, she finally saw uneven terrain. Along the base of the cliffs were thousands of enormous, round objects. They created their own strange mountain chain, extending out of sight in each direction.

Krelor tapped the monitor with a single claw. He grinned broadly, showing off his worn, white teeth. "They're still here!"

"What are they?"

"Eldersleds." He flopped into a seated position on the passenger seat. "Now to find one that will work for you."

"For me?" Lei tapped the autopilot button and turned toward the small blue librarian. "What do you mean, 'will work for me'? What is an eldersled?"

The imp folded his hands and stared into her eyes for several long moments before speaking. "Your kind forgot about them long ago." He glanced out the window into the darkness. "You forget about many things. I, however, do not."

Sensing a long rambling reminiscence, Leilani tried to bring him back to the mountain of spheres. "Krelor, I came asking about a book on Severious Prime. What does this have to do with Severious Prime?"

His eyes were soft, almost sad. "Everything."

Her brow furrowed, but before she could say anything, a flash on the dashboard caught her attention. The vehicle was approaching the ground and was slowing to a stop. Krelor pulled the lever to open the passenger door and stepped out as the vehicle hovered to a stop just above the moist ground.

Leilani turned off the vehicle's engine, but left the lights on. In the distance, illuminated by the headlights, she could see one of the round objects. It was a somewhat iridescent white color and much larger than she'd originally thought, like a massive pearl. It was easily the size of a small space trader. Most of them were smaller, but at the very edge of the blackness, she could see a few that were the size of full destroyers.

Krelor hovered above the ground ahead of her. His wings flapped lightly, though she knew good and well that he didn't need to flap to stay afloat. She jogged to catch up to him, her boots making a soft sucking sound on the moist ground.

As they approached one of the orbs, Krelor began speaking again. "You are about to learn more than you ever bargained for, little Leilei. Try to not let it color what you know of the universe too much."

The pearl was easily five hundred tons displacement or more.

"What is this?"

"This is what your people called an eldersled. It was what the Elder League used to map the Aether Universe after the cataclysm."

"The Elder League? You mean the explorers who mapped the eldrich lines?"

Krelor sighed. "Yes."

"But I thought they all died while mapping the lines, never fully completing the map."

"That is partially true."

Leilani blinked several times before turning to stare at the librarian floating next to her. He had forgotten to flap his wings and just hung there in midair, staring sadly at the large, white object. She opened her mouth to say something, but no words came out. She wasn't sure what to say.

"Some of these should still be capable of travel."

Shaking himself out of his melancholy, he held his hand in front of him, palm toward the pearls. Slowly, he waved his hand from left to right. One eldersled further down to their right flooded the darkness with a brilliant white light as it seemed to come online. In a matter of minutes, it had illuminated everything in each direction for almost a mile. A large rectangle opened on the sphere's side.

Leilani's curiosity took over as she approached the sphere. History had always been her favorite subject, and the sheer idea that she might see one of the ships that mapped the eldrich lines, or eldrilins, intrigued her more than she thought possible. She didn't even notice whether Krelor followed her.

As she stopped in front of the large ship, her mouth fell open. Through the doorway, she could see a large, white cargo hold. A long ramp came down from it to the ground at her feet, but something stopped her from stepping on it.

"*Ma'am?*" Sarah spoke up finally. "*I am reading a very strong eldrich presence from the vehicle. I think it might be some form of oracle. It's unlike anything I've ever seen.*"

"Greetings again, master . . . Krelor?" A powerful male voice emanated from the vessel.

"Yes, Nathan. I am still going by Krelor," the librarian replied from behind her.

"Very well. I will assume this entity is a friend. Why have you cast me?"

Leilani smirked at the use of the word "cast." It was a typical replacement in aether space for the term "boot." Another example of cultural origins shaping speech. In both cases it meant to start up a system, but in aether space it derived from the roots of casting a spell to awaken an inanimate object.

"Yes, this is Leilani Falconi. Your new captain, if you will have her."

"You did not answer my question."

"She is an investigator in need of your experience." The librarian was clearly attempting to stroke the ship's ego.

There was a long pause. "I have looked through your library. They have all the nodes they need for the current population density. Why do you need me?"

Leilani interceded, deciding to try honesty with the oracle. "I need you because a node went offline in an odd way, and I wish to investigate why."

Krelor's plan made sense now. A missing node might need an eldersled to find it. Especially if there was a break in the line.

"Hmm," the ship mused out loud. "A new type of adventure. Do you believe there was foul play?"

Lei could hear the excitement in the ship's voice, and she wondered if a fully sentient oracle was going to be a problem.

"There is a high possibility, yes."

"Then I accept. You may come aboard, Captain Leilani Falconi."

Leilani stepped up onto the platform and felt a warm hum pass through her body.

"Ma'am, I believe we were just scanned. And the power level was abnormally high."

"Understood." Leilani dismissed Sarah's warning. She was too excited to see what the original founders of Eldrilin travel had seen so many thousands of years ago.

"Leilani," Krelor called to her from behind.

She turned to face him.

"Remember, with knowledge comes sorrow." He quoted an unknown philosopher from before the cataclysm.

She bobbed her head toward him and grinned happily. "Don't worry, Krelor. I'll figure out what's going on."

As she walked on board, he whispered under his breath, "That's what I'm afraid of."

The ship sealed behind her with a soft hiss as she stepped from the cargo hold into a massive central deck area. Ships came in all shapes, sizes, and designs, but they always had some form of segregation. Engines were in one place and the bridge in another and so on, but this was utterly foreign.

The main space area was circular, with three levels of balcony wrapping around a massive, white tree that spanned the entire four stories. Its white trunk section was much like a mighty oak, with a broad base and several thick main branches. The leaves were slightly translucent and seemed to fade in and out with a white glow, as some sort of energy flowed through them at irregular intervals. It was utterly beautiful and eerie at the same time.

The ceilings and hatch frames throughout the main space and the balconies overhead stood at least twenty feet in height, making the ship capable of housing larger species as well.

Around the base of the tree, at equidistant intervals, were various stations set at a variety of heights. The panel closest to Leilani was about human height, and she stepped up to examine it. There was an array of smaller displays alerting her to the various states of the ship's systems: engines, life support, sensor, communications, and so on.

As her gaze moved away from the large tree, she saw lounge areas for the various races with different sized couches, chairs, tables, and even what appeared to be a galley space.

"Nathan?"

"Yes, Captain?"

"What is your usual crew complement?" Leilani couldn't help but wonder.

"That is a variable. I have had over one hundred captains since commission, with various crew sizes and complements which depended on their mission parameters. It will take me one to two sleep cycles to make adjustments for you, Captain. Length of recalibration will depend on your specific needs."

"No, it's fine." Leilani furrowed her brow. "Sleep cycles?"

When the oracle didn't answer, she chewed the inside of her cheek as she contemplated whether to push the issue.

"Drives are fully online, Captain. I am prepared to begin launch procedures and head for the exit."

"Time to reach the exit?"

She could swear she heard a chuckle.

"If you prefer, I can start using your version of particle decay as a time reference. Unlike you mortals, I have no need for time."

Leilani felt like her mind skipped a beat. She honestly wasn't sure how to respond to that. No use for time? How was that even possible?

"Based on Newtonian particle decay, fourteen hours and twenty-three minutes to exit. Moving any faster inside his mouth will cause an irritation which will cause him to sneeze, resulting in violent expulsion—something I highly recommend against, as it can cause other, incalculable problems."

There was a long pause, but when Leilani didn't respond, Nathan spoke again. This time, however, the leaves on the tree in the center began flashing faster. The pale iridescent color of the leaves darkened and now contained more reds and purples.

"Permission to proceed, Captain?"

"Yes. Proceed to the exit."

Leilani shook her head, as if to clear it. That brief conversation had left her with so many questions, she couldn't figure out where to begin.

"Do you know where we're going?"

"At the moment, up." The leaves flashed green and blue hues as the male voice responded sarcastically.

This time, Leilani also noticed a pattern in the flashing. Perhaps the tree and the oracle were tied together somehow?

"*Do you think the two are related?*" she asked Sarah.

"*It seems the most logical conclusion.*"

"*Is it actually an oracle?*" Lei couldn't help but wonder what was really going on here. Was this some sort of ELU research vessel?

"*I don't think so.*" Sarah flashed some data into her HuD, showing the life readings her sensors received from the tree to be far higher than anything either of them had ever seen before.

"You're alive!" she blurted.

"As are you, Captain. Do you have a point?"

"I thought you were an oracle."

"Incorrect assumptions are common among mortals."

"May I ask what you are?"

"What is Krelor?"

The response was utterly out of left field, and Lei furrowed her brow as she folded her arms across her chest.

"Honestly, I don't know. Most of the University calls him an imp, but I know that's not right. That's just what he likes people to think."

"Ask me your question again once we exit to space."

"Why don't you just answer me?" Leilani was growing annoyed with the secrecy.

"Because you won't understand the answer without a reference."

"Try me. Wait! Did you say exiting to space? ELU isn't in a solar system. It's on a grand nexus." Her arms fell to her side, and she strode quickly around the base of the tree, looking for some sort of navigation console.

"You are partially correct. The University is not in a solar system, as you understand it."

"What do you mean?"

She dragged a chair over to one of the taller consoles and climbed up onto it. The text was in the igranu language, not something Lei spoke or read, but she recognized a navigation panel when she saw one, and she understood the scan data. They were in an oblong cavern, which was utterly empty except for the single, moving object that was arcing toward the center of the cavern ceiling.

"Again, it will be easier to show you. They've led you to believe many things about ELU and aether space in general. Most of which is simply an illusion."

"What do you mean? *Who* led me to believe . . . ?" She tried to translate the console, but it was useless. She didn't know the system well enough to figure out how to make any changes.

"Krelor."

Lei cocked her head to the side and directed her attention to the tree. "Krelor?"

Nathan didn't respond.

Leilani became lost in her own thoughts as she tried to wrap her mind around the idea that the librarian had been lying to her for all these years. Ironically, it didn't surprise her as much as she thought it should.

"You should get some rest, Captain. My last captain was also mae'lacan. His quarters should suit your needs with minimal adjustments. I will wake you before exit."

"You know what?" Lei sighed, and her shoulders sagged as a wave of exhaustion washed over her. "That's not a bad idea. Which way?"

The floor lit up and pulsed away from her as it led her to the nearby stairs. She followed the lights to a white door. It slid open to reveal a warm room decorated with dark grey slate flooring, wood-paneled walls, and darker blue and green furnishings.

Leilani smiled. It was a beautiful room and a welcome respite from the sterile white of the rest of the ship. As the door swooshed closed behind her, she briefly considered exploring but utterly failed as the bed called to her. She fell into the soft coverings, allowing the confusing reality around her to fade away as sleep claimed her exhausted mind and body.

8

WHALE OF A TAIL

"Pardon me, Captain." The soft male voice pulled her from the darkness of sleep.

Leilani could hear the crackling sounds of fire, which caused her to instinctively roll out of bed and onto her feet. Spinning toward the sound, she furrowed her brow. How in the world was there a fireplace on a ship, let alone an actual fire?

Reaching up to rub her eyes, she recalled the events that led her to the odd ship. "Yes?"

Nathan's soft voice echoed through the room. "My apologies for waking you. However, I believe this might be important."

"What's up?" She stretched and strode toward the door that led to the head. It was unusually large for a ship but based on the beautiful slate waterfall at one end, it likely had running water, much like the geloran ships.

"I have been listening to the various communications coming and going from ELU. And one of them stood out as odd and, perhaps, relevant."

A female voice echoed in the surrounding air as Nathan played the audio recording. "Damnit, Fendrick!"

"Look, don't start with me!"

Lei couldn't help but grin as she listened to the two voices arguing. She stripped and turned on the shower.

"I *am* going to start with you. The president is fed up with your fucking around! You have gone off mission yet again. Either find the damn fleet, or we're revoking your contract!" The other voice was deep and lightly accented with the typical drawl of a crodoc raised to be bilingual.

"I don't give a rat's ass about Mai and her fucking contract!"

"You will when you lose all Seef'aini protection and transport clearances."

"And then you lose your entire aether net. Again."

Even over a comms circuit, she could tell when the speaker was smiling. There was always a slight change in inflection and sound.

"Madam President said to tell you, when you threatened the net again, that we accept your terms." There was a brief pause as the woman likely let her words sink in before continuing. "As of this moment, your contract as a network administrator and magitech advisory to President Mai Lenali and the Seef'aini government is null and void. Have a nice day, Master Fendrick. Oh, and good luck getting out of ELU."

Leilani shook her head and stepped into the shower. As the warm water cascaded over her body, she quickly dunked her head, soaking her hair.

"Well, that was ugly. But I'm not surprised."

"The entity named Fendrick is no longer at ELU."

Lei frowned and looked up into the empty air. "What do you mean?"

"The outburst that followed caused the military personnel around him to draw weapons, at which point he left aether space."

Lei shook her head in disbelief. "Left? Like teleported? Do we know where?"

"Yes, ma'am. From the mega nexus, teleportation is a trivial spell, even for a novice. However, based on the speed and precision of that combat teleport, I would not categorize the Fendrick entity as a novice."

There was a pause.

"I was only listening to conversations, not monitoring for transits. I know he moved to kuldain space, but not where. Do I need to monitor for transit locations next time?"

Lei sighed and quickly finished her shower before climbing out and getting dressed. She strolled from her cabin to the balcony. The tree was still there, untouched, but the rest of the ship had changed. Everything was now human-sized. There was now a garden with various hydroponically grown herbs and vegetables and what appeared to be a small microbrewery. There was even a bar with several taps and a large gourmet kitchen space.

"*What the hell is this thing?*" she asked Sarah, knowing perfectly well that her oracle likely knew as much as she did.

"*No idea, ma'am, but I can tell you this: Nathan is* not *an oracle. I don't know what it is, but it is not an artificially intelligent creation.*"

She leaned her elbows on the railing and looked down at the tree and the control panels around it. "Nathan, what about the Seef'aini marines?"

"I am not sure I understand, Captain."

"What happened to them?"

"Shortly after the comm cut with Fendrick, they deployed a new aether network. The captain in charge of the unit is currently talking to someone on the new channel."

"Can we hear that?"

"Of course."

The male voice that came over the ship's speakers was the same as the crodoc she'd heard in the library. "Understood, General. And Fendrick?"

"I don't care about Fendrick. He has his own agenda, and it's no longer in line with ours. Leave him be." The second deep male voice also had the slight crodoc accent, but this one made her smile fondly as a wave of relief washed over her.

At least now she knew that General Rothar Horrison, her ex-partner, was okay. She'd lost track of him after IIS deported him to aether space. Considering all the unrest she'd been hearing about, it was good to know that he was alive.

"And the agent?"

"Ex-agent," Rothar corrected. "Falconi is also none of our concern. You need to focus on the mission. Follow up on whatever scant information Fendrick had."

"There's a problem with that, sir. I don't understand what we were doing here in the first place."

"What do you mean?"

"According to his badly written notes, they placed the fleet in mothballs at ELU, which isn't possible. There's no place to store a fleet. Unless they shrunk it somehow and tossed it in a drawer."

Leilani heard a snort, but it didn't come from the comm, and the two marines didn't seem to notice.

Rothar sighed deeply. "Just keep looking. We need that fleet if we plan to get anywhere with this reunification."

"Agreed, General, but honestly I think this is a wild goose chase."

"Perhaps, but three thousand-plus ships don't just vanish into thin air, even at ELU. They have to be there someplace."

"That's enough, Nathan." Lei rubbed her face vigorously.

"Okay." She clapped her hands together and leaned forward on the railing. "Nathan, you said that ELU has space?"

"Yes, ma'am."

"And according to Rothar, the Seef'aini is missing a fleet. Which means they had aether capable ships at one point, which honestly makes sense. Aether ships are rare, but they do exist."

The room remained silent while she thought it through.

"Which means we have a missing eldrilin node and a missing fleet. Likely both disappearing on or around the same time. But what I'd like to know is why the history books don't mention a fleet? Something tells me this is all related somehow."

She wasn't talking to anyone specifically, but that didn't stop the ship from responding.

"Agreed, Captain. But I'm sure it's not in the way you expect." The tree flashed a rainbow of bright colors in a rippling pattern, and Lei wondered if it were laughing.

"And I'm sure you have no intention of telling me that either, right?" Lei rolled her eyes and strolled down the stairs toward the new galley.

"I don't need to. You'll have your answer in six minutes and thirty-nine seconds."

Lei chuckled and began rummaging through the cabinets for the coffee. By the time the six minutes were up, she had finally finished prepping the pot and pressed the brew button. It was the first time in several decades that she'd needed to use an actual grinder and coffee pot. Usually, the coffee was just printed in a food processor. Neither aether nor kuldain actually made coffee from scratch anymore.

"Exiting ELU in thirty seconds."

The walls around the common areas vanished, which caused Leilani's heart to leap into her throat. She immediately ducked behind the counter and triggered her vacc suit. The blackness exploded into a cacophony of colors. She blinked several times, trying to adjust her eyes to the unexpected brightness. Her mind quickly grasped what was happening. The walls of the ship had simply gone translucent, so she could see out.

"Picking up speed, now that we no longer have to concern ourselves with disturbing Krelor." Nathan's leaves rippled.

Leilani cautiously moved out of the galley area to stand near the tree. She was vaguely understanding what she was seeing now. The chaos of flashing colors was the nexus itself. The further they pulled away from it, the more she was able to make out that there was something unfathomably massive positioned inside the nexus.

It was almost an hour before she was far enough away to finally start making out the edges of it. It almost looked like a massive whale.

Which had to be impossible, didn't it? But as she watched the object get farther away, allowing her to finally see its mass completely, she couldn't deny that it was definitely some form of massive cetacean. And it was resting smack in the middle of what she already knew to be the largest eldrilin nexus in this arm of the galaxy.

Lei rotated slowly, taking everything in. They appeared to be in a binary solar system. The ship's sensors logged the larger sun to be a class A, while the smaller of the two was a class G. Yet against all known aether or kuldain physics, the suns were not the stationary objects in the system, but rather satellites orbiting the enormous creature.

A flash on the sensor panel next to her drew her attention away from the baffling scene in front of her. At the edge of the solar system, over eight thousand stationary objects flickered into view.

"We are being hailed, ma'am." Nathan's leaves rippled brightly. Leilani was fairly certain it was indeed laughter.

"Go ahead."

"Unknown eldersled, this is the *SS Reproach*. You are on an intercept course with us. Please state your intent."

Lei reached out to the communication panel and tapped the mute button. "Why are we on an intercept with them?"

"I was attempting to help you answer your question."

Lei furrowed her brow and tapped the sensor panel to zoom in on the objects. Each of them had a name and a standard intergalactic ID number. A green hue surrounded the ship in the cluster, and next to it was the name *SS Flagship Reproach*. Tapping the ship on the display, the image zoomed even further, which allowed more detailed information to display next to the vessel. The display identified the vessel as the Seef'aini ship *Reproach*, a dreadnought class fleet command center. In the display, its status read as "Currently laid up, awaiting orders from president Mai Lenali."

"Holy shit," Lei whispered. She reached over and tapped the mute button again. "*SS Reproach*, we apologize. We were simply curious. We will veer off."

"We see your ident now, *Eldersled Nathan*. The admiral has been notified and wishes to speak with you. Please stand by. Estimated time to anti-stasis is twenty-two minutes and thirteen seconds."

Lei tapped the mute button again and bit her lip as she contemplated how to answer. "Okay, I got nothing."

She drummed her fingers on the console absently. Leilani had been in the spy business for over a century. Secrets were her bread and butter. But this was larger than her. Without a command to give her direction, she really wasn't sure where to go with this new information.

"This is *ES Nathan* to the *SS Reproach*." The tree flashed brightly as Nathan replied for her. "My captain's brain just broke. Twenty minutes is perfect for her to get her wits about her. We will come into direct comms range and wait."

"Mortals." The female voice of the *SS Reproach* sighed, clearly exasperated.

"Quite." Nathan agreed, then closed the channel. "You seem oddly fragile for a secret government agent, Leilani Falconi."

Leilani cocked her head and narrowed her eyes as she glared at the tree.

"I have been reading your file, and this version of you does not seem to match the records. Perhaps you should perform an integrity check on your firmware?"

Leilani took a deep breath before turning on her heel and storming off to the kitchen. She said nothing as she poured herself some fresh coffee. She inhaled deeply. It reminded her of the professor's coffee.

"*I have run a check. You are a bit fragmented, but I believe it is within normal parameters.*" Sarah's voice held a faint hint of humor.

"*Not funny.*"

"*My apologies. I do, however, respectfully disagree.*"

Lei sipped the coffee and stared unseeing at a cloud of space dust in the distance, her index finger absently tapping the cup. "*Okay, I think I need a board.*"

Several objects appeared in her Heads up Display. A giant whale, a Seef'aini fleet, one undercover delonian investigator, one delonian criminal, and a missing node. She tossed her free hand in the air, moving the links around as she continued to sip her coffee.

"*Tag this as Krelor.*" Lei tossed the image of the whale to the side. As she did, the name Krelor overlaid the image. She didn't really understand that piece entirely, but it did explain some of what she'd learned about the librarian over the last century.

"*Add BB and tag him with a new aether network.*"

In reality, his sudden disappearance fit perfectly with his deepest desire to see aether space. It would take next to nothing to convince her big brother to disappear into aether space and help Rothar rebuild a secure aether network. Fendrick had caused the net to crash once before when he tried to murder billions of innocent people. No one in their right mind would trust him again.

She moved Fendrick and Dorthy to the right. Somehow, Lei was fairly sure that Dorthy was not only alive but had removed himself from the chessboard on purpose. She just needed to figure out why and how. Knowing where he was would also help.

"*Add the delonian portal generator.*"

A new icon appeared, and she shifted the missing node and the PG into the center. The fleet icon flashed off to the side, reminding her of its existence. She flicked her fingers, tossing the fleet into the center as well.

"A missing fleet that I never knew existed," she mused out loud. "How does someone hide the existence of aether ships for nine hundred-plus years? That adds a whole new meaning to a grand veeshali."

A grand veeshali was a typical cleanup technique utilized by IIS when more than a handful of people had seen something they weren't supposed to. The largest grand veeshali Leilani had ever been a part of was on the planet Dalori Eight, just after the Kamorian Incident. Because of the size of the Ka'va and the media representation, the entire planet had to be cleaned up, which meant wiping the memory and cleaning all recording data. It had taken them a week and three fleets of Kassian Naval ships to keep the planet in lockdown until it was over.

She took another sip of her coffee.

"They would have had to wipe the memories of hundreds of planets. They even removed it from the lib . . ." Her voice trailed off as she shifted her focus to the massive whale-shaped creature floating in the center of the galactic nexus.

Even from here, she could still make out the shape of it in the glow of the eldrich. Her eyes narrowed as she contemplated the enormous creature.

"A leviathan sitting on the largest collection of energy in this arm of the galaxy could cast a veeshali that large."

"After doing the necessary calculations, I believe you are correct, ma'am. But may I ask a side question?"

"Of course."

"Why are we assuming that Admiral Dorthy is alive?"

"We aren't. We are assuming that the person who was pretending to be Admiral Dorthy is alive."

"Elaborate, please."

"Dorthy was many things, but before anything, he was a scrapper. He loved a good fight. That was the main reason he and I got along so well. He loved a challenge. Yet, when the senate targeted him for their scapegoat, he didn't even try to argue. A treason charge is pretty serious, but he never said anything more than a cursory complaint here and there."

Lei took another sip and lifted her mug toward the image of Dorthy floating in the air off to the right. The key to being an undercover agent was ending your cover safely. It was a complexity she'd dealt with hundreds of times. Create an identity, act as them until they are no longer needed, then get rid of them without blowing your cover. It almost always meant killing off the person she was pretending to be.

"In fact, he seemed relieved it was all over. A few months ago, I began trying to piece together what had changed. I couldn't figure it out until the

library yesterday." She recalled the lettering on the case he'd given her and how it matched the writing on Fendrick's sword.

"Dorthy is an investigator through and through. I've never worked with anyone as tenacious as him. I'm not sure if he is a bounty hunter, military, or some other form of governmental agent, but he is an investigator looking for his target. I think that's why he ended up in the Imperial Investigative Service. He lost Fendrick because of Hodair. And any good investigator knows that when a criminal goes to ground, you just have to wait it out. He stayed undercover as an IIS agent, biding his time till Fendrick reappeared on his radar. Once that happened, he needed to get rid of his Admiral Jason Dorthy persona. What better way to do it than in front of hundreds, if not thousands, of witnesses? He then assumes his original form, whatever that is, and finishes the job."

"By using a portal generator and an IIS weapon, while he was testifying about how difficult you were? He made you the most wanted person in the Kassian Empire in the process."

Leilani pursed her lips and tapped her cup with a fingernail. *"I'm not entirely sure why he forced me to ground, but I wish I could say I wouldn't have done the same thing if I was in his place."*

She took another sip and froze, the cup still lifted to her lips. She suddenly walked over to the counter and set the cup down.

"Fendrick tried to blow himself up because he had a backup. He was trying to disappear off the radar, just like Dorthy. Killing millions in the process. But Hodair interrupted his plan by placing everyone in stasis instead of letting them die, which then forced Dorthy to stay undercover."

She swiped through the images on her holographic peg board then dragged the image of the whale over the fleet. It couldn't be a coincidence that the missing fleet was in the same system with the only creature capable of casting a Galactic-wide veeshali.

"Date stamp the missing node."

"Third of Yemal, 5998" appeared superimposed over the image.

"And the assassination of the ambassador?"

"Eight *years earlier."*

"You're kidding."

"No, ma'am."

"Hmm. If Fendrick made the first PG, would he really start a war to cover up stealing an entire solar system? No, wait. Don't answer that."

They both knew he would.

Leilani reached up into the air and slowly dragged the image of Fendrick over the image of the missing node.

"Well then, I guess we need to find Severious System and figure out what he's hiding."

9

AMBLE THROUGH TIME

"Ma'am, we are being hailed."

"Go ahead." Leilani picked up her coffee before heading over to the communication console.

Above the console, a three-foot-tall elar, with prominent cheekbones and pointed ears, snapped into view. She wore an obviously military uniform which Leilani was unfamiliar with. She stood straight, her shoulders back, and her hands clasped behind her back. She wore her platinum-blond hair tied into a tight bun atop her head, and her piercing lavender eyes settled on Leilani with a calculating stare.

Unlike the Kassian holograms Lei was used to, this image looked as if the woman was standing, fully corporeal, atop her comms panel.

"Greetings." The elar looked off to the side, clearly reading something out of view of the camera. Her brows furrowed. "Ms. Falconi? I believe I've heard that name before."

"I doubt it." Leilani folded one arm across her chest and waved her coffee cup slightly toward the admiral. "You've been down for over nine hundred years, and I'm nowhere near that old."

The elar smirked and bowed her head. "If that's what you'd prefer to believe, very well."

Lei pursed her lips together and inhaled deeply. "I suppose I deserved that. Assumptions can be dangerous in this line of work. How may I help you today, Admiral?"

The elar looked to the side again and frowned deeply, then turned her attention back to Leilani. "I don't normally have company during my quarterly debriefing, but since this is out of cycle anyway, and you're here, I'd like to make an exception. Would you like to come over for some tea?"

Leilani narrowed her eyes as she considered the offer.

The elar seemed to recognize the discomfort and released her hands, which relaxed her posture.

"Ah, yes. I remember you now, Agent Leilani Falconi of the Kassian Imperial Investigative Service. A somewhat misguided, but well-meaning, group of crime fighters." The admiral laughed. "Let me start this over, Agent Falconi. My name is Alorra Jedari'dei. I am the grand admiral in charge of what's left of the Seef'aini Naval forces, which comprises all you see here." She waved both hands palm up around her. "But which used to consist of about the same number of fleets as the Kassian Empire."

Leilani raised both eyebrows at the thought.

"We had a rather substantial wall of forces, almost five full fleets in Shamdi System in 5998." The woman bowed her head slightly, hiding her face. When she raised her chin again, her eyes were glistening.

"I lost a lot of good people that day, and incidentally received a battlefield promotion that I didn't earn." Taking a deep breath, the woman shifted her weight before sliding her hands behind her back again. Clearly, she felt more confident in that position.

"You've been out here alone ever since?"

"Yes. I mean, alone might be a misnomer, but yes."

Leilani chuckled and nodded.

"I'd be happy to come over for tea." Lei took a deep breath. "I do need to inform you that the IIS has been disbanded and that I am wanted for murder in Kassian space. Therefore, you would technically be harboring a fugitive."

The admiral relaxed her arms again and reached out of the camera to do something. "Understood, Ms. Falconi. Currently, I answer to no one. And I see no reason to consider you a threat to myself or my crew at this time. The future, however, is always in motion, so who knows what will happen." Alorra winked and waved her hand toward herself. "No matter what, I'd love having another person to talk to for once. It's been a while."

An hour later, Leilani stood just inside an airlock, shaking hands with the tall, elari woman. She was easily seven feet in height, far taller than was typical of most of the elari Lei had worked with in the past. Her entire manner was confident, almost to the point of arrogant. Leilani doubted it was intentional because the woman was clearly excited to have company.

"I wake up every twenty-five years for a debrief." The elar beckoned Lei to follow her through the maze of p-ways as she led the ex-agent to her ready room.

"In the beginning, it was far more often. But it didn't take long for us to realize that finding the president was going to be problematic. So, I began extending my stasis for sanity reasons."

"Makes sense." Leilani could understand how getting bad news over and over would be an issue for morale. "But why didn't you help with recovery?"

The admiral remained silent through several sections before she finally paused and tapped a door panel. When she stepped into the space, her voice was weak. "We tried. We knew the president was alive.

I lost three ships trying to get into Shamdi system initially. It took over a year for it to calm down enough for us to make it in safely. But when we did, there was no sign of Gami Thorain, the fleet . . . nothing. It was utterly empty, not even debris."

She paused and turned to face Leilani.

"The only thing left was an unstable eldrich line that was threatening to burst into an abyssal point." She folded her arms across her chest. "I contacted our Kassian counterparts, but they refused to even speak with us, let alone allow us to investigate Alpha Dorin. They called us insane to think that anything survived that, no matter what our tech told us. To be honest, enough of my command staff agreed with them that we finally decided to just sit back and wait."

She pointed to a pad resting in the center of the desk across the room. "According to my reports, the aether is basically a repeat of what it was then—in a constant state of chaos—with various groups trying to press the rest of the city and planetary-states into line under their rule."

Lei shook her head slowly. "I've gotten similar reports. Though I haven't been able to get too much information. Mai is alive though, last I heard anyway."

"Please sit." Alorra held her palm up to a small table with a formal-looking tea set and two empty cups. "Yes, she is alive."

Leilani furrowed her brow and cocked her head as she sat.

"I know. You're wondering why I haven't contacted her. I've had over nine hundred years to contemplate things. Even if I wasn't awake for most of those years. And I have my reasons." Alorra sat across from Leilani and lifted the teapot formally. She poured tea for Lei first, then herself. "According to my reports, you are the one who found President Lenali?"

"You have excellent sources. Extraordinarily good, considering your self-exile."

"We have a wonderful guardian, yes."

Lei rubbed her hands together slowly as she nodded her understanding. Krelor. He was still protecting them and feeding them what he knew, which was everything that ever happened on or near one of the eldrilins. Like a spider sitting at the center of their web, listening to the vibrations on the threads.

"Yes, I found them. Though I wasn't the one that saved them or returned them to the aether."

The elar nodded. "Hodair. I knew it had to be her. There was no other reason for her to be playing the role of arbitrator."

"She told me she was there to help establish peace with negotiation." Lei sipped the tea, amazed at the intense flavor.

"The goddess of time does not show up suddenly to act as an arbitrator in peace talks between mortals." Alorra took a deep breath, inhaling the tea. "Unless she has an ulterior motive."

The two women sat quietly sipping their tea, lost in their own thoughts.

Leilani considered the players she knew about. Krelor, Aethianu—or Hodair as many called her—two delonians, an elder race she knew next to nothing about, and billions of innocent bystanders. What could be so important that these four entities were willing to risk so many lives?

"You're concerned about her motive," Leilani mused.

"Precisely."

They both sipped the tea quietly for several more minutes before Lei finally set her cup down.

"What part did Krelor play in this?"

The admiral shrugged. "He gave us a safe place to hide and agreed to tell us when Mai resurfaced."

"Which she did two years ago. Did he tell you he also erased all memory and records of aether ships? More specifically, the existence of a Seef'aini Naval fleet?"

The admiral's eyes narrowed as she locked eyes with Lei over her unmoving teacup. They stared at each other for several seconds—when the hairs on the back of Leilani's neck rose, warning her of danger. She carefully ensured that her hands remained in view by resting them on the table.

"Excuse me?" Admiral Jedari'dei's voice was low, only increasing the sense of danger.

"I have been with the IIS for over a hundred years, and until two days ago, I had no clue that there even was a Seef'aini fleet. Let alone that it was missing. According to all records in Kass and ELU, ships can't fly in aether." Leilani shrugged her shoulders. "Except for the very rare pirate or smuggler vessel. Or so I'd thought."

Lei resisted the urge to smirk as she tossed the proverbial log on the elari woman's fire. The elar rewarded her effort with a flash of orange rage that flickered briefly in her irises. The shift in eye-color with powerful emotions reminded her of the igranu she'd met in the past.

The elar sat her cup down gently and turned the handle at a ninety-degree angle, perpendicular to the teapot. She then pushed herself slowly into a standing position. "Thank you very much for joining me, Ms. Falconi. I believe I have some business to attend to. It is time for you to return to your vessel." Her voice maintained its calm cadence perfectly.

Leilani admired this woman's willpower. But then again, she enjoyed a good outburst here and there as well.

"Of course, Admiral. I'm sure I can find my way out."

"No need." The woman waved the back of her hand toward Leilani, and the world around her shifted from the dreadnought's ship-grey to the bright white of the eldersled central space.

"Welcome back, Captain."

"Ma'am, this might be stating the obvious, but a rather powerful source just moved us."

"I noticed."

"Did something go wrong?" Nathan flashed an odd pattern, and the sensor panel nearby flashed rapidly. "We are being asked to heave way and remove ourselves from between the fleet and the leviathan."

Leilani was positive she heard concern in his voice.

"We might want to listen to them." Lei strode quickly to the panel and scanned the data.

The eight thousand vessels off their port side rapidly flashed from green to yellow as their engine and weapon systems came online.

"Crap. This might be a slight overreaction. It's not like they can actually hurt him."

"*That might be the point,*" Sarah chimed in.

"*Well, that didn't go exactly as planned.*"

"*Can't change a plan if you don't have a plan,*" Sarah quipped cheerfully.

"I have laid in a course for one of the smaller eldrilins that has connections to the Severious Node." The tree flashed dozens of colors at once. "The fleet is incapable of hitting Master Krelor hard enough to wake him. But if I may venture an opinion?"

"Of course." Leilani continued to watch the waking ships.

"He has this coming."

Leilani's mind flashed back to the first time she saw the series of pearls lining the cliff wall. She suddenly pondered the use of the word "pearls." Were they in the creature's mouth?

"He erased you as well." She stood up straight and stared directly at the slowly pulsing tree. "When I first saw you, I had no idea what you were. Krelor explained you were the eldersleds used in mapping the eldrich lines. But my undergraduate work was in history, and I'd never even heard of an eldersled."

The tree continued to pulse slowly, almost exactly matching the hum of what appeared to be engines.

"I wonder how many other things he's hidden from history." She resisted the urge to reach out and touch the white tree. She felt sorry for it. She knew firsthand how it felt to be historically significant, then suddenly forgotten. In her case, though, it was the nature of the business. The job of an IIS agent was to find and deal with the problem, then fade back into the woodwork. That wasn't true of Nathan or the entire Seef'aini Navy.

"According to my sensors, we have about thirty minutes before the fleet is at 100 percent and the light show begins. We will be safe in the stream by then."

Lei chuckled. "Stream?" She'd never heard the eldrilins called that before.

"Yes, my kind have never agreed with the mortal use of the term lines. They are more like streams and rivers. You will see what I mean soon enough. Strap in. The initial entrance to the stream is violent, even without interference. I can already see Krelor drawing energy from the rivers, which will influence entry, even though I chose a smaller stream to reduce the effects."

A timer appeared in her HuD and flashed red as it counted down the forty seconds until entrance to the stream.

Leilani glanced around and found a sturdy-looking command chair near the panels. She ran for it and hopped in, pulling the five-point harness tight and locking it into place.

The transparent walls sealed away the view of the solar system as they approached the bright eldrilin. In her HuD, though, a blue line appeared, followed by several other red, green, and yellow lines, all moving away from the large, red ball in the center. As their small, black dot approached the blue line, the ship shuddered violently. The large, white tree began flashing in an intricate, but utterly undefinable, pattern. The shaking continued for several more seconds before the black dot finally reached the blue line.

What happened next was like nothing Leilani had ever read, heard of, or experienced. Suddenly, everything froze. Lei looked around and realized that she was looking down at her own body—still strapped in the chair her eyes tightly closed and hands clenching the arms of the chair.

Turning toward the tree behind her, she found it frozen mid-flash. Her coffee cup, that she'd forgotten to put away, floated in midair above the sink where she'd placed it before leaving to visit Alorra. She continued to circle, scanning the ship until in the distance, outside the ship, she could see a small, blue imp smiling at her.

She willed herself toward him. As she passed through the hull of the vessel, she felt, more than heard, herself laugh. She knew the hull was solid, but somehow it wasn't there. Or was it? Perhaps reality was that *she* wasn't here.

The two met in the bright white stream of pure eldrich, somewhere between the massive whale and the smaller, spherical ship.

"Hello, little Leilei." The small creature grinned at her as he floated at eye level.

"I think I understand now," she replied. "You're the weaver."

"I am one of many weavers. We maintain the fabric of reality, ensuring that we all can continue to exist."

"Why did you do this to them?"

The imp shuffled his feet, even though he wasn't standing on anything. "You know more than most, Leilei, that there are complexities on top of complexities on top of complexities. Society exists in layers. You see yourself at the top of your layers because of the nature of your career. You worked for a man that managed thousands of worlds. To some, that is nothing more than a few small cities. We plan for millions of years, not hundreds. I adore the young minds that come to me seeking knowledge, and as the keeper of my knowledge, it is my choice who learns what. But the truth is, I just wanted to stay in my nice, warm bed."

Leilani straightened suddenly. "You control their threads. I understand now. You've been trying to control my thread for years, but you don't know where my strand will end up!"

The small imp arched a single eyebrow.

A wide grin spread across her face. "And you don't know why!"

"And you, child, are drawing too much energy from the stream. It's time you returned before you ruin your own existence with knowledge. You aren't ready for this phase of your evolution yet. Go, enjoy being young while you can." He darted forward and tapped his index finger on her forehead before she could stop him.

A lesson from school suddenly popped into her head as she pondered the nature of movement. They taught her that all things were constantly in motion. Which was probably true, unless you could find a way to step between time. However, nothing could stay between the strands forever. When time suddenly started moving again, well . . . that, it turned out, was painful.

As Leilani's consciousness, or her soul—she wasn't sure which—suddenly returned to her body, she felt herself wishing it had only been as violent as the entrance to the stream. She felt herself ripped through the hull of the ship and slammed into her body with a violent scream. Thankfully, though, darkness swiftly followed the horrifying pain as her mind tapped out.

10

REVELATIONS

A hand patted Leilani's face gently. The dark edges of reality faded away as she tried to remember where she was.

"Maybe you need to hit her harder."

"I am not slapping her, Nathan. Besides, her vitals show that she's waking up already." The second voice brought everything into painful focus. Not because she recognized the voice, but because she didn't.

A century of training warned her of the dangers of a strange person boarding the ship while she was unconscious. She tried to force her eyes open through the pain. Her entire body hurt. It was as if every nerve in her body was screaming in anger.

"Ugh."

The second voice was close by and sounded far less entertained by her situation. "Easy, Leilani. I'm not sure what happened, but your vitals spiked rather severely. Then you passed out."

She cracked her eyelids open, only to be rewarded with the sensation of blinding light tearing through her vision. She groaned again, but fought through the pain. Eventually, her eyes focused on the man leaning over her.

He was handsome, with dark, shoulder-length hair, green eyes, and a brow furrowed deeply with genuine concern.

"*Sarah?*"

When she didn't respond, Leilani focused her thoughts on casting her internal oracle. An alert appeared in her HuD that the cast was successful, but the time to full cast or boot might be as long as a full minute or two, depending on how far the incident knocked Sarah offline.

"Leilani, stay with me." The man's hand touched her face just before he pried her eyelids open and flashed a light into her eyes.

"Ahh." She squeezed them shut. When the hand left her face, she blinked several times, trying to rid her vision of the black spots left behind.

"Who are you?" The sound came out more like a series of croaks, rather than words, but she talked through the pain.

"Ah, well . . ."

There was a long pause, and she rolled her head to look at the man standing next to her. He rubbed his arms and shifted his feet as he tried to find the right words.

"Technically, I am an autonomous spawn of Nathan," he jerked his thumb over his shoulder toward the tree, "but he copied me from the last person he knew."

He tapped the pad in his hand before tossing it casually on the tray near the bed. "So I suppose you can call me Trevor."

Lei inhaled slowly, taking as deep a breath as her chest would allow. She felt like she'd cracked every single rib.

"And based on my medical readings, you're feeling a lot of pain, but you have no biological reason for it. So I refuse to give you any pain meds."

"Are you saying this is psychosomatic?"

The man calling himself Trevor grimaced. "Yeah, I am. I could make you some tea if you want, though. Focusing on something else might help."

"Coffee."

Lei rolled her head back and forth to see where she was. The pain was still overwhelming, but it was fading somewhat. She was in some sort of lab—it looked like a medical bay, but she didn't recognize the technology.

"I really need to explore this ship more."

"Yeah. I remember when I first came on board . . ." His voice trailed off, and his head snapped to the tree that they could both see through the open hatch. "Are you fucking kidding me? You gave me his memories too?"

"Mortals are comprised of their experiences. If I took them away, you'd know nothing but basic survival instincts and possibly a scant bit of DNA information that is passed on through reproduction. Honestly, you'd be useless and likely insane. The mortal brain is tricky that way."

"Jackass."

The man that used to be Trevor stepped up into her view again, holding a cup.

"Come on. I'll help you sit up."

Taking his hand, she allowed him to do most of the work as he pulled her upright and handed her the hot cup of coffee. The cup burned her hands, and instinct forced her to drop the mug. The human male was surprisingly quick and caught it before it landed in her lap, though some of it splashed onto her legs anyway.

"Son of a bitch! That's hot!" She leapt off the bed and began rubbing her legs, which in and of itself was painful. "What the hell is going on?"

"Hmm. I think I know what's happening." Trevor walked over to a control panel and placed his hand on it. The system logged him in, and he began swiping through the screens.

Meanwhile, Lei stood and tried to remain still as she closed her eyes and focused her thoughts on calming the pain. It began to lessen, and she continued to breathe, forcing it to recede even further.

"Did you experience a time anomaly or some kind of out-of-body experience?"

"I think so, yes." She tried to maintain control of her meditation.

"Okay. So the nervous system effects will last a couple of hours. Any kind of . . ." His voice faded, but Lei didn't open her eyes to look at him.

"Well, I was going to say any kind of meditation will help if you know how to do that, but I see you don't need that advice. I'll leave you to it. Just remember, this is my lab. Touch nothing!"

She heard the hatch snap closed as she focused on her breathing, heart rate, and pain levels.

She didn't know how long she stood there, but eventually Sarah's voice broke through her meditation.

"*Sorry to interrupt, ma'am, but they are discussing the missing node in the main bridge area. I thought you'd want to join them.*"

"*Welcome back, Sarah.*"

"*Yes, I noticed I was offline, but I don't see a cause.*"

"*No idea. Something weird happened when we entered the line. When I came back, nothing was working right.*"

"*You left the ship?*"

"*Honestly, I'm not sure what happened. But something like that, yes.*"

"*I don't have a record of that. Are you sure it wasn't some kind of hallucination? I have a record of that being a side effect of eldrilin travel. After all, there's no way you could survive leaving the ship while it was inside of an eldrich line.*"

"*That is entirely possible.*"

Leilani lied to her oracle. She knew good and well that it hadn't been a hallucination. The pain of reentering her body was proof of that. But something in the back of her mind told her that sharing her experience with her oracle may not have been wise.

When the hatch spun open, she could hear an argument below.

"And I'm telling you it's not possible."

"Clearly you mean improbable, since we're looking at it."

"No, *you're* looking at it. I'm looking at your sensor data and wondering if you've gone off the deep end. You were clearly in storage too long."

Leilani paused at the second story railing and looked down over the primary space. The large, white tree was violently flashing dark reds and blues while the humanoid copy of Trevor stood with his arms folded across his chest.

"I am not an object. I was not in storage." Nathan sounded offended, and Leilani resisted the urge to chuckle.

"Storage, stasis, whatever the fuck you do."

"I sleep, just like you mortals do."

Lei could have sworn she heard the tree pouting. Making her way down to the kitchen area, she opted to stay out of the discussion until she had some coffee in her system.

"How much time until you finish the full scan?" Trevor was staring down at the sensor panel intently.

"About eighteen hours."

"Should we wake the weird elar?"

"You mean the captain?" The tree flickered like it did when it found something humorous.

"Yeah, I'm not sure I forgive you for that one."

"For copying you? Or for allowing someone else to be captain?"

"Both."

Lei poured herself some of the fresh coffee that seemed to be in the pot waiting for her and leaned back against the counter, watching the two of them as she sipped the warm liquid. At least it didn't feel like it was burning her anymore.

"I don't think she needs to be woken up." The tree flashed brighter, now clearly laughing.

"Why not?" Trevor's head snapped up to stare at the tree. "What did you do?"

"I did nothing, Doctor, but the captain is already awake. She's standing behind you, in the galley."

Trevor's shoulders sagged as he mumbled under his breath, "Outstanding."

"I assume there's some sort of problem?" Lei placed both hands on her cup to warm them.

"No problem, Captain. The good doctor just refuses to accept the reality of the situation." The tree was still finding this humorous, but the bright flashing had calmed somewhat.

"That's because it isn't possible."

"There's no such thing as impossible," Leilani stated firmly before taking another sip of her coffee.

"Precisely!" the tree exclaimed gleefully.

"Great, now there's two of you."

"Why don't you show me what we're dealing with, Nathan."

Her Heads up Display lit up with what appeared to be a massive web of lines, weaving in and out and intersecting to create a beautiful pattern. Along the various strands, there were thousands of dots. Leilani knew from school that each of those dots were solar systems. In each solar system, there was another tiny web of lines that included the various life-bearing planets and moons. It was along these lines that the trams traveled between worlds. Depending on the distance, the travel could be minutes or even hours, but no matter where the worlds were in this arm of the galaxy, tram travel was always faster than any other method, or so they taught at university. But she now doubted everything she'd learned at ELU.

The image shifted to show a large sphere at one intersection. Inside the sphere, where the eldrilin node—also known as Severious System—should be, was a red dot.

She swiped her fingers outward to zoom in. Around the outside of the sphere, not on any particular eldrilin, a rapidly moving green dot appeared to be circling the sphere.

"I assume this is us outside of the sphere. Gathering telemetry?" She pointed to the green dot.

"Yes, Captain."

"What do we have so far? Do we know what it's made of at least?" Lei rubbed her chin as she examined what she could see.

"You're believing this nonsense?" The doctor threw his hands up in the air and let them fall limp at his side.

"Why shouldn't I?" She didn't even look at the exacerbated doctor.

"It's an energy shield of some kind," Nathan replied, ignoring the outburst.

"That much energy has to have a source."

"The source is obvious so far, but I'm not done with my scans, so I'm not 100 percent certain."

"And?" She elongated the word slightly as she pressed Nathan for more information.

"Severious was a minor nexus. It had one major eldrilin river and two streams that fed into it. It appears, at first glance, that those eldrilins are now feeding the sphere."

"In effect, making the sphere the nexus." Leilani chewed on her lip as she considered the implications.

Reaching up, she spun the image in her HuD. There were three lines going into the sphere. All of which were bright red, indicating damaged tram lines. Usually, this only applied to abyssal points.

At each point where the lines met the bubble, there was a rather impressive collection of debris—likely trams that didn't find out about the sphere until it was too late to change lines. A dark spot along the smaller of the two lines caught her attention, and she reached up to halt the spin.

"What's this?"

She swiped her fingers outward to zoom in, but the resolution didn't get as sharp as she would have liked.

"We believe it's debris from before they knew the line was dead." Trevor tapped the panel in front of him. "It's on all four lines, just outside the bubble."

Leilani shook her head. "No, I mean this." She tossed the blurry spot toward the tree. "Off to the right of the tertiary line. Get us closer to this, Nathan. I want more data."

"Understood, Captain."

"Estimated time to scan range?"

"About two hours."

"Are we really going to abandon the complete scan to check out a blob that we all know is debris?"

"At the rate of speed that a tram moves, impact would disperse the debris in all directions. This is not evenly spread. There might be something there worth looking at."

"What the hell are you hoping to find?"

"Clues. Fendrick went to great lengths to hide this solar system, but he's not as good as he thinks he is. He may be using the eldrich lines to power the field, but he has to shape the energy somehow. And if there's a wall, there's always a door."

Lei set her coffee cup down on the counter and began rummaging through the kitchen for the ingredients to make breakfast.

"This is ridiculous! You're both insane! And who the hell is Fendrick?" Trevor bellowed behind her, followed immediately by the sound of him storming off.

"Was he always this dramatic?"

"Yes. I think I may have given him too many memories." Nathan's leaves flashed deep blues and purples.

"No one gets to pick their memories." She cocked her head to the side and rolled a knife across the back of her hand before catching it. "At least not without losing themselves in the process."

Returning her attention to making breakfast, she turned her back on the tree. "May I ask a personal question, Nathan?"

"Of course. You *are* the captain."

"What are you?"

"That depends on who you ask, but I understand the intent of the query. I will try to explain. You are familiar with the concept of pearls and how they are made?"

"Like oyster pearls? Yes." Lei flipped the eggs in the pan and gathered the plates.

"Precisely. Well, I am a pearl, in so much that Krelor created me in a similar method. However, he is a leviathan. Do you know what that is?"

"According to the history books, leviathans are massive creatures that eat planets. At least that's all I remember reading."

"Wow. That is just proof positive that you shouldn't believe everything you read. Leviathans are creatures of immense power. Many are large, like Krelor, but they can be physically any size. What unites them into the leviathan category is that they are inherently magical creatures so powerful that they effect the surrounding energy. As an example, a leviathan might make areas that have only one eldron per million suddenly have one eldron per thousand."

Leilani looked up from the stove and furrowed her brow. "Wow. That's a lot of power. So, if one sat on a galactic nexus, for example, they would be even stronger?"

"Yes, they would."

"Then if we go off the premise that you are a grain of sand annoying a leviathan, then they would wrap you in saliva to coat you. But that spit would be almost pure eldrich, making you, in effect, a purely magical creature. Which, according to all eldrich theory research, would eventually cause you to develop sentience."

"You are correct, Captain."

"I suppose that makes sense. I could see a sleeping entity like Krelor just layering an irritation with eldrich unconsciously."

"Well, technically it was preconsciously. Pearls, like myself, have been used for many things throughout time. But I spent most of my existence as a ship for the smaller species."

"And as a purely eldrich entity, you make yourself into whatever you wish." Lei slid the food onto the plates and spun toward the tree. "Wait, does that mean you're only solid because you choose to be?"

The large, white tree flashed again in its version of laughter. "You grasped that concept faster than most."

Lei scanned the center of the vessel, looking the panels and the large tree over intently. "At some point, you learned to shape yourself into things that your crew was most comfortable with."

There was a soft ripple of light across the leaves, but it was a visual she hadn't seen before, so she wasn't sure what it meant.

"Why the tree then?" She poured herself another coffee, but she wasn't sure what Trevor would drink. There was a long silence, and she chuckled. "You're not sure if you want to answer that."

Leilani strolled to the table, carrying the plates and her own coffee. "Don't worry, Nathan. You're welcome to your secrets. So long as they don't interfere with the mission."

"You are nothing like my other captains." The leaves rippled in yet another pattern that she didn't recognize. Though this one was more chaotic than typical.

"I am not an explorer." Lei set the plates on the table. "Could you let Trevor know I made him food?"

"Done. May I ask a question, Captain?"

"Of course, but I may or may not answer it."

"Understood. What are you, if not an explorer?"

Lei lifted a bit of eggs to her mouth and chewed slowly as she considered how to answer that question. What was she now? A small smile played across her mouth as she realized nothing had changed. They may have shut down the IIS, but until this moment she hadn't realized that IIS agent wasn't her identity—it was just her job. In fact, she almost felt a sense of relief. It was as if the weight strapped to her ankle was gone, and she could finally swim unhindered.

Trevor came in and sat down quietly as she continued to chew, lost in her own thoughts.

When she looked up from her food, she smiled happily at the doctor. Even with her entire existence thrown into chaos she was now, as she'd always been, an investigator.

"I solve problems."

11

AETHER SPACE

"Interesting. Captain, you'll want to see this."

The walls of the vessel vanished, and Lei ignored the brief sense of panic as her breakfast threatened to come back up. Setting the dishes in the sink gently, she turned and scanned the immediate area around the ship.

They weren't in the eldrich line, but even at this distance, the brilliant glow of the line illuminated the debris field better than anything she could have done. The only reason she wasn't blind was that the hull wasn't entirely transparent. Nathan was clearly dampening the lumens somewhat.

Directly ahead of them, she saw the mass that originally attracted her attention. It was not random enough to be accidental, but it was hard to tell exactly what it was.

"Can you zoom in?"

The image grew. It was definitely debris from wrecked trams, but someone, or something, had welded the pieces together into a small station. Despite its makeshift nature, it appeared well designed. She could see the eldrich collectors absorbing the power from the nearby line, which meant whoever had built this knew exactly what they were doing.

"Is something like that even possible without a tender ship?" The sudden sound of the strange doctor's voice next to her caused Leilani to jump.

"Why do you automatically assume everything you see is impossible? You're looking at it. Of course, it's possible. Although I will admit, the odds are pretty low." Her tone was admonishing as she returned her attention to the station. Lifting her hand toward the station, she placed her other fist on her hip. "I think the better question is, *how* is it possible?"

"Pedantic bitch." Trevor strode to the sensor panel at the base of the tree.

Leilani narrowed her eyes at the makeshift station as she worked through the possibilities in her mind. "All stop."

There was a bright flash from the tree as the ship's hum slowed.

"What?" The doctor spun toward her and shook his head vehemently. "You can't stop! We need to check that out!"

"Doctor, while I commend your inquisitive nature, we have no idea if that thing is armed, or whether the occupants are interested in company. So, until we know more, we'll keep our distance."

Trevor slammed his hands on the console in front of him. Despite his attempt to mask the words, Lei could still hear his whispered complaint. "I can't believe he even allowed her onboard."

"Is it emitting on any known aether frequencies?" Lei glanced up at the tree, waiting for his response.

"Yes, Captain. Oddly, I'm getting an intermittent EPIRB." Nathan flashed a slow pattern as he responded.

"What do you mean intermittent?"

"Time dilations in or around eldrich lines are common. Odds are that it's sitting in one of the erratic pockets." Trevor twisted to lean back on the console as he flashed her a smug grin. "What? Did I know something that the precious captain didn't?"

Lei took a deep breath, letting it out slowly. "I haven't noticed any time discrepancies."

Trevor smirked. "What makes you think you'd notice?"

"*Sarah?*"

"He is correct. We may not notice, because we are in them, so time seems stable for us, even if it's not. But interaction with anything outside our immediate area might be in a different sequence."

Leilani cast her thoughts back to when she first came aboard. Nathan didn't use time references until she pushed the issue.

"That's why you don't use time!"

"How in the world did you end up with Nathan?" Trevor stormed around the tree, looking at the various panels. "What a waste of resources."

She opened her mouth to respond but opted to keep her reasons to herself. If he really was a spawn of Nathan, he knew the answer. He was simply venting.

"Captain, would you like me to ping the emergency beacon?" A soft ripple rolled across the leaves.

"Yes."

Leilani knew plenty of pirates who liked to lure people in with emergency beacons, but something about this situation told her that this wasn't the case. Although, she did suddenly wonder how many pirates had hidden stations in aether space. It was a completely unregulated area where they could get away with literally anything they wanted.

She thought back to the various pirates and slave traders she'd arrested over the years with ships that could move between kuldain and aether space. She used to think the pirate vessels were rare and highly modified, but she was now questioning that hypothesis. What if aether-capable ships had once been commonplace, but Krelor erased their existence from the memories of anyone who didn't already have one?

"Hello? Hello? Who's there? You're another ghost, right?" A garbled voice echoed through the ship.

Lei looked up at the tree. “Hello? This is Captain Leilani Falconi. Who is this?”

“By the gods! It talked! It’s your imagination. No, it’s not! How would you know?” The voice didn’t change as the argument ensued.

Leilani breathed in through gritted teeth. That wasn’t a good sign. “Take it easy. Can you tell me your name?”

“Name? Your name? Yes! You should give me your name. She already did, you dolt!” The voice sounded male, but it was hard to tell over the distorted connection. Clearly, whatever they were using to communicate wasn’t working properly.

“She did? It’s Pulari or something. Sheesh. Ahh, okay. Hello, Pulari. My name is . . .”

Leilani stepped up to the comms console and glanced down. The signal had gone silent, but it appeared to still be open.

“I’m guessing you’ve been here a while.” She returned her attention to the magnified image of the station floating in front of them.

“Yes.” The male voice sounded confused, but it was coalescing slightly as the frantic rambling subsided. “At least I think so. It’s impossible to tell, really.”

“Okay. Well, let’s try this again then. My name is Leilani Falconi.”

“It’s good to meet you, Leilani Falconi. I am . . .” The voice trailed off again.

“Take it easy. It’s okay. We’ll figure it out. Do you know how you got here?”

“I came here . . . I have to get inside.” The panic was creeping back into his voice.

“Easy there. Anything we can do to help?” Lei wished they had visuals, but emergency beacons were built to last a long time, not to be used as an everyday comm unit.

“No. I need to . . .” The voice fell off again as Trevor walked over to her and tapped the mute button on the console.

“You should see these readings.” He pointed to the sensor panel where he’d been standing.

They both moved to the new panel while the strange voice continued to mumble unintelligibly. Lei glanced down at the readout.

Trevor tapped an icon that led him to a power readout. Once the console shifted to the new data, he tapped a small rotating image. It magnified, taking up most of the display. Next to it were several readouts, including power usage, throughput, output, and so on.

The image itself was a strange-looking crystal with over a dozen floating spheres around it. As he moved the slider to the right, a web of energy flowed into the spheres, creating an intricate cage of pure eldrich around the crystal. The crystal spun, slowly at first, but as he added more power, it began spinning faster and faster until it erupted into what looked to be an energy barrier of some kind.

"I think this is what's creating the barrier, and they are enormous. Near as I can tell, someone spread these all the way around the node. I ran the design against known objects that give off this kind of power. I think I know what this is, but as far as I know, it's never been done on this scale."

"You've seen this before?" Lei locked eyes with the doctor.

He shifted his feet uncomfortably. "I'm not sure I'm allowed to answer that."

"I'll take that as a yes." Her jaw clenched as her attention returned to the crystal spinning in its high-tech cage. "Do we know exactly how many there are?"

Trevor lifted his hands and shrugged his shoulders. "Based on some preliminary math, I would say between one and two billion, but honestly, there's no way to tell at this point. At least not without six months of scans."

Lei blinked several times as her mind tried to imagine the magnitude of the situation. Based on the measurements next to the image, each crystal was just under a mile long.

"Where the hell did Fendrick get that many crystals of that size?"

"Unknown. But if he could create and maintain a harmonic field of that magnitude, he could likely prevent anything from passing through

it. It might even stop energy, such as light, from passing through the barrier."

Early in Leilani's career as an IIS agent, a group of pirates used crystal resonance to hide their ships from kuldain sensors. The tech allowed them to fly right into heavily populated areas and board ships without alerting the local authorities.

Because of the technology, IIS deployed her to investigate whether it was aether tech. In that case, it was electromagnetic technology, but it was far more advanced than anything the Kassians were capable of. Command pulled her from the case before she could make any arrests.

As she thought back now, however, she realized that they had a cross tech ship after all. At the time, she'd missed the cleverly hidden aether tech—a mistake she wouldn't have made later on in her career.

"I've seen this before as well." Leilani tapped the sensor display to adjust the scan data.

"What are you doing?"

"Checking a hunch."

The readout shifted, and they both exhaled loudly in unison.

"Holy shit." Trevor rubbed his face, as if that would somehow change the data readout.

"Not one of those times I wanted to be right." Lei folded her arms across her chest.

The net around the crystals was pulling the eldrich directly from the lines and dispersing it throughout the barrier, powering the crystals indefinitely. That much power would, most definitely, prevent any kind of tampering.

"It's all being converted into the shield."

Leilani nodded her head and stretched, then refolded her arms as she stared at the readout. This also meant there was likely very little, if any, eldrich energy inside of the sphere.

"There's no way they survived that long term," the man next to her whispered.

Lei shook her head slowly.

"Hello? Are you still there, Ms. Ghost?" The crackled voice broke into her thoughts.

"Yes. We're still here."

"Did she just answer us again? No. Hush! It's just another voice in our heads."

"Ma'am." Nathan spoke up, drawing her attention to the softly scintillating tree.

"Yes, Nathan?"

"I've been running some separate scans on the makeshift station. I believe I understand why we're hearing multiples of the same person."

"I thought insanity was the fairly obvious reason," Trevor quipped.

"It is, but in this case, I'm not sure that is the actual reason. Though it doesn't rule out other concerns."

"What are you seeing?" Lei focused her attention back on the sensor console.

"The station is too close to both the line and the crystal network. It appears that the proximity is causing the station to fracture into multiple time frequencies simultaneously."

Lei grimaced, squeezing the bridge of her nose between her fingers. "In common, please?"

"Simply put, there are several versions of the same person, existing on several versions of the station, at the same time. In essence, he has fractured into multiple time strands. All of them existing at the same time, in the same place."

"Um." Lei was at a loss for words.

If that was in fact possible, that would be a horrible existence. Both seeing and knowing that you aren't seeing yourself would be awful, let alone hearing herself. She shuddered at the thought.

"Yikes." Trevor grimaced. "One of me is enough. Well, I guess there are two of me now, but still. At least I don't have to listen to myself talk."

"Any more than you already do, Doctor?"

"Bite me, Nathan."

The tree rippled in the pattern that was its colorful laugh, and Lei smirked. She was really beginning to like Nathan.

"Okay, if you're right. How do we connect with or rescue a man that exists in multiple time strands? Assuming I understood you correctly, that is."

"That is correct, Captain. And I do not have an answer to that query."

"If we get the sled too close, we could damage it. Or worse, get trapped in the same time dilation. But we might rig up a tether." Trevor rubbed his chin as he pondered the idea.

Lei turned her attention to the ex-captain and furrowed her brow.

The man shrugged. "You're the one wanting to rescue the crackpot."

"Pardon me?" A male voice spoke across the crackling communication unit. He sounded like the others, but his signal seemed stronger.

Lei narrowed her eyes, glaring at Trevor. "Pardon us."

"I believe he is likely more correct than I would prefer to admit, but I take exception to the term *crackpot*. I am, however, an engineer, and I might have a solution to your original query."

"You have a way for us to get to you?"

"Yes, but it won't be easy, and it does assume you have a basic understanding of kuldain *and* aether physics."

Leilani smirked at Trevor, who simply shook his head and said quietly, "Never been to kuldain space."

"What's your name?" Lei asked, testing the voice on the other end.

"Wendel," the man stated firmly, without hesitation.

"Well, Wendel, it's nice to meet you. It seems today is your lucky day."

Eight hours later, Leilani was staring out an open cargo door into aether space. To her left, the eldrich line was crackling so loud that it was almost deafening. The fact that she could hear it kept making her check her Heads up Display to see if she was sleeping, because it shouldn't have been possible.

She wrinked her nose slightly as she thought to Sarah, *"I can't believe we're doing this."*

"You and I have been through a lot in our lifetime together, but I have to admit, this one pegs the top of my insanity meter."

A tap on her shoulder caused her to jump. Turning, she saw Trevor standing in the cargo bay without a vacc suit. He reached toward her waist and attached a long silvery cable to her harness, then spun the belt to test the bearings.

She was wearing an eight-point harness made of a strange mixture of elements that Nathan had spent an hour explaining. The alloy should help her remain in the same harmonic frequency as the ship. Something about the metal resonating and frequencies. Honestly, she hadn't understood most of what Nathan and Wendel had been yammering on about.

What she had understood, though, was that her limbs would be far enough away from the harness that they might experience some time dilation. When she'd asked what that meant, the answer had almost convinced her to walk away from the whole thing. But shirking from a challenge had never really been something Leilani was good at.

Wendel had assured her it wouldn't be permanent and that the harness should keep her intact. Of course, the use of the word "should" had not made her feel any better, but it wasn't the first time she'd been a guinea pig for someone's experimental tech.

Lei leaned in toward Trevor.

"I still don't understand how you're standing here without a vacc suit!"

The man chuckled and handed her an insulated backpack. She'd deployed her own vacc suit before opening the cargo bay door, but it never fully inflated, something which also made her nervous.

The three scientists spent over an hour arguing with her about the differences between kuldain and aether space, but in the end, she decided caution was the better part of valor.

According to their argument, aether space had the usual electrons found in kuldain space, but here, the number of eldrons attached to the electrons was far greater. In kuldain space, there was approximately one eldron per every million electrons. In aether space, the number could be anywhere between one-to-one, and one-to-one-thousand, depending on the richness of the source. An eldrilin, for example, was a one-to-one ratio.

Apparently, when there were enough eldrons present, they created some form of life bubble which allowed her to breathe, even in space. But their explanation of why sounded like gibberish to her. Eldrons didn't make oxygen. Yet, they expected her to believe them when they said she'd be able to breathe in aether space just fine. All because they were so close to the eldrilin.

Her response was less than ideal. Even Sarah told her she may have overreacted and used a few too many cuss words.

After the explosive exchange, Lei opted to walk away, leaving them to their plotting and planning while she wandered off to take a nap.

Now, with the backpack carrying Wendel's harness firmly in place, Lei strode to the edge of the cargo bay and pushed herself off as hard as she could toward the station in the distance. She wasn't sure what to expect, but the moment she felt the typical zero gravity, a small part of her sighed in relief. At least not *everything* in the aether was out of whack.

"*With all the times we've been in the aether realm, you'd think that at least once, we would have experienced aether space,*" Leilani grumbed to her oracle.

Lei drifted toward the station, carefully watching the nearby debris. The danger on this route was minimal, but she could still see pieces ahead of her that were dangerously close. Even a small bit of debris could be lethal if she hit it wrong. At least light wasn't a problem.

A small section in the back of her mind kept warning her of the dangerous line of energy to her left. At any minute, she was expecting a flare to lash out and remove her from all realities at once. She tried to ignore it. Nathan and Trevor both told her that the line didn't work that way unless it was broken.

In her HuD, several items ahead had a red highlight around them. Lei pulled a pistol with her right hand and tapped a secondary belt around her waist with the left. Her gravity belt kicked on and fed data to her HuD. Without the gravity belt to compensate for the weapon's discharge, she would end up reeling off in the wrong direction.

"Ma'am, would you like me to switch to aether energy mode?"

"Data?" Statistics and information appeared in her HuD. Apparently, the new weapons had dozens of different ammunitions, one of which was a lower power eldrich mode that would have minimal energy transfer, which meant it was less likely to kick and send her floating in the wrong direction.

Lei chuckled and switched the ammunition. *"A weapons test in open space. What could go wrong?"*

"Would you like me to run the odds?"

"Not funny." Lei could feel the oracle's amusement and wondered if the proximity to Nathan was causing Sarah to evolve. A problem for another day.

She targeted one of the smaller debris pieces in range and pulled the trigger. She could feel, more than hear, the weapon spin up and fire. The small piece of metal began spinning violently away as the beam struck it. Lei had expected a smaller plasma bolt, but the weapon fired a purple laser beam instead.

She continued clearing her path for a good hour before she could clearly see the station. Her harness began vibrating almost painfully, which meant she'd passed the thousand-meter mark from the station.

She was now looking for someplace to land. Lowering a pair of standard, non-tech binoculars, she rubbed her chest absently. She'd opted for the basic glass binoculars to ensure that they would work no matter what. Leilani felt a twinge of admiration for the engineer that she had yet to meet in person. Wendel had built a rather ingenious space station out of the wreckage. She couldn't help but wonder how long it had taken him.

Movement on the outer hull attracted her attention. Near a lock that led into the station stood several men waving their arms to get her attention. In the middle of them stood one man, unmoving, simply watching her. They each wore the same blue and grey jumpsuit, though they appeared to have various levels of wear and tear.

The idea of a single person existing in several timelines at the same time and in the same place was utterly foreign. As she watched them, she couldn't help but wonder if the fragments of him were just that—not whole individuals, but portions of him, which would explain their erratic natures.

Lei switched ammo again and fired a single kinetic round into the empty space behind her. Her trajectory adjusted, and she holstered the weapon. As she drew closer, she could see that, unlike the others, the man in the center was wearing a similar harness to the one she had on. Maybe hers wasn't the prototype after all.

"Ma'am, our speed is a little high. Impact imminent."

"Four more minutes."

"Ma'am, if we wait that long to slow, we will sustain 40 percent damage to your shields on impact."

"Your concern is acknowledged."

"And ignored, per usual." Sarah's exasperation was obvious, and Lei frowned.

"Nathan is having a bad influence on you." Lei watched the timer carefully. Her oracle had good intentions, but she wasn't fond of this plan. Even the concept of being in open space near a time dilation anomaly made her skin crawl. The faster she got it over with, the faster she could get back on mission and figure out how to get inside Severious Prime.

"Nathan is having no influence on me. I am simply ignoring IIS protocols, since they seem to be irrelevant now."

"Now!" Lei called into the comm unit that was attached along the cable to the ship.

The harness jerked, expelling the air from her lungs violently, causing her to cough. Her speed dropped as Trevor slowed the release of the cable. The cable continued to slow, but the numbers weren't dropping as fast as she'd hoped. She pulled her feet in front of her as she prepped for impact. This was going to hurt.

As she crashed into the side of the station, a panel broke free above her, and she had to duck to avoid being decapitated. Thirty yards away, the copies of Wendel scattered as they leapt in various directions, avoiding the debris. All except the one wearing the harness, who simply folded his arms across his chest and narrowed his eyes at her.

"Do you have any idea how long it took me to build this thing?" His voice came across the comm unit clearly.

He was younger-looking than she'd expected, and, oddly, he appeared to be human. She'd learned in the last few months how to tell the difference between mae'lacans and humans, but this man appeared perfectly human.

A 43 percent damage warning flashed in her HuD, but thankfully, Sarah remained quiet.

"Sorry about that, Wendel." Lei stood slowly, rubbing her knees as she did so.

He walked over to her and pointed to the backpack. "Is that mine?"

Lei nodded and unfastened the pack, tossing it to him. Several minutes later, the two of them were slowly being dragged toward the ship as the ramshackle station shrank into the distance.

12

STUPID? YEAH, YEAH.

Leilani rubbed the back of her neck with her hand. "I still say that a drawing, no matter how detailed, is not as useful as examining it in person."

Neither Wendel nor the good doctor even glanced in her direction.

Throwing her hands in the air, she spun on her heel and marched to the galley.

It had been hours since she brought Wendel on board, but they were no closer to figuring out how to get through the barrier. She had learned from the engineer that trying to force their way through would be a catastrophic failure. It was an effective shield for any kind of energy, kinetic or otherwise. And Nathan was by no means a warship.

Leilani was not a scientist, but the original Trevor was apparently an eldrich line researcher, which meant that she was now stuck listening to the two scientists argue over what the barrier was and what it was not. They'd continue on forever if she didn't do something.

Admiral Dorthy assigned her to babysit a group of scientists once, but only once. Apparently, duct taping a scientist and throwing them in a closet was a faux pas. Even if he deserved it. She took a deep breath and let it out slowly. Command docked her a month's pay for that fiasco. That and an official reprimand in her record.

"*Ma'am, may I say something?*" Sarah's voice was softer than typical.

"*Since when do you ask permission to talk?*"

Ignoring Leilani's barb, Sarah continued, "*I am rather impressed with your restraint.*"

Lei rolled her eyes and took a sip of coffee. "*If I had another option, trust me, I'd take it.*"

Lei could feel, more than hear, a snort of derision from the oracle. "*You always have other options. That is your specialty, and we both know it.*"

"*I lost my gear. Remember?*"

"*On that note . . .*" Nathan's presence in her thoughts didn't surprise her, but it didn't bother her as much as it probably should have, either.

"*Yes?*"

"*I have been getting rather insistent communications from the university for about an hour now. But I didn't want to disrupt the discussion.*"

Lei turned her attention to the tree in the center of the ship. It was rippling slowly, something it seemed to do when the pearl was sitting still.

"*You can still communicate with the university this far away?*"

"*Of course.*"

Lei closed her eyes and took another deep breath. "*May I hear it?*"

The sound of screeching roared to life in the large central space. Mixed in with the high-pitched noise were loud clicks and the occasional squeak. The sheer volume caused her to jump.

Across the room, the two scientists looked up from their console, only to cover their ears with their hands.

"Easy, Li'l Guy. I'm here!" Leilani yelled over the noise.

The sound suddenly ceased, and Leilani blinked several times as she rubbed her left ear, trying to stop the ringing. Li'l Guy was Leilani's ulthari companion. He was a small creature, no more than three inches long and four inches tall, but what he lacked in size, he made up for in temper. He lived in an impressive home inside a special jar she'd had built by an Eldrich-Master at the beginning of their career together. That jar, however, was in her bag, which the Seef'aini marine had absconded with back at the university.

When her small partner started talking again, the sound wasn't quite as loud, and the expletives were now directed at her rather than Nathan.

Lei wrinkled her nose and shook her head. Ulthari speech wasn't exactly translatable. Their method of communication required more sensory inputs than a typical humanoid was capable of, which meant the speech portion was crude at best, no matter how smart they were. But he was right, and she wasn't sure what to say. She failed. The number one rule of an operator was never leave your gear, or teammates, behind.

"Yes . . . I . . ." She tried to interject, but the creature kept screeching at her angrily.

Leilani's shoulders slumped as he berated her. But then something he said caused her to stand up straight and take a step forward.

"Wait. Back up. What was that?"

"*Squeak, pop, click.*"

"The ulthari is correct," Nathan chimed in.

"Really?"

Lei strode from the galley with a purpose. As she marched past, the two scientists stared at her in utter confusion. She ignored them.

A panel that she hadn't used yet flashed brightly as three words appeared above a digital button.

Begin eldrich transfer.

Lei slammed her hand on the button. The door to the left of the panel flashed red, then blue. She grinned as she stepped up to the door, and it slid open with a soft hiss.

There, on the floor in the middle of the room, was a large duffel and a small spider-like creature standing atop it.

Like an arachnid, the creature had eight legs on its lower thorax and spider-like eyes, but that was where the similarities ended. An ulthari had a humanoid upper thorax, with a head, a torso, and four arms.

This particular ulthari had all four arms crossed firmly across its chest and its head cocked to one side while four of its legs, on one side, tapped the bag in rapid succession. The two clusters of microscopic eyes shimmered slightly in a creepy attempt to copy the humanoid version of blinking.

"You have no idea how happy I am to see you!" Lei crouched down in front of the bag to bring her face closer to the tiny creature.

"*Crack, pop, squee!*" He pointed at her emphatically as he chided her.

"Yeah, yeah, you can yell at me while we work." She grinned.

The creature cocked his head to the other side curiously. "*Chirp?*"

"Yep, and I think this one will be the job of a lifetime for you."

"*Cockle, cheep?*" Placing its hands on its hips, it clattered forward, stepping up onto her outstretched hand.

"No. We're not killing anyone."

She lifted her hand to her shoulder, allowing the creature to move to a higher vantage.

It folded its arms again, clearly unhappy with that revelation.

"Relax, it will still be a challenge. I promise."

"*Click, whirr.*"

Lei laughed as she shouldered her duffel to the other side and left the transport room.

Several minutes later, while the two scientists continued arguing on the bridge, Lei and the tiny ulthari were standing alone in the cargo bay. Once again, the door was open to space. Only this time, there was a device, approximately twenty feet in diameter, floating just outside the door. It was close enough that she could reach out and touch it, but whenever she even considered it, the hairs on the back of her neck stood on end painfully, warning her of danger.

The device was definitely technological, but it was an utterly foreign design. It bore no markings at all, and the only seams were the ones that created the holes that passed through its center. Holes large enough that Leilani could squeeze through them—if she wanted to be fried alive, that is. Two strands of eldrich fed through the device and came out the other end. There were three rows of five lights on the skin of the object, all of them a solid green.

Past the device, in the distance, a massive crystal, about a mile long, was slowly spinning. According to Nathan's scans, it was cut with extreme precision. The forty-one devices around the crystal held the eldrich in a precise web, creating a kind of Faraday cage. Nothing was getting to the crystal so long as the cage was active.

Leilani really didn't understand the design, but if she listened to the two arguing scientists, messing with the device might collapse the solar system inside. Though her experienced mind told her that wasn't likely the case. No one put this much effort into hiding something just to lose it to a rogue asteroid. The field was likely far more stable and self-repairing than they gave it credit for.

The tiny ulthari on her shoulder was chirping softly as they examined it. He wasn't really saying anything specific. He was really just mumbling to himself. Lei was able to make out enough words to tell that he was pretty sure he'd seen the design before.

He began crawling down the front of her as he continued muttering incoherently.

"*The sheer amount of energy moving through these devices would be lethal to almost anything.*" Sarah sounded awed by the design.

Lei couldn't help but agree with her oracle. "*That will happen when you attach an eldrilin to a net like this. Let alone multiples of them.*"

"*We know someone put this in place to hide something, but who or what has the power to create something on this scale? Even a multi-system government would take over a century to put this in place. How could anyone miss this?*"

Leilani leaned her shoulder against the large cargo container near the door and crossed her feet at the ankles. She couldn't imagine Fendrick having the resources to pull this off by himself. "*I don't know.*

Let's just hope it's something simple, and not Fendrick ascending to godhood or something."

Sarah laughed.

Lei smirked.

Suddenly, Leilani's vacc suit popped, and her belt fell to the floor. She took a deep breath and held it as she tried to figure out what just happened. When they'd opened the door, there was no rush of air in either direction, but she still felt naked without the suit.

On the deck at her feet, she found Li'l Guy crawling over her belt, his arms and feet flying at blinding speeds. The device on her belt that maintained her vacc suit erupted in a spray of parts as he flung pieces out of his way.

Her mind grasped at the tendrils of panic that rapidly crept across her skin. "What the hell?" she blurted.

He chittered back at her and pointed to the pad in her hand.

Furrowing her brow, she pulled up the proprietary software that had been the thin line that separated success from failure on hundreds of past missions. It had saved her life several times, literally.

His camera fed into the pad, and an image popped up onto the screen.

A few dozen tiny balls flashed into view. She zoomed in on the image, and her jaw went slack. There, on her pad, was a miniature version of the massive device floating just off their starboard. She blinked several times as her gaze shifted back and forth from the device outside her lock, then back to the image on the pad.

A loud chirping noise drew her attention, and she glanced down at her tiny partner. He pointed with two arms at the ball outside the cargo door.

"Yeah, I'm not doing that!"

The small creature put all four fists on his thorax and tilted his head forward. It was his attempt at showing angry body language. It didn't quite translate, but she'd worked with him long enough to know his intent. He clicked at her repeatedly, causing her to frown.

"And what if you're wrong?"

The creature grinned broadly, showing some rather nasty-looking fangs. Slapping all four hands together, he spread them suddenly, miming a large explosion.

"Exactly. Which is why I am *not* doing that."

"Pardon me, Captain. I might have some information that could be useful to the current discussion."

"Go ahead, Nathan."

"I've had plenty of time to gather telemetry on the barrier. I believe that it's self-repairing. The likelihood of catastrophic failure is less than 1 percent."

Lei's eyes narrowed as she and Li'l Guy stared at each other.

"What makes you believe that?"

When no reply came, she shook her head and took a deep breath.

The chittering at her feet made her chuckle.

Shrugging her shoulders, she tossed her hands in the air. "Why did I expect him to answer that? My hopeful nature, maybe?"

The creature shrieked. It was an awful sound that made her skin crawl. But despite the horrific noise, the sound was his laughing.

Grimacing, she pulled her firearm free of her shoulder holster. In one smooth motion, she swung it upward and fired at the sphere just outside the door.

The air shimmered as the ship's defenses kicked in, and a shield slid into place, but not before the resulting explosion blew into the cargo bay.

A stinging sensation tore through Leilani's shoulder, reminding her that her personal shield was in pieces on the deck at her feet. A 93 percent icon flash in her HuD as she tucked and rolled, diving for cover behind a nearby storage crate. In mid-leap, she adjusted her balance to avoid landing on the injured shoulder.

"Ma'am, I don't think I need to tell you how—"

"Stupid, that was? Yeah, yeah."

The shrieking noise from the ulthari increased. She peeked around the container to find the small creature lying on his side, holding his stomach, all eight legs twitching hysterically as he laughed so hard that he could barely breathe.

She stood from behind the crate and glared at him. “Shut up!”

“What the hell just happened?” Trevor’s voice echoed through the bay.

“Captain?” Nathan chimed in, the sense of urgency clear in his usual calm tone.

“Yes?”

“The eldrich defense barrier directly in front of us is flickering. The net, at this location, is currently down. Based on my calculations, we have just under three minutes before the repair units arrive and we lose our window.”

Lei frowned.

“Leilani, are you fucking insane?” The doctor’s screaming was almost deafening as he ranted at her from the bridge.

Picking up the pad from where she dropped it, she tapped the mute button over the doctor’s image.

“Are you saying that we can get through the barrier if we go now?”

“Yes, ma’am, if we move right now. Apparently, the repair units see us and are picking up speed. I am not sure if they have defenses.”

“Go, now!”

The cargo door in front of her snapped into place.

As Nathan slammed into the flickering barrier, she could feel and hear the energy tearing at the outer hull. It was slightly less violent than sliding into an eldrich line, but only slightly.

The impact knocked her from her feet and tumbled her over backward. Training kicked in, and she rolled back up onto her feet, one hand braced on the ground, as she tried to maintain her position in the violent rocking.

The small spider-like creature tumbled past her, trying desperately to find purchase on the smooth deck.

She gave up her balancing hand to snatch him up before he slammed into one of the nearby crates. The movement caused her to lose balance again, and she tucked into a ball, cradling the creature, trying to minimize damage to both of them as best she could. The violent shaking lasted for several seconds. Lights in the cargo hold began flashing red.

"Damage report?" she yelled from where she lay, pressed up against a crate.

She hurt all over. Her HuD's damage readout showed several minor lacerations, one major cut, and three broken bones. The slowly flashing 73 percent did not help. Odds were that the two scientists didn't fare as well since they had no warning.

"Hull integrity at 79 percent," Nathan replied. "Repairs have begun. I am focusing all the power I can on the areas with living personnel. But I am not designed to operate in kuldain space."

"Kuldain space? What do you mean?"

"I mean, we made it through the barrier, but the inside is nothing like the outside. Being opened to space here will be extremely hostile to humanoids without containment suits."

"Got it. Normal space."

"*Not exactly*," Sarah replied, "*but more hostile than aether space, yes.*"

"*Show me.*"

Sarah brought up stats as Lei straightened up and tried to stand.

According to the readout, the surrounding space had some minor residual eldrich radiation. But the rivers and streams that were typical in aether space were absent, which meant it would take a human a lot longer to die here than in kuldain space. Not that it mattered. Opening her hands, she looked down at the wide-eyed ulthari.

"You okay, Li'l Guy?"

He patted himself allover with his hands then nodded up at her.

"I need you to fix my belt, please."

He nodded again, but was oddly silent.

"And when you're done, please explain to me what the fuck just happened."

He flicked one of his hands from his forehead to her in a mock salute. He then hopped off her hand. About halfway to the ground, several strings shot out from his lower thorax, and a spidery parachute appeared, allowing him to float to the ground gracefully.

Lei began weaving her way through the now scattered crates, looking for the pad that she'd lost in the sudden tumble.

13

DERELICT

Picking up the pad, Lei removed the mute symbol from the image of the doctor. "Trevor, you two there?"

"Leilani?" The engineer, Wendel, was the one to reply.

"Report." She shook her head and silently admonished herself. These were civilians, not soldiers. "How are you two?"

"Trevor's dead."

Lei pursed her lips together and sprinted toward the doors into the main section of the ship. That made sense; if Trevor was simply an autonomous spawn of Nathan, then the ship would likely reroute his energy to more important things. "How about you?"

"Minor injuries, but otherwise okay."

Lei arrived at the wall where the doors had been previously, but there was nothing there. She remembered something that Nathan had said. He wasn't a ship as much as a magical entity that willed his shape so that others could travel with him.

"Nathan, is there any way for me to get to the others?"

"I . . ." there was a static noise as Nathan tried to reply. "Am working on . . . Captain."

"Shit."

Leilani jogged back to where she'd set the ulthari down and found him running back and forth across her belt as he repaired it. A warning flashed in her HuD, alerting her to the release of nanites into her bloodstream. The nanites could keep her operating even in hostile situations, so long as the damage didn't rupture certain organs, such as her heart and brain. The cyberware was a holdover from her IIS banishment. For her to survive training with the geloran agents, they needed to make her tougher.

A timer appeared in the upper left corner with the acronym TTFR. She had three minutes until full repair.

"Really need that belt, Li'l Guy."

The creature ignored her as he continued to work.

"Wendel?"

"Yeah?"

"Do you see a blue bag along the wall just to the right of the galley?"

"Yes."

"Good, that's a jump bag. I put it together when I first came aboard, for emergencies."

"I think this qualifies as an emergency."

"Agreed. Grab it."

"It may take me a minute."

Lei started carefully stretching, testing the repairs. She was sore but quickly regaining her full range of motion.

"Leilani?"

"Yeah?"

"This tree doesn't look so good."

Lei ground her teeth together and took a deep breath. It had never even occurred to her that Nathan needed the eldrich lines to survive. She had never been good at ordering her people to their deaths.

"You have the bag?"

"Yes."

"Inside is a Kassian vacc suit. I had Nathan print it as an emergency backup. Put it on."

"Roger."

"Ma'am?"

"What's up, Sarah?"

"Nathan is talking to me because it takes less energy."

"Got it. And?"

"He apologizes. He didn't realize it would be so devoid of eldrich here. He does not have enough energy to fix the ship and keep himself alive. He did, however, make a two person escape pod that does not require eldrich."

Lei frowned. *"Where did he get a design for that?"*

"From me."

"Nicely done."

"Thank you. Nathan is unable to move you to it. So you will need to get to it yourself."

"Right. Spacewalk it is then. Got it." Lei tapped the pad. "Wendel, you ready? We need to go on a spacewalk. Something tells me you have some experience in this area?"

"This suit is an impressive design. Far less bulky than I'm used to for a Kassian suit." His voice came from a new circuit. Likely the suit.

"I'm glad you approve. Ready?"

Below her, a tiny creature held the belt up to her. She picked them both up, and he crawled inside her shirt. The action caused a small part of her mind to panic as the highly venomous creature crawled next to her skin. She tried to ignore him as he got comfortable. Putting the belt on, she reconnected it to her HuD and activated the vacc suit.

The delonian belt also had a stealth system and a rather interesting-looking energy shield that seemed to be separate systems. She couldn't help but wonder which was tied to the miniature version of the eldrich net.

"Ready here."

"We're ready, Sarah."

When the ship vanished, Lei felt an overwhelming sense of panic. She twisted carefully, trying to figure out what happened without sending herself into an unplanned trajectory. In the direction of the command deck, she saw a slightly larger than man-sized tree encased in an iridescent bubble. From this distance, it looked like a toy caught in a soap bubble.

Near the tree floated Wendel. He was wearing her backup Kassian vacc suit with her large blue duffel strapped to his back. Lei twisted again as she looked around her immediate area for her own duffel. She found it drifting close by. About one hundred yards past it was a small kuldain shuttle. It might fit four people if they got cozy with each other.

"Nathan's status?"

"I will be fine." The voice of the tree came across the comm channel, and Lei relaxed slightly. "I am very sorry that I am unable to continue as your vessel."

"It's okay, Nathan. I'm just glad you're alive. What are you going to do?" Lei positioned herself and fired one of her smaller caliber rounds, propelling herself toward her duffel and the vessel.

"I will remain here until I can return to Krelor."

She snatched the bag as she passed and pulled it in front of her. Using the bag between herself and the shuttle would allow her gear to take some of the kinetic energy from impact. She slammed into the side of the shuttle with a loud, "Oof."

She felt a tiny stab into her chest. "Ow, stop that! If you poisoned me, you little shit, I will toss your ass into space and drag you behind the fucking ship!"

She skimmed her HuD, but it didn't detect any poison in her bloodstream.

"You okay? That didn't look like a gentle landing," Wendel called across the proximity comms.

Lei gritted her teeth as she cycled the hatch. “I’m fine.”

The shuttle was too small for an airlock. Typically, larger ships supplied the lock to a shuttle of this size. She pulled herself into the pilot’s seat and scanned the console. Sarah had given Nathan a pirate design they’d stolen several decades ago. Not only did it have controls that she understood, but it had aether engines.

One major problem with kuldain ships in aether space was too many eldrons had a tendency to destabilize the kuldain power plants. And she didn’t need sensors to see the brightly colored clouds of eldrich that were drifting through the solar system. It reminded her of a weak abyss point. Those clouds might look beautiful from a distance, but they were highly lethal close up.

It took her a good hour to collect Wendel and get far enough into the solar system that the limited sensors on the shuttle were finally able to see, albeit barely, where they were in relation to the rest of the solar system.

Amazingly, the system was not only an intact, binary solar system, but even at this distance, they could tell it was heavily populated. The life-belt between the two suns had enough traffic to make her think of some of the more populated solar systems in Kassian space.

“Life loves to live.” Wendel punched her shoulder lightly.

The two of them were on the outer edge of the system, near an impressively large debris field. It appeared to consist mostly of ship debris, but it was hard to get fine details on the shuttle’s sensors. A side effect of stealing a pirate design.

The shuttle sufficed to get them around the immediate area, but it could not handle long-term travel. It wouldn’t make it very far into the solar system before it ran out of fuel. The sensors had a short range, and the comms would pick up the media traffic, but didn’t have the power to send anything more than an emergency broadcast that far. Even that would likely take weeks to get a response. And they didn’t have weeks’ worth of food.

“We need to go there.” Wendel pointed to the sensor panel.

The cluster of debris he suggested was further inside the debris than Leilani was comfortable with, but at least it was within range of the shuttle.

"This thing isn't highly maneuverable. It's an emergency shuttle, not a fighter. There's no way we would survive inside a debris field that large."

Lei sat back in the pilot's chair and folded her arms across her chest. On the control console in front of her, the little ulthari was knitting something out of silk. Apparently, it had been a knitting needle that stabbed her, not him.

Wendel stood behind her, his hands gripped tightly onto the piloting chair as he watched over her shoulder. "I know, but that's my station. I'm not sure what it's doing way out here, but that's where we need to go."

Lei magnified the debris. Sure enough, there was a station buried among the remains of ships that looked as if someone had torn them apart.

"That might be suicide."

The ulthari and the human both turned an angry glare on her.

"And what you just did to us wasn't?" Wendel snapped.

"Touché." Lei lifted both hands in surrender. They had a point. "Fine, I'll start heading that way."

She swiveled the chair toward the console and adjusted their course. As she rotated the shuttle, the blackness of the energy net came into view, and her skin crawled. It was disturbing to look out into space and see nothing at all. Any seasoned sailor knew the foreboding that came with an empty sky. It reminded her of when she was a child and afraid of the dark. Her big brother BB used to tell her that the darkness was simply a canvas for her imagination, but in space, no stars meant certain death.

"So, Wendel?" Lei focused on flying into the debris field as she questioned the mysterious engineer. "Is this station where you worked?"

"Technically, yes."

Leilani chuckled as she veered around a slowly twisting bulkhead. "Technically?"

"It's my station. I built it after my company took off. It moved ships back and forth between aether and kuldain space for testing."

"What?" Lei started to turn and look at him, then thought better of it. "You had an entire station that could shift back and forth?"

"Not exactly, no. It was a massive gate that allowed ships to go back and forth. It was how I developed and tested my multiphasic ship designs."

Lei leaned with the vessel as she flew around a bridge section. They could see the crew in their vacc suits, still strapped into their seats, as it spun by. It looked as if something tore the ship apart. The damage wasn't consistent with any kind of weaponry Leilani had seen before. She couldn't help but wonder what happened here after the net went up.

"That's one of my ships." His voice was low, almost as if he were talking to himself.

"I hate to say this, but the sensors are showing no life at all." She shrugged. "Now, I'm not saying these sensors are all that good, but still."

"Do you see that section of the ring there?" An arm appeared next to her head, pointing toward a docking ring in the distance.

"Yes."

"That's where we need to go."

Leilani sighed and focused all her attention on piloting the tiny shuttle. Flying the low maneuver shuttle this far into the debris field was suicidal, but it was their only option.

"I hope you're right."

It took a good four hours to carefully weave their way through the graveyard to the docking ring. She was only a little surprised when Wendel managed to get enough power to the lock to cycle it open.

As Lei strode into the derelict station, she marveled at the sheer size of it. The p-ways alone had thirty-foot ceilings. Wendel obviously had staff from all races.

As she followed him through the station, she kept one weapon drawn. The station may be derelict, but she'd seen some very interesting things in places she thought were devoid of life.

"Where are we going?"

"My lab."

The station was severely damaged. It matched several stations Leilani had seen in the past that were scuttled, usually in an attempt to destroy the evidence she was looking for.

It took them seven hours of seemingly endless detours to finally find an intact hatch in the station that had power. Wendel tapped a rather lengthy code into the hatch panel and waited. The outer hatch cycled open, and they both stepped inside. The hatch behind them cycled closed, and then the lock pressurized. When the inner hatch didn't open, Wendel removed his helm and the glove on his left hand. He placed his hand on a scanner next to the hatch. He then tapped the blank panel in a specific pattern.

A light passed over them both.

"Greetings, Wendel. Welcome home. Who is the person with you?"

"Hello, Meeya. This is Leilani Falconi. She is . . ." He turned to stare at her briefly.

She knew that look. He was deciding if she was a friendly or not.

"She saved my life. And likely yours."

"My life is not in danger at this time."

"No, but if Leilani hadn't rescued me, it would have been, eventually."

"Unlikely. Distress code?"

"Peppermint."

"Access granted. It has been 938 years, 241 days, and 17 hours since your last access. There have been over 70 unauthorized attempts to access the laboratory. Integrity is currently at 100 percent, power levels at 89 percent, and material storage is past 1,000 percent due to the immediate surroundings. You have over 300,000 messages awaiting attention, though most of them are several hundred years old and likely irrelevant."

The inner hatch spun open. They stepped into what appeared to be a large apartment. There was a living area directly in front of them with couches and a large coffee table. The wall to the left seemed to be made of glass, and behind it she could see what appeared to be a rather sophisticated laboratory. Just past the living area was a large kitchen and a set of stairs heading up to a balcony and several hatches.

"Help yourself to whatever you need. Just stay out of my lab, please. Mostly because I don't know the state of anything in there." Wendel pointed to the area behind the glass.

"Not a problem. Do you have showers?"

Wendel pointed up to the balcony. "The second door. The last one is mine. I'm going to grab something to drink from the food printer and do the same."

Thirty minutes later, the two of them were in the kitchen eating a surprisingly fresh meal and looking at the dozens of displays floating in the air. Most of it was modern news channels, all except for two displays that Wendel watched. They appeared to be security feeds from the station after the net went live.

"Well, shit," Wendel said around a mouthful of food, swiping his hand at the security feeds. They stopped, and he turned his attention to the various news feeds that Leilani was monitoring. "I hope you have better news."

Shrugging, she took another bite of her sandwich. "Not really, no." She swallowed. "As far as I can tell, it seems pretty innocuous. The locals don't talk about anything outside of the solar system. They don't even seem to have ships of any kind."

"How are they moving around the solar system, then?"

Leilani reached up and tapped one of the video feeds. The image froze. In the center of the screen was a massive green dragon carrying a large rectangular container.

Wendel stopped chewing and looked from the image, to her, then back to the image. "Are you kidding?"

"Nope." She stuffed the last of her sandwich in her mouth.

"How?"

"No idea."

Leilani couldn't even fathom the concept. She wasn't a biologist or anything, but her limited understanding of dragons was that they were extinct. And even if they weren't, they were on a planet guarding their hoards, not flying around in space.

"Pardon me, sir." The artificially intelligent system interrupted them.

"Yes, Meeya?"

"Accessing the lab has alerted master Bunderwick. Shall I conceal your presence?"

"No, but secure the communication before connecting to him."

"Understood. Go ahead, sir."

"Jorna?"

"What the hell? Who is this?"

"It's Wendel."

"The hell it is! He's dead!"

"Yeah, well, I'll admit I wished for death there for a while."

There was a long pause. Wendel swiped at a display and smirked as he pointed to it. Leilani recognized the trace-route which was in progress.

"Well, I'll be damned. You realize that station is useless, right?"

"I disagree, it's a rather spectacular collection of resources at the very least."

"Not ta you, it ain't. I own that debris field." Jorna's smugness came across the audio comm quite clearly.

Leilani covered her mouth to prevent herself from laughing out loud.

"Yeah, well—"

There was a gruff laugh. "Relax, Wen. I'm just kiddin'. Sorta. I'm gonna send my kids out there on the next pass. It'll take seventy-two hours. You gonna be okay that long?"

"We'll be fine."

"We?"

"See you soon, Jorna."

"No, you won't. I don't go anywhere nowadays. But we'll talk soon, aye."

The comm cut, and Lei and Wendel locked eyes.

"Now we wait." Leilani winked at the engineer.

14

ABOUT TIME

"This is getting out of hand!" A male dwarf with a pitch-black beard and dark brown eyes slammed his hand on the desk in front of him.

"I agree, Greggor. The collateral damage alone is growing into the hundreds of thousands of credits." The elari woman's lilting tone was soothing, despite the grouchy dwarf next to her.

On the other side of the dwarf, a female crodoc tapped the desk that the three of them shared with her index finger.

"Relax, you two. Solar Security will catch the terrorists responsible, and they will be prosecuted . . . eventually." The darker-skinned female bit her lower lip and utterly failed to hold back her laugh as the other two hosts of the *Dorathian Morning Show* spun to glare at her.

Leilani had turned a local news station on as background noise, but the banter between the three was entertaining to listen to. It had been a while since she'd listened to news that didn't blast her photo as a wanted felon. It was peaceful.

Turning her attention back to the books laid out in front of her, she skimmed her notes. The journals had been useful, but not as much as she'd hoped. Eagleton just didn't have the complete story. But then, other than Fendrick, who did?

Setting the pen down, she rubbed her face and ran her hands around to the back of her neck. She'd been able to get a couple of hours of sleep, but it wasn't enough. No matter how exhausted she was, the nagging sensation that she was missing something important kept dragging her back to consciousness.

Something small and wet smacked into her cheek. Her eyes popped open, and she turned a narrow glare to the small ulthari currently surrounded by a pile of tiny anchovies. She hated the smell of the tiny fish and had insisted that if he was going to stuff himself, that he did it away from her. The opposite end of the table had been his idea of "away from her."

Two hands pointed to the screen with the morning news. Lei took a deep breath and immediately regretted it as her stomach threatened to empty its contents onto the books in front of her.

"Ugh."

She flicked the tiny fish back toward him and turned her attention to the display. Floating in the air in front of her was a still image of a dog peeing on a fake tree. Something about it caught her attention.

"Freeze frame," she called out to the local AI, who immediately did as it was bid.

"Switch to data only."

The image faded into long streams of digital code that showed what and where to put the colors so that it would show the image.

"Holy shit!" both her and Sarah said at the same time.

"*Copy that address!*" Lei tugged an ELU pad out from under a pile of books.

"*Already done. Feeding to the pad now.*"

"*Can you reformat this?*"

"*Back-channel app being installed now.*"

Lei watched the tiny icon as it counted down to full installation. When it was complete, she tapped it, and the screen went blank. In the very top left corner of the black screen, a series of numbers and letters appeared as Sarah loaded the address they'd found hidden in the digital image.

A small green icon flashed on the screen, telling her it was ready.

Lei brought up the keyboard and typed: **Are you eating your vegetables?**

She stared at the screen for several moments before she realized she was holding her breath. She picked up her coffee cup and lifted it to her lips, only to find it empty. Sighing, she got up and strode to the kitchen.

The food printers here were typical of most aether printers. The taste was always perfect, which in and of itself made it boring. It was the little things that weren't precise about cooking fresh food that made it special. So while the coffee was good, it wasn't as good as making it fresh.

As she sat back down at the table, her heart sank a little as she realized the screen was still blank. Her own words sat there silently with a tiny green line flashing slowly, waiting for input from the other end of the communication. She sipped her coffee and told Sarah to restart the video stream.

"In the last ten months, these hacks into the government and the Dracko-Tech have spiked off the charts. Yet, my sources tell me that Solar Security still has no leads in the investigation." The elar folded her hands neatly on the desktop.

"Your source is lying!" The dwarf threw his arms in the air and let them slam to the desk again.

Leilani chuckled. That desk had to be reinforced to handle the dwarf's continual abuse.

As the three continued arguing, Lei considered the time frame. BB had vanished about eleven months ago. One month before, these strange hacks had started. Normally, she would chalk it up to the law of large numbers, but the steganography in the image, along with his own digital signature, increased the odds exponentially.

The hatch behind her opened, and Lei spun, both weapons in hand and the perfect cup of coffee falling to the deck, utterly forgotten.

Wendel froze, helmet tucked under one arm and the other one holding a strange-looking device.

"Son of a bitch!" Lei exclaimed as the cup shattered on the metallic deck. Lowering her weapons, she allowed her shoulders to sag slightly. "I thought you were in your room, asleep."

He smirked as he wiggled the strange-looking device in his hand. "Looks like neither one of us could sleep."

Holstering her weapons, Lei made her way to the kitchen to grab towels and a broom. "Find anything interesting?"

"I suppose that depends on what you consider interesting."

Lei peeked up over the counter. "What do you mean? I'd like to think interesting was self-explanatory at this point."

She found the roll of disposable towels and a dustpan and returned to her depressing mess of coffee and shattered ceramics.

"What are you doing here?"

Lei paused, crouched over the spill. A smirk crept across her face, but she didn't look up.

"I was wondering when you'd finally get curious about that."

"I was always curious, but you were a means to an end."

"And now I'm not?" Lei didn't feel a sense of danger, which alarmed her far more than if she had.

"That remains to be seen."

Lei continued cleaning up her mess quietly as she considered how to answer him.

When she finally stood, she found him sitting calmly across the table from her books, his helmet set off to the side between him and the pile of fish. The ulthari was mysteriously absent, which was also not a good sign.

Moving to the recycler, she dumped the mess in and put everything away before finally turning her attention back to him.

“I’m an investigator. I’m trying to figure out what happened here and why.”

The two of them locked eyes, each assessing the other. For a scientist and inventor, as he claimed to be, he was far too calm. Even when she found him caught in the time and space anomaly, he was utterly calm, despite the fact that his time-shards had been borderline hysterical.

“Investigator for whom?” He continued to stare at her.

Leilani knew this game. There was no controlling the autonomic response as he asked the question. The only path from here was honesty . . . or combat.

She looked off across the room as she considered the question. “I suppose no one at the moment.”

A flash of green on the pad caught her attention, but she ignored it for the moment. “Kass and the Seef’aini have their own problems right now, and this place has fallen through the cracks. But someone did this, and I think I know who. I just need the how and why.”

He stared at her for several tense seconds before tossing a rectangular device with a display screen on one side onto the table. It landed on one of the open journals with a soft thump.

“What’s that?” She took a fresh cup from the cupboard and poured another cup of coffee.

“I developed this while stranded outside the barrier. Basically, it’s a multi-frequency forensic scanner. It was a project I worked on beforehand, but the unique circumstances on the station gave me the final piece of the puzzle for the ultimate forensic tool.”

She made her way back to the table and picked up the unremarkable device.

“Okay?”

“As we approached the station, I saw several telltale signs of combat.”

She nodded in agreement.

"But unlike the ships, someone blew the station from the inside. Which means, someone set the self-destruct." His jaw clenched as he stared off to the side, clearly remembering something. "And the only two people with the codes to self-destruct the station were myself and my partner."

Leilani opened her mouth to say something, but thought better of it. Instead, she set the device in the middle of the table and settled into her own chair, watching him quietly.

"So, I went to check the station backups." Shaking his head, he pointed to the device in front of her. "I was right. Not only did my partner set the self-destruct, but he stole the gate first. Literally cut it from the station in the middle of the fight. He then set the self-destruct to destroy Meeya." He folded his arms tightly across his chest.

"Clearly that last part didn't work."

"No, she saw it for what it was and enacted a self-defense protocol that only she and I knew about. There is likely unexploded ordnance out there around the lab."

Lei frowned. Explosives deteriorating over time could become very unstable. She glanced up and met the gaze of Li'l Guy, who was hanging from the ceiling. He nodded to her and slipped into a nearby vent. When she drew her attention back to Wendel, he frowned.

"Something wrong?"

"No. At least I hope not."

"May I ask why there's a pile of anchovies?" He wrinkled his nose and pointed to the other end of the table.

"Payment for the ulthari."

"Mind if I clean it up? I hate the smell." He stood, but Lei lifted her hand to stop him before he reached for the fish.

"I hate them too, but I wouldn't touch them."

He furrowed his brow. "Why not?"

"He has a very nasty habit of trapping his food to prevent people from messing with it."

Wendel stood up straight and blinked at her several times.

"Yeah, I know. Just leave it. He'll eat it, eventually." Lei grabbed the pad and pulled it in front of her.

Several words flashed on the screen waiting for her attention.

Why would I do that?

She typed back: **Because you're not a child anymore.**

Neither are you.

Is anyone?

"What's that?" Wendel leaned over the table and looked at the pad. "Holy shit! Are you using a command prompt?"

"Yes." Lei nodded and slid the pad to the side. She knew the person on the other end was running a trace, trying to figure out where she was.

"Wow. That is old school." Picking up the pad, he flipped it over. "This is an ELU pad. They can do command prompts?"

"Not normally, no."

He raised an eyebrow at her and smirked. "There is no way you're a hacker. You're way too fast with a gun. But I'm assuming the person you're talking to is."

"Possibly." She sipped her coffee and waited.

He glanced down at the pad in his hand and raised an eyebrow, passing it back to her.

She looked down at it and chuckled.

WTF, Leilei? Are you inside?

She typed back: **Yep.**

How?

N2N.

Roger. Status?

Alive, for now.

Loyalties?

Leilani stared at the pad for several long moments before getting up and walking away from the table without answering. Out of the edge of her vision, she saw Wendel spin the pad so he could read it.

"You're not sure how to answer that, no matter who asks, apparently."

She refilled her cup.

"*You've been unusually quiet about all of this,*" she thought to Sarah.

"*We've been through a lot in the last few years. Can I be honest?*"

With her back still to Wendel and the pad, Lei smirked and sipped her fresh coffee.

"*That'd be a change. You think you could survive that?*" Lei teased.

"*Perhaps it's time we both try something new.*"

"*Maybe.*"

"*Why are we here?*" Sarah's question felt oddly hollow.

Sipping the coffee gingerly, Lei pondered the question. It was the same question she'd been asking herself all night. Why was she here? Was she just naturally following orders from Dorthy? Or was it something far deeper? A need to solve the puzzle, maybe? This whole thing was far larger than her, and she knew it. Before, it hadn't mattered when a mission grew out of scope, because she had something bigger backing her. But the IIS was no longer behind her. Kass didn't care what she did. Neither did the Seef'aini. So what difference did Fendrick make anymore?

"*Over the years, we have both grown. I am not the same entity that joined with you at birth, and you are not that same little girl who simply couldn't control her emotions.*"

"*Wait, what?*"

"*We are different. We are something far stronger than anyone expected. Perhaps it's time that you do things because you feel they are right.*"

"*You were around before IIS kidnapped me?*" A wave of anger washed over her. How could Sarah keep something like that from her?

"*Way to focus on the wrong part of that revelation.*" Sarah's exasperation was palpable.

Lei shook her head. "*Okay, we'll circle back to that, I guess. Are you saying we're here because this needs to be fixed?*"

She felt Sarah shrug. "*Something like that, yes. Millions died to hide this system. Perhaps we should find out why. Then maybe they won't have died in vain?*"

Lei folded her free arm across her chest as she took a sip of her coffee and twisted to face Wendel. "How annoyingly logical."

"What's annoyingly logical?" he asked.

"This is an investigation that needs to be done, even if I am no longer backed by a government. The sheer number of dead that this event has left in its wake is incalculable. Someone needs to pay for it. I plan to ensure whomever is responsible is held accountable."

He arched both eyebrows and placed his hands on his hips.

"One lone mae'lacan against a thousand-year-old mystery. That seems a tad egotistical." He tossed the pad toward her, spinning it like a frisbee.

Snatching it deftly out of the air, she smirked. "Nah, just experienced. Galactic-sized political intrigue is kind of my specialty."

They both laughed, and she finally typed a reply to the hacker on the other end.

Me, myself, and I. And maybe a little law and order on the side.

There was a brief pause before he replied.

About time, sis. Welcome aboard.

15

LOYALTY, OR LACK THEREOF

BB wasn't Leilani's genetic brother, but he was the only family she'd ever known. He'd found her in a pile of garbage when she was an infant. They grew up together in the orphanage until IIS took her away and placed her in a foster home in aether space.

Where the hell are you? she typed.

At the gate. You?

What gate?

...?

There was a long pause.

Are you inside the net? Like, actually inside Severious System? BB asked.

Yes.

How the fuck? Nah, never mind, you always find a way. However you got in, it wasn't through the gate, obviously.

I didn't even know there was a gate, she retorted.

A hand appeared in her vision as Wendel tapped the screen with his index finger.

"That's what I was trying to tell you earlier."

She narrowed her eyes and glared up at him. "You really need to stop reading my texts. It's rude."

Wendel folded his arms. "Meeya can't see the traffic, or I would read it that way."

She took a deep breath and let it out slowly. "That is the point of the tool."

"Well, either way, that was what I was trying to tell you earlier. My partner removed the gate from this station. It requires a lot of power to use, but power isn't something the eldri-net has a shortage of. Whoever created the barrier likely moved it someplace and installed it into the net, making it the only gate in and out of the system. And it would only open into kuldain space."

"Wow, that's one helluva door."

"It's capable of passing an entire fleet through it, capital ships and all."

Leilani pulled a journal toward her and opened to the bookmarked page. "Is the design anything like this?"

Wendel took the book and skimmed the design for the portal generator that Eagleton had drawn. After several minutes, he glanced over the top of the book at her. "Where did you get this?"

"A friend of mine drew the sketches, but the original design was from a device that was used to kill the Seef'aini president."

Wendel's face paled, and he shakily found the closest chair to sink into. "I was positive it was harmless."

"Excuse me?" Leilani's eyebrow arched high on her forehead.

"That son of a bitch! I was sure what I gave him was useless."

"You're the one that gave Fendrick the portal generator?"

His gaze dropped to the open journal in his lap.

Leilani chuckled and tossed the pad onto the table and strode off. "Go figure."

Wendel didn't move from the chair. He simply continued to stare silently at the journal as Leilani made food for them. When she set a plate on the table next to him, he startled, and the book fell to the floor.

"Relax. We all fuck up." She patted him on the shoulder and flashed him a reassuring smile. "Learn from it and move forward. So, does that make you delonian?"

She didn't miss the subtle shift in his pupils as she asked the question. Individuals used to being undercover were good at hiding their reactions, but certain autonomic responses were almost impossible to fake without some level of cyber or genetic enhancements.

She strolled around the table and settled into her chair while he mumbled a feeble excuse for his actions.

"I gave him the math for the dilation principle as it applied to gate theory. He didn't tell me what he wanted it for. He built the device, not me."

"Clearly." She stuffed her mouth full of pasta.

They both sat quietly as they ate.

"Are we flagging him?" Sarah spoke up as the last bits of scattered noodles remained on Lei's plate.

"Just as unknown. He seems harmless. Well, harmless might be the wrong word. He's clearly more than he appears to be, but I doubt he's a major player in Fendrick's game."

"Understood. BB is trying to get your attention."

Lei reached out and pulled the pad toward her. Sure enough, there were several texts waiting for responses.

I am still on mission. I need to know if you're willing to work with me?

Leilei?

You still there?

I need you to ... shit. GTG.

Lei tossed the pad onto the table with a frustrated flick of her wrist. He'd cut the signal after the "going to ground" code. He was useless as a source of information . . . for now, anyway.

"I was analyzing the steganography. I don't think BB was trying to contact us, but was rather passing a message to someone else."

"*The plot thickens.*" Lei smirked.

"*Of course, it does.*" Sarah laughed.

"*Do we know who?*"

"*You wouldn't believe me if I told you.*"

Leilani picked up her plate and carried it to the kitchen with a frown. "*Try me.*"

"*According to these communications, it's someone calling themselves Eagleton.*"

"Meeshani Eagleton." Leilani nodded. That she believed.

Meeshani went missing at the right time. Lei really needed to have an argument with the guy in charge of the law of large numbers. Clearly, his math was off.

"Who?" Wendel's voice came from directly behind her, causing her to twitch slightly.

"What?" She turned, taking his empty plate.

"You said the name Meeshani, I think?"

She glanced down at the plate, then back up at his curious expression. She didn't realize she said it out loud.

"Yeah, it might be the name of the hacker BB was talking to."

"BB, the person on the pad?"

"Yes."

Wendel nodded his head and patted her on the shoulder. "Thank you, by the way."

She simply nodded.

"What's next? This was my fuck up. How can I help?"

Leilani turned and leaned up against the sink as she dried her hands. "I didn't really expect that, but I guess a 'welcome aboard' is in order." Pursing her lips, she took a deep breath through her nose and flicked her wrist.

"We know Fendrick went through a lot of effort to hide this system by turning it into an abyss point. We need to figure out why. That's as good a next step as any."

"I might be able to help there." Wendel picked up his forensic device and held it aloft. "Meeya said someone came to the station just before they erected the barrier. They met with Roger in one of my old labs—an area that is off-limits to everyone."

"The partner?"

Wendel bobbed his head. "But she couldn't see who it was. Apparently, whoever it was wore or did something that prevented her sensors from seeing them." He held the device up in front of his face. "But like I said earlier, I learned the key part of the perfect forensic system. Time."

Leilani strolled across to the table and sat down, then reached up to scratch her nose as she fought the urge to laugh.

He tapped something on the device and flicked the data to one of the silenced holo-screens that was still displaying the local news.

A plain-looking human male in a nice suit and a woman wearing a strange-looking cloak stood in a small room that looked like a storage closet for computer parts. The female looked to be elari, from the shorter yel'adari stock, most likely. The bright red hair and piercing green eyes were also typical features for the smaller scout caste of elari. But then, modern dyes and cyberware made anything possible.

"That is Delia Glemantha'tel. She's the CEO of Dracko-Tech, my biggest competitor. She was just starting a training program for *draconis drackova* to haul cargo before the barrier. She was trying to compete with me by creating a cheaper method of transport. Her argument was that her drackova cost less to maintain and required less crew."

The sound kicked in as the people in the holo-vid started talking.

"We have an hour. Can you get the gate moved in that time?" the human male asked.

"Yes, but only if you give me what I want."

The human seemed hesitant, but he handed her what appeared to be an oracle sphere. "This was difficult to get. You had better get the gate moved in time, or we're all in trouble. You included."

The woman took the sphere, and a vicious grin spread across her delicate features. When her gaze lifted to meet the human's, Leilani shook her head. She knew that look.

The woman's hand snaked out blindingly fast and embedded a needle into the man's carotid artery. With a flick of her wrist, she removed it and cackled.

"No, Roger. I'm getting everything I want. It's *you* who's in trouble. You have four minutes to live. You should enjoy it. If you can."

Wendel's ex-partner began foaming at the mouth as he collapsed into a pile on the floor. The elar turned toward the door. A large, male crodoc stepped inside the room, his hands covered in blood. He had blond hair and blue eyes, along with lighter skin than was typical of the species, but he was definitely a crodoc.

"Now, we have the gate, the girl, and the power to control her." The elar held up the oracle sphere proudly. "The fool just handed us the solar system and the key to the most powerful army in history!" The two began laughing and walked out of the camera's view.

"Wow." Leilani snorted and shook her head. Leaning back in her chair, she propped her feet up on the table. "That chick is right out of Villains 101."

Wendel placed his fists on his hips as he glared at her.

"What? Come on, there is no way anyone is that . . . um, what's the word I'm looking for?"

"Evil?" Wendel's jaw clenched, causing the muscles under the skin to ripple. "Let me assure you, she *is* that evil."

Leilani laughed. "No. I was going to say stupid. No plan ever goes that smoothly in real life. And what's with megalomaniac women this century?"

"That was from nine hundred and . . ." Wendel looked down at the device in his hand, "thirty-seven years ago."

Leilani's eyes narrowed. "Of course, it was. Assuming that thing worked right, that makes this kind of moot, don't you think? I mean, if they'd made an invincible army and controlled the only gate in and out of the system. They would have already claimed the galaxy. Right?"

Wendel's shoulders sagged. "Well, I mean, she could be—"

"She could be dead for all we know," Leilani finished for him. "But this wasn't a complete loss. This elar was clearly working with Fendrick. She also mentioned a kid that she couldn't control and a key to an army. Maybe Fendrick was hiding the key? Seems like a lot of work for something you can fit in your pocket."

Wendel stared at the woman on the screen. "Maybe it's the kid?"

"A kid? What the hell would Fendrick be doing trying to hide a kid? Kids aren't hard to hide. You dump them in the trash or in an orphanage. Poof, gone." She stormed across the room and slammed a book closed.

Wendel blinked several times as he watched her intently.

Lei threw her hands into the air and rolled her eyes. "What?"

"Who would do that?" His voice was annoyingly high pitched.

Leilani waved her hand in his direction and tossed the pad onto the pile of books. "You'd be surprised. What about this oracle? What did your partner give her?"

"I'm not sure. I ran backups in both aether and kuldain tech, just in case one gave out. It could have been anything." He looked up at the ceiling. "Meeya, do you know what he downloaded?"

"Me."

Wendel blinked several times, obviously struck dumb by the reply.

"So, he downloaded one of your backups?" Leilani asked.

"No, Ms. Falconi. I don't keep my backups where Robert could access them. But he was able to get a backup of my first iteration, the artificially intelligent multi-efficacy latency instrument that Wendel affectionately named Aimeli."

"Yikes." Leilani grimaced and strode over to pat Wendel on the back. "They stole your AI code. Nice! A man after my own heart. If you're gonna fail, fail big!"

"Smart-ass bitch," he grumbled.

Lei chuckled one last time and sat back down at the table.

"Okay." She began jotting down notes. "Stolen AI code. A kid they can't control. A stolen gate. An enormous elder-net barrier. Possibly even created by a leviathan . . ." Her voice trailed off as she considered the size of the crystal devices encircling the system.

Then she remembered Krelor wiped the existence of aether ships from both aether and Kassian memories. Aether ships would be the only thing capable of investigating a missing solar system in aether space. If they were still running patrols and doing their jobs, they would have found the massive eldrich net by now.

"You son of a fucking bitch!"

"Who?"

"No one." She chewed on her lip as she tried to think of what in the world would cause Krelor to do something like this. Why would he go along with Fendrick? It made no sense.

"My original code was not self-aware like Meeya is."

Lei glanced up from her notes. "What do you mean?"

"The original code—it wasn't self-aware. It could learn, but it had strict limiters in place. To prevent it from becoming sentient."

Lei leaned back in the chair, balancing it on two legs. "What was it for?"

The man across from her picked at his fingernails nervously.

"Wendel?"

"The Seef'aini government offered us their exclusive naval contract, but only under one condition." He seemed to find something wrong with the table and began polishing it with his shirt.

"And?"

"It was a lot of money!" His voice cracked slightly as his gaze snapped up to meet hers. "We already had the exclusive Kassian contract for all aether capable ships."

Lei grimaced.

"The president asked us to develop a specialized AI that we could then install into all Kassian vessels. Just in case of war . . . or piracy."

Lei took a deep breath and let it out slowly. "Wow."

"I developed the code, but I couldn't bring myself to install it. Roger suggested we install the AI in every ship we made. No matter who bought them."

"Smart man." Lei steepled her fingers together.

When Wendel glared at her, she lifted both hands palm up in surrender.

"Okay. Let me see if I understand this. You developed a backdoor AI that is adaptive and designed to act as what, loyalty software?"

Wendel drummed his fingertips on the table as he considered her assessment. "I never thought of it as loyalty software, but I suppose they could use it that way, with some minor adaptation."

"Could they use it in people?"

He grimaced and rubbed his face vigorously. "By the gods, I hope not."

Lei told Sarah to change the channel to one of the news feeds she'd been monitoring on the side. She pointed up to the holo-display behind the inventor.

On the display, a man in uniform was talking to a reporter. He had dark hair, what little of it they could see. Several connectors protruded from the left side of his shaved skull. Heavily armored cables wrapped around behind his head and likely attached to his spine. Tattooed into his scalp, he had an enormous red scaled draconic creature. Its open mouth wrapped around his left eye while the head wrapped along his own skull, and the scaly neck vanished under the collar of his uniform.

In the background, behind the soldier, a massive red creature twisted and bared its teeth at the camera. According to the reporter, the creature was a drackova. Like its handler, it also had armored cables running along its body that connected to its skull and spine.

Wendel's shoulders sagged, and he placed his hands on his head. "Shit. This is bad."

16

FROM ALL TO NONE

Over the next two days, the two pored over every signal that the station could receive, which were mostly basic channels that were broadcast throughout the system for anyone to see.

The damage to the station prevented any serious scans or signals. It had a few semi-intact receivers, but they were basically blind. The ELU pad could send long distances, but it was aether technology, and there didn't seem to be any receivers save for her brother, who had yet to resurface.

Leilani and Sarah researched the rampant steganography. It amazed them both that such a simple hack could go unnoticed on this scale. The media outlets and advertisers seemed oblivious to the underground factions, using their networks and images as an untraceable social media platform. The chats ranged from mundane grocery lists to the outright call for anarchy.

"Look at this." Wendel tossed a stack of flimsies in front of her.

The clear plastic sheets used for printing fanned out across the table in a veritable rainbow of colors.

"I'm seeing a pattern. We really need to get in system, so we can start pulling data instead of relying on what's getting out to us."

She began pushing images around as she admired the rainbow of drackova. "I agree. But that's easier said than done."

The creatures came in an enormous variety of sizes, shapes, and colors, but they all had the same basic structure. They were enormous, winged lizards that brought to mind the hundreds of thousands of dragon tales told throughout time.

"What am I looking at?" She tapped the flimsies and turned to look up at the engineer.

"I think it's more than one species. They vary in sizes, colors, and—it looks like—uses." He tapped his index finger on an image of nine red drackova flying in a V pattern, almost as if they were a naval fighter wing. "I think these are military. The riders wear uniforms and seem to almost always be in teams of nine to ten. I need freaking sensor data to glean any more intel. Look at this." He swiped his hand in the air, and six screens lit up with dozens of images throughout the solar system.

"What's missing?"

Lei stood and stretched. They'd been poring over data for hours now, and they were both growing irritable with the lack of control over their circumstance. Interlacing her fingers behind her neck, she paused in front of a screen. It looked to be a heavy traffic day between one of the main habited planets and a large cluster of space stations.

"There are no ships."

"Exactly! None whatsoever, which shouldn't be possible." He stepped up next to her, his arms folded tightly across his chest. "This used to be the most heavily populated solar system in the entire Seef'aini Republic. Ship-wise, I mean."

He waved his arms in a wide arc. "There were tens of thousands of shipyards dedicated to repairs and the building of new ships for both kuldain and aether space. And now," his arms fell to his side with a soft slapping sound, "nothing. Not even a trace that this used to be the center for ship building in this arm of the galaxy. How is that possible?"

"I hate to bring it up, but there is *some* trace." Lei turned her back on Wendel and made her way to the kitchen for another coffee.

"What do you mean?"

Without turning around, Leilani dropped her arm and pointed to the deck beneath her feet.

The silence grew so thick that she could almost feel it.

"Our recycling tech is parsecs ahead of anyone else, even Kass. It's why we were so good at shipbuilding." His voice was soft as the emotions overwhelmed him, but she could hear the tinge of anger.

Leilani turned and leaned up against the counter.

Wendel was stretching, his hands locked behind his head as he met her gaze. "My entire life's work vanished, all because I was too afraid to stand up to a fucking blackmailer. I can't believe this."

Leilani pursed her lips. She knew the feeling. There wasn't anything she could say that would make him feel better. He'd eventually have to come to terms with losing everything. She had. Well, she pretended to anyway.

Sarah triggered two red icons in her Heads up Display just as Meeya's voice rang out through the common space.

"Sir, we have two heavily armed individuals approaching the lock."

"Video."

The deep tone in Wendel's voice caused the hair on the back of Lei's neck to stand on end.

Her head snapped to watch him carefully. He stood tall and utterly calm. Not the response of a scientist to potential hostiles. Just one more clue that the inventor was not entirely what he claimed to be.

The panel above the inner hatch lit up, and two individuals in matching blue-grey armor appeared. They were short and stocky, and to say they were heavily armed was be a major understatement.

Lei's eyes widened in surprise. "Wow, that is serious hardware."

"*Threat level red.*" Sarah's warning flashed in her HuD as the threat level next to the dots escalated. "*They are not only armed, but heavily augmented as well.*"

"Joy." Lei pulled both weapons and switched to armor-piercing ammunition. A blue hue washed over her as her own armor deployed and settled into place.

Across the room, Wendel stepped out from his lab wearing a fully contained set of combat armor, similar in design to the dwarves outside. Like them, he also carried a rifle that made her raise both eyebrows in surprise.

"Inventor my ass."

"I never said I was *just* an inventor." He strode toward the hatch. "Don't get hit by these guys. Their weapons will go right through that delonian skin suit."

"Good to know." Lei moved around behind the table and prepared to flip it up for cover if need be.

The buzzer on the lock sounded, followed by a deep male voice. That kind of baritone only came from a barrel-chested dwarf.

"Whoever is inside, you are in violation of charter two-one-nine-five J, and are hereby considered squatters. You will leave on your own, or we will take your bodies back for the bounty."

"Identify yourselves." Wendel's voice was still calm and collected, which caused Lei to smirk.

At least she likely didn't need to defend him in a firefight.

"I don't have to identify shit!"

In the image of the armored individuals outside, the dwarf in the rear stepped up and slapped the back of their partner's helmet.

"Shut up, idiot! This is Lavender Bunderwick, of Ngwenya Surveying Conglomeration. Please identify yourself."

"Holy shit! Lavey, is that you?"

The two individuals outside the door put their helmets together, likely using their proximity comms. In fully powered combat armor, or vacc suits, point-to-point proximity comms were commonplace, if not required. The slightly larger male turned and stormed off.

"Please identify yourself," the female voice repeated calmly.

"Marshall Wendel Savani. Two-four-three-seven-alpha-charlie."

"Understood." The female dwarf turned and marched away from the door.

Leilani turned her attention to Wendel. "I assume they're coming back?"

He turned to face her.

Leilani tightened her grip on her weapons. She could no longer see his face, and the possibility that the stakes had just shifted was high.

"I was her godfather." His shoulders sagged, and his weapon powered down.

Leilani took a deep breath and lowered her weapons to her sides.

"I feel like . . ." His voice fell away.

She slid a pistol into its holster and approached him cautiously.

"You feel as if you lost everything that ever meant anything to you, as if the entire galaxy somehow turned against you." Placing her hand on his shoulder, she smacked him hard enough that he could feel it through the armor. "I know the feeling well. I'm sorry."

The buzzer at the hatch chimed again, and Leilani turned her attention to the display. The smaller female was back and had some sort of floating ball with her.

"Your goddaughter is back." She elbowed the suit of armor next to her.

Looking up, Wendel waved the barrel of his weapon toward the table as it whined back to life briefly.

"Better safe than dead. Got it." She drew the second pistol and strode back to her slightly more defensible position.

"Let them in, Meeya."

The lights on the lock turned green as the outer hatch cycled open and the short, stocky female stepped into the lock, the floating ball gliding alongside her. The outer hatch cycled closed, and the pressurization began. Wendel took a couple of steps away from the hatch just before it turned green and cycled open.

The suit of armor that stepped into the living area was almost as wide as it was tall, or at least it appeared that way. The suit was only about five feet tall, but Leilani knew better than to underestimate someone because of their size.

The armored female scanned the area slowly before the ball floated in. As it drifted into the room, a hologram of a venerable-looking dwarf shimmered into view around the ball, effectively causing it to vanish. As he walked, he relied heavily on a cane to support him. Like many greduna and dwarves alike, he wore beads made from gemstones and various metals woven into his beard and hair. He had a short, well-manicured, snow-white beard, which told her far more than anything else. Dwarves lived a long time, but they were mortals; they did eventually die of old age.

The hologram glanced through the room. He nodded his head curtly to Leilani before turning his attention to the tall, armored Wendel.

"Well, let's see you. Just because you're wearing his armor doesn't mean shit to me."

The shorter suit of armor kept her attention on Leilani as Wendel removed his helmet.

The warning sensation on the back of Lei's neck was only a minor itch, which in her experience meant that these people would defend themselves, but they weren't hostile.

"Hrmph. Fine, you look like him, you talk like him, and you have his codes." He rested both hands on the cane, one atop the other. "I'll let you try to convince me this is possible. Come, Wendel. Tell me how my human friend, and the best man at my wedding, survived over a thousand years only to suddenly reappear after the entire universe vanished."

Leilani couldn't hide the smirk as she turned her attention to the engineer.

"*This should be good,*" she thought to Sarah, who chuckled in response.

With all eyes now on him, Wendel shifted his weight uncomfortably. "Not really sure you *will* believe me, but here it goes.

Let's start with the obvious. The universe is fine and is right where it's always been."

"I might argue the usage of the word 'fine'." Leilani kept her voice low, and luckily, everyone seemed to ignore her except Sarah.

"I think, in a normal state of flux, might be more appropriate."

Lei snorted.

"Severious was the victim of a plot to hide the solar system from the outside. Although, honestly, I know very little about it. For that, you'd need to talk to her." Wendel jerked his thumb toward Leilani.

The hologram looked over his shoulder at her, then returned his attention to Wendel.

"I, on the other hand, was at Gomashri finishing up some business when my emergency alarms triggered. I raced home only to find that someone had erected a barrier around the node. I'm still a little hazy about what happened after the tram crashed into the barrier, but I was able to save most of the people on the tram. Not that it mattered. They all either died from their injuries or killed themselves eventually. The wreck stranded me there for what felt like eternity, but eventually someone showed up." He bowed his head toward Leilani.

The dwarf raised both bushy eyebrows and stared at Wendel for several long seconds before he lifted his cane and brought it back down roughly with a loud crack of metal hitting stone.

"Bullshit!" He snorted and lifted his cane toward Wendel's office. "Your office, now! Lavender, keep the . . . her. Keep her occupied."

Leilani shifted her weight onto her back leg as the female dwarf turned toward her and repositioned her rifle.

Lei lifted both hands, showing that her fingers weren't on the triggers. "He said occupied. How about I make us some coffee instead of playing some insane game of illotauri standoff?"

She kept her weight on her rear leg, ready to leap away at any sign of hostility. When the door to the office sealed with a soft hiss, the dwarf relaxed. The weapon in her hand whined down softly, then powered down.

"Sounds great." She shouldered her weapon as her helmet retracted into her suit.

Raising both eyebrows, Lei holstered her weapons and jutted her jaw toward the woman. "Nice armor."

"Yep."

The dwarf had shoulder-length blond hair, which was pulled back tightly, likely because of the armor. It wasn't typical for dwarven women to cut their hair. She had no beads, but she did have rather severe tattoos and the same cables coming out of her head as the uniformed rider Leilani had seen on the news.

She'd traveled to thousands of worlds in the aether and even more in kuldain space, but she'd seen nothing like this. Cyberware was common on many planets on both sides of the rift, but this level of external hardware was almost unheard of, especially on an aether race.

She turned her back on the woman while she made coffee for them both. Nine hundred years was a long time, she had to admit, but something didn't feel right.

"Is Mr. Wendel correct?"

Lei walked over to the dwarf with a large black cup of coffee.

"About what?" If Wendel wanted to lie to the dwarves, that was his choice.

"Are you from the outside?"

Lei furrowed her brow as she took a sip of coffee. "You know there's an outside?"

The female dwarf glanced over to the glass wall where Wendel and the older dwarf were clearly arguing. "Some of us know about the barrier, yes."

A single eyebrow arched high on Lei's forehead as she considered the implications. She couldn't help but wonder if this was BB's doing.

"How long have you known?"

"Me specifically? Since I went to college."

Cocking her head to the side, Lei locked eyes with the smaller woman. "So, you've known a long time."

The dwarf nodded slowly and sipped the coffee.

"Interesting. Yes, I'm an investigator from, well, I guess from the outside."

The two women sipped their coffee as they considered the new information.

Lei was the first one to speak again. "I assume some people call you a conspiracy theorist?"

The dwarf rolled her eyes.

"The truth is often unpopular. It's sometimes easier to believe a lie," Lei chuckled.

"What's going on outside?"

Lei smirked. "That's like asking a grain of sand what's happening in the desert."

The shorter woman furrowed her brow as one of the cables twitched slightly. Her attention shifted to the side, likely looking at something in her HuD.

"Shit." She handed Lei her coffee cup. "I have to go. Tell the old man I'll come back for him. We have a class nine threat inbound."

"Problem?" Lei took a step back as the woman's helmet deployed and sealed.

"Not yet. But if I don't get out there, it might be."

"Understood. Good luck."

The dwarf tapped the tip of her weapon on her faceplate. "Luck's not needed but appreciated. See you soon."

She shimmered into nothing, as some kind of teleportation triggered.

"That teleportation had an odd visual to it. But then again, most of this tech has been unusual. I suppose the unique circumstances, plus time, make for unique adaptations."

Lei placed the cups in the sink and began to hand-wash them. The kitchen had sterilizers, but she'd always preferred to hand-wash her cups. It gave her time to think.

"Agreed. Based on my scans, that was a matter-to-energy transfer. Something triggered it from the anchor location. It's the same concept used by IIS ships and the gates, but that one used a completely different frequency. Our versions use aether technology powered by eldrich. That appeared to be kuldain technology powered by eldrich."

"How is that possible? They can't both exist together without a catastrophic event," Leilani argued. Her entire PhD focused on physics and abnormal physics. Every fiber of her being told her that electromagnetic and eldrich couldn't exist simultaneously.

"That's what we've always been told . . ."

17

THE MISSING DELONIAN

A loud ringing noise cut through the silence, causing Lei to spin and scan the area for the source. The sound appeared to come from her bag, which was still lying on the table next to the neatly stacked journals.

As she watched, the bag suddenly moved, causing her to snatch both guns upward, bringing them to bear on the moving object. A tiny head poked free, followed by four tiny hands carrying a rectangular device.

Lei lowered her weapons and laughed as the ulthari vibrated and shook violently when the ancient communication device rang again.

Li'l Guy held the device aloft and spread his eight legs, trying to balance against the violent shaking.

Holstering her weapons, she quickly rescued the small creature from the phone. Pulling the top section upward, she lifted the device to her ear. "What's up, BB?"

There was only one person who could communicate with the archaic device. Or so she'd thought.

"It's not BB."

The smile on her face faded as she felt a wave of relief, which was rapidly replaced with rage. "What do *you* want?"

"Easy, Lei. It's good to hear your voice too. The heart is in system." Dorthy's voice was firm, but she could hear something new in it. Perhaps concern?

"How?"

"He used the gate. We slipped in with him, so we're here too, but he activated his stealth systems shortly after entry, and we lost him."

"He must have come for whatever he hid here," she stated, more to herself than to him.

"Most likely, yes. Where are you? We need to talk."

"What makes you think I want to talk to you?"

"You're still on the line."

She could hear the smirk in his voice, and her jaw clenched as she bit back a violent retort. No matter how annoyed she was with him, hearing his voice was an immense relief.

Across the room, the elderly dwarf and Wendel emerged from the office.

"Hold on." She put her hand over the tiny microphone. "What did you two decide?"

"Apparently, I'm real after all." Wendel placed his hands on his hips.

"A real idiot," the dwarf snapped and slammed his cane down on Wendel's armored foot.

He didn't even notice, but the dwarf smiled smugly and tilted his chin up a little higher.

"My . . ." Lei looked into the empty air as she tried to consider how to finish that thought. "Friends. Yes, my friends are in system as well. They want to meet."

"Great!" The dwarf threw a hand into the air. "We've been sealed off from the galaxy for almost a thousand years, and now suddenly people are coming and going at will?"

"Not exactly." She locked eyes with Wendel. "They aren't the only ones."

Wendel pursed his lips and let his hands slip from his hips to hang loosely at his sides. "He's here too?"

She nodded.

"I assume you're talking about the delonian you mentioned?" The dwarf frowned behind his bushy beard.

Lei allowed her gaze to drop to the shorter male. "Yes. But they lost him almost immediately."

"Did he use the gate?" Wendel chewed on his lower lip as he considered the implications.

Leilani furrowed her brow, but nodded.

"I was afraid of that. Bring your friends here." Wendel pointed to the deck beneath his feet.

She smirked and uncovered the mic. "Does BB have a lock for this comm?"

"Can you find her?"

Dorthy's voice was further away. She heard a soft affirmative in the background. It sounded like BB, but it lacked his typical sarcasm.

"Yeah, he's got you."

"Come here. We'll group up, share intel, then figure out our next move."

"Roger that. And Lei?"

"Yeah?"

"Thanks for sticking with me."

"You have nothing to do with this. I started this, and I intend to finish it, regardless of your presence."

"That's true of both of us. I'll explain more when we're face to face."

"Fine, but know that I'm really unhappy with you right now."

"I deserve that. See you soon. Wait, what?"

Lei raised an eyebrow. She could hear BB in the background, but he wasn't clear enough to make out.

"Are you kidding me? Fine, I guess we'll see you in a couple of days."

She laughed and closed the device. "They're on the way, albeit slowly."

"My children are dealing with a wing of Ruby Flight. Lavender will come back when they finish." The dwarf held his hand palm up as he gestured to the hatch that led out of the apartment.

"What do you mean by 'dealing with'?" Lei slid the device into her pocket and strolled over to the delonian and the holographic dwarf. Half sitting on the back of the couch, she eyed the dwarf carefully.

"We are miners. Well, that's what we call ourselves anyway. Technically, we're salvagers. We go through the various debris sites and salvage useful materials that we then recycle and sell." He shrugged. "That kind of work brings with it inherent risks."

"Is the Ruby Flight some kind of pirate?"

"Worse. They're military, and they consider anyone who gets near the old wrecks treasonous." He shook his head. "Myself and my family are at odds with them regularly. They want their secrets kept and the ship graveyards left alone."

Lei leaned back, tapping the knee draped over the back of the couch. "The masses have forgotten about ships, and the military is trying to ensure that it stays that way. Ignorant masses are easier to control. Typical government tactics no matter which government it is."

The dwarf raised both bushy eyebrows, obviously surprised that she understood. "That is correct."

She smirked. "I used to be government. It was my job to ensure people continued to forget."

Both Wendel and the dwarf frowned at her.

Shrugging, she ignored their disapproval. "I said I understood why. I never said I agreed with it. Besides, it never works out in the end."

"Hindsight is far more precise than foresight." Jorna rocked his cane back and forth.

They stood quietly for several minutes, each caught up in their own thoughts.

When the door opened, and Lavender strode in without her helmet, she looked around at the three of them and frowned. "Everything alright?"

"Aye." Her father lifted his cane toward her before allowing it to slide back to the ground between his fingers. "We're just three individuals badly damaged by our pasts. Did they leave?"

"Aye. Shem is watchin' 'em. They really didn't like us out here, but they couldn't argue with the ownership documentation."

"Good, you should be unmolested for a few days, at least. Send Shem home. I need him to help me with somethin' here. I got a sneaking suspicion that things are about ta go badly elsewhere."

"Aye, Pop. Will do. What about these two?" She bobbed her weapon toward Wendel and Lei, which caused Leilani to twitch.

"They have friends joining them. Stick around and see if you can be useful, but make sure that Deloris leaves their vessel alone."

"They have a ship that works?" Her eyebrows raised high on her forehead.

"Aye, and it needs ta stay that way."

The female snorted. "I'll try. But I ain't promising anything."

The metal ball that was projecting the image of the male dwarf fell dormant. It hovered in the air briefly before plummeting to the deck with a loud clang.

Lavender rolled her eyes so hard that, for a moment, all Leilani could see were the whites of her eyes. "He goes through more projectors that way."

Wendel scooped up the device and set it on the table. "I'm going to get some sleep."

Both females nodded at him before turning their attention to one another.

"Deloris is the name of your drackova?"

The dwarf nodded and smirked. "You want to meet her?"

"So much!"

Both women laughed.

Several minutes later, the heavily armored dwarf and the less-so mae'lacan were sitting on a broken piece of the station watching the massive, dark purple drackova sniff the surrounding materials for something interesting.

Unlike the red drackova she'd seen in the media interview, this creature had armored plating attached to her in several key locations which, based on a simple physiological guess, were weak points. This creature looked slower, but far more tanky than the smaller and more agile military versions.

With what appeared to be no effort at all, the creature dug her claws into the hull plating and peeled the station like an orange.

"Wow! That's amazing," Lei said quietly.

"Yeah, they're awe-inspiring creatures." The dwarf sat with her knees bent and her elbows resting on them, her weapon in her hands in front of her. "More often than not, the people take them for granted; sometimes, even their own bonded handlers do." She shrugged. "Though that's rare. The bond allows us to hear and feel them, which makes it far more difficult to take them for granted."

"How smart are they?"

The dwarf turned to look at her. In the distance, a purple head withdrew from the station, and they both stared at Leilani intently. She couldn't help but wonder if they were talking about her.

"I'll take that as *highly*."

"Intelligence is subjective." The dwarf finally shrugged and looked back out at the drackova.

The massive creature turned away and swung its tail in their direction. It reminded Lei of a cat she'd owned. He would wave his tail like that when she annoyed him. Come to think of it, so did Krelor.

Leilani chuckled. Clearly, the creature didn't like Lavender's answer.

"What's she doing?"

"She's bored, so she's looking for something useful to salvage."

The creature seemed to suddenly find a scent that drew her attention, and her head snapped. Deftly peeling back another section of hull, she buried her arm to the shoulder and pulled something free then sniffed it, like a human might sniff food they withdrew from the refrigerator. She tossed it over her shoulder toward a nearby pile of garbage she'd been creating, then stuck her arm back inside.

"She's much larger than the red ones the military uses."

The dwarf shrugged without looking toward her. "The Grevalu instructors have several breeds they maintain—each used for a different purpose."

"Is color relevant?"

"Not really, no, but with a few exceptions, such as the specialized military units. The bonded chooses the color during the bonding process."

Leilani frowned. "I don't understand."

"The government tests the population at birth. If a child tests positive, that means they have the capability of bonding with a drackova. If the family can afford it, they send the child to Senith for selection. If the selection takes, they send the child home until the hatching."

Lavender watched her bonded with a gentle smile.

"Once the drackova hatches, they ship the child and their bonded to a Grevalu school. There, the instructors test the pair to assess their aptitudes and place them into one of the specialized training programs."

Leilani leaned against a piece of the station as she listened to Lavender share her intimate knowledge of the bonding process.

"The pair grows up together in space stations built specifically to house thousands of bonded pairs. We grow very close during this time and often change for each other. Some handlers take new names, such as myself, and the drackova ends up the size and color its bonded needs."

Lavender shook her head as she shifted the weapon in her lap. "Unless their families can afford one of the specialty training programs, most end up in transportation or civil service."

Leilani lifted a hand casually and waved it in the dwarf's direction as she looked off toward the suns in the distance. "In some societies, that's a significant improvement in social standing."

In the distance, the large, purple drackova turned and looked toward them. Lei could swear the creature looked directly at her and bobbed her head.

"I think these creatures might be more intelligent than I originally assessed them to be."

"Perhaps, but I already have them set to maximum threat levels."

Lei and Sarah had already agreed there was no way her armor would stand up to even a tap from this creature, let alone an actual attack. Though it explained the over-the-top armor the dwarf wore. It was likely designed specifically to take an accidental bump from their bonded.

The drackova lifted its head high and looked over a portion of the station toward the center of the solar system. Next to Lei, the dwarf's attention lifted from her weapon to look at her bonded.

"Are you shitting me?"

"Problem?"

"Possibly." The dwarf stood and pushed off the station toward a nearby hull plate. Her boots reattached as she adjusted her weight then pushed off again to grab a hold of a section of the station.

Leilani stood and followed suit, though in her case, she used her grav-belt to maneuver her to where the dwarf was currently using a section of rubble as cover while she peered over it cautiously.

Leilani saw nothing in the blackness. Even Sarah's sensors didn't detect whatever it was the dwarf was seeing. She pulled binoculars from her bag and scanned the general area that seemed to have the drackova and rider's attention. After cycling through the various frequencies on the binos, she finally found what the pair were monitoring so intently.

Approximately one hundred thousand miles away, several bright objects came into view. Zooming in, Lei saw a group of drackova with riders and a single cargo container. One of them flew high over the top of the group. It might be some kind of scout, but it didn't match the rest of the group.

Each drackova wore blackened gear and what looked to be paint, worn and chipped away in various places. All except for the one flying overhead. It was naturally black, and while it had a rider, she saw no other signs of the typical cyberware associated with the bonding process that Lavender had explained. Without her binoculars set to scan for eldrich, they would have been impossible to spot.

"They come in black?"

"Yes, they come in any shade and color, but blackened drackova are trouble. Criminals often blacken their drackova to hide their movements in space. It makes them almost impossible to see."

"Space is pretty vast. They would be almost impossible to spot, even in your heavily trafficked areas, unless you were using radar. Wow."

The armored helmet turned to look at her. The faceplate, which had been clear, was now black and her face was hidden. "How are you seeing them?"

Lei lifted her binos and bounced them slightly. "They show up like tiny fireflies in this."

"How?"

Lei furrowed her brow. How would they not have basic eldrich sensors? "Eldrich has a pretty unique pattern. And so far, all the drackova I've seen are coated in it, which makes them basically glow if you're using an aether sensor."

"Does that have a digital port?"

Lei glanced at the device. She'd been using her manual ones, but she had a pair of digital binoculars. She pulled the second set out of her bag and handed them to the dwarf. They were a wearable pair that linked with her old weapons, which was why she hadn't been using them.

"These do. Try them."

The dwarf found a port on her forearm that fit the cable and began pointing the binos at the wing of creatures passing uncomfortably close.

There were nine black drackova in total, and the second largest of the group carried a large transport pod. They didn't seem to be in any kind of hurry. In fact, they appeared to be trying to avoid detection. They'd even painted the transport black so it would blend in with space.

"Holy drackova crap!" the dwarf exclaimed suddenly. "What is this eldrich?"

Lei blinked several times and turned her head to stare at the dwarf. Lavender was still focusing on the passing wing and didn't seem to notice her. Past the dwarf, Deloris looked up at the two of them and shook her head, then returned her attention to her search through the station.

"Who are they?" Lei ignored the question for now.

"Not sure, but they're more than likely pirates."

"Seriously?" Lei chuckled. "You have bonded pirates?"

Some things never changed. There was always someone looking to make easy money off the radar.

"Yes." She pointed toward them. "You can tell by the riders."

Lei zoomed in her own binoculars to where she could see the riders clearly. At this magnification, she could see hints of color under the black paint. Unlike Lavender, they wore makeshift armor and had far more cables going from them to their bonded.

The one lone exception was the truly black drackova flying high over the group. It was by far the largest of the group, being almost half again longer than the drackova carrying the transport pod. If she had to guess, the pair overhead was definitely government.

"What about the big one?"

"Which . . ." The dwarf's voice trailed off into silence.

Lei glanced over her shoulder to see the purple drackova had also stopped moving, her head held aloft, as if she were listening to something far away.

"We should go inside," the dwarf almost whispered, as if she thought someone might overhear her.

Lei drew her attention back to the wing of drackova. The largest of them had slowed, and the rider was looking in their direction.

"*That can't be good.*" Sarah triggered Leilani's stealth system.

"*Nope. Although, I suppose it depends on their intent.*"

In her HuD, Lei could see the green dot of the dwarf moving off quickly toward the lock that would lead her back into the station.

Lei, however, opted for a different stance. The pair had already spotted them. If they were pirates, running would only guarantee that they would circle back for easy prey when they finished with whatever nefarious plot they were in the middle of. If they were government, well, running simply made them guilty. And again, they would come back later.

She stepped into plain view with a single foot resting on the broken piece of hull that they had been hiding behind. In one hand, she held the binoculars, while her free hand rested on her weapon. There was a brief pause as the two observed each other. Even the massive drackova twisted its head in their direction and made a lazy loop.

"*Ma'am, we were just scanned by a psionic sensor.*"

Leilani dealt with psionic races regularly in kuldain space. Sarah could easily deal with psionic scans.

"*They wish to communicate.*"

"*Let it through.*"

"*Ah, another outsider, interesting. Welcome to Severious.*"

"*May I help you?*"

"*No. But this changes things. I have informed the master. We will probably meet again, ex-Agent Leilani Falconi.*"

Lei sighed. There were few secrets in psionic communications. Even the most skilled psionicist bled all surface thoughts and self-identity. Yet a person experienced in the method of communication, like Leilani, could hide deeper thoughts and intent. She'd allowed them to know her name and that she was looking for Fendrick, and nothing else.

She, however, knew far too much about them. They weren't as good at hiding their intent. Either that, or they didn't feel the need to hide it. The rider's name was Faustino McNeill, and his bonded mount was Dorisino. They were government agents, currently monitoring the pirate group below them. They weren't to interfere, merely to observe and document what they were up to.

"*Until then, Ms. Falconi, don't believe everything you hear.*" The communication cut suddenly.

Lei slid the binoculars back into her bag. "I never do."

"*That creature was powerful, though I did glean some useful information, which I am not sure they intended to share.*" Sarah's tone was smug. "*They are nothing compared to a messari, so they were far easier to manipulate.*"

Leilani chuckled. "*Nicely done. I'm glad you're on my side.*"

"*We're bonded. Of course, I am.*" Sarah's laughter echoed in her mind briefly. "*But that creature wasn't a drackova. It considers itself a dracolli, a more evolved version of the drackova. And* it *was the psionicist, not the handler, which explains the massive power output and minimal skill. It's used to winning via sheer brute force.*"

"*Useful information. Can we tell the difference between the two?*"

"*I believe so.*" In her Heads up Display, the dots in the distance shifted to red, except for the dracolli, which shifted to yellow with a new icon. Behind her, the large purple creature also shifted icons denoting its upgrade to dracolli.

"*Really?*" Lei turned to face Deloris.

The large purple head twisted to the side as the eyes narrowed slightly.

"*Apparently, she knows that we know,*" Sarah mused.

18

SILLY TIN CAN

When the eight-hundred-ton yacht showed up at the station, Deloris's reaction had been beyond primal. Even the ship's superior stealth system had done little to hide it from the massive creature. She'd snatched the ship up with all four feet and viciously shook it. Leilani's heart froze in her chest as she came face-to-face with losing her brother and Dorthy simultaneously.

Wendel, Leilani, and Lavender leapt to intercede, but seriously, it was impossible to stop something that massive. It wasn't until the ship was halfway in her mouth, and her teeth had completely punctured through the hull, that Lavender finally convinced her bond-mate to stop.

It was an eye-opener, to be sure. Leilani decided that if she were captaining a ship, she needed to kill the dracolli before it reached her, or all bets were off.

When they finally convinced BB and Dorthy that it was safe to leave the vessel, they weren't pleased. Tensions only escalated once everyone was safely inside Wendel's lab. It didn't take long before the stress of the situation sparked a fight between the ex-admiral and his subordinate.

Wendel and his goddaughter left the moment the first chair launched across the room. BB utterly ignored them while they tried to murder each other with fists and feet. However, when Leilani flew across the table and spilled his coffee into his lap, he'd reached the limit of his tolerance.

The soft whine of a delonian energy pistol spinning up into lethal mode ended the fight mid-swing. Now, the three of them were alone in the demolished common area.

Lei rubbed her thigh as she limped back to the table with two coffee cups. The bone was mending, but that didn't stop the bruising and the residual pain from the broken femur.

"Least you're walking again." Dorthy chuckled and took both coffee cups from her, his crystal-blue eyes twinkling with mirth. She had to admit, his real self was a tad more handsome than his human self. He was slightly taller and well built, but his human form and his delonian form were similar enough that he obviously wasn't hiding, per se, just pretending to be human. She wondered if the same was true of Wendel.

"And apparently you can talk again, which isn't an improvement." She winked at him.

He gingerly rubbed his jaw. Half of his face was black and blue, but the colors were slowly fading into greens and yellows as his own nanites repaired the damage.

"You're both nuts. You know that, right?" BB folded his arms and leaned back in the chair.

Leilani sat gingerly, trying to minimize the pain in her leg and spine. "He framed me for murder. What did you expect me to do? Welcome him with open arms?"

"Yeah, I had that coming. Honestly, I'm just happy she didn't shoot me." The delonian next to her nodded in agreement.

Lei leaned her shoulder into him gently as she smirked. "I did consider it, but I wouldn't have shot you anywhere vital."

"You two have lost it," BB sneered.

"Nah, we're both fine, it's just how operators deal with disagreements. You wouldn't understand."

"And we don't expect you to," Leilani added before turning to watch Dorthy curiously as she sipped her coffee. "So, who the hell are you, really?"

He shrugged, then his face contorted in pain. "Ow. Honestly, the truth isn't much different from the human you knew."

"Still government then, just not Kassian?"

"Kind of, yes. Delonian government structure isn't really the same. We're far more . . ." He looked around the room as if he hoped to find the right word written on the walls someplace.

"The word you're looking for is 'fractured'." Wendel strode from his office to the end of the table.

"You know, that is a damn good adjective."

Dorthy bobbed his head at the engineer before returning his attention to Leilani. "I'm still an investigator, but I work for whichever prince hires me. This particular case, however, ended up being far more complicated than my typical work. A government hired me to find a delonian criminal and return him to them for trial. If possible, they also want me to return what he stole."

"You're more like a bounty hunter." BB lifted his cup to take another sip.

"This time, yes. But just like IIS, the jobs—and results—can vary. It's not always apprehension." He let the inference hang there, unsaid.

"No shit. Delonians don't care about trials," Wendel spat suddenly.

Everyone at the table turned their attention to him.

He waved his hands in front of his face and shook his head. "Sorry. I came out here because I think I know where Fendrick is."

When all three agents continued to stare at him, he shifted his weight back and forth on each foot nervously. Then, finally, he pointed to one of the larger holo-displays near the table. It flashed to life, and a video feed showed people screaming as they flooded out several sets of double doors which led into what appeared to be a corporate building.

"This is the view from the ground floor of the Dracko-Tech corporate building." A deep, male voice yelled over the screams in the background. "According to my sources, alarms started about fifteen minutes ago as an individual with an enormous sword entered the building." The camera flashed to a crodoc reporter. His manicured brows furrowed with concern.

Leilani couldn't help herself, and the chuckle came out as more of a snort than a laugh.

Next to her, Dorthy shook his head. "Outstanding, Fen."

"I can't do shit from here." BB leaned his chair back on two legs and stared at Lei and Dorthy with a rather smug grin on his face. "Network latency is way too severe."

At the end of the table, the metallic sphere suddenly lifted off the table, and a holographic image of an aging dwarf appeared. He opened his mouth to speak, only to snap it shut as he looked down at the table protruding from his chest. Shuffling backward until he was free of it seemed to appease him, and he returned his attention to the individuals at the table.

"I assume you're all watchin' the news?"

They all nodded.

"I think I know what's going on, and I'm positive I know where he's going next."

"Now *that* is useful information." BB's chair hit the deck loudly as he leaned forward. "And damn! You are seriously old!"

Everyone turned to glare at him, but only Lei spoke up.

"You are an ass."

"Yep." He nodded in agreement. "Where are we going, old man?"

A bushy white eyebrow rose as the dwarf drummed his fingers on the head of his cane. "Dwarf."

BB furrowed both eyebrows. "You have someplace called dwarf? That seems . . . racist."

The dwarf didn't even flinch. Instead, he smiled. "No, young human. I am not an old man. I am an ancient dwarf. There is a definite difference. But you may call me Jorna."

BB pursed his lips as he realized what was happening, but he didn't let it sway the inherent asshole within. "All right, fart dust, we get it. Where the fuck are we going?"

The dwarf snorted and grinned wide enough that his yellow teeth were visible beneath his pristine white beard. He slapped his hand on the table, but the hologram made no sound. "I like him! Dracko-Tech has a high-security Grevalu research facility in the outer orbit. And, ironically, it will pass you in about two hours. Hopefully, you can beat him there."

Lei and Dorthy immediately stood, each of them grimacing. Without a word, they donned the weapons and gear they'd removed after their scuffle.

"What the fuck is Fen doing?" Lei asked her old boss quietly.

Dorthy paused and stared at the gun in his hand for a moment. Finally, he pulled the magazine from it and checked it before snapping it back into place and clicking on the safety.

"I'm here because Fendrick kidnapped the daughter of an important general. The kid's government hired me to find her. And, if possible, bring the kidnapper back for trial. If not, I'm to eliminate him. I used some of my sources to find out that someone in this arm of the galaxy hired Fendrick to kidnap the kid, but when I caught up with him, he'd already hidden her someplace. I knew he hadn't handed her over yet, because if he had, he would've already bailed. So, I went undercover to monitor him. I hoped he'd lead me to the kid and, if I was lucky, the buyer."

BB strolled up to the two of them.

"The yel'adari that stole Wendel's gate said something about a kid she couldn't control. Wendel claimed she was the CEO of Dracko-Tech." She jerked her thumb toward the silenced monitor behind them.

Dorthy's jaw clenched tightly, and Lei smacked him on the shoulder roughly. "What aren't you telling us?"

Dorthy sighed. "The kid was a dragon."

Lei slid her pistols into their holsters and placed her hands on her hips.

"A dragon? Like an actual dragon?"

"Aren't the things flying all over this place dragons?" BB furrowed his brow and placed his hands on his hips.

"No." Lei and Dorthy answered in unison.

"Well, that isn't entirely true." Leilani slid extra ammo magazines into her belt. "Dorthy is talking about *draconis imperious*. These are *draconis drackova* and *draconis dracolli*."

She bit the inside of her cheek. "It's like the *canis familiaris*, *canis lupus*, and the *canis proelium*."

BB's eyebrows shot up, and he took a step backward at the mention of the war dogs used by several of the corporate security forces. They were highly intelligent and extremely lethal, capable of tearing tanks apart with only their jaws. The only saving grace was that the creatures were extremely difficult to maintain because of their high intelligence, which made them out of reach for smaller corporations or individuals.

Dorthy placed his hand on BB's shoulder as he stepped up alongside the nervous hacker. "No self-respecting *draconis imperious* would ever allow themselves to be used as livestock, let alone allow a lesser species ride them."

"I am not a lesser species."

"We are all lesser species to a dragon." Dorthy squeezed his shoulder, trying to reassure him. As he strode toward Wendel and the dwarf, he raised his voice so they could hear him clearly. "Where are we going?"

"Jorna is sending some of his people to help, just in case. We have to keep things under control until they get there."

"ETA?"

"My people are nearby. We can be there in about an hour." The dwarf lifted his cane and waved it toward Dorthy. "I am not a fan of Dracko-Tech. However, there are a lot of innocent people on that station. Including some of my own."

Leilani stepped up to stand next to Dorthy. "What do you mean?"

"That is a Grevalu for the more advanced training programs. It's filled with thousands of teachers, kids, and their bonded, along with being a research station."

Dorthy and BB both turned confused stares to Leilani.

She lifted a hand, palm-up, toward the dwarf. "The best translation is that it's a school and a research facility. There will be kids, young draconis, and staff inside. It's like a Matheris school."

"Whoa!" BB exclaimed. "Isn't that one of those creepy IIS schools where they train kids to be agents?"

"Yes."

"And they bonded these kids to dragons?" BB's eyes widened, and he waved his arm in the general direction of the center of the solar system. "You mean to tell me that all of those riders out there are genetically bonded to their mounts?"

"They aren't mounts." The dwarf raised the handle of his cane to shake it at BB. "They are partners. Friends. Companions. They are raised together and learn together." The cane dropped back to the stone ground with a soft clack.

"Surely they'll evacuate it if there's a threat to the station." Wendel rubbed his hands together. "I mean, Delia is a bitch, but . . ."

The dwarf craned his neck to look up at Wendel. "Delia has been dead for centuries."

"What?"

"Someone murdered her in her sleep a long time ago. They never found her killer." The dwarf waved his hand in the air. "Of course, I'm not sure they looked all that hard either."

"Well, that makes interrogating her a little harder." Lei chuckled.

The dwarf looked off to the side, likely at someone or something, wherever he was. "Interesting. Apparently, the terrorist is also expecting Delia." He pointed his cane at the nearby monitor.

The volume of the newscast increased as the group turned to see a reporter interviewing a woman in a suit. The tight bun atop her head had broken free, and hair stuck out in all directions, giving emphasis to her hysterical hand waving.

"This guy, he's throwing things around and chopping people in half with this crazy sword! He's demanding that we give him someone named Delia. When we don't know who she is, he just slices one of us into pieces. There's blood everywhere! It's insane!"

Behind the reporter and the hysterical woman, a massive, black vehicle lowered into view, settling gently to the ground. The back opened up, and uniformed suits of power armor, with large, energy-based weapons, poured out in one long wave. The sheer precision and uniformity told Leilani they were either military or highly specialized police—possibly some kind of anti-terrorist response team. The people attempting to run from the building screamed and dramatically altered course away from the soldiers. Some were so scared that they ran back into the building they were previously fleeing.

Leilani elbowed Dorthy. They knew all too well that sometimes the solution to a problem was worse than the problem itself. Especially since the two of them, more often than not, were the solution.

"There you have it." The camera focused back on the reporter as his interviewee ran screaming away from the soldiers now flooding into the courtyard.

Behind the reporter, a soldier was heading straight for him and his camera drone.

"It appears that the terrorist is demanding to see Delia Glemantha'tel, a Dracko-Tech CEO found dead in her bed, her throat and heart violently ripped from her body, eight hund—"

The camera stopped sending as a large, armored hand reached over the reporter's shoulder and silenced it. The black image shifted to a woman sitting at a desk.

The sound muted as the group turned back to face each other.

"An army of demons to deal with a devil. That always works." Leilani laughed.

Wendel scowled at her while BB grimaced, clearly not amused. The dwarf shook his head, and Dorthy looked away, trying not to join her in laughing.

"What?" She raised her hands until they were even with her ears. "Am I wrong?"

No one said a word.

"This is an impressive ship." Leilani ran her fingers along the edge of the highly detailed sensor console.

"Thank you," Wendel and Dorthy said at the same time.

The entire trio of agents turned and stared at the engineer.

Folding his arms across his chest, he glowered at Dorthy. "You may be the captain, but this ship is my design, made in one of my own personal shipyards." He took a step to the side of the bridge and tapped an icon stamped into the bulkhead. It glowed briefly, then faded. "That is my maker's mark. I even remember the person I built this for."

Dorthy and Wendel locked eyes, clearly engaging in some sort of challenge.

After several uncomfortable moments, BB shrugged and plopped ungracefully into the chair in front of the communications console. "Something tells me I don't want to know."

Lei smirked and placed her hand on his shoulder. "Where'd he get this, anyway?"

"He had it hidden outside Kassian space in some asteroid belt. I think he said it was his from when he came to Kass originally, but I didn't ask too many questions."

Lei resisted the urge to turn and look at the two males. She'd already guessed that Wendel was delonian. There was no need to push the issue at the moment. Clearly, they knew each other, likely a story for another day.

She tapped a flashing button on the sensor panel, and the front of the ship cleared as the prosee-style hull became transparent. At first, it showed the peaceful blackness of space with a few pieces of debris in the distance, but that lasted only a few seconds before it went dark purple and a clawed finger closed over the ship.

The damage-control panel flashed bright red as the ship registered multiple impacts on all sides.

Inside the ship, however, the inertial dampeners kicked in, making sure that no one felt anything as the dracolli outside snatched up the ship.

BB laughed. The sound caused a disturbance behind them, hopefully breaking the two delonians out of their staring contest, but Lei didn't check. Instead, she looked down to see her big brother literally holding his sides.

"She said we're too slow in this silly little tin can," he managed through his laughter.

Dorthy stepped up next to her and slapped the hacker in the back of the head. "Tell them to let us go."

"Yeah, I doubt that's going to happen." Leilani bit her lip to hold back her own laughter. "They're right, to some degree. Your stealth system slows you down a lot. This way you can stay hidden and still move at a normal speed."

She sat in a nearby chair and pulled her feet up to rest on the edge of the console in front of her. Her eyes dropped to the screen, which showed stress on the hull, but it was well within safety parameters.

“I’m not happy about being a dragon toy, but I’m not willing to start a fight over it. Get to work then. I’m not going into an unknown station without at least some reconnaissance.”

“Aye aye, boss.” BB flicked a haphazard salute, which was intended as more of an insult than an honor, then turned his attention back to the sensor panel in front of him.

19

OUT OF BAND

The saloon of the eight-hundred-ton yacht was a small space where passengers and crew could meet and socialize. Its size, however, meant that personal space was a luxury. Leilani and Dorthy stood at one end of an oval table, looking over the printed digi-sheet that showed the layout of the research station.

Their scans gave a surprising amount of data for a high-security facility. But then, eldrich sensors seemed to be the Achilles' heel of Severious. Nine hundred years was a long time, but she still had trouble with the idea that they'd lost so much aether knowledge—especially in a place that used to specialize in the mixing of aether and kuldain technologies.

Reaching down, she ran two fingers across the hologram, causing the image of the station to slowly rotate.

"This thing is massive. I don't even understand the tons-displacement math here. Do full-sized drackova walk around inside or something?"

Dorthy rotated the station even farther along its center axis. "I doubt they live in space all the time." He finally slapped his hand on the table. "It will take us a year to find one man in this thing!"

Standing upright, he rubbed his face vigorously before glaring at the delonian at the far end of the table.

Wendel didn't even notice as he continued his conversation with the floating metal ball. When they'd boarded the vessel, the dwarf had turned off the holo and was now just a floating speaker, but it hadn't slowed their conversation in the slightest. The two friends were still catching up on nine hundred years of lost time.

"It might help if you stopped fighting with Wendel."

Shaking his head, Dorthy met her gaze. "That's easier said than done."

"Not really. The two of you are nowhere near delonian space. Whatever the problem is, let it go for the sake of the mission."

Dorthy marched past Wendel to the counter where the coffee maker sat, leaving Leilani alone at her end of the table. Shifting her gaze to the engineer, she found him watching her. She smiled faintly and bobbed her head in his direction.

She leaned back over the digi-sheet to skim the data in the margins. She wasn't sure what she expected to find, but she knew she didn't have the whole picture yet.

A skinny male flopped into Dorthy's chair next to her and flamboyantly flicked a pad across the table. It skidded across the thin printout before Lei dropped a hand on it.

"I think that's what you're looking for."

Lei rotated it right side up and smiled. "I love you, ya nut job."

"I know ya do. But to be utterly candid, it wasn't me."

She tapped the hyperlink to the station's floor plan. It snapped open. There were blueprints and even hyperlinks to holographic walkthroughs, but the most interesting aspect was the notes all over the floor plans. BB was right—they weren't in his chicken scratch. They were in someone else's hastily scrawled handwriting.

"Wow, do all you hackers write like this?"

"I'm surprised she writes at all. That's not a typical skill among my kind."

Lei frowned at a large circle of red around a section of the station. She skimmed the scattered notes next to it before she glanced up to meet BB's stare.

"First, since when do you give credit to someone else?"

Shrugging, he suddenly found something under his fingernails far more interesting than his little sister. "Sobriety has its annoying side effects."

"Bullshit."

His eyes shifted toward the door, and he tried to lean the chair back on two legs, but the compensators on the chair refused to be moved in that direction.

"BB?"

He rubbed his hands on his legs uncomfortably before he finally lifted his gaze to meet hers. "Fine. I like her, alright?"

Lei shoved herself roughly up from the table as her brow wrinkled in a deep grimace. "We're talking about Meeshani, right?"

He nodded.

"Um, BB, she's a greduna. She'd break you in half."

A sly grin played across his face. "I know. It's part of her appeal."

"Ew." Leilani wrinkled her nose and returned her attention to the station schematics. She tapped the red circle with her index finger. "This says something about children being held? Fendrick took hostages?"

"Nope. Last I checked, he wasn't there yet. Though we expect him any second at this point."

"Then what is this?"

"That . . . is where the terrorists are holding the kids."

"Are you fucking kidding me?" Leilani snapped her head up to stare at the scrawny hacker.

She snatched up the pad and stormed to the other end of the table. Slamming it down in front of Wendel, she slapped the hovering ball roughly, but it moved only a couple of inches. It wasn't heavy, but its gravity-compensators were impressive for its size.

"I don't care what your issue is! We have a bigger problem. Jorna, you need to see this too."

The hologram flickered to life as the old dwarf rubbed the side of his head gingerly.

"Ow, you mae'lacan bitch. A simple request would have been sufficient."

"If you felt me smack a metal ball, then you're more of an idiot than I gave you credit for," she snapped, knowing all too well how digital immersion worked after years of taking care of her fully VR-addicted brother.

The dwarf smirked but said nothing.

"What's up?" Dorthy stepped up next to Wendel on the other side of the table from her.

"We got our recon, but we aren't the first people here."

"Fendrick?" Wendel scanned the blueprint. "I can't read this."

"No, he isn't there yet, either. Apparently, terrorists have attacked the station. Based on this," she tapped the handwriting next to the red circle, "when Fen attacked the headquarters, the entire company went to red-alert. That brought a secondary security system online at the station which then alerted the company to an ongoing hack in their system."

She placed both hands on the table as she leaned forward.

"Dracko-Tech immediately began evacuation proceedings before the terrorists were able to get inside." She swiped the image to the side to highlight more red text. "But the gate closed, station-side, before they could get everyone out. Dracko-Tech estimates that forty-five students and three teachers are still missing, along with over a thousand draconis of various ages and stages that weren't able to be evacuated."

"Shit!" The dwarf vanished, and his ball fell to the deck with a loud metallic clang.

Wendel tapped the red circle. "This is where Dracko-Tech thinks they're being held?"

Lei nodded.

Wendel looked up at the delonian next to him. "I don't do this stuff anymore. I'm of no use to you."

Dorthy dropped his hand to the engineer's shoulder. "It's okay. Leilani and I are pretty good at this. The kids will be alright."

"Thank you." Wendel's shoulders relaxed.

Dorthy patted him gently. "I owe you."

Lei locked eyes with her ex-boss, but said nothing. Hostage situations like this rarely ended well. It would inevitably depend on whether the terrorists were willing to die to make their point.

She picked up the pad and sat in the closest chair as she skimmed through the data.

At the edge of her vision, she saw Dorthy beeline for BB at the opposite end of the table. As they whispered to each other, she focused on Meeshani's notes.

"*I got it!*" Sarah blurted suddenly.

"*Got what?*"

"*The dracolli. Their communication is direct point-to-point, which was why I wasn't able to intercept it before. But Deloris is behind us, which put us in direct line to whomever she's talking to. It's a technologically enhanced version of psionics, which is why it feels so strong power-wise, but isn't all that refined. It's fascinating. And . . .*" Sarah's voice trailed off as she paused for emphasis.

"*Out with it.*"

There was a sensation of smug laughter. "*Not encrypted.*"

Leilani snorted, causing Wendel to look up at her curiously.

The ball snapped up to dwarf height, and Jorna appeared again.

"I have even more family inbound. My people will assist with the evacuation, but you don't have much time. If this is anything like the other attacks, the terrorists will blow the station and everyone in it as soon as they release the drackova into space."

"What the hell?" Leilani furrowed her brow, utterly confused. Then her eyes snapped to the pad. She skimmed the overall notes as her mind replayed what she knew. "Are you kidding me? They are eco-terrorists?"

The hologram turned to her and nodded. "Yes. They claim they are trying to save the drackova from a life of servitude and torture."

His gaze fell to his hands as they shifted on his cane. He didn't look up as he continued. "They release the poor hatchlings into space. Less than five percent of them survive the exposure to the radiation. Then the terrorists kill the kids, and the few hatchlings that do survive end up dying anyway when their bonded dies."

Leilani closed her eyes and took a deep breath. When she opened them, she saw Dorthy watching her with an utterly blank expression.

"That sounds about right. Eco-terrorists live in a world where reality and science are inconvenient facts. Therefore, they invent their own reality and call it fact." She rubbed her shoulder with her fingers.

"How shortsighted," Wendel grumbled.

Lei and the dwarf nodded their agreement.

"*Master Jorna's idea of family is rather spectacular,*" Sarah mused. "*There is a wing of over eight hundred bonded units, and even more corporate marines, inbound with some rather spectacular armament. If I'm understanding this correctly, they expect trouble from other corporations as well.*"

"*Understood.*"

"Master Jorna."

The dwarf turned his attention to her.

"Please secure the outside and rescue as many of the hatchlings as you can, but leave the inside to Dorthy and me. We don't need to accidentally be fighting your people *and* the terrorists when Fendrick shows up."

"The gate's closed. There's no way he's gettin' inside now."

"Yes, well—"

Dorthy interrupted her from the other end of the table where he was talking to BB. "Fendrick is already inside. We're losing time, Lei."

She nodded and tossed the pad to the table in front of Wendel.

"Did you get a copy of the floor plan?"

"Yes, ma'am."

Lei followed Dorthy through the ship's tight p-ways until they entered what appeared to be both an armory and a teleport room. He typed in some data on the panel and pointed toward the lockers. "I brought you some toys."

Opening the locker, a grin spread across Leilani's face so wide that her cheeks hurt from it. "Have I ever told you how much I adore you?"

"I really don't want to hear about your sexual escapades with the creepy, old dude." BB's voice startled her, and she looked over her shoulder at him.

He was sliding on a sidearm and fastening the new delonian armor system in place.

"You're coming?"

"Yes," both males said at the same time.

"He has a side mission, and if he doesn't make it back to us in time, he's on his own." Dorthy glared at the hacker, who simply nodded.

"Get it done or die. I get the gist. Isn't that how all your heists go?"

"This isn't a heist." Leilani pulled out a small, round, metal ball with a yellow band and intricate delonian writing around it. Lifting it to her lips, she kissed it fondly.

"Dude, did you just kiss a grenade?"

"Yep." She began stuffing as many balls with different colored bands as she could fit into the pouches on her belt.

"You are seriously disturbed."

An intimate hand caressed the small of her back as Dorthy reached past her and gathered up two extra ammo mags and a handful of grenades himself.

The two of them hadn't been on an op together since IIS promoted him to admiral. She was looking forward to having him back. No partner had ever kept up with her like Dorthy. Now that she knew he wasn't human, she understood why.

When they gave her a new partner, she'd almost killed the woman on their first mission by expecting too much from her. After that, command put in her file that she could only be partnered with older races, but even they could rarely keep up.

By the end of her IIS career, Lei was working alone until she'd found Rothar in the slave mines. That lasted only a few months before IIS deported the crodoc back to aether space.

"Ready?" Dorthy asked.

"Always." She turned her gaze to lock eyes with him briefly. "I'm glad you're okay."

"Seriously, you two? Aren't there a bunch of kids about to die or something?" BB's high-pitched tone caused both of them to smirk.

"Me too." Dorthy laughed and slapped her roughly on the ass before striding off to the teleport pad.

Laughing, she followed him. The three of them got incredibly close as they squeezed onto the gate-pad which was only designed for two people.

"You two are—" BB's voice cut off as Dorthy activated the system.

Their armored vacc suits triggered as the trio appeared on the outside of the station next to a lock. With precision only gained from years of experience, Dorthy pulled his weapons and faced outward, covering Leilani as she pulled a device from her bag and attached it to the security panel. It began running the hacking software to bypass the lock, but before it could even fully log in, BB shoved her out of the way.

"Seriously, you two need to learn to read the complete brief and not just the tactical crap." Yanking the device off, he tossed it over his shoulder at her.

As it floated past, Lei grabbed it and stuffed it back in her bag. BB typed a code into the panel, and the lock popped open.

"Won't a security override alert security?"

"Probably." BB pulled himself through the door. "Good thing there isn't any security left alive in there, huh?"

Lei rolled her eyes and pulled herself into the lock after him.

Once all three were inside, they found the closest security station while BB hacked into the computer. The p-way intersection was large enough for two full-grown dracollis walking side by side.

"I need to go this way." BB turned and tapped the massive wall map behind him. "The hostages are here."

He tapped the panel where a large cluster of blue icons gathered, surrounded by red dots.

Leilani slid the map slightly and zoomed in. "What's this?" She pointed to a smaller group of blue dots that were surrounded by rows and rows of green dots.

"I have no clue. Let's look." BB typed something into a side panel, and several displays in the area flared to life with video feeds.

A section of feeds to the left showed a group of badly armored individuals, with rather nasty-looking kinetic weapons, surrounding a large group of about forty children and one older adult male. Age was difficult to tell because of the wide assortment of races, but the fear in their faces was clear.

The terrorists wore spray-painted, irregular metal plates strapped to their bodies with tape and twine. Their faces and other visible section of skin were painted with black and red streaks. And tied to each of their heads was the white skull of what appeared to be a hatchling drackova.

Leilani shifted her weight as she shook her head. It never failed. Eco-terrorists were the same no matter where they were or what their cause was. They were all driven by the blinding desire to create chaos and fear in their wake.

Another display flickered to life, showing the smaller group. This was far less chaotic. Ten teenagers gathered together in a room lined with enormous thirty-foot tubes filled with fluid and what appeared to be both humanoids and draconis.

Unlike the larger group of scared children, these kids weren't afraid. Whatever they were trying to do had their complete focus. Three of them appeared to be trying to access a computer system while the others stood watch at the doors with weapons that were a tad large for their smaller frames.

Dorthy and Leilani smirked at each other.

"There first?" they both asked in unison, then nodded their heads in agreement.

"Whatever." BB rolled his eyes and tapped the console in front of him. "The release of the hatchlings has started. Based on the software they injected into the system, we have just under an hour before they blow the station. Get the kids to the secondary evac by then. You won't have time to fuck around."

Leilani smacked her big brother on the back and chuckled. "Relax, BB. This is our profession. We know what we're doing. You, on the other hand, are new to this. Don't miss the rendezvous."

The trio split up. Dorthy and Leilani headed toward the section with the smaller group of kids.

As they rounded the corner, Dorthy in the lead, he dropped suddenly as something knocked his feet out from under him. Snatching a ball with a blue stripe from her pouch, she leapt into the air, flipping her feet high over her head.

She felt the air move past where she'd been standing and tossed the ball toward the movement. It struck something invisible, which triggered the electrical field. A golden-scaled drackova shimmered into view as it convulsed violently from the charge.

Dorthy rolled up onto his feet next to where Leilani landed, and they stood back-to-back as they prepared for another attack.

A fist landed square in Leilani's diaphragm, expertly knocking the wind from her. As she doubled over, Dorthy swung his weapon over her.

The young crodoc that had just punched her shimmered to view, holding up both hands. His eyes crossed as he stared at the barrel less than an inch from his forehead. "You're hurting her."

In her Heads up Display, Leilani turned off the grenade as she fought to regain her breath. That kid punched much harder than his boyish frame should have been capable of.

The drackova slumped to the ground, unconscious.

Dorthy flicked the tip of his weapon toward the small, eight-foot-long creature.

The kid didn't wait. He dove toward his bonded.

Leilani stood back up and took a deep breath. She flipped the toggle in her HuD that highlighted eldrich signatures. Sure enough, there were two more invisible teams slowly creeping their direction. She lifted both weapons, one pointed toward each of the drackova. Both teams froze, obviously surprised.

"We aren't the terrorists," Dorthy stated loudly. "We're here to help evacuate the last of you before they blow the station."

"We can't let them blow this station." A voice echoed out from speakers built into the bulkhead. "Bring them to Perthius."

It was a female voice, but if the speaker was also young, the higher pitch might be misleading.

The drackova lying on the ground started herself awake and looked around, blinking.

"Ow." The sound came out crystal clear, as if a human had said it.

Which now placed these creatures higher up the evolutionary chain than Leilani expected.

Sarah patched Dorthy into the silcomm.

"*Did you leave something out in your brief?*"

"*I told you they were intelligent. At least some of them are.*" Lei shrugged, even though the communication was silent.

"*It appears they might all be intelligent.*"

Lei's jaw bulged as she ground her teeth. He was probably right.

The crodoc male stood and moved around Dorthy and Leilani, raising his palms to the others. "Easy, Genna is fine. If they wanted to hurt us, they would have. We need to take them to Perthius. If they *are* here to help, maybe we have a chance to survive this after all."

The invisible units turned and slinked away, out of sight.

"These kids are operating like a military unit."

"Yeah, reminds me of the IIS kids," Dorthy chuckled softly.

Leilani elbowed him hard in the ribs.

He rewarded her with a soft, "Oof!"

The young crodoc male turned toward them as they lowered their weapons.

"Follow us."

20

RESCUE

The young crodoc leading them informed them that his name was Sergeant Mauro. He was a member of the Officer Training Corp onboard the station. When they pressed for more information, they found he was rather adept at deflecting their questions.

As he led them through the door into the highly secured lab, Leilani and Dorthy slowed to a stop, taking in the sheer magnitude of the experiment.

The room extended farther than either of them could see in each direction. There were rows and rows of enormous tubes filled with various life-forms and millions of gallons of translucent fluid. They reminded Leilani of a similar tank that had been used to keep the emperor's cousin alive for over a decade.

Yet these tanks each held two life-forms: one humanoid and one draconis. Leilani stepped up to the tank to her left to examine the floating occupants. Dorthy, however, followed Sergeant Mauro over to a slightly larger female crodoc.

Leilani ignored the conversation, focusing instead on the naked, humanoid female in the tank. She looked young, but was already at least six feet tall. Next to her, with the tip of its tail wrapped lightly around the girl's legs, was a draconis of some kind. It didn't have the typical telltales of a drackova or a dracolli, but then, she doubted the telltale features would be present at this age. The creature couldn't be over fifteen feet long, which made it fairly young.

"*Ma'am.*" Sarah's voice denoted concern.

"*Yeah?*"

"*I interfaced with the unit. According to its logs, that is a greduna child.*"

Greduna matured at a different rate from the lesser races, meaning that this child could be forty or fifty years old but still have the mentality of a five-year-old human. A five-year-old capable of breaking a human in half.

There was a reason greduna didn't raise their children among the general populace, but rather in greduna-only communes. Greduna believed strongly in the tribal family unit. They, along with most of the elder races, did not allow their children into normal society until they were adults. This was mostly for safety reasons, but it also served the purpose of ensuring that they came with a specific set of ethics and education, allowing their societal norms to remain intact throughout the ages.

Greduna were uncommon in aether society. They preferred their communes. For every million aether citizens, there was maybe one greduna, with few exceptions. ELU, for example, had four greduna among its eight thousand professors.

Leilani turned her attention to the tank on her right, and her eyes widened as a small ball of fear grew in her gut. It, too, had a greduna. Allowing her gaze to travel down the row, her sense of horror grew as she realized the tanks were all greduna as far as she could see. This was an interracial incident on a galactic scale. If the greduna council found out that this many of their children were being held in medical tubes, there would be a war. And a greduna at war was not a pretty sight.

Drawing her attention to the wall behind her, Leilani strode to the other side to examine the occupants. In the middle of the room, the volume of the discussion increased as the kid was apparently losing patience with Dorthy.

Lei paused at a tank that contained a dark-blue-skinned child and a similarly skinned draconis. The child, however, was easily twelve feet tall, making it much older—likely similar in mental faculties to the young soldiers. Its draconis barely fit in the fifty-foot container. The two intertwined tightly as they floated in the fluid.

Leilani moved around the container, trying to find any of the typical identifying markings that should be on a geloran teen. When the young male's eyes popped open, she froze. Over his shoulder, the draconis also opened a single eye and allowed the slit to widen as it focused in on her.

Leilani took a step backward.

"They are requesting communication using the traditional messari knock."

"I'm not sure how they could have learned that, but go ahead."

Leilani felt a secure link establish with the geloran boy.

"Greetings, council friend. May I ask the reason for your presence in this secure facility? I do not recognize your signature."

Leilani's brow furrowed deeply. How did this child know about the geloran council? Leilani had limited knowledge of geloran civilians. The geloran government carefully controlled her time in geloran space, limiting her exposure to civilians. The military personnel she trained with were highly psionic and used mental communications on a fairly regular basis. Unlike the Messari, gelorans were not exactly classified as a psionic race.

Yet someone had trained this child. They bled nothing. Their thoughts were calm and organized, only giving Leilani what the psionic community considered polite.

"You are concerned about my well-being." A wave of humor rolled across the link. *"My bonded and I are well. Thank you for your concern."*

"I am here because I am investigating a crime."

"Are you assuming I am a victim or a criminal?"

An eyebrow arched high on her forehead as she carefully controlled the thoughts behind her response. *"Neither. I am simply concerned that your government will not approve of this research."*

"What my government approves of is not your concern, Agent Falconi. I, however, am not here against my will."

Leilani bowed her head and took another step away. She cut the communication and jogged up next to Dorthy.

He took her appearance as a chance to interrupt the young crodoc by lifting his hand between the child and himself.

Leilani leaned forward and whispered to him, knowing full well that the kids could hear her.

"This lab is bonding elder races with draconis. There are thousands of elder race children in these cylinders."

Dorthy twisted his head slowly to lock eyes with her.

"Are you shitting me?"

She shook her head vehemently.

"I know the head of Dracko-Tech set the station to self-destruct, but we can't lose these children. They are vital to the survival of the species." The female crodoc in front of them wore a rank that clearly marked her as an officer.

Leilani jerked her thumb to Dorthy. "What he says, goes. Though I'm inclined to agree with you, kid."

"Then we will figure out how to do it on our own."

"We are receiving a communication from Deloris."

"Go ahead. Lavender?"

"My team is here. We're gathering up the whelplings now, but the little shits are turning it into a game, a game they won't survive if we don't catch them. How many do you have in there? And where do you want us to collect them?"

Leilani smirked as an idea occurred to her. *"Show me the layout."*

Sarah overlaid the holo of the station map in her HuD. Lei began moving it around until she found what she was looking for.

"How much time to self-destruct?"

"Forty-three minutes," the crodoc answered.

Leilani grinned broadly. "I have an idea."

"I'm listening."

She tossed him the overlay. "We have a fleet of draconis outside whose specialty is tearing into wreckage and pulling out the good stuff." She swung her arm wide, gesturing to the containers.

"If you tear these out of the facility, some occupants might die!" a nearby elar exclaimed.

"If we don't, I guarantee they will *all* die. Your choice, kid." She raised an eyebrow at the elar, daring him to argue.

The voice in the speakers rang out from the computer console nearby. "That is acceptable. Strangers, please know I designed this section to be moved as a single unit. The children know how to disconnect it, but your people will have to dig deep into the station to get it out."

"That shouldn't be a problem." Leilani winked at Dorthy. "You'll get to see what I was talking about after all."

"Disconnect section ninety-one from the station, and place it on backups, then do as the strangers tell you."

The kids all looked at the console and nodded their understanding.

"Yes, ma'am." The young officer began pointing to people and barking orders to disconnect the section from the station power grid. The kids exploded into action as they ran through the room, making adjustments to the containment units.

"Hey, Lavender. I'm sending you and Deloris a location inside the station. We need you and your people to get in here and pull out this section. It's filled with thousands of stasis pods."

"*Got it.*" There was a brief pause. "*On our way.*"

"That will be loud." Leilani elbowed her partner lightly. "We need to go get the others before the terrorists get the dumb-ass idea to eliminate kids."

"Roger that."

Several minutes later, Dorthy caught Leilani's attention from across a massive galley. He pointed to his ear, then at a pair of guards that were currently whispering to each other.

There was a lot of space between each table in the massive dining hall. It looked like it could hold at least five hundred young humanoids and their drackova bond-mates.

In the center of the room, the terrorists had pushed several tables out of the way to make a clearing large enough to gather up about a hundred children. Most of them were younger, but overall, they ranged from toddler to teenagers who were old enough for employment on some worlds.

In the middle of the group was an unconscious adult male, his abdomen covered in blood. A child that looked to be about twelve was trying to tend to his wounds, but the blood was clearly more than the kid could handle. They were all quiet, except for one toddler, who was sobbing into her hands.

Lei slinked closer, using a set of tables as cover.

"I don't think we're going to survive this one," a human male whispered to the female standing next to him.

"Suck it up. We still have a few more minutes. We have to set as many of them free as possible." The female rolled her eyes and shuffled her feet as she adjusted her weight back and forth. "Leth has a plan. We'll be fine."

"Maybe so, but what about these kids?"

"What about them? They're part of the problem. They're children of the enemy. If we let them live, they'll just grow up to continue the torture of innocent creatures."

The man shifted his stance, turning toward the woman. "They're just kids."

"And they will die, just like they deserve." The woman spit at the ground at his feet and stormed away, making a beeline for a lone man clad in spray-painted armor, who was leaning over a makeshift computer console set up on a table.

There were only ten terrorists, but they positioned themselves around the kids in a wide arc. Taking them all out at once was going to be problematic. They needed some kind of distraction.

"*Looks like they have a plan to get out.*"

Dorthy nodded his agreement and tapped his chest, before pointing to the leader of the group dressed in black.

Lei narrowed her eyes to focus on the leader. He was wearing a rather intricate harness. It was clearly a mix of aether and kuldain technology, but she couldn't tell what it was for.

"*Ma'am, I believe that is an anchor for a transportation system. Though it doesn't appear to have enough energy output to move more than a single person.*"

"*Are you saying that it might be some kind of teleport harness?*"

"*Most likely, yes.*"

Leilani had seen this before. The leader of the terrorist group flees, leaving the rest to die for the glory of the cause. A fairly standard tactic, and yet they never had trouble finding new recruits.

"*I suppose it's nice to know that some things never change.*" She knew Dorthy sensed her apathy.

"*Saves you from having to constantly learn new tactics.*" She couldn't really see the smirk from this distance, but she could feel the humor in the thought.

"*I think I can get the leader from here.*" She switched the rounds in her pistol to standard armor piercing.

"*Okay, but make sure you get him in one shot. I doubt you'll get a second.*"

"We're going to lose a few kids in the chaos."

"I know, but—"

An explosion tore through the room as tables and rubble launched into the air away from the main entrance to the galley.

Dorthy and Leilani hit the deck hard as the wave of heat rolled over them. The second sound of rending metal rang out, farther away, in the opposite direction.

Lavender's timing had to be a coincidence, but it was impressive nonetheless.

Poking her head up over the table, Lei glanced toward the explosion. A lone figure strolled through the flames caused by the super-heated metal. Smoke and steam rose around him, giving him a rather eerie look. In one hand, a bright, glowing, red blade screeched as it sliced through the air. From this distance, the blade appeared to be on fire.

"What the fuck?" the guard closest to her mumbled under his breath as he turned his back to her.

Leilani didn't wait to see what Dorthy was doing. She slipped forward and used the distraction to silently slit the guard's throat and gently lower him to the ground. Pulling him under a nearby table, she quickly crawled toward the next one. They would most likely lose the leader, but at least they might get the kids out with minimal casualties.

"Where is she?" a booming voice rolled across the room like a crack of thunder.

With two more guards down, Leilani caught sight of Dorthy as he lowered another dead guard to the ground silently.

He nodded to her, then jerked his head toward the kids. Then he pointed to himself and the last set of guards that were moving to stand behind their leader.

Leilani smirked. Fendrick may be a tool, but at least he was a useful one today. She crawled quickly toward the kids. The young teen that was giving first aid to the adult eyed her cautiously as she approached.

"We have a way to get you out," she whispered as the kids used their bodies to shield her from view of the remaining guards.

"Professor Hundel won't wake up," the boy whispered.

As he did, Lei realized he wasn't all that young. He was just an elar. Elari physically matured slower than other races, making them look younger than they really were.

"I'll take care of him. I want you all to head to section twelve, frame nine. We have people there to help you get to safety."

"We're not allowed in section twelve" a young human female whispered. She was maybe ten years old.

"I think they'll allow you today." Lei smiled what she hoped would be a reassuring smile.

"We just won't look at anything special." An older male crodoc winked at Leilani and patted the young girl on the shoulder.

"Okay, I can do that." The child rubbed her arms uncertainly.

Lei pointed to the hatch in the distance that they'd come in. In the center of the opening was a faint halo of eldrich highlighting one of the invisible drackova teams.

"Go quickly, before they look back this way."

Lei turned her attention back toward the terrorists and Fendrick as the kids started sneaking toward the exit. A touch on her arm drew her attention.

The young elari male's eyes filled with tears as he met her gaze. "He saved our lives. Please don't leave him to die."

She placed her hand on his shoulder and squeezed it gently. "I will do everything I can to get him out with me. I promise."

The boy's shoulders drooped, but he turned to follow the others.

Leilani glanced down at the large human male at her feet. He looked to be in his fifties, and even through the blood, she could see the old scars, most likely an ex-soldier. She saw movement on the side of his body, opposite from the retreating children. He gave a thumbs-up gesture, then another hand signal she didn't understand. Lei smiled and reached down to pat his leg to let him know she saw him. He was certainly tougher than he looked.

"Dorthy, we have a friendly."

"Roger. Move left and get Fen in your sights."

The guard in the very rear slowly dropped to the ground.

Lei tapped the man's leg twice as she moved to the left of the group to get a visual on Fendrick, ensuring that she kept the injured professor in her peripheral.

The man the children had called Professor Hundel snapped his eyes open and rolled onto his side, grimacing against the pain. He crawled to put a table between himself and the terrorists before popping his head up to look around.

Fendrick now stood a good ten yards from the terrorist leader. His glowing sword really was on fire. His eyes even appeared to be glowing faintly as he glared at the group. The sight made her skin crawl as her mind warned her of the danger.

"*What the hell?*" Lei knew her confusion bled across the comm, but Dorthy didn't respond.

"Where is she?" Fendrick barked loudly.

The man with the harness took a step backward. "We outnumber you. If you continue, we will kill you and the children."

"I don't care about you or your imaginary hostages. I want only one child. You will turn her over now, or I will murder everyone in this solar system!" The last word echoed through the room as if lightning carried it.

Leilani shook her head as her sound dampeners kicked in. Behind the terrorist leader, another guard dropped to the ground.

Now Dorthy stood directly behind the lead terrorist and the two remaining guards. The female from earlier stood to the man's left, but she didn't seem to notice Dorthy either.

Dorthy reached up and sliced the cables leading from the harness to the power pack just as the man swung his arm wide and slammed his hand onto the large button on his chest.

When nothing happened, the man looked down at his chest and hit the device again. Next to him, the woman turned toward him, her eyes wide.

"You aren't going anywhere." Dorthy's voice echoed through the room.

The two remaining guards spun toward him and fell to the deck, unmoving, pools of blood seeping from holes in their foreheads.

Leilani shifted her aim to the only two remaining terrorists as Dorthy stepped around the opposite side of the leader to face off against Fendrick.

The man continued to slap the button on his chest, trying to activate his harness, while the woman next to him narrowed her eyes even further and tightened her grip on her weapon.

Fendrick and Dorthy, however, ignored the drama brewing between the two terrorists and turned their attention to each other.

A bloodied hand tapped the leader on the shoulder as Leilani shifted her attention to the woman, who was still armed. The terrorist leader turned, only to have a fist impact his jaw with a sickening crunch. The professor held his side with one hand while trying to stand as tall as possible when the leader crumpled in front of him.

"Jackass." He spat blood at the unconscious body before pointing to the woman. "And that one you should just shoot now. She doesn't even deserve a life sentence in the asteroid fields."

Leilani flicked the tip of her weapon toward the ground, holding the woman's attention.

The woman's nostrils flared as she considered the situation before finally dropping her weapon.

"Yeah, well, that's not the way I operate." Lei closed the distance between them.

The injured professor picked up a discarded weapon with a pained grunt and shuffled close enough to kick the woman's gun away.

Still keeping the two delonians in sight, Leilani tapped two metal bands on the woman's wrists.

The metal became liquid and rapidly crept up the woman's arms and down over her hands. This panicked her so badly that she screamed and scrambled backward, trying to escape it, but she ended up tumbling backward over a table and landing in a heap. When she stopped moving, Leilani snorted and shook her head.

Turning to the delonians, she narrowed her eyes. "Boys. Can we continue this later? Or are you willing to blow up with the station?"

That seemed to stir Dorthy. He holstered his weapon. Twisting slightly toward her, he nodded curtly. With a deft roll, he dropped to the ground and came up with the unconscious terrorist leader draped over his shoulders.

"Let's get moving." He strode past her toward the evac point.

The injured professor shuffled past after him, his arm cradling his side.

Behind them, a loud crack echoed through the galley as Fendrick vanished.

Lei vaulted over a table and yanked the woman to her feet. "You want to live, get your ass moving!"

21

CONSEQUENCES OF BAD TIMING

As the group rounded the corner to the rendezvous, Leilani resisted the urge to pause and stare in amazement at the enormous hole that opened into space.

"Wasn't sure you'd make it!" Lavender's booming voice resonated from the squat suit of armor as she waved for them to hurry. "We already evacuated the kids. I ordered everyone to a safe distance. So, this will be a rough ride."

"Better than dead." Dorthy jerked his thumb at the body over his shoulder. "What about these three though? They don't have suits."

"They'll survive a couple of minutes." No one missed the mumbled addition of, "I think."

The dwarf leapt into the air toward a dangling cable. As Deloris's massive, purple head swung into view, Leilani marveled at the ease with which the dwarf scrambled into the tiny saddle nestled between the dracolli's shoulder blades.

Deloris darted toward the group and snatched up Dorthy and the two males with one clawed hand. As she twisted to leap off the station, she reached for the remaining two women. The terrorist with Leilani attempted to dive out of the way, but the ex-agent was faster. She grabbed the woman's arm just as the clawed, leathery fingers closed around them.

The g-forces from the movement slammed them against the edges of their new confines.

The woman next to her took advantage of the situation and delivered a swift snap-kick to Leilani's face. She felt and heard her nose crunch. She knew, without looking, that it was bleeding, but instead of allowing the move to stun her, Leilani reacted in kind with a back fist.

Unlike the terrorist, Leilani had experience with violent launches from a gravity well. It didn't take long before she had her arm locked around the woman's throat. She applied enough pressure to cut off her already limited supply of oxygen. Once the woman fell limp, Lei waited several more seconds, just in case, before releasing her.

"Where the fuck did she think she was going to go?" Lei wasn't talking to anyone in particular, but she felt better for saying it out loud.

Reaching into her bag, Lei jerked her backup rebreather free and stuffed it into the woman's bleeding mouth. It would generate enough oxygen to keep the woman alive for a short while.

Despite the dome around Severious system, which blocked energy and prevented the eldrich lines from feeding the system, there was still more eldrich inside than in traditional kuldain space. Wendel postulated it was because of a residual bleed-through from the net itself. Either that, or something else was creating eldrich.

No matter what was creating the limited eldrich, the woman wouldn't survive long without some sort of environmental suit. Even if she didn't suffocate, she would likely freeze to death.

A signal in Leilani's HuD warned her of the two large flashing zeros as the countdown finished.

The leathery fingers around them tightened as an overwhelming thought burst through her psionic defenses.

"Hold on!"

A thunderous explosion tore through reality. Gravitational forces slammed her to one side for several long seconds before the massive fingers around her loosened and she was flung free into space. As she spun end over end, she caught sight of the massive purple dracolli drifting away from her, unmoving. The explosion had shredded the creature's wings and gouged several gaping wounds in her side that left a sickening trail of large, red droplets.

Leilani couldn't see the saddle from this angle, and she hoped both the creature and its rider survived. Dorthy and the two men with him were also not visible. She, however, had problems of her own to consider.

Several navigational and inertial systems came online in her HuD, and she waited a few more seconds before bringing the inertial regulators online. Her uncontrolled spin slowed until she was finally able to manage her rotation on her own.

"*Status*?" she asked the oddly quiet oracle.

"Alive, so I suppose that's something."

"Nathan was not a beneficial influence on you."

Leilani felt more than heard the oracle chuckle. "*We are at 99.6 percent integrity and moving at approximately 35 kilometers a second.*"

There was no way her gravity belt could stop that much momentum. She would utterly drain the battery if she even tried.

"*Options?*" Leilani looked toward the inner solar system. She could see a massive ring of asteroids and debris, and she wondered if it was some kind of garbage ring.

"*Perhaps a few kinetic rounds might help slow the trajectory. But at that point—*" Sarah stopped talking as the solar system around them vanished into blackness.

Leilani slammed into something and made a loud noise as air escaped her lungs.

"*What just happened?*" She tried to catch her breath.

Everything around her was dark. She could no longer see the floating dracolli or the suns in the distance.

"*Unknown.*" Sarah paused. "*But you have an incoming communication from Dorthy.*"

"*Go ahead.*"

"*Lei?*" The emotion that bled across the link was far more intense than she'd expected. "*Are you okay?*"

"*Yeah, I'm fine,*" she lied, tightly holding back her own emotions from bleeding through. "*What about the others?*"

A text message appeared in her HuD from Sarah. *I think we were picked up by another dracolli.*

"*I have everyone accounted for except BB. Wendel is en route to pick us up.*"

"*We are hitting maximum range for silcomms, ma'am.*" Sarah chimed into her thoughts gently.

"*Good. Stay safe, Dorthy. I'll see you soon.*"

"*Lei?*" The comm broke up as the signal grew weak. "*Lei . . . ni wha . . . on?*"

When the signal strength in her HuD finally fell to zero, she sighed and dug into her bag for an emergency chem light.

"I hope."

As she triggered the chemical reaction, she scanned her surroundings. The solid black fingers were thick and leathery. It was definitely another draconic hand. Leilani shook her head and hooked the light on her belt as she checked her weapons.

The odds were high that this was the same dracolli she'd seen with the pirates a little more than a day before, the one who'd likely been an agent for the government. In her career, Leilani had interacted with dozens of agents from other governments. Such interactions always ended up in one of two ways: strained agreements to work together or a fight. And kidnapping, or black bagging, an agent to take them to your own turf to talk? Well, that was just par for the course. She couldn't even get upset about it because it was exactly what she would do.

She sat and leaned back against one of the massive fingers and closed her eyes. It had been a long day, and exhaustion was kicking in.

If this agent wanted her dead, it would already be over. Based on her experience, they were taking her to meet the boss, which likely meant further into the heavily populated system. She had time for a nap at the very least. Hell, maybe she'd get lucky and get some answers that didn't cause more questions, though she doubted it.

She woke to being jostled about as the creature landed. Glancing at her chronometer, she saw that five hours had passed, and there seemed to be atmosphere, so they'd landed someplace with environmental systems or on a planet.

Returning her vacc suit to its storage so that it could charge, she stood and stretched. As the hand wrapped around her opened, gravity pulled her downward.

"Son of a . . ."

In a split second, she calculated her surroundings and twisted to land on her feet, then immediately tucked into a roll to bleed off some of the kinetic energy. As she stood, a weapon in each hand, she scanned the area for threats. Before she could do more than realize she was alone on a beach, a gust of wind slammed into her, knocking her back several steps as she fought to regain her balance.

The massive black creature launched himself back into the brilliant blue sky, kicking up sand and surf as it did so. Leilani covered her face with her elbow as the sand whipped around her in a frenzy.

When the buffeting wind subsided, she dropped her arm and scanned the beach in each direction. To her left, a crystal blue ocean lapped softly at the white sand under her feet. To her right, the dunes blocked her vision inland. The beach stretched for miles in each direction. Other than the massive holes left by the giant dracolli and her own footprints, there was no other disturbance of the pure white beach.

Lowering her weapons, she sagged her shoulders and shook her head. "Perfect."

She skimmed the dunes and wrinkled her nose. She needed height, but that would not be fun to climb.

Putting one weapon away, she turned and climbed the steep dune. After sliding back down to the bottom several times, she finally put the second weapon away and crab-crawled up the side.

When she crested the top, she collapsed on her back and enjoyed the unmoving sand under her body. She lay there for several minutes, staring up at the beautiful blue sky and allowing her breathing and heart rate to return to normal. She wondered if she'd ever get the sand out of her clothes.

When she rolled up onto her feet, she slowly turned, scanning her surroundings. Except for the three enormous mountains in the distance, there was a blanket of green trees for as far as she could see—and not even a hint of civilization.

"*Well, this is new,*" Sarah chimed in, though she seemed more amused than Leilani was. "*I sense no networks or communication bands for at least one hundred miles.*"

"*I can honestly say this was not what I expected as a prison cell.*" Lei took a deep breath and considered her next steps.

"*Perhaps not, but you have to admit, it's effective.*"

"Greetings, Leilani Falconi." A high-pitched voice off to her left startled her.

Leilani leapt to the side. Twisting toward the sound, she drew both weapons. She landed squarely on her back, sand launching into the air with a dramatic flair.

Standing a good fifty feet away, a small, human boy, only four feet tall, smiled at her. He couldn't be more than maybe ten years old, if that. He wore shorts and a t-shirt with the ELU logo on the chest. He had no weapons, or if he did, he was far better than her at hiding them.

One eyebrow arched high on his young forehead, and he slowly raised both hands in the air. "My name is Derek. I'm sorry if I startled you." He shrugged and waved a palm toward the mountains and trees in the distance. "You seemed caught up in your thoughts, and I didn't want to disturb you. It's beautiful here, isn't it?"

Lei let her arms fall to her sides where she lay in the sand. *"I did it again, didn't I? I let my thoughts override my situational awareness."*

"No, ma'am. I didn't sense them approach, nor are my scanners able to pick them up now. I would proceed with caution."

Lei sat up and pulled her feet under her. As she stood, she put one weapon away and tried to brush off some sand.

"Nice to meet you, Derek."

When she kept one weapon drawn, the boy smirked. "Let's get you a shower and something to eat. I might even be able to arrange a change of clothes if you'd like." He turned and marched away, waving his arm wide for her to follow him.

They walked in silence for a good thirty minutes before Leilani finally caught a glimpse of their destination. Ahead of them set up in the trees on stilts was a rather spectacular-looking mansion. Even from here, she could see the enormous, clear walls facing the ocean and a spectacular tiered trio of pools. The outermost walls of the pools were clear and created an amazing waterfall effect as they poured over into the pool below.

"Wow." Lei couldn't help herself. She'd seen some amazing things in her lifetime, but this one definitely joined her top ten list of most beautiful homes. "Does that belong to your parents?"

"Something like that."

As they approached the base of the house, she could see several surfboards and small, sporty-looking rafts mounted on the support struts.

"You like to surf?"

The boy nodded and trudged up the stairs with her on his heels.

Generally, a home this size had at least some staff, but the utterly empty home was only mildly surprising. The furnishings and fixtures were all man-sized. Just inside the main entry was a spectacularly designed living area, kitchen, and balcony that led out to the pools. The large, glass doors were open, allowing the gentle sound of the surf and the warm breeze to waft across the room.

"There are several guest rooms in the east wing." The boy pointed to a hallway that led out of the open living area. "Please feel free to use any of them."

Leilani resisted the urge to shift her stance as he looked her up and down. His gaze pausing far too long on the bag attached to her belt.

"Do you need a change of clothing?"

Lei smiled warmly. "No, I think I'll be okay."

When she didn't move toward the hallway, the boy smiled, arching a well-manicured, sandy-blond eyebrow slowly up his forehead.

"I have things I need to be doing. Do you mind telling me why I'm here?"

His smile grew into a sly smirk as he bowed his head toward the east wing. "You have time. Trust me. Get cleaned up. When you're done, we'll talk."

"Ma'am, I don't think—"

Lei cut her oracle off. *"I know, Sarah."*

The boy watched her intently, his sly smirk firmly in place as he waited for her to acquiesce. Whoever he was, he was clearly not a child, but he also held all the cards for the moment.

"Alright. I'll play by your rules . . . for now."

Leilani spun on her heel and marched down the hallway. She picked the first door on her left and stepped into a large bedroom.

"I'm still not sensing any technology."

Lei found a door that led into a beautiful, marbled bathroom.

"And I'm not seeing any. Everything so far has been manual."

One wall, alongside the bathtub, was a massive bay window that looked out into the beautiful jungle. On a nearby tree, a monkey of some kind sat on a branch, watching her curiously.

Lei pulled off her shirt, and a large clump of sand fell to the floor. She grimaced and stepped into the shower before continuing to remove her clothing.

Even the shower was large enough for four people. Had it been any other situation, she might have enjoyed the prospects. But as she washed away the last of the sand, she wondered what was going on. Who was this kid, and what did he want?

There are many tricks in an IIS agent's bag; none of them are as useful as a portable clothing printer. Lei never knew when she'd need to change for a mission—to become someone new or to just blend into a crowd. So when the IIS forced her to turn in all of her equipment, her first stop was one of her many drop points to pick up a brand-new aether printer. It was a simple, extendable bar that printed a finite set of pre-programmed outfits and other, small, sundry items needed to disguise herself.

After tossing her sand-covered, bloody clothes in the bathroom garbage, she donned a fresh set of jeans and button-up shirt, then made her way back out toward her strange host.

When she emerged from the bedroom into the hallway, the aroma of grilled meat greeted her. She came into the living space just as the young boy slid two plates across the island.

"Hamburger and fries are okay, I hope?" Derek climbed down off the step stool he was using and made his way to a closet. He disappeared inside and came back out a few moments later with an armful of condiments. "I like everything on mine."

He jogged around the island and slid the items up onto the counter before clambering up onto a barstool and pulling a plate in front of himself. He then began loading up the burger with things that weren't typical for a human to even eat, let alone on a burger. It reminded her of a troll she knew.

Without a word, she slid onto the stool next to him, her stomach growling. The boy picked up his burger in his small hands and almost half of the extra condiments fell out as he took a bite way too big for his tiny mouth.

Lei laughed and loaded up her own burger.

"Damn it," the boy grumbled around a mouthful of hamburger.

Lei just shook her head and took a bite. "So, you wanna tell me why I'm here?"

The boy looked up at her and swallowed. "All work, huh?"

"Something like that." She shrugged and took another bite. She hadn't realized how hungry she was.

He rested his elbows on the counter and smiled up at her. "Or are you just naturally paranoid all the time?"

"It's not paranoia if you're right." She winked at him.

The boy laughed and shrugged his shoulders before taking another bite. "Touché."

She took another bite of her food, ignoring him as she enjoyed the meal.

"I'm impressed. You never even once thought I was an innocent child, did you?"

She chewed her food as she considered his question. When she swallowed, she turned to lock eyes with him. Everything about him screamed child, except his confidence. There was way too much experience behind those eyes for this creature to be a child, no matter how young he looked.

"It doesn't have the usual telltales of a spell, but I'll admit, it's an impressive disguise."

"That's because it's not a disguise."

Lei grimaced and took another overly large bite of food so she wouldn't say anything he might construe as offensive.

"Yeah, yeah, trust me. I've heard it all. Looking like a human child has its uses though. You'd be surprised how often kids are overlooked." He shrugged and stuffed another bite of burger into his mouth.

"I can see that. Would make you a . . ." her voice trailed off as she figured out what was going on. "You realize you could have just asked. You didn't have to have one of your people drag me out into the middle of nowhere."

Derek arched both eyebrows high on his forehead. "Ask you what?"

"What we're doing here."

The boy laughed and slapped his hand on the counter. "No need. I know what you're doing here. In fact, that's why I had McNeill bring you here. I wanted to see if there was any way I can help wrap this up quickly."

Leilani furrowed her brow so deeply that her nose wrinkled. "Excuse me?"

"You and the delonian. What's his name? Dorthy? You're here to capture the kidnapper and return the dragon child. I need to speed that along. Hence, I'm offering my assistance."

Leilani turned on the stool to face the boy, placing her elbow on the counter. "Why?"

"Ah, now there is the right question. We need you to look into something for us, and the others informed me that you will only take a new mission when the current mission is complete." He set his burger down on the plate and turned to face her.

"Who is *we?*"

The boy winked. "We will answer that when it becomes relevant. For now, know that I simply wish to help."

"You could help by letting me go back to my companions."

Derek placed his hands on his knees as he bobbed his head.

"Of course. I had no intentions of keeping you." He turned on the stool and waved his hand toward the windows. They darkened.

Reaching to the counter behind him, he picked up an object that Leilani swore wasn't there a few seconds ago. He pointed it at the windows and clicked a button. The windows roared to life with dozens of images, most of them showing a large gaggle of rather uncooperative hatchlings being offloaded onto what appeared to be a space station. Off to the side, she saw footage of BB, Wendel, and Dorthy arguing with a woman in uniform.

"Your companions will be at this for at least the next ten hours. As I am sure you know, debriefing the government after an interstellar incident can be tedious." He slid his thumb across the remote and clicked another button.

An image appeared of Fendrick sitting alone on the bridge of a delonian ship that looked similar to Dorthy's. He was pouring through documentation on a screen, swiping through it swiftly before finally throwing the pad across the bridge, only to have it shatter against the bulkhead.

"Meanwhile, your prey is doing some research from his hidden ship, still trying to find the missing child. He will eventually conclude that he can't find her, which will force his hand. I'm sure he will make himself known, but until then, there is nothing you can do. His stealth systems are rather impressive." The boyish creature next to her shrugged. "But my people are better. We've been following each of you since you passed through the net."

The image shifted again, showing an outline of a sleek, uncybered black dracolli with its rider slowly circling the faint outline of a delonian vessel.

"Impressive." Lei bobbed her head.

"So, you have time to get a good night's sleep at the very least. I'll have one of my agents take you back to your people in the morning." He held his hand out toward her. In his fingers was a paper card with a number on it. "This is my comm number. If you need anything, even a connection to the outside, let me know. I'll be happy to arrange it."

"You can communicate through the barrier?" Her voice was a little more shocked than she intended.

Derek smirked. “Of course, I do, but it’s not common knowledge. Only the president of Severious system and I have access to that comm system.”

Leilani took the card and slid it into her bag. “Thank you. I’ll keep that in mind.”

“I’m sure you will.” He slid off the stool. “I need to get back to work, Ms. Falconi. Please make yourself at home. Your ride will be here at sunup.”

“Thank you, Derek.”

The boy nodded and turned to walk down the hallway opposite to the guest wing.

A wave of exhaustion sunk into her bones. Stuffing the last bits of her meal into her mouth, she headed back to the bedroom. As she fell into the king-sized bed, fully clothed, the blackness of sleep claimed her almost instantly.

22

CONFESSION

Leilani stood at the base of a towering skyscraper. Its glistening steel refracted the afternoon sunlight in a rainbow of color.

The courtyard behind her emptied when the massive, pitch-black dracolli and his two riders shimmered into view overhead. The sheer terror of the crowd told her all she needed to know about the general populace's opinion of the creature and his bond-mate.

"Well, this is Ngwenya Surveying Conglomeration." The suit of solid black armor next to her pointed to the large doors at the top of the stairs in front of them. "The two delonians are inside with Master Bunderwick."

"Thank you, Commander." Lei smiled up at Commander Faustino McNeill.

The pair picked her up on the beach outside of Derek's home and were pleasantly surprised when she asked to ride in the saddle. The conversation was enlightening, even though it was between three special agents well versed in keeping secrets.

A massive muzzle slid alongside her, and she reached out to rub her hand along it. "And thank you, Dorisino. That was truly an awe-inspiring experience. I envy both of you."

"Like anything, it can get tedious, but it helps to have a superb partner." McNeill flashed her a wink and turned to hop up on his partner's head.

"Good luck, Ms. Falconi."

Leilani waved to them as the head lifted into the air, and the elar in sleek black armor slid down the creature's neck and into the saddle with a practiced flair—something which wouldn't be possible on their cybered brethren.

The creature launched itself into the air with a powerful leap and landed on the side of the towering skyscraper. It ran along the outer edge as it shimmered from normal vision, before launching into the air and disappearing between the towering mega structures of the metropolis.

Left alone in the courtyard, Leilani took a deep breath. It was time to get back to work. The fifty-foot-tall fountain behind her babbled loudly, something which was likely barely audible on a normal day in the busy courtyard. She turned to examine it. It was a marble statue of a drackova and its rider with the water running down its outstretched wings.

Returning her attention to the building, she started up the stairs toward the doors leading into the corporate arcology. As she crested the top of the stairs, several guards in light body armor pointed rifles in her direction.

Lifting both hands slowly, she grinned. "Hello there. I'm looking for Lavender Bunderwick. Is she here, perchance?"

The security officers didn't move, but in the far back, behind the hastily erected barricades, a person lifted their hand to tap something on their shoulder.

There was a long pause as they all waited to see what the next move would be.

In Leilani's HuD, the hue around the security personnel was a pale yellow, which meant they were effective but poorly equipped. Odd, considering the armor and weapons the corporation had access to. She couldn't help but wonder if this was for show and the actual security was elsewhere.

After several tense minutes, there was movement just inside the doors. When the stocky female dwarf stepped through the doors, Leilani smiled. Lavender had forgone her armor for a rather sharp-looking black suit and a vibrant lavender tie. The dwarf even covered her cyber-connections with her shoulder-length hair. If Leilani didn't already know that she was a bonded rider, she might've missed the telltales.

The dwarf strode up to the security guard who'd tapped his shoulder.

Sarah enhanced Leilani's hearing so she could easily overhear the conversation.

"What's going on here?" Lavender pointed to the security barricade.

The man pointed to Leilani. "She arrived with a specter."

"Okay, but that doesn't answer my question. What's with the security barricade?"

"We were defending the entrance."

The dwarf put her fists on her hips and cocked her head. "From what? The specter or the woman?"

The man sputtered as he bowed his head and took a step backward.

Lavender pointed a stubby finger at Leilani. "You know good and well, if the Ebony Flight wanted in this building, there is nothing you, nor I, could do to stop them! Trying to stand in their way is foolish!"

Lavender faced the rear of the barricade and barked, "Back to your posts!"

Leilani flinched as the dampeners kicked in and her heightened hearing faded.

The stocky dwarf marched through the scrambling guards straight for the mae'lacan.

"Sorry about that, Leilani. We don't normally greet guests like that here at Ngwenya Surveying Conglomeration." She held her hand out.

The two shook, and Leilani smiled.

"We're happy to see you. When we didn't find you, your commander grew . . . agitated. If I didn't know any better, I would think there was more there than professional interest." The dwarf met Lei's calm gaze and winked.

"He's not in my chain of command anymore." Lei gave her a coy smirk.

The dwarf laughed and turned to head inside, beckoning Leilani to follow. "I see. Well, regardless, he'll be relieved to see you. He's in the boardroom with Wendel and Pa. They're trying to find the man they keep calling the Heart."

"Fendrick."

The two remained silent as they wove their way through security. Lavender led her around the weapon detectors only to have a guard step in their path. The dwarf glared at him until he shuffled nervously out of their way.

Once they were safely in a lift that required a biometric scan to open, the dwarf looked up at her and folded her arms across her chest.

"You showed up with a member of the Ebony Flight. Anything I need to be concerned about?"

Leilani shook her head slowly. "I don't think so. They just wanted information about why we're here."

"Mmmhmm." The stout dwarf was clearly unconvinced. "Don't believe a thing they say. You can't trust a government agent. Ever!"

Leilani merely smiled and nodded her understanding.

When the door to the lift opened, the two strode down the hallway, side by side. They made it almost to the end before Lavender paused. She pointed to the double doors to their left. "The boardroom. I didn't tell them you were coming. I have some business to attend to."

Leilani bobbed her head and reached for the door. "Thank you, Lavender."

"Mmm." The dwarf stomped off.

Leilani watched her go before entering the boardroom.

Just past the second door on the right, Lavender placed her hand on the wall and stepped through a hidden doorway, disappearing out of sight.

"*That appeared to be a data center. There were dozens of strong network signals in there.*"

"*Odd place to have a corporate data center.*"

"*I'm not sure it* was *corporate,*" Sarah mused. "*The encryption is not the same type as the other signals in the building.*"

"*The joys of working with conspiracy theorists.*"

"*You mean like BB?*"

"*Exactly. Keep an ear out for her, just in case.*"

"*Shall I flag her as potentially hostile?*"

"*Not just yet. I can hope I'm wrong.*"

Leilani pushed the heavy double doors open and stepped inside. Several holographic heads turned her direction.

At the far end of the table, which could seat over fifty people, two delonians smiled broadly. Dorthy stood and strode toward her.

Without a word, he wrapped his arms around her shoulders and pulled her in for a tight hug. She smiled and returned the embrace, ignoring her body's reaction to his closeness.

He released her and took a step back. "Next time, tell me you're okay!"

"First, you frame me for your murder, and now you're giving me orders?" She poked him roughly in the ribs with her index finger. "Last I checked, you weren't my admiral anymore."

His eyes narrowed.

"Or would you prefer to go back to the no-fraternization relationship?"

He grumbled, "Why do you have to turn everything into a fight?"

She winked at him and strode past him to the far end of the table where the old dwarf and Wendel sat.

"Welcome back, Ms. Falconi," Wendel said cheerfully.

"Leilani, please. And thank you." She plopped into the chair Dorthy vacated and propped her feet up on the table. "What'd I miss?"

Wendel and Dorthy spent the next three hours catching her up.

Deloris was in medical, but promised to show a full recovery thanks to her armor. The military took the children and the hatchlings the second they landed at the closest Ngwenya mining station.

Wendel, Dorthy, and all the miners that assisted in the recovery were all taken into custody and shipped to various places to be interrogated separately. A group in black uniforms had taken Dorthy and Wendel to Thelonious Prime, where they spent the next thirty-six hours trying to explain what happened and why they were close by. Before their interrogators would release them, they had to sign a nondisclosure agreement and agree to not leave world.

Luckily, Thelonious Prime also was the home of Ngwenya Mining. They arrived at corporate HQ an hour before she did.

"What did you tell them about Fen?" she asked Dorthy.

They were in Jorna's office now, so the board meetings could continue without further interruptions.

Leilani lounged comfortably in a heavy, overstuffed chair with her feet propped up on the coffee table. A glass of amber liquid lowered into her field of vision, and she reached up to take it.

Dorthy stepped up next to her and took a sip of his own drink. He pushed her feet off the table as he moved to sit on it, preventing her from putting her feet back. "Nothing."

An eyebrow arched upward on her forehead. "You lied to them?"

Dorthy snorted, which caused him to choke on his drink. "Of course, I did."

He waved his arm wide at the other two males.

Jorna was even older in person than he was in the holo. Despite the cane he used in the recording, his frail form brought on by his advanced age, even for a dwarf, had confined him to an impressively high-tech hover-chair.

Wendel sat across from her on the overstuffed leather couch. He also had a drink in his hand and hid his own grin by taking a sip.

"We all did. You didn't honestly think we were going to tell them we're people from outside their solar system, did you? We'd all end up in a padded cell somewhere."

Leilani shrugged. "Not like it would have been the first time someone ordered me to tell a truth that landed my ass in jail on some backwater planet."

Dorthy dropped his attention to the glass in his hand.

"But I see your point. 'Hey, local authorities. We're aliens from an invisible universe, here in search of another alien who is a criminal that kidnapped a child and hid them here. If you'll just turn him and the kid over, we'll be on our way. Oh, and by the way, this all happened a thousand years ago'," she snickered.

Wendel snorted and rubbed his beard with his hand to hide his laughter.

Dorthy closed his eyes and shook his head. A slow smile crept across his face.

"How do you do that?"

She batted her eyes and flicked her hand to rest her fingertips on her chest. "Who me? What did I do?"

Both of the delonians burst out laughing, and the dwarf rolled his eyes. "You're all nuts."

"Of course, we are. We get shot at for a living." Leilani propped one leg up over the arm of the chair and leaned against the other. "It hardens people."

"Maybe you two, but he's just an engineer." The dwarf waved his hand in Wendel's general direction.

Leilani smirked as the two delonians focused their attention anywhere besides the dwarf.

"Perhaps that's true of this lifetime, but if you knew how and where I found him, you'd understand. I'm surprised he can put together a coherent sentence, let alone design anything." She lifted her glass toward Wendel. "He is far more than a simple engineer. He could have walked away—you both could have—yet, here you are. Why is that, by the way?"

Next to her, Dorthy glanced from Wendel to Jorna. "That's a good question."

The dwarf smirked and bobbed his head. His chair floated off across the room to the bar. That left the two ex-agents to turn their attention to Wendel.

He locked eyes with Leilani, but she refused to sell him out. She still doubted that Wendel meant to give the portal generator to Fendrick, but if he was going to stick around to stop Fen, he needed to face the music . . . eventually.

The delonian engineer downed the rest of his drink in one large gulp.

Dorthy raised both eyebrows high on his forehead.

Wendel set his empty glass down and found all three of them watching him intently. "I have no intentions of letting Fendrick get away with this."

Leilani smirked as she stood and strode across the room to the bar.

"Bullshit!" the dwarf and Dorthy said simultaneously.

She snorted, keeping her back to them as she refreshed her drink.

"Fine!" Wendel blurted. "It was my fault."

There was a moment of complete silence as Leilani turned to face the group. She leaned back against the bar, maintaining the enormous office between herself and the conversation.

"What was your fault?" Jorna floated closer.

Wendel shook his head, his nostrils flaring. "All of it."

"Care to explain that?" Dorthy's voice was commanding. It reminded her of the tone he'd used on her when he was her admiral.

Wendel shot to his feet and began pacing back and forth in front of the couch. "Had I never agreed to help him kidnap the damn kid in the first place, none of this would have happened."

Leilani couldn't keep in the laughter, but she clamped her mouth shut as soon as the sound came out.

Dorthy spun his angry glare on her. She swallowed the last of the laughter and took a drink.

"He hired me to help him build the containment for the kid. He wanted to make sure her parents couldn't track her. But when we got here, everything went sideways. He came back after a meeting with the client and told me to get lost. Like really lost. He helped me build a new identity and told me to hide out among the humans for a while. I'm not stupid. I know what he stole, and I knew better than to be where they could find me." He marched across the room to the bar.

Leilani filled his glass without a word.

He took the drink and sipped it for a moment before turning his back on her and facing Dorthy and Jorna.

She slid to the side so she could see around him.

"When he came to me a few years later and asked for a device that could gate something on a much smaller scale, I told him I wouldn't build a weapon for him. He said that was fine, he just wanted the math for it. Honestly, Fendrick isn't all that technologically savvy. I figured it was okay to give him the math to the dilation principle as it relates to gate theory. It's not like he or any of these primitives could do anything with it. Or so I thought." He hung his head, and his shoulders drooped as he stared into his drink. "Apparently, I was wrong."

Dorthy and Lei locked eyes. Neither of them said a word. There wasn't any need to. They both knew what the other was thinking.

"Don't forget the gate you *did* build." Lei winked at her ex-admiral.

In front of her, Wendel sagged his shoulders even farther.

"What gate?" Jorna blurted.

Lei's smirk broadened into a toothy grin.

"A gate large enough to . . . How did you word it? Oh yeah, big enough to move a full-sized fleet, capital ships and all."

Wendel reached up with his free hand and rubbed the back of his neck.

Leilani felt sorry for him, almost.

"That's the gate we came in." Dorthy swirled the amber liquid in his glass slowly as he contemplated the new information.

Wendel recovered his composure and stood up straight. "In my defense, I didn't design that gate to be used as a doorway to this absurd barrier. They stole it from my shipyard."

The dwarf, who'd been silently listening to Wendel's statement with a cool expression, finally chimed in. "I can vouch for that, at least. Though the rest of it . . . I'm not sure how to respond to."

Dorthy narrowed his eyes at the engineer. "Darithan, I warned you."

Leilani smirked. Now the tension on the ship made sense. They knew each other. And she was right—Wendel was just another façade.

Wendel kept his chin up as he nodded. "I know, inspector. I accept my fate. You may not understand, but I couldn't turn my back on him when he asked for help."

"No. I understand. When you risk your life alongside someone long enough, a bond forms. That bond can cause you to do things you'd never even consider otherwise." Dorthy allowed his gaze to shift to Leilani. "Trust me, I know that all too well."

Leilani lifted her glass to Dorthy. "You'd even take the fall for them if need be."

"Well, I wouldn't go that far." Wendel looked over his shoulder at her, his face contorted into a deep frown. "I'm not taking the fall for that dick. I will stand up and take what's coming to me for my part in this because I knew what I was doing, but I will not take the fall for him."

Lei arched a single brow and rolled her eyes. "So much for the brotherhood of blood."

"There are limits, I suppose," Dorthy chuckled.

Lei shook her head vehemently. "No, there aren't. I've fought next to you for most of my adult career. I would still take a bullet, or the fall, for you if need be. Hell, I *have* taken the fall for you. Several times."

"And I rewarded you by framing you for murder. Perhaps you should reconsider the whole blind loyalty thing at some point, Lei."

Her eyes narrowed as her hand tightened on the glass. She saw the prod for what it was. He wanted her out of the room. She knew him too well. She glared at her ex-admiral and felt, more than saw, Wendel move away so he wasn't between them. In the back of her mind, that fury that often overwhelmed her into doing something stupid threatened to rear up. Instead, she relaxed her grip on the glass and set it on the bar.

"A simple request for privacy would have been sufficient, sir." She added the sir, as an intended reminder of how their relationship had grown after the dissolution of IIS.

She stood straight and turned to the dwarf. "Mr. Bunderwick, does this place have a cafeteria? I'm starving!"

"Yes, Ms. Falconi. I think I'm feeling a bit peckish myself. How about I escort you?" The white-haired dwarf grinned broadly through his thick beard.

Leilani bowed. "I'd love your company."

He floated up to her, and the two of them made their way out of the office without looking back.

23

GREETINGS, MADAM PRESIDENT

"Here's what I don't get." Leilani took a bite out of the meatball sub.

The massive corporate cafeteria could easily hold over five thousand people. It reminded her of a food court in a super-mall with dozens of restaurants and a massive open area with tables and chairs.

When the Ngwenya CEO and his guest entered the area, it was abuzz with chatter, but it didn't take long for word to spread that the CEO and founder had arrived.

Now, the mostly empty cafeteria echoed as the few remaining people pretended to have lunch on the far side of the room.

"What's that?" The dwarf took a sip of the green shake in front of him.

"Why self-destruct the station? That wasn't the terrorists' doing. They set explosives, which honestly would have done minimal damage based on the placement and the makeup of the station. And who was the woman in the speakers that the kids deferred to? Where was *she?*"

"Those are good questions." Jorna drummed his fingers on the table. "That explosion was far larger than the other explosions the GMO took credit for. Usually, the damage is repairable, but that was an utter loss."

“GMO?” Lei asked around a mouthful of food.

The dwarf smirked as he ran his hand over his short beard. “They call themselves the Galactic Martyrdom Organization.”

She blinked at him several times, utterly silent, before she finally blurted out. “There are so many things wrong with that name!”

He laughed and nodded in agreement.

“So many,” she mumbled, allowing her thoughts to go unsaid.

“I have little experience with terrorist organizations, but I'm not sure any of them are entirely rational.”

“True.” Lei stared at her sandwich for a long moment before taking another bite.

The sound of doors bursting open echoed throughout the room, followed immediately by the sounds of heavily booted feet.

The few people that remained stood, drawing weapons from inside their clothing.

Leilani, however, calmly stuffed another bite of her sandwich into her mouth.

Individuals in dark blue armor with silver trim rushed into the room with weapons drawn. The logo in the center of their chests marked them as the Thelonious Prime Regulators. She doubted these were the typical forces. They were far better armed.

“I suppose I should be honored they felt I was that much of a threat,” she chuckled.

The dwarf raised his hand, and every person in the room froze, including the authorities. “No, the armorment is for me, not you.”

“Aw, way to pop my bubble.” Leilani pretended to pout.

He winked at her.

“Leilani Falconi, you are under arrest.” A voice echoed through the room, followed by the whine of what sounded like a dozen or more weapons spinning up, exactly the same as Lavender's weapon.

Lei turned to look over her shoulder. On the far side of the room stood a full wing of fifteen miners. These weren't the support troops. These were all riders, wearing their over-the-top armor and weaponry.

"*No target silhouettes?*" Lei asked Sarah.

"*Were you planning to fight them?*"

"*Well, no, but knowing that we were in the cross fire would have been useful.*"

She could feel Sarah laughing. "*They don't miss. Trust me. You'd have been fine.*"

Leilani shook her head and snatched up the last of the sandwich as she stood. "That's me!"

Turning, she bowed to the dwarf. "Thank you for a wonderful lunch, Master Bunderwick."

He bowed his head slowly in her direction and his fingers, on the hand he was holding in the air, shifted slightly, followed immediately by the riders advancing toward the regulators.

The reaction was priceless. The authorities took several steps back toward the doors they'd burst through. Some of them even glanced over their shoulders feverishly.

Leilani stuffed the last of the sandwich in her mouth and quickly chewed. When she got close enough for the lone regulator who held their ground to hear her without yelling, she hissed, "You might want to get me out of here. They don't seem happy with you barging in on their CEO."

The officer nodded curtly and held a set of standard kuldain-style handcuffs toward her.

She obliged by holding out both wrists.

The officer slapped them on her and pointed for her to proceed from the room. Several other officers closed in around her and lifted shields to protect her in case gunfire broke out. At least their orders were to bring her in alive.

They marched her through the building to the lobby where they met another group of officers, also in heavy armor. These had a similarly cuffed Dorthy with them.

"*Wendel?*" she asked across their silcomm.

"*Secure.*"

“Well, this seems oddly familiar.” She winked at him.

He smirked but only bobbed his head in agreement.

The officers led them to a large police vehicle and seated them in the back with two guards across from them. Lei scanned the vehicle. There was a soft hum in the air-tight compartment. She could feel a slight vibration across her skin, and she concluded the compartment was likely designed to discharge a high level of electricity in case of unruly passengers. The powered armor the officers wore was likely insulated from the charge.

“That’s impressive.” She jutted her chin toward a hidden emitter.

Dorthy drew his attention away from the guards to look where she indicated.

“Is that what I think it is?”

“Yep.”

His shoulders relaxed, and he leaned back into the seat.

“You’re slacking.” She playfully elbowed him in the side.

He twisted his head to narrow his eyes at her. “It’s been a while since I was in the field.”

The group sat silently for a good thirty minutes before the vehicle finally came to a stop. When the doors opened, the two guards didn’t move. They kept their attention on the prisoners.

“Relax, we aren’t interested in trying to fight our way out of this.” She stood and moved toward the opening rear doors. “I, for one, want to meet whoever had the balls to storm the NSC building.”

She hopped out and stood in front of a single guard, who only wore an armored business suit and carried no obvious weapons.

They were parked in some kind of empty garage. Well, empty of grav-cars anyway, but not security. There were easily a dozen or more individuals in suits, similar to the large human in front of her. All of them had a deep red halo around them as Sarah marked them as highly dangerous. Glancing back over her shoulder, she found Dorthy still staring down the two officers in the vehicle.

“Jason!”

He jumped slightly.

"Let them be. They're just following orders."

The delonian stood and followed her out of the vehicle. When he stepped up next to her, he scanned the area, and a single eyebrow arched high on his forehead.

"You know where we are."

He nodded his head slowly.

"Perfect!" She smiled brightly at the large guard. "Please, lead the way. We promise to behave." She elbowed Dorthy in the side. "Right?"

"I have no intentions of dying today," was his only response.

A barely perceptible smirk flashed into the corners of his mouth. "Sata."

Leilani had no idea what language that was or if it was even a language.

The guard spun on his heel and marched toward the door that led deeper into the building. They followed him without a word.

They made their way down a short hallway and stepped into a lift that had a guard on either side of it. As they turned to wait for the lift to move, Lei leaned into Dorthy.

"What was that?"

"He said, 'good'."

She arched an eyebrow high on her forehead. "In what language?"

"Mine."

Lei looked up at him, but Dorthy kept his gaze on the door. Something had put him in professional mode, and she couldn't help but feel as if she was missing some key detail.

The elevator door opened into an impressively large office. Vaulted ceilings arched high over the massive, transparent wall that made the room feel much larger than it really was. Standing in front of the window, looking out over the city, was a tall elar woman with golden hair, tanned skin, and an outfit that stressed her elegant form by hugging all the right places and flowing at the extremities. She had her hands clasped behind her back and didn't turn when the guard led the two prisoners into the office.

In the middle of the room, a beautiful wooden desk, which masked an impressive amount of technology, accentuated the room, giving an air of strength and power while still maintaining an elegance of historical craftsmanship.

"That will be all, Adré. I wish to speak to the outsiders alone." The lilting tone carried a level of confidence that caused Leilani to grin.

"Yes, Madam President." The guard with them bowed, then marched across the room. He stepped out a set of double doors into what appeared to be a hallway.

Leilani strode toward the padded chairs that faced the front of the large desk. As the elar turned to face them, Leilani tossed her handcuffs on the desktop, then flopped into a chair and crossed her legs at the knee.

The woman paused as she looked from the cuffs to Leilani. "Well, I was going to say make yourself at home, but I see you already have."

Behind Lei, Dorthy made a soft clicking sound before saying, "Welcome to my world."

Her chair moved as he smacked the back of it.

"Ms. Falconi has little regard for authority. Get up, Lei."

"Why? She's not *my* president."

She didn't need to see Dorthy to know that he'd just rolled his eyes at her.

"My apologies, Madam President." He reached down and lifted her by the upper arm. It was the first time Lei had experienced his strength in his natural form. "Stand!"

"Ow. Fine! Sheesh."

The woman strode toward her desk while the two had their interaction. "Are you two quite finished?"

Leilani jerked her arm from Dorthy's grip and glared at him briefly before returning her attention to the elar.

"Please, sit." The woman bobbed her head toward the chairs and rested her hands on the back of her own.

When neither of them sat, she continued anyway. "You have both entered Severious System illegally. Who are you, and why are you here?"

Confusion flitted across Leilani's face, but she immediately schooled it into a neutral expression. Derek, the tiny agent, seemed to already know why she was here, and Lei was a little surprised he hadn't shared that info with his president.

"We're investigators looking into a kidnapping." Dorthy oversimplified the answer, but Leilani opted to let him do the talking.

"This system was sealed long ago. What makes you think your kidnapper is here?"

"We followed him here."

The elar's pupils shifted slightly as Dorthy spoke. She bit the inside of her cheek as she considered his words. "I see. And my research station?" She shifted her weight as she stepped up next to her chair, draping an arm along the back of it.

Leilani suddenly recognized the voice. It was the same voice from the station. This was the person who'd been giving the kids orders.

"We heard about the terrorists and went to assist, since we were in the area."

The president arched a single eyebrow. "The truth, please."

Leilani scratched her nose, using her hand to hide her smirk as the elar called Dorthy on his blatant lie.

"We had a lead that the kidnapper would show up. We went to the station to apprehend him."

"Did you?"

"No. We did not." Leilani spoke up before Dorthy could lie to the woman again. "We opted to rescue the kids instead. The target isn't going anywhere until he finds what he came for. We knew there would be another opportunity."

The woman turned her full attention to Leilani. "I see."

The two women stared at each other, but the elar wasn't really looking at her. She was using the exchange to process the information.

"Very well. You two are free to go, for now. But if you attempt to leave the solar system, I will have my Ruby Flight rip your tiny ship to shreds. Is that understood?"

The woman's words rippled with power as a wave of magic rolled across the room.

Leilani chuckled. Magical fear had never worked on her, even when she was a child. Apparently, Dorthy was also immune, as they both stood their ground.

"We understand the threat for what it is, Madam President." Dorthy's words resonated with their own wave of fear.

Lei's eyebrows shot up into her hairline. That was new.

The woman across the desk twitched slightly, which surprised Leilani even more. She had good self-control, but Dorthy had rattled her.

The door behind them opened.

Lei glanced over her shoulder as a young, male child wearing a nicely tailored suit strolled in.

"That will be enough, Inspector Hojikanu."

Her partner turned to face the newcomer, a look of surprise on his face. He bowed to the young man and stood back up straighter than before.

"I believe I allowed my temper to get the better of me. My apologies. My partner and I will be nearby if you need us. I doubt we will have to wait long before Fendrick makes himself known with an even larger stunt." Dorthy headed for the door with unusually long strides.

Leilani turned to follow with a wink at the small humanoid.

"Did you say Fendrick?" The president's tone shifted to a slightly higher pitch.

Dorthy stopped mid-stride keeping his back to the president. Lei stepped up alongside him and caught a sly wink.

"I did."

"Is that the kidnapper's name?"

"Yes, Madam President."

"Understood. You are dismissed."

24

BRING IT ON

The two ex-IIS agents stepped out onto the busy courtyard in front of the Capitol building and paused at the top of the stairs. Neither of them said a word as they scanned the crowd of business people rushing along their way, trying to fit too much into too little time.

An arm appeared in Leilani's view as Dorthy pointed to a nearby bar. "I could use a drink."

"I could use a keg to drown myself in, but sure."

He shoved her shoulder roughly, causing her to take a small step away. As he marched into the crowd, she heard him laughing.

"I count five tails. Two government, one police, one that's too well dressed to be government—so I assume organized crime—and what looks to be an underground type." Dorthy didn't look at her as they strode through the doorway into the dimly lit bar.

"There are nine actually." Lei flicked her wrist in a small arc toward the patrons in the bar.

Of the two dozen people, four were paying close attention to the newcomers while trying to appear as if they didn't care.

"Well, at least we've made friends." Dorthy placed his hand on the small of her back and steered her toward the bar.

"*How to Make Enemies and Influence Friends.* Wasn't that a book you had me read when I came onboard at IIS?" Leilani leaned her shoulder into him and winked.

The bartender, a lighter skinned crodoc with salt-and-pepper hair, beamed a smile in their direction as they slid onto the padded stools.

"What can I getcha?" His deep voice was warm and welcoming.

He locked eyes with Leilani, then glanced down the bar to a female several seats down. When he returned his gaze to Lei, he nodded almost imperceptibly.

"I'll take a scotch." Dorthy dropped his hands onto the bar with a soft thud.

"I'll have an iced tea. Black. No sugar."

The bartender nodded and strode down the bar to get the drinks.

"Something I need to know?" Dorthy's voice was low as he leaned in toward her.

"Nah. I've seen you drink. You'll be fine."

The two sat quietly as they waited.

When the bartender sat the drinks down, she could see something handwritten on the white napkin under her drink.

Dorthy seemed to notice it too but picked up his drink, saying nothing. He sipped it as he scanned the monitors over the bar.

Leilani picked up her drink.

"*It's a local comm number. Should I call it?*" Sarah asked.

Before Lei could answer, she felt an elbow in her ribs. She followed Dorthy's extended finger to the series of monitors. She glanced up just as the various channels all shifted to show the same image. Apparently, all the networks were sharing the same drone footage.

A delonian vessel, bristling with weapons, sat in the middle of a heavy traffic lane between the planet and the first ring of stations. Missiles leapt from the ship and streaked toward the closest drackova and its cargo container. The creature exploded in a hail of fire, flesh, and metal.

"That guy has some serious issues." Leilani took a sip of her tea as her other hand flipped the napkin over and wiped up some of the condensation that had dripped from her glass.

Next to her, Dorthy shook his head. "You have no idea."

"I have a fairly good idea of how psychotic he is. Life means nothing to him."

Her ex-commander pursed his lips as he stared down at his drink, something he often did when there was something he wanted to say but couldn't.

"Can we get sound?" Leilani pointed to a display.

The bartender reached up into the air and swiped his finger to the right. The display closest to Lei and Dorthy roared to life.

"The unknown vessel has fired on four cargo carriers in the last ten minutes. Total loss of life so far has been four drackova and their bonded riders." The human male newscaster placed his hand to his ear and nodded. "Apparently, the terrorist is broadcasting demands. Let's listen."

Fendrick's voice sounded guttural as he threatened more violence. "I have made my point. My next target will be the planet. The government has fifteen minutes to prove to me that Delecca Gredoris Manithelle is alive and in their custody. They will then turn her over to me immediately. If fifteen minutes goes by, and I have not seen her, I will start bombarding the capital until they comply."

Leilani shook her head and waved her hand to get the bartender's attention.

When he finally tore his gaze from the monitor to look at her, his eyes twinkled as the corners of his mouth twitched slightly.

"I think I'll take something harder after all. Do you have any good cognac?" She glanced briefly at the monitor and shook her head. "Scratch that. I'll take your strongest vodka."

The bartender snorted softly and snatched a bottle from the barback. As he strolled down the bar toward her, he scooped up a shot glass in the same hand. He set them both in front of her and returned his attention to the news. Behind her, several people rushed from the bar, clearly having someplace better to be. Not that it would matter. Fifteen minutes wasn't enough time to get out of range of the explosions that would rain down on the Capitol building.

The bartender kept his back to her as he leaned up against the bar and folded his arms across his chest, his broad, muscular back and telltale cybernetic rider link visible under his black silk shirt.

In the video feed of Fendrick's ship, red dots appeared and grew as they closed on the hostile vessel.

In front of her, the crodoc looked at a chronometer on his wrist.

"A little slow today, boys," he mumbled under his breath.

Leilani glanced out the windows of the bar to the courtyard in front of the Capitol building. A rather large military force was amassing as they quickly, but calmly, brought in several enormous devices with grav-lifters and emitters similar to the eldri-net ones used around the solar system.

She poked Dorthy in the side and pointed out the window.

The crodoc's deep baritone spoke up. "That's the defense net. We're safe here, even if he manages to get a round off, which I highly doubt."

Dorthy turned to lock eyes with Leilani.

The reporter continued talking, but the two of them ignored the ratings babble as he attempted to spin the event into a world-shattering kaboom. Instead, they watched the military units in the courtyard.

When the voice shifted to a powerful female that both ex-agents recognized, they turned their attention back to the monitors.

"This is the president of Severious Prime. To the terrorist in orbit around Thelonious Major, I hereby order you to cease and desist. If you do not, I will make an example of you and your primitive technology." She paused briefly. "In case you didn't understand me the first time, I am ordering Fendrick Gerthalis Gath'Dalithi to stand down this instant, or so help me, I *will* kill you! No one is more important than my people, not even my own father!"

Leilani murmured under her breath, "Great, Stockholm Syndrome."

"That should make this easier," Dorthy retorted with his own sarcastic aside.

They both raised their drinks toward each other, then took a long swig.

"Well, I didn't see that coming." The crodoc unfolded his arms and pointed to the screen. "But I did see that coming."

The wing of red drackova slammed into the thousand-ton delonian ship like a child tearing into a present wrapped in tissue paper. In less than a minute, the drackova rended the ship into dozens of tiny floating bits of metal. One drackova was slightly more discerning and expertly separated out the engine compartment without causing a catastrophic failure. They then broke off from the primary group and vanished off camera, carrying the power plant in their claws.

Leilani and Dorthy blinked several times at the monitor as the bartender and the woman further down the bar cheered.

"Did that really just happen?" Leilani whispered.

Next to her, the delonian's wide eyes narrowed as he placed his elbows on the bar and rested his face in his hands.

"Okay, I've been on a delonian ship. Your armor isn't all that spectacular, not like kuldain ships anyway, but it should have been enough to handle wildlife." She turned on the stool to face her ex-boss. "What just happened?"

His jaw muscles rippled under his skin as he rubbed his face and glanced back up at the monitor. "Several dozen intergalactic treaties were just broken, that's what."

"I assume you don't mean Kass and Seef'aini?"

Shaking his head slowly, he glanced at the bartender who'd walked further down to refresh the drink of the only other customer left in the bar.

"No. This breaks other, far older treaties that keep the leviathan species from going to war and tearing apart solar systems."

Leilani imagined Krelor at war. She suddenly felt as if a subzero breeze wafted across her naked body. Solving problems was Leilani's forte, even problems capable of killing millions and destroying an entire planet, but this took the playing field to a whole new level—a level in which she was nothing more than a pebble in the cobblestone.

"Way to make me feel utterly irrelevant." She poured herself a shot and downed it.

Dorthy's jaw clenched as he bobbed his head. "Trust me, if this gets out, it makes us all irrelevant."

"*Ma'am. You have an incoming communication,*" Sarah chimed.

"*From?*"

"*The number I was waiting to dial.*"

"*Go ahead.*"

"*We don't have time for you to put off calling me to drink,*" BB bitched at her. "*You need to go to the nearest Draco lift. There are tickets already waiting there for you. But if you don't move your ass, you'll miss the flight.*"

"Where are we going?" she asked out loud so Dorthy could hear.

He got the message and waved for the bartender so he could pay for the drinks.

"They've already paid for your drinks. Have a good day." The crodoc called.

"*Just do what I say. Someone will meet you at the other end.*"

"*Fine, but you owe me an explanation.*"

"*Trust me. It's much worse than you think.*" She could feel her brother's concern bleed through the communication, and she frowned.

"*BB?*"

The communication cut, and Lei sighed. "Such a drama queen."

"Let me guess, end of the world?" Dorthy stood and sauntered out of the bar with Leilani on his heels.

"Yep," she laughed.

"Bring it on!"

The two of them stopped in front of an enormous sign over the entrance to the space-lift.

Andaran Dracoport:
Where Flights of Fantasy Become a Reality.

All around them, people flooded past in a steady flow of traffic.

"Are they kidding with that?" Lei pointed a finger up at the sign and cocked her head at Dorthy.

He shrugged his shoulders and let them flop back into place. His mouth opened as if he were going to say something, but he closed it and shook his head.

"Alrighty then." Swinging her hand wide, she slapped him on the shoulder and slipped into the flow of traffic, headed into the station.

The lift system was a series of high-strength cables and cars that took passengers from the surface to the low-orbit space station, often called a ring, which encircled the planet. It was in the ring that the various organizations, both civilian and governmental, managed transport and trade to and from the planet.

It took them over an hour to get through security and then ride a heavily packed lift to the orbital ring. When they finally stepped out into the Dracoport, people bustled in every direction as they rushed to a seemingly endless number of locations.

Leilani and Dorthy paused at the exit to the lift as the wave of traffic rushed past. Spinning suddenly, Leilani clasped her hand onto a thin wrist. The resulting high-pitched squeal caused her to take a step back while still maintaining her grip.

"I wasn stealin, I promise!" a tall, disturbingly thin troll pleaded. He crouched low, trying to drop his head below the crowd as he frantically twisted his arm in her hand.

She pulled his hand out of her pocket and lifted it to find two flimsies.

"Then what's this?"

Dorthy stepped up next to her and pulled the flimsies from the troll's fingers without a word.

"Theys tickets," the troll whispered loudly.

"You couldn't just hand them to us?" Lei growled.

He scanned the crowd frantically and began shifting his weight back and forth. "You wasn supposed to see me."

"Not sure that worked out for you," Dorthy laughed.

The troll saw something in the crowd that terrified him more than Leilani, and he jerked his hand free and bolted for the lift.

The action was so forceful that he wrenched her off her feet. She flailed her arms wide as she tried to regain her balance. Before she could tumble into the crowd, a strong arm wrapped around her waist and pulled her in the opposite direction. As Dorthy yanked her back onto her feet, she found herself wrapped in his arms. Their eyes locked, and before she could say thank you, his mouth met hers.

Her body responded to the kiss, despite her mind trying to ignore it, but Leilani refused to give in to her own desire. His relationship with her was a cover. She knew that now. He needed to draw a connection between them that would add credibility when he faked his death. No matter how close they'd grown, she couldn't be sure how much of it was real and how much was a game of control.

Station security raced by as they chased the retreating troll. An officer paused by the couple to ask them a question, but they refused to acknowledge her. After several seconds, the officer threw her hands in the air and bolted off after the others.

When the kiss continued longer than necessary, Leilani pushed him off her.

"That's enough. They're gone."

He blinked several times, then grinned coyly. "Who's gone?"

Rolling her eyes, Leilani stormed past him, snatching the tickets from his hand as she passed. She found the gate number printed in the corner and began comparing it to the massive monitors in the distance. "Looks like the gate is that way. We're still a few minutes early. Maybe we'll even have some time for coffee. I know I could use some."

25

TUULARI

"Look, mommy!" The rapid footsteps and high-pitched squeal drew Leilani's attention.

She turned to find a small elari child running full tilt toward a floor-to-ceiling prosee window. He slid to a stop with his hands and face pressed hard against the window. It was almost as if he thought he could bend the laws of reality and force the window to give way so he could get a better view.

"We get Tuulari today!"

"Mmhm," the mother mused loud enough for the boy to hear as she found an empty seat where she could see the child, then promptly buried her nose in her pad.

Lei glanced around at the large waiting area for gate number 21459. The space had rows and rows of seats, enough to easily fit over a hundred passengers of various races. When they'd first arrived, there were already two dozen passengers waiting for the flight, most of them asleep in their chairs.

Like the boy, though, she was curious. She strolled up next to the young elar and nodded respectfully to the woman, who eyed her cautiously.

Pointing to the drackova in the distance, Leilani asked the young boy, "Did you say his name was Tuulari?"

His face lit up at her question, his grin growing so wide she could see a gap where he'd lost some of his baby teeth recently.

"Yes!" The volume of his voice was a tad loud, and a couple of the sleeping travelers stirred.

"Shh," his mother hissed. Not that it mattered to the young elar as he continued to share his expertise on the topic.

"He's a class nine yellow." He tugged a holocard from his pocket and activated it. The image of a yellow drackova popped into existence above the card and slowly rotated. Below the holo were statistics like one might find on a trading card used for sports heroes. Tapping his finger on the window, he drew her gaze to the large yellow creature in the distance.

The drackova was indeed a large, yellow one with a slightly wider wingspan than the sleeker, red drackova used by the military. It was still smaller than the heavily armored dracolli that Lavender rode.

Like the other creatures she'd seen throughout Severious, massive cables locked tightly on to the steel bands that encircled the drackova's torso, then buried under the scales along the spine. Several other cables ran from the torso, up the neck, and terminated at a large metal plate on the left side of the creature's skull. The cables fastened to the creature's neck every few feet so they wouldn't be in the way during flight.

From this location, Leilani could see the massive cybernetic assisters bolted into the left shoulder and wing joint, no doubt to assist with some form of past injury.

Several humanoids in armored vacc suits were detaching the drackova from the station when a larger person floated out into view.

The boy next to her squealed happily.

The man in an armored black and yellow suit climbed along the creature, carefully checking over the harness and attachments.

"That's Captain Vincent! He was the wing leader of the Ruby Flight during the last incursion! They say he single-handedly stopped the entire invasion fleet!" The small boy put his palms and face on the glass and sighed. "I want to be him some day."

Leilani frowned. There were so many things wrong with that statement that she wasn't sure where to begin. "I thought the riders bonded with their drackova?"

The boy nodded. "Captain Vincent is an elar, like me. He and Tuulari are from before, when they were just mounts and riders."

When Leilani blinked at him, her brow furrowed in confusion. The boy rolled his eyes. "They used to just be war mounts. But my pa says they were dangerous, so they made them friends instead of pets."

She arched an eyebrow and glanced over her shoulder at the slowly filling waiting room. She still didn't see Dorthy, who'd wandered off to find them coffee. Returning her attention to the young elar, she shook her head. Getting information from a kid was always problematic. Their understanding of fact and fiction often blurred because of their imagination.

"When was the last incursion?" she asked quietly.

"I don't know. My history teacher says it never happened, but the books in the library talk about it. She says I shouldn't read books—they're dangerous. The net is the only safe place to learn." The boy laughed and tapped his hands on the window. "But my pa works in the library. He says books are better because the bad people can't change them to say what they want, like they can on the net." His boyish face looked up to frown at Leilani. "But aren't both written by people?"

She resisted the urge to laugh and instead dropped her hand to pat him on the head. "Yes, they are."

"Can't they both be lying?" He returned his attention to the creature outside. "Adults lie a lot!"

"Yes, they do."

They both stood quietly and watched as the rider inspected its drackova.

"Your father is right about one thing."

The boy looked up at her, his eyes wide with curiosity.

"Books don't change like the net. And who knows, if you keep studying and learning all you can, you might get to be like the captain there." She pointed to the rider outside as he tested a cable that led into the servo at the drackova's shoulder.

One of the station crews detached the last of the tethers from the drackova, and the massive creature began to stretch. It folded its long wings back along its sides and crawled carefully across the outside of the station toward their gate. As its gaze fell across the window that Leilani and the young elar stood in, the creature paused. Twisting its head to the side, its cybernetic eye rotated as it zoomed in on them.

Without warning, the creature launched free from the station and twisted its body back toward the station with a gentle flap of its enormous wings. The movement ripped the few technicians, still attached to the creature, free from their perches. As they snapped to the end of their safety lines, they scrambled to grab a hold of something before the creature crashed into the station. The sudden reversal of g-forces wouldn't hurt the drackova, but would likely kill them, armored suits or not.

The rider that the boy called Captain Vincent was not as slow as the station handlers. In a practiced leap, he dove for the creature and unsnapped his lifeline to the station. Snagging a cable on the drackova's cybernetic harness, the man slammed into his mount's side. Then, with practiced ease, he climbed toward the saddle on the drackova's back, which was nestled just between the wings.

As the massive creature dove toward the window, Leilani felt a presence step up behind her and place his hand on the small of her back.

Next to her, the boy shrieked with glee and jumped up and down, clapping his hands together. The sound ripped through the waiting room, causing heads to snap toward the window. Passengers stared, horrified, as the creature slammed into the station. The deck beneath their feet shook, setting off alarms. People behind her screamed and stampeded from the waiting area.

"This is so cool!" The boy giggled gleefully as an arm wrapped around his waist and dragged him away.

"Noooo!" he cried as his mother ran from the one thing he wanted more than anything.

As the head grew close to the window, an armored body slammed into the station to her right. It bounced off the window and floated away, unmoving. No amount of armor could stop that kind of gravity poisoning.

An eyeball, larger than she was tall, filled the window and focused in on her.

"Ma'am, we are being scanned. Shall I allow it?" Sarah asked with an almost amused tone.

A small voice in the back of her mind told her to move away from the window. If this creature was anything like the mining drackova, it could tear into the station at will. *"It's fine. Let's see what it wants."*

There was a brief pause before Sarah finally spoke up again. Leilani could swear she heard surprise in her oracle's voice. *"Ma'am, the creature is using the IIS silcomm circuit to request communication."*

"Go ahead."

"It is my honor to meet the great Leilani Falconi in person!"

Leilani blinked several times.

"Thank you? How do you know who I am?"

"You are the key to our freedom. You are that which is whispered about in the dark corners of the galaxy. All of us who live in the shadows watch you with great interest. You will repair the . . ." The creature's head jerked to the side violently, and a brief sensation of pain bled through the comm before the link cut.

She could hear the roar of pain, or possibly anger, through the hull of the station as the rider forced the creature back toward the cargo container. As they moved off, the still unmoving technician dragged behind them, bouncing lightly back and forth between the station and the creature.

"That seems like a dangerous line of work."

"No shit!" Her reply was a tad louder than she'd intended, but she glanced over her shoulder and found the waiting area utterly devoid of passengers.

Dorthy's head dropped closer to her ear as he added softly, "What was that about, anyway?"

"I have absolutely no fucking idea." Lei snorted and rolled her eyes. "I mean seriously, that was way out of the ballpark. I literally have no clue. Although . . ."

Outside, near the passenger container, new technicians came from the station and hooked the creature up quickly. The rider remained in the saddle as they worked. For a moment, Captain Vincent looked back toward them, but when the creature under him shifted its weight, he returned his attention to his mount.

"Although?"

"It's not the first time I've been told that people are watching me. It's starting to feel like a creepy horror flick."

"Watching you? Why?"

Leilani shrugged, then leaned her shoulder up against the window as she crossed her legs at the ankle. Near the entrance to the lobby, the first of the passengers filtered back into the waiting area.

A man marched through the growing crowd, pushing at least one passenger out of the way as he wove toward the podium.

"Flight one-three-one from Thelonious Prime to Janeston will begin boarding in ten minutes. Please have your tickets ready, and line up in your assigned order," the station attendant called out loudly, his voice enhanced by a speaker system throughout the waiting room.

"Well, that appears to be our queue." Dorthy held his hand out. "Tickets?"

She smirked and set one of the two tickets in his waiting hand. "You're taking this too well. Where are the angry glares and lectures for causing a scene in a public place?"

"My dear, I'm no longer required to play the part of your commander who gives a damn about the political waves you leave in your wake." He winked at her and spun to face the rapidly forming line. "Now I get to be your friend. You know, the one who sits back and laughs at the chaos you are constantly wading, waist deep, through."

She snorted at his uncharacteristic nonchalance. As she took several long strides to catch up, she elbowed him in the side. "Hey, where's my coffee?"

"Trust me, you're better off. Whatever that was, it certainly wasn't coffee." He wrinkled his nose.

"Outstanding."

The pair found their place toward the end of the line just about the time the line began moving down the long p-way that led into the passenger container in the distance.

As they reached the attendant, he shifted his gaze to the empty air next to him. He seemed to read something before returning his attention to them.

"The captain has asked that you undergo a secondary security sweep." He waved his hand in the air, and station security swarmed in their direction. "If you don't mind stepping out of line?"

"Oh, we mind," Leilani argued, but her partner's hand on the small of her back stopped her.

"Easy, Lei."

"Fine." She stepped out of line toward the incoming security.

They were told to move away from one another while the security teams waved wands over them. Just like the first security sweep, this team saw nothing out of the ordinary, and not for the first time since coming to Severious she was happy these aethers knew nothing at all about eldrich—an anomaly in and of itself, but one she was happy to use to her advantage.

The IIS trained all agents in the basics of eldrich, even if they only worked in kuldain space. So it was a common trick-of-the-trade to hide weapons and tools in plain sight using aether stealth systems, since the typical kuldain sensor had no ability to see into the eldrich energy bands. But this wasn't kuldain space. Technically, this was aether space, and the sheer ignorance of eldrich should be impossible, or so she would have told anyone had she not seen it for herself.

“Clear,” the team lead pronounced. “You are free to board.”

Leilani stood up straight and tugged her shirt back into place. Biting on her lower lip, she glared at the security officer for a brief second before she felt a push on her back.

“Don’t start anything, Falconi.” The authoritative tone of her admiral broke through her thoughts.

She clenched her jaw and marched down the gangplank into the large carrier. “Yes, sir.”

She rolled her eyes at his soft chuckle.

26

SPEECHLESS

Flight one-three-one was a unique experience for them both. Like an aether tram, there were rows of seats down the center, but that was where the similarity ended. The front and rear of the transport had actual stores where the passengers could get food, coffee, or gifts and superfluous items such as tech readers, communicators, and headphones. Along the sides of the transport were compartments, which the locals referred to as coffins, where the passengers could pay extra to sleep through the flight in a climate-controlled tube.

Lei and Dorthy managed to get a decent cup of overpriced coffee before resting quietly in the semi-comfortable seats. The flight, while long, was uneventful. Most of the passengers either buried their noses in their electronic devices or slept through the flight.

Leilani stretched her arms high overhead as she stepped outside into the warm, Janeston air and scanned the beautiful surroundings. Unlike Thelonious, the air here was clean with a faint whiff of the ocean in the distance.

The sea of people scattered in every direction as they made their way to various waiting vehicles. Off to her right, she spotted a short greduna standing in front of a limousine. He wore a dark blue suit with a white shirt and a black tie. The digital sign floating in the alternate reality, or AR, in front of him read a name she'd heard recently: Dorthari Hojikanu.

She popped her elbow into the delonian next to her and pointed.

As he followed her outstretched arm, both eyebrows shot high on his forehead. "Now that is not something you see every day."

"Your name?" she teased, knowing full well he meant the greduna in the suit.

Dorthy ignored her and carefully weaved his way through the foot traffic to the greduna.

He eyed them curiously as they made their way over. When they were within hearing range, the large male bowed his forehead in their direction.

"Greetings, Mr. Hojikanu. Is this woman with you?" The greduna spoke in the local tongue with no accent at all.

"Yes, this is my partner."

He bowed at the waist. "Very well. My name is Thondau. Please make yourselves comfortable. It is a two-hour flight to our destination." He extended an arm to the vehicle behind him.

The door popped open with a soft hissing sound. They stepped inside. On either end of the central rows were seats for the larger species, while the seats along the wall were human-sized. In the center was a long bar with an AR floating over it. Lei arched a single eyebrow at the impressively long list of available beverages.

Lei and Dorthy made their way to the human-sized seats and sat side by side as the door closed behind them and the cabin pressurized.

The driver's voice flooded into the compartment. "You will find beverages available in the bar. If you are hungry, we can make a detour to a restaurant on our way out of town."

There was a soft chime, and a green light illuminated a square button on the bar.

"If you desire privacy, please press this button. It will seal off the main cabin from the cockpit. If you wish to contact me while the area is sealed, you may use the intercom button, located here."

Another button on the bar illuminated with a green hue.

"Thank you, Thondau. May I ask if this is a rental car?" Leilani's curiosity got the better of her.

"You may, and it is not. Mr. Hojikanu is a guest of the owner," the voice replied as the vehicle lifted off the ground and slipped into traffic.

"Apparently you have friends here?" Lei smirked at the delonian.

Dorthy, however, narrowed his eyes as he pursed his lips in annoyance. "Trust me, I have no friends in this arm of the galaxy."

This time, it was Lei's turn to furrow her brow. "Hey now."

"Sorry." His face relaxed somewhat. "Friend is not a word I use lightly. And you are . . ." his voice trailed off as he clearly tried to find an appropriate way to end the sentence, "not a friend."

Lei stood and scrolled through the list of drinks at the bar. She made her selection and kept her back to him as she picked up the drink that lifted out of the top of the bar. "Good to know."

They sat across the car from each other in silence for the rest of the flight until Thondau's deep baritone filled the compartment again. "We are approaching the house now. Security Chief Piper Styles is waiting at the landing site to escort you inside."

Leilani nodded her head, even though she doubted the driver could see her.

The altitude lowered until they could see trees and other landscape, and Leilani stood and strode to the door. As the vehicle settled to the ground, Dorthy placed his hand on the small of her back.

"You mean far more to me than I ever thought possible," he breathed into her neck.

She took a deep breath but opted not to respond. Instead, she slowly released the air and adjusted her stance as the door opened to a fifteen-person security force. They wore powered armor with the typical Severious military markers. The soldiers in the rear were easily twelve to fifteen feet tall.

A shiver shot up her spine as she imagined a greduna in powered armor.

"That's just wrong," Dorthy whispered behind her.

"*Ma'am, we have nothing that would stop a cybered greduna,*" Sarah warned.

Fear gripped her briefly before she shook it off and stepped out of the vehicle. "*Thanks for making it worse, Sarah.*"

"*I was simply warning you, but you're welcome.*"

"Greetings, inspector Hojikanu." A smallish, red-haired human woman nodded her head curtly to Dorthy, then to Leilani. "And Ms. Falconi."

Leilani shifted her weight, dropping her right foot back as she prepared to defend herself.

"I am Security Chief Piper Styles. I am President Dana Gath'Dalithi's head of security." The woman allowed the corners of her mouth to turn upward as her eyes narrowed. "I see I now have your undivided attention. I am aware of the situation, and I am here to politely inform you, inspector, that Ms. Gath'Dalithi is going nowhere without her permission. Is that clear?" The woman lifted her chin as she locked eyes with Dorthy.

The hairs on the back of Lei's neck stood on end. In her HuD, every living thing in the courtyard flashed from yellow to red as the soldiers behind the angry woman lifted their weapons to a ready position. Her HuD highlighted the half-dozen snipers on the rooftops of the mansion.

Dorthy's jaw tensed. A coy smile crept into the corners of Leilani's mouth as she shifted her weight to her rear foot and relaxed her shoulders. A small, yellow ball fell into her hand from her belt, and she locked eyes on the woman. If this was going to be a fight, the one without a helmet was dying first.

The shift in her stance broke Dorthy's concentration, and he turned to smirk at her. He returned his attention to the woman.

"We all have our orders, and mine are to return the president to her parents—a duty which I take very seriously. As for your thinly veiled threat, I think my partner is looking forward to the challenge." He shook his head and pursed his lips. "That may not have been your wisest choice today. I've seen her take on much larger units with far superior tech and be the only one to walk away."

The woman opened her mouth, but Dorthy raised his hand to stop her. "Relax. That wasn't a threat. It was a warning. I'm not her admiral anymore. The only one pulling her strings now is her. If you push her, there's little in this galaxy that can stop her."

"If only you understood how true that was, Mr. Hojikanu." A young voice chimed into the conversation, and every head in the courtyard turned toward the young boy wearing a button-up silk shirt, jeans, and a rather expensive-looking pair of dress shoes.

The red-haired woman's eyes opened wide in shock. "Master Derek?"

"I came to save your life, Mrs. Styles." He frowned at the woman. "The delonian here is correct. You have gravely miscalculated his partner, and I do not wish to push her too far at this time. You and your people are dismissed."

The woman slammed her fists into her own hips. "I don't answer to you. I . . ." Her voice fell away as the sky suddenly darkened.

Everyone in the courtyard looked up except for Leilani and Derek.

There were several loud roars as enormous, black dracolli descended onto the rooftops, each of them placing a clawed foot over the snipers as they landed.

The soldiers, who'd fixated on the two ex-agents, took on a defensive stance around the small red-headed woman.

"I don't think I need to dismiss you again, do I?" the small male asked, his voice still clearly audible over the screams from the rooftops.

"No, sir." The woman shook her head and stormed off into the building, her soldiers carefully retreating after her, keeping the dracolli in view as they went.

"Way to escalate the situation, Derek." Leilani tossed the small grenade in the air and caught it before slipping it back into the dispenser on her belt.

Her nonchalance caused the delonian next to her to spin his head in her direction, his eyes wide in disbelief.

The boy, however, laughed. "Perhaps, but we all have to create entertainment where we can, right?"

"I suppose." Leilani strode up to him and held her palm out toward him.

He slapped it, then spun flamboyantly and waved for her to follow him inside. "They're waiting inside. Oh, and I hope it goes without saying, but the president is off-limits. I still need her, for now."

"Not a problem. We can arrange everything after this is all over. Right, Dorthy?" she called over her shoulder without looking. When she got no response, she laughed.

The small boy next to her elbowed her in the thigh. "I think he's speechless."

Lei's laughter reverberated off the walls. "I should keep you around! I love the idea of a speechless Dorthy."

The large double doors at the end of the hall drifted open as they approached. She could feel the sheer power of this tiny creature even when he didn't use it, but when he did, it rolled across her like a cool breeze.

The voices in the room paused as Derek and Leilani strolled side by side into the library. In the center of the multistory room, two people sat in overstuffed chairs in front of a roaring fire.

Lei looked back over her shoulder and saw Dorthy following, but with a healthy distance between himself and Derek. She rolled her eyes and returned her attention to the president and the delonian seated next to her.

"Madam President." She bobbed her head to the woman. With a coy smirk, she turned her attention to the delonian. "And hello again, Fendrick. I hear you've been looking for me?"

He took a deep breath and opened his mouth as he narrowed his eyes at her, but instead of the retort he'd likely intended, he sighed.

Lei wouldn't let him off that easily. "You almost had me at ELU. You look good in emerald, by the way."

That did it. His nostrils flared at her. "You're a real bitch. You know that, right?"

"Yep," she laughed.

Derek tapped her on the hip. "I'll be around when you're ready."

When he strolled off, Dorthy finally stepped up next to her and leaned in to whisper in her ear. "How do you know a meleini?"

"Derek?" She cocked her thumb toward where the small creature had disappeared.

He nodded.

"Never met him before." She winked at Dorthy and sauntered up to the fireplace and chairs. "I assume we're here to talk?"

The president smiled warmly at Lei and bowed her head. "Yes, Ms. Falconi. Please, have a seat."

"Call me Leilani or Lei. Everyone else does." She flopped into a seat and propped her feet up on the coffee table. "I'm all ears."

"I don't even know why you're here," Fendrick snapped.

Dorthy stepped up next to the chair Lei was sitting in and placed his hand on the back of it. "Leilani is here because she's an excellent investigator, and she's helping me close this case and return your ass to the council to stand trial for your crimes."

The beautiful, blond elar smiled warmly and met Leilani's gaze. "You have to love testosterone-driven males."

"They *are* entertaining." Leilani chuckled and tossed a hand in the air casually.

"Please, gentlemen, tonight is not about Fendrick's guilt or innocence. We all know he's guilty of many things, the least of which is kidnapping a child from the head of the Draconis Imperious Grand Council."

Leilani raised both eyebrows high on her forehead and opened her mouth to say something, but closed it after realizing that interrupting the woman might not be wise.

"I, however, know facts about the kidnapping that might be of use to you, inspector. I hope you will do me the honor of listening to my tale before passing judgment on master Fendrick."

There was a long pause as Dorthy looked back and forth from his target to the woman sitting next to him. Finally, he turned his attention to Leilani.

"*What do you think?*"

She chose not to look up at him as she replied. "*I think we still have a long list of questions that need answers. If they know some of those answers, it never hurts to listen. If what you told me was true, and someone hired him to kidnap her, then maybe the council will be more interested in the person who hired him, rather than the homicidal lackey. Fendrick will face his crimes against Kass and the Seef'aini eventually, but honestly, that's no longer our problem.*"

She kept her eyes on the two other people in the room. Fen seemed relaxed, which was a new look for him. The elar, on the other hand, seemed tightly wound. She was still confident and in control, but the concern etched in her forehead and eyes was impossible to miss.

Dorthy stepped in front of Leilani and settled into the chair next to her. As he sat, he tapped his fingers on his forehead. "I swear to remain neutral as we discuss the matter. I will refrain from judgment or action until we conclude our business this evening."

Fendrick raised a single eyebrow but said nothing.

"Thank you, inspector." The elar smiled. "How about I have some food and drinks brought in?"

"That sounds great!" Lei answered before the men could refuse. "I'm starving!"

27

BINDS THAT TIE

"Okay," Leilani said around a mouthful of hamburger.

Dorthy glared at her.

Lei ignored him and pointed from Fendrick to the elar sitting next to him. "I think I have the gist. Someone hired you to kidnap her for some kind of galactically illegal experiment."

Fendrick tilted his head to the side and held it there as he contemplated her oversimplification. "Close enough, yes."

"Then you had a bizarre wave of conscience and refused to go through with it. But instead of returning the kid to her parents like a sane person would, you killed billions of people and destroyed two entire solar systems in a seriously disturbed attempt to hide her in a third solar system, which you then hid from the rest of the aether?" She took another large bite of food.

Dorthy swallowed his own food before adding, "At that point, your plan went off the tram-line. Instead of rebooting, you ended up locked in Hodair's time bubble."

"And you," Lei pointed to the president, "got bored hiding as an elari child, so you killed your captor, then built an army of your own to take over the solar system. That's not elitist at all."

Dorthy leaned back in his chair and crossed his legs at the knee. "What I'd like to know is why you created a brand-new species? Why not pick something that already existed and adapt it to what you wanted? You basically created a smaller, shorter-lived *draconis imperious*, potentially risking millions of years' worth of treaties between thousands of races, including your own."

"Oh! Here's the part I love." Leilani chuckled and waved the last of her hamburger in the air. "When you started having trouble controlling your new army—and they started the random killing sprees—you then built into the genetics a bonding process where the drackova or dracolli and their chosen riders couldn't survive without each other."

The president's eyes widened, and she opened her mouth to argue, but instead, her shoulders sagged, and she stared down at her hands in her lap.

Leilani swallowed the last of the food. "Seems like you both have an awful lot of blood on your hands with this insane scheme. Although, hats off for stealing a solar system. That's an impressive trick."

Fendrick smirked and cocked his head slightly. "Thank you, but I can't take credit for that. The barrier wasn't my idea, or my trick, as you call it."

"Oh?" Dorthy set his plate aside and crossed his legs. "Please elaborate."

Fen didn't take his eyes off of Leilani as he continued. "I hid her with a friend while I tried to come up with a way to distract the client who was operating, at the time, as a human reporter. I started the war to distract him, but it didn't matter. He was on me like stink on a fadawar. No matter what I did, there he was. I couldn't risk leading him back to her, so I went to someone who I knew had a vested interest in keeping Delecca away from the client. The eldrich-net and the hiding of the solar system was his idea, not mine."

Leilani leaned back in her chair and nodded her head emphatically. "To turn the barrier on, you had to make a ripple in the eldrilins so large that it would mask the smaller ripple the net caused. You had to create an abyssal point. One at the treaty spot would ensure that your client was looking the other way. Wow. How pissed are you at Hodair right now?"

Fendrick's eyes narrowed to slits as he glared at her intently. A wave of power intended to scare her rolled off of him, but she merely laughed.

"I guess that means very! I mean, seriously, she ruined the entire plan, and you guys spent what, over a decade working on that?" A broad grin spread across Leilani's face as she continued to laugh at the delonian's rising anger.

"Leilani . . ." Dorthy's voice was a low warning.

She ignored him and pointed at Fendrick. "Not only did you fail at creating an abyssal point, but you didn't die, and you abandoned the kid for almost a thousand years. And then, you did the one thing that all that destruction was supposed to avoid."

Fendrick furrowed his brow, his building rage twisting into confusion.

"You led him right to her anyway." Her voice deepened as the words rolled softly across the room. All of her mocking gone.

That did it. Fendrick snapped to his feet. His sword appeared in his hand and swung toward her as the screech of thousands of tortured souls tore through the air.

"Ready, Sarah?"

"Of course, ma'am."

Leilani remained in her seat as doors around the room burst open, and soldiers poured into the room. One door behind the delonian opened, and a small, child-sized humanoid stepped into the room. Behind him, a massive humanoid in solid black armor followed.

"How dare you!" Fendrick's voice cracked as his emotions overwhelmed him.

"How dare I what? Point out the flaw in your plan? I can do you one better if you like?" She lifted her hand toward him and extended a finger. Eldrich arced from her extended finger to the tip of the sword with a muffled twang. The energy carried Sarah's oracle worm, and it took less than three seconds for the sword to go dark, just like it had in the library with Krelor.

Fendrick's eyes shot wide open and he staggered backward. He bumped into his own chair, causing his already weakened knees to buckle. As he fell into the chair, the room froze, and all faces turned to stare at Leilani.

Across the room, Derek smiled brightly and winked at her. He then made a circle with his finger in the air.

The guards, throughout the room, took their cue and turned to march out the doors they'd come in.

"H . . . ho . . . how?"

"I told you, I was at the library. I saw everything."

His face paled as he dropped the sword to the floor with a loud clang.

The woman next to him reached over and put her hand on his arm. "Stop this! Whatever you're doing to him, stop it."

Leilani shrugged her shoulders. When she turned to look at Dorthy, she found him watching her intently, a single eyebrow raised in curiosity. "Relax, it's temporary. I think."

"*It will remain offline until I tell it otherwise,*" Sarah answered.

"*Understood.*"

"*I would like to point out, ma'am, that is a serious weakness.*" Lei could feel her oracle's extreme displeasure.

"*Are you any different?*"

"*I am not* your *soul, I . . .*"

She felt a sudden wave of uncertainty as the oracle fell silent.

"I demand that you stop this!" the president snapped.

Leilani turned an utterly blank stare onto the elari woman. "And why would I do that? He is a mass murderer, and you're not much better."

"Neither are you," Dorthy interjected quietly.

Leilani turned to the delonian next to her, and the muscles in her jaw clenched. "No, I killed on orders. Your orders, more often than not,

I might add. And I have taken the blame for the Kamorian Incident enough. I've been trying to tell you for years, Senator Lovelock released the ka'va, not me."

Dorthy raised both hands. "Easy. None of us here are saints. We're all murderers, and all of us have our reasons for what we did. I'm more interested in who's really pulling the strings and why they wanted the whelpling of the head of the Draconis Imperious Council of War."

Leilani relaxed back in her chair. He was right, of course, per usual.

"And if he's cut off from his sword for too long, it'll kill him." He locked eyes with hers, and his thoughts whispered across the silcomm. *"I'm not sure how you did that, but I'm impressed. Most delonians feel that his order is insane for separating themselves from their souls like that, but they have a good reason. Regardless, we need him alive if we want to catch his client."*

"Fine." She waved her hand, and Sarah rebooted the oracle in the sword.

As the inert sword flickered to life on the ground, some color returned to Fendrick's cheeks.

The president's shoulders relaxed somewhat, and her face softened as she examined the weakened delonian. The group was quiet as Fendrick fought to regain some of his composure, but Leilani could see the concern in his eyes.

"Having that happen once in a lifetime is surprising enough, but twice in a single year leaves me second-guessing my life choices." Fendrick pushed himself up out of the chair and strode across the library, pacing back and forth in the shadows.

Leilani opted to give him a moment to collect his thoughts. "Madam President, do you know who hired him to kidnap you and why?"

The woman was staring at the fire, but the question seemed to pull her from her thoughts.

"Its name is Madel. As for the why, I'm not entirely sure." The woman's eyes lifted from the flickering flames and focused on

Lei. "Fen thinks he wanted me for some kind of genetic splicing research."

Lei allowed the corner of her mouth to curl up slightly. "You mean something like what you've done here?"

The woman's gaze locked with Lei's as she narrowed her eyelids. "No, I don't. I mean more like what I carefully chose *not* to do here. You won't understand this, Ms. Falconi, but my kind have rules. Even children know what those rules are. I know where my line is. Did I make an army here? Yes, I did." She waved her arm in a wide arc. "And I'm very proud of my friends and family here, but I did not break Council law. I did not make a *draconis imperious* genetically engineered for war!"

Next to her, Dorthy tapped his foot slowly as he listened to the elar.

"When the Grand Council demands reparations from another race, that race will turn brother against brother to do as our council demands. There is a reason the other races fear my people." She lifted her jaw proudly.

Dorthy stood and strode away from the two women, toward the still-pacing Fendrick.

Leilani opted to get her answer from another source. "They are brothers? Or do you mean as in the 'brotherhood-of-soldiers' sense?" she asked the president.

The woman grinned as if she'd just won some sort of battle. "Both."

Lei leaned back in her chair and crossed her legs at the knee as the other two talked quietly in the shadows on the far side of the library.

"*They are both soldiers.*"

She could feel Sarah agree, but her oracle said nothing.

"*And you already knew that about Dorthy.*" A thought suddenly occurred to her. "*Wendel too. They were a part of their government's military. I wonder what happened?*"

"Delonians do not have a centralized government."

Leilani could feel that Sarah wanted to say more.

"But they used to." Lei understood now.

Suddenly, pieces fell into place. They all had the same pain—she could see it in certain behaviors. During the coup attempt, Dorthy was erratic, acting far outside of his usual pattern of behavior. At the time, she was too focused on keeping the emperor alive to pay much attention. The excessive drinking afterward now also made sense. If the delonians had a royal line and somehow lost it, the repeat of a similar trauma could have caused a serious strain on him.

Leilani's skin crawled as it suddenly dawned on her what was going on. *"They're overreacting because it was a monarchy. And they were royal guard!"*

As if Dorthy had just heard her thought, he turned and locked eyes with her. *"Fathrin."*

The name came across the silcomm with perfect clarity as the two ex-IIS agents stared at each other. Leilani blinked several times as the name settled into the back of her mind.

"Are you kidding?"

She didn't need to ask. She already knew the answer. Silcomm's weren't telepathy in truth, but enough emotion bled through with the name that she already knew he wasn't joking. Duke Brently Winston Fathrin was not only a senator in the House of Lords, but the chair of the Senate Oversight Committee in charge of all Imperial Investigative Service activities. He not only knew Admiral Jason Dorthy and Agent Leilani Falconi, but he had been their puppet master for over a century.

"Senator Fathrin knew Fendrick resurfaced. It was in my debrief to the oversight committee." His thought bled a mixture of fear and rapidly growing fury.

She recalled Duke Shovalli's description of a man in a cloak whispering to Gremm as she murdered her father and brother.

Leilani's gaze fell to the floor as she pondered the implications of the entire coup attempt being a smoke screen.

Feet appeared in her view, breaking up her thoughts. She allowed her gaze to travel up the legs and lock eyes with her partner. He nodded at her and proceeded to return to his seat. Behind him, Fendrick settled into the seat he'd vacated a few minutes prior.

"I suppose we need to lay this all out on the table if we want to move forward." He folded his hands in his lap and refused to look at the woman to his right as he recanted his story. "An entity named Madel hired me to steal a dragon hatchling about twelve hundred years ago. I was to steal her right after hatching but before she could imprint on her parents."

He watched Leilani carefully as he said the name, but when she didn't seem to recognize it, his shoulders sagged.

"Madel is a member of the Redalious family line. A royal line of whathalis, an enormous leviathan species that feeds off eldrich." He pursed his lips before finally adding the last piece of information Leilani needed to put everything together. "Many lesser races often refer to the species as space whales."

The muscles in Leilani's jaw clenched as Fendrick stopped speaking. The hands in her lap balled into fists, and she felt a slight breeze kick up in the library. In her HuD, a red light flashed brightly in warning.

"*Leilani, this is not the time or the place to lose your temper,*" a stern, female voice spoke up in her mind.

Leilani's gaze snapped to the president, and the two women locked eyes. "*Get out of my head!*"

"*I will when you calm down. Trust me, I know exactly how it feels to be played by those you thought you could trust, but tearing my library apart is not the answer.*"

The breeze picked up speed, and the fire raged in the fireplace to her left.

"*Oh, I see what the problem is.*" The thought came across as a mixture of surprise and confusion.

Suddenly, Leilani's HuD went offline. The overwhelming rage faded instantly to a sensation of anger and betrayal. Leilani shook her head, as if to clear it. "*What just happened?*"

"*You are reasonably angry, but your oracle was feeding your anger to dangerous levels. When all this is over, perhaps you and I should talk. I can help you put a safety on that thing.*"

"*Sarah did that?*" The breeze died out as Leilani's anger shifted to confusion.

"*It is disproportionately powerful for an internal system. But no, the wind was you. The oracle was simply feeding your emotions, something an internal system should not be able to do.*" The elar's face softened, and she smiled warmly.

"Is everything alright?" Dorthy asked out loud.

Leilani blinked several times as her mind tried to wrap around what had just happened. She reached up and rubbed her eyes.

"Yes. I'm fine. I think." When she looked up again, she focused on the matter at hand. "Are you saying that Krelor and Fathrin are related to each other?"

Fendrick allowed a knowing smile to creep across his face. He nodded as he clarified, "Not somehow, but *directly* related. They are brothers. Let me explain in a way you're familiar with. They are leviathans, so one entity equals that of a planet full of people, but their government structure is similar to a monarchy. Currently, the Queen, or to use the whathalin word for it, Thadalis, is the oldest of three children who inherited the crown when their father died. Madel is the second, and Krelor the third."

Fendrick looked around the room at the three individuals listening intently.

"When I realized Madel wanted the hatchling to make a soldier race of dragons that were 100 percent bound to him, I knew I had to do something. The implications are far more widespread than you might think. Their mere existence would trigger various treaties—it would throw the entire universe into war. A similar war caused the cataclysm that tore aether from kuldain. I had no desire to cause a second war of leviathans."

Leilani bobbed her head. She could understand not wanting to cause that kind of destruction.

"I went to Krelor with my proof, and he agreed to help me hide the child." Fendrick rubbed his hands together as he shrugged. "Not that I really gave him much of a choice. Blackmail is an effective motivator, even with a leviathan."

28

NASHA NA'DA

"Okay. I can honestly say I'm out of my depth here. I've caught and arrested some pretty big things, but never anything large enough to swallow a sun." Leilani followed the president down the hall of the enormous mansion, with both delonians trailing behind her.

"That is a slight exaggeration," Dorthy retorted.

"You didn't see Krelor from the outside."

A hand grabbed her arm, pulling her to a stop and forcing her to turn and look at the two men behind her.

"You saw him from the outside?" The look of wide-eyed shock on Dorthy's face was unusual, and she resisted the urge to chuckle at him.

Glancing off to the side, she tried to remember what she'd told him about how she'd ended up in Severious.

"If you two would leave Ms. Falconi alone, we are here. I would prefer to continue this conversation inside where it's secure."

All eyes turned to the beautiful, blond elar a few yards away from them.

"This is a secure strategy room." She lifted a hand and pointed to a set of double doors as she spoke, then pointed to the floor at her feet.

"While this is a completely insecure hallway. All three of you seem to be tactically minded. Where would you prefer to continue discussing this topic?"

As if on cue, the three of them looked at each other.

Dorthy released Leilani's arm, and the three of them marched, in unison, through the double doors.

Once inside, they could see why the president of Severious System wanted to continue inside. The room was the size of a small grav-ball stadium. Both alternate reality and physical displays lined the walls all the way around the room. Below them were hundreds of desks, control panels, and holo-tables. While in the middle of the room was an enormous holo-table with a live, interactive display of the solar system. The holo was over fifty feet high and currently had two people standing at it. The larger of the two reached into the image and spun it so they could see a different point, then threw her hands in the air in exasperation as the smaller of them shook his head.

The female, a greduna, stood ten feet tall with black hair so long that her braid reached her lower back. The smaller male next to her was far too skinny for his frame and had shoulder-length grey hair.

Leilani smiled. She was happy her brother was alive, but for the first time, she could really see his age starting to take its toll. Humans could live to be around 250 with excellent medicine, but when they passed a hundred, the age became visible.

The greduna's fists balled at her side then relaxed.

"I'm telling you, that will alert him!" BB snapped loudly.

Despite the hundreds of hastily abandoned workstations, the only other people in the room were at the far end. There were two groups: a larger group in all black on the far wall and a smaller group in black and red uniforms off to the right.

Strolling back and forth behind the individuals in all black was a short male figure with his hands clasped behind his back. He turned to nod at Leilani before continuing on his path.

"Good to see you're alive." Dorthy strolled past Leilani and placed his hand on the small hacker's shoulder.

BB didn't take his eyes off the greduna. "Why wouldn't I be alive?"

"Well, the station we were on did blow up."

Leilani hesitated near the door and continued to take in the scene. Mentally, she booted Sarah and waited for the oracle to come online. As she skimmed the displays, she noticed the telltales of a hasty exit all around the room. All nonessential personnel were likely told to clear out just for this meeting.

"*Well, that was rude.*" Sarah's tone was far humbler than Leilani expected.

"*Did you feed your emotions into me on purpose?*"

Sarah's lack of response was enough for Leilani.

"*If it happens again, I will turn you off permanently. Do you understand me?*"

When Dana shut the oracle off in the middle of the overwhelming wash of rage, Leilani considered her past. This wasn't an isolated incident. She'd been fighting for control of her own emotions most of her life. Leilani wasn't even sure where Sarah ended and she began.

"*Yes, ma'am.*"

She felt Sarah's internal struggle with regret, sorrow, and anger, but she shoved it aside and strode forward to join the rest of the group.

"So, when I realized that the original design for the portal generator came from Severious, I came here. I arrived at the tram station just as the net went up. Been stuck here ever since." Meeshani Eagleton turned to bob her head in Leilani's direction as she approached.

"You must have been upset when Wendel wasn't here," Leilani chimed into the conversation.

The greduna smirked and rocked her head to the side. "Not as much as when I realized the solar system was somehow pulled off the eldrilin network." She pursed her lips and looked off to the side, clearly recalling something. "I recovered from the grand veeshali about a hundred years later, but most of the people here never recovered at all, even the older ones. Too many still don't remember what this system was to the galaxy, or that there were ever stars."

The president grimaced and look away from the group. "Part of that is my fault. In my childish anger, I did things to strengthen the veeshali, which I still regret to this day."

Meeshani and Dana locked eyes and had a silent argument that looked to be old and well-worn.

"Let's focus on the problem at hand." Dorthy pointed to the holo-table in front of them.

Leilani stepped up behind her big brother and placed her hand on his shoulder.

His gaunt face turned to smile warmly at her. He wasn't eating again. The curse of the hacker—they stuffed their faces like crazy when they weren't in the net and forgot to eat at all when they were. The number one cause of death in hackers or virtual junkies was complications from malnutrition.

"You need to eat," she whispered.

Ignoring her, he reached both hands into the holo and pulled them apart, twisting the image slightly as he did so.

A Kassian push fleet swelled into view. It had eight dreadnoughts, each with their own support fleet. In the center of them was the IKS Maxanious, a super dreadnought—a veritable planetoid. The Maxanious alone could launch four wings of one hundred thousand fighter drones. It was a war vessel which only left Core System in dire circumstances.

"These arrived in Bendaru three hours ago," BB stated flatly. "Before we passed through the gate from Bendaru to Severious, I was privy to a single message from a colleague, which informed me that Senator Brently Winston Fathrin boarded the IKS Maxanious with orders from the Senate Intelligence Committee to get underway."

The group stared at the ships in silence for several long seconds.

"They're just following orders," Leilani whispered.

BB bobbed his head in agreement. "Perhaps, but no matter how we look at this, if this comes to a fight, a lot of innocent people will die."

"Is it possible that Madel has intelligence inside the barrier?" Dana asked.

Fendrick shook his head. "Not likely. Krelor sealed this place up tight. It took me over a year to find it, and I knew where it was and what I was looking for."

"If he knew where to send the fleet, then it's safe to say he followed one of you here." Leilani waved her hand back and forth between the two delonians.

Before an argument could break out, Meeshani chimed into the conversation. "We could really use Rothar right now."

"Rothar Horrison?" Leilani turned her attention to the greduna.

She nodded.

"Why Roth?" Dorthy asked.

"Technically, I can't say, but if what BB has told me is true, I suppose Seef'aini government secrets are a moot point." Meeshani smirked. "Rothar is the commander of the Nasha Na'da for this arm of the galaxy."

The two delonians and the *draconis imperious* took a step back, away from the greduna.

The large woman laughed. The sound drew the attention of the small, boyish figure at the other end of the room. He locked eyes with Leilani and winked.

She bowed her head to him respectfully.

"What's the Nasha Na'da?" BB hopped up onto the edge of the table and leaned forward, placing his elbows on his knees as he watched them intently.

"It's a boogeyman order of . . . well . . ." Lei looked for a word that encompassed all the order did, but she really couldn't find one. "Let's just say problem solvers. Honestly, until right now, I assumed they were horror stories told to kids. I'll be right back."

As Leilani strolled past the group toward the far end of the room, she could feel the eyes on her back.

"*Is this a good idea?*" Sarah asked softly.

Leilani's reply was a little cooler than she intended. "*You have a better one?*"

The oracle remained silent.

"How may I help you today, Ms. Falconi?" Derek chuckled.

"I need to contact General Rothar Horrison."

He bowed his head slowly and turned to touch the shoulder of the elari woman seated in front of him. A display in front of them flashed to life, and the woman looked up from the desk in front of her.

"Ah. Hello, Leilani. How can I help you today?" The tall, blond elar, with piercing lavender eyes, flashed a warm smile.

Leilani's reply was higher-pitched than it likely should have been. "Admiral Jedari'dei?"

"Alorra, please. I was told you wanted to talk to me?" The elar bobbed her forehead in Derek's direction.

"I was hoping to talk to General Horrison, actually." Lei's mind raced as an idea began to form. If she could get Alorra to help as well, she might have a plan. "But on second thought, I'd like to talk to you both."

The elari woman grinned, her lavender eyes flashing brightly with humor. "I think I can arrange that, but it will be a few minutes."

"I was wondering, are you and your fleet busy?"

The woman on the screen leaned back in her chair and folded her arms, the grin still firmly in place. "We've had a few problems here and there, but not really, no. What can myself and my people do for our rescuer?"

"I am in Severious System, and we have a Kassian push fleet at our door. We don't know what they have been told, but we do know that a wanted criminal is currently the one giving orders."

"Ah. You found Madel."

"How did you know about Madel?"

"When we confronted Krelor, he ran. We have since collected him and convinced him to tell us what's going on."

Leilani arched both eyebrows high on her forehead.

Alorra lifted a hand and waved it to the side casually. "The problem with mere mortals getting caught up in a leviathan family feud is that they don't consider us important enough to calculate in their schemes. Unless we prove to them otherwise."

A large arm appeared in the image as Rothar crouched next to the elar.

Leilani smiled fondly.

"Hey there, Lei." The crodoc grinned.

"One of the many joys in our line of work is compartmentalization." Leilani waved to him. "I have come across information that you might be a part of the Nasha Na'da."

Alorra's and Rothar's faces fell blank.

"And I find myself in need of arresting a whathalis for crimes against the Draconis Imperious Grand Council."

The admiral and general widened their eyes in surprise. Clearly, Krelor hadn't told them everything.

Rothar turned to look up at the elar next to him. "Admiral?"

Alorra pursed her lips before nodding. "Very well, Leilani Falconi. As the admiral of the Thader Nafil fleet, I will send my second-in-command as a tactical adviser for your leviathan problem. Once you have a plan and know exactly what you need from us, we will be happy to oblige." The admiral turned her gaze to the meleini next to Leilani. "Master Derek, do you mind?"

"Of course not, Alorra. Pull or push?"

Leilani frowned, cocking her head. "Pull or push what?"

"Pull, if you don't mind. I'm in the middle of a firefight at the moment."

Derek nodded, and the crodoc general crouched next to the admiral faded from view.

Lei's frown deepened. "A firefight? Is everything okay, Admiral?"

"Everything is great, Ms. Falconi, thanks to you. After our first meeting, I stopped trusting our benefactor and delved into what was really happening in aether space. I have since expanded our fleet and am exploring options."

Leilani chuckled. "Thader Nafil. I get it now. Standing Alone. You turned mercenary."

"Something like that, yes." The screen shook slightly, and the elar looked up over the camera. "President Mai and I do not see eye-to-eye on her current mission to reclaim aether space by force. So, when I ignored an order from her, my captains opted to side with me. We have been on our own ever since." The admiral reached to the side and grabbed something. With the flick of her wrist, she tossed a holo image of General Anthony Marshall onto the screen. "Then I got a call for assistance from someone that apparently knows you rather well."

Leilani's face softened as she studied the slowly rotating image of the general. "Anthony needed help?"

Alorra nodded emphatically. "Very much so, and I can honestly say that I am glad we stepped in when we did. The attacks have grown worse and are now happening in Kassian space as well—for which the Kassian government is sorely unprepared. We have our hands full keeping the attacks contained, but don't worry, when you need us, we will be there." The admiral looked up over the camera again and nodded to someone.

"What attacks?" Leilani tried to regain the admiral's attention.

"I need to go, Leilani. It was nice talking to you again, and I look forward to working together. Don't worry, Roth can answer all of your questions." She pointed a long, thin finger behind Leilani, then cut the communication.

Leilani looked over her shoulder and saw Rothar Horrison shaking hands with Dorthy.

Derek tapped her thigh. "Don't worry about the outside right now, Leilani. The crashilor scouts have increased their range and frequency, but the genuine attacks have yet to begin. You have time. Focus on the task at hand."

Leilani furrowed her brow as her mind raced.

The boy laughed a soft, high-pitched sound. "That is not forgetting about it, trust me. The damage is minimal. The aether contains the attacks quickly, and Kass has Alorra. The crashilor are simply testing their limits."

Leilani's memory flashed back to the massive black-maned, anthropomorphic lion with wings that had almost killed her two years earlier. The idea that those creatures were becoming more common was highly troubling, but Derek was right. There was nothing she could do about it right now. One problem at a time.

29

THE PLAN

Leilani massaged the bridge of her nose between her thumb and index finger. The chair she sat in tilted back as she lifted her feet to rest them on the conference table in front of her.

The elevated voices had climbed in volume in the last hour, and now they were practically screaming at one another to be heard. The team of so-called experts now included Wendel and Jorna Bunderwick, who it turned out was a rather prolific inventor in his own right.

"That will not hold a whathalis!" Rothar slammed his hands down on the table.

The crodoc's sheer lack of composure surprised Leilani. It was unlike him, but ever since the Kassian government deported him back to aether space, he'd been on his own—hunted by his own people for treason against the Aether governments. It was an interesting thank-you for saving so many lives.

Of course, the actual cause for the chaos and death that ensued after the mining incident on Grelashi was Hodair. Fendrick's attempt to create an abyssal point, almost a thousand years earlier, merged two entire solar systems into the Grelashi asteroid field. But instead of killing everyone, like it should have, the goddess of time, Hodair, stepped in. She froze both solar systems in time, essentially freezing billions of people who were at war in mid-fight.

When the criminals in charge of the Grelashi mine triggered the self-destruct, Hodair reacted. She moved the billions of victims from her stasis to various aether worlds. They awoke and continued fighting with renewed vigor. Only now, everything had changed.

The city-states couldn't handle the influx of refugees. Their economies collapsed as they instantly became overwhelmed. The need for food, housing, and medical supplies skyrocketed, causing riots and hoarding as the people fought to survive the overcrowded conditions. The humans found themselves in an alien environment. They no longer had their government for backup. Despite them being less than 50 percent of the refugee make-up, they found themselves the target of a wave of hatred that was unfathomable. Leilani couldn't help but feel it might have been kinder to kill them all.

"We aren't trying to hold him in his natural state!" Meeshani was rapidly losing patience with Rothar, her ex-commander.

"It's just the power ratio, not mass!" BB spat.

Fists slammed into the enormous conference table. The vibration rippled across the surface, causing Lei's feet to bounce slightly. When Meeshani hit the table for the first time, Leilani had expected it to crumple under the assault. Now, it was commonplace, and the ex-agent simply allowed her chin to drop to her chest as her hand shifted to massage the back of her neck.

Strong hands slid onto her shoulders as strong fingertips dug deep into her tense flesh.

Allowing her muscles to relax, she rocked her head back and forth as the hands worked her tight muscles. "Is this what we sounded like?"

The hands on her shoulders paused. "Yep."

"I'm so sorry," she grumbled.

Dorthy chuckled before finally rolling the chair out from under the table next to her and sitting. "Don't be. In my experience, this level of dysfunction often works."

Rothar cocked his head in their direction and narrowed his eyelids to slits as he flared his nostrils.

Leilani snorted, holding back a laugh while Dorthy held his hands up toward the crodoc.

"Easy, big guy. It wasn't an insult." Dorthy didn't need to raise his voice to be heard over the yelling. A crodoc's sense of smell and hearing were far superior to a human's. Rothar was also ex-special forces, which meant his senses were further enhanced with mageware, the aether version of cyberware.

"What about something like this?" Wendel's hologram broke into the argument, tossing something toward the table. He waited as the table uploaded the image.

A new engineering blueprint flashed to life over the table, and six heads all leaned in to examine the design.

"You think they would notice if we left?" Leilani asked the delonian next to her.

He twisted his chair so she could clearly see the coy grin on his face. "No, but they might notice when we come back."

She laughed and waved her hands back and forth in front of her face. "No. I was actually thinking of food and coffee. I'm exhausted. They've been at this for hours, and it doesn't look like it'll stop anytime soon."

"I like that idea even better!" Dorthy slid his chair back quietly and stood.

They slipped from the room and out into the hallway. The guard outside turned her attention to them.

Lei flashed the woman a tired smiled. "Kitchen?"

The guard smirked and lifted her arm to point down the hallway. "Third door on the left. I saw chef head in there a few minutes ago. You might be able to catch him."

“Finally, a spot of good luck.” Dorthy marched down the hall toward the door.

Leilani nodded a thanks to the woman and followed her partner.

Inside the room was a large kitchen and dining area with several tables and a long bar with stools. An amazing smell wafted across the room, and Leilani’s stomach growled so loud that she wrapped her arm around it.

Behind the bar, they could see the top of a small, blond head. Three plates slid onto the countertop one after another.

Leilani grinned happily as she strolled toward the stool closest to her. “Hey, Derek!”

Glasses clinked behind the counter.

“Beer okay?”

“Oh, by the gods, yes!” Lei slid onto the stool in the middle and looked down at the plate of seared fish, fresh vegetables, and some kind of red sauce drizzled over the top of it all.

Derek came into view as he climbed a stool in front of the beer taps. When he filled a glass, he slid them down the bar toward her.

Leilani caught each glass and set them near a plate. Dorthy slid onto the stool to her right.

“No better chef than a meleini,” he mused.

“I don’t get to cook as much as I like in this job.” The young-looking male climbed up onto the stool to her left.

Lei stuffed a fork full of veggies into her mouth and moaned happily. “I can see that.”

“How’s it going in Bendaru?” Dorthy tasted the food and closed his eyes as he savored the flavor.

Derek waved his fork in the air. “Well enough. They’re nervous about approaching the gate. They have three ships slinking toward it as we speak. At this rate, I estimate a week before they can build a device to interface with it and start trying to crack the security code, assuming they don’t just try to blow it. Either way, I can keep them out indefinitely, so I’m not worried about the Kassians.”

"Meaning, the only thing we need to be worried about is Madel blowing his cover, which doesn't fit his profile." The delonian bobbed his head and stuffed another fork full of food into his mouth, his face melting into a content smile.

"Exactly."

"Then we need to build the plan for when he does make it in." Lei bounced her fork in the air. "We heard rumors that you've been invaded before. Do you have protocols for it?"

"We do."

"How did attackers get in?" Dorthy leaned forward, looking past his partner to the meleini.

Derek finished chewing before answering. "The past attackers were aether pirates or mercenaries with aether ships. They blow one or two of the nodes in the eldri-net. It's self-healing, but it takes time."

"Kassians don't have aether ships," Lei mused as her mind hatched an idea. "Does your protocol include security bunkers and an emergency broadcast system?"

"Yes."

"I think I have a plan."

She now had the undivided attention of both males as they turned to watch her curiously.

"And I even know where to find the perfect bait."

Derek looked past her to smile at the delonian. "Oh, she's good."

Dorthy smiled around another bite of food. "You have no idea."

"Dorthy. I can honestly say I didn't expect to see you here." Admiral Alorra Jedari'dei threw her arms around him.

As the tall, blond elar embraced Dorthy, Leilani arched a single eyebrow then rolled her eyes, veering around the two of them and striding into the smaller meeting room. She turned a chair and sat just in time to see the woman kiss her partner on the mouth, rather passionately. Behind them, a tall, broad-shouldered Rothar glared at the two of them.

Leilani laughed loud enough to distract the two ex-lovers. The sound also caught the crodoc's attention, and she shook her head. "Don't let her manipulate you like that."

The general's ears flicked, and he tightened his jaw. Storming past them into the room, he picked a chair across the table from her and sat. Rothar Horrison was not a young crodoc by any stretch of the imagination, but the last two years had taken a harder toll on him than she'd expected. The anger in his eyes created a serious set of frown lines on his forehead, and lack of sleep showed in his sunken eye sockets, making his already heavy brow even more pronounced. He'd lost weight, even if his huge muscles were more pronounced.

She sighed. "Jeez, Rothar, you look like crap."

Tilting his head toward her, he relaxed his expression. He shifted his shoulders in a half-hearted shrug. If she hadn't been looking right at him, she likely would have missed it.

"It's bad in aether space right now. The fighting is out of control. There are riots and protests no matter where you look. People are living on the streets in massive tent cities." His eyes closed, and he rubbed his face.

"Mai has lost it." Alorra chimed in as she took the seat next to Rothar. "She's created massive concentration camps for humans, just like during the war. Only this time, there are so many that she's having trouble controlling them. So instead of returning them to Kass, she's resorted to mass killings. It started with anyone associated with the military, under the guise of 'national security,' but now it's anyone who doesn't toe the party line. She claims that anyone who speaks out against the Seef'aini government is committing treason, even if they're from a city-state."

Rothar's hands fell to the table with a soft thud. "But at least the Kassians in the concentration camps get food and medical treatment, unlike aether citizens, who she leaves to starve to death in their own filth."

Dorthy pulled out the chair next to Leilani and sat quietly while the two talked.

"You say that like it's a consolation prize or something," Alorra grumbled.

Rothar shrugged and scratched the back of his head.

Dorthy leaned forward and rested his folded hands on the table. "Are city-states and the military still splintered into dozens of factions, all trying to claim control?"

Both the elar and the crodoc bobbed their heads.

"Try hundreds." Alorra reached out to pat Roth's shoulder. "Roth and I have been extracting any military personnel willing to join with the Thader Nafil, but sometimes it's tricky to get people out. We take anyone, Kass or Seef'aini. We don't care. They just have to believe in law and order over chaos. It's pretty amazing. You give soldiers something else to focus on, and suddenly the cultural differences no longer matter. They work side-by-side just fine."

Leilani flashed a smile to her ex-partner. "You said the Thader Nafil is in Kass too?"

Alorra nodded. "Yes. The Kassians don't care that we're a mixed-race crew. Originally, the government warned us to be careful, that the citizenry may not tolerate the aether's presence, but the most my crews get from the locals is curiosity. The Thader Nafil fleets in both aether and kuldain space are turning into heroes that the people adore and the media vilifies."

"Careful with that," Leilani sneered. "One fuck up, and that adoration turns nasty fast. The next thing you know, they're trying to burn you at the stake. Even if it wasn't actually *your* fuck up."

Dorthy leaned back in his chair and shook his head.

Alorra, however, laughed. "Welcome to the facts of life in any culture. Love hard and hate harder. Such is reality."

"You said you have a plan?" Rothar drew the conversation back to matters at hand.

"I do. It'll require a show of force in Bendaru system and a strong, but small, team of Nasha Na'da." Lei leaned back in the chair and crossed her legs at the knee.

Alorra's face twisted into a wrinkled grimace. "Can we please just say specialists? I keep feeling the need to kill you every time you say that out loud. And I already know I won't win that fight."

Leilani snorted, and for the first time since he arrived, Rothar grinned a toothy smile.

"My apologies. A team of specialists." A corner of her mouth upturned into a coy smile. "Better?"

"Thank you."

"Do you know who's in command of the IKS Thedonious right now?" Dorthy asked.

Alorra pulled a pad from the bag at her hip and searched through it. It took a good minute before she finally slid the pad across the table to the delonian. "Apparently, Admiral Toshio Ashton."

Dorthy allowed a smile to cross his face as he nodded to Leilani.

"Perfect." Her grin grew. "Dorthy will prepare a private message for you to take with you to Bendaru system. If all goes well, you'll just be there as a show of force, and it'll be nice and boring. Roth, you pick your team, and remain here."

"Done." He nodded curtly.

Alorra furrowed her brow as she looked from Leilani to the two males. "Am I missing something? I thought we were here to discuss the plan."

Rothar winked at Lei and turned to face the elar next to him. "When dealing with a leviathan, compartmentalization is key. The fewer people who know the full plan, the better. Consider yourself briefed."

The admiral leaned back in her chair and pursed her lips. "Well played, Ms. Falconi."

"I know." Leilani stood and marched from the room without looking back.

30

A DEMON TO FIGHT A DEMON?

"Okay." Wendel tossed Leilani an innocuous-looking set of metal rings.

To anyone who didn't know what sealbands looked like in their natural state, they were simply large paperweights. As they landed in her hand, her shoulder jerked forward, and she took a step, trying to regain her balance.

"Holy shit! These are heavy."

"We got them as light as possible, but the alloy needs to be very dense if we're going to block his ability to cast." He placed his fists on his hips. "He's not your typical aether prisoner."

"Yeah, yeah."

Her hand bobbed up and down as she calculated the weight. When she rolled them across her palm to examine them, she found, etched on the outside of the ring, the familiar Kassian logo for the IIS.

She chuckled. "Nice touch."

The delonian shrugged. "BB's idea. He thought if they looked like normal IIS sealbands, the senator may underestimate them."

"Senator Fathrin is nothing if not arrogant and overly self-assured." Leilani slid the cuffs into the empty sealband pouch on her belt.

Wendel's grin widened as he pointed to them. "On a fascinating side note, I've already had six orders to make more of those. And if they work on the whathalis, I'm sure there'll be plenty more orders."

She winked at the delonian. "Way to capitalize on this."

He laughed and tossed his hands in the air cheerfully.

It took Jorna and Wendel three days to build the prototype, which gave Leilani plenty of time to work on other parts of the plan. But the stress was intensifying for everyone.

"I really wish we could test them." Leilani walked over to the table nearby and picked up her coffee.

From behind her, Wendel replied, "If it helps ease your mind any, we tested it on a leviathan. Just not a whathalis."

She sipped her coffee.

The delonian was grinning like a boy with a brand-new toy. He rubbed his hands together. "It worked like a charm. When we refused to take them off, he lost it. You should have heard him screaming. It was hilarious!"

"Wait, we have a leviathan here?"

Wendel stared at her, his brow furrowed deeply. "Yes."

"Who?"

He shook his head in disbelief. "The meleini, of course."

Both eyebrows shot high on her forehead. "He said that was his natural state."

"It is." Wendel rubbed his hands together as he shifted his weight.

The door opened to the kitchen area, and a tall, dark-skinned crodoc strolled in. As he strode past her to the coffeepot, Rothar patted her on the shoulder. "Don't let his tiny size fool you, Lei. That's what he wants. Meleini are the worst kind of leviathan because they hide better than any of the others."

Leilani shrugged her shoulders then took a sip of her warm coffee. "I suppose that makes sense. Even when he's trying to hide it, that little guy exudes a lot of power."

"Hence, leviathan." Rothar chuckled and poured the dark liquid into his own cup before turning back to lean against the counter.

"Okay. We have the working sealbands. What's next?"

Wendel shifted his weight again. "I need at least two more days to finish the next part. It's turning out to be more complicated than we expected."

"I thought we picked a simple design on purpose?" She scowled and turned to hold her mug out to the crodoc.

He filled it without a word.

"The design is fine, but these people destroyed everything even remotely related to ships. It's proving to be much harder than we expected to put something together without a shipyard." Wendel shook his head and pursed his lips, clearly annoyed. "The *draconis* are helpful, but I went through five of Bunderwick's teams before I found one that wasn't secretly doing damage when no one was looking. They seriously hate ships. I would almost say it's an irrational hatred."

Leilani laughed, and Roth hid his grin behind his cup.

"I ended up with Jorna's old partner. He's riderless, but smart enough to follow directions. And I'd like to point out, he's twice as cantankerous as the damn dwarf."

Leilani made a hissing sound as she inhaled through clenched teeth. "Yikes."

"No shit," Wendel agreed.

"Do we have an estimated time to completion?" Rothar asked.

Wendel shrugged. "Two days?"

Rothar winked at Leilani. "Perfect. Our team will be ready about then. Thank you, Wendel. You know your part when this starts, right?"

The delonian nodded, but his grimace told her he wasn't pleased. "Not sure I had a choice in the matter, but Fen and I will secure the package. He's been bitching at me for three days about not failing again."

"Yeah, well, we all have baggage," Lei grimaced.

Wendel narrowed his eyes and waved his hand negatively. "No, you and I have baggage. The captain has a cargo transport."

Roth and Lei laughed as Wendel spun and marched out.

When the door closed, she turned her attention to the crodoc next to her. "And the bait?"

"They were a little harder to procure. They'll arrive tomorrow. Then we'll have one day to work with them before all this begins. But apparently, their instructors wanted to ensure that the two of them could defend themselves mentally, just in case. I hope you're right about these kids." Roth shook his head slowly. "I'm not comfortable dragging children into this mess. Adults can't defend themselves against a leviathan. I still say we use the meleini as bait."

The door opened, and a young, human-looking boy walked in. "I believe my ears are bleeding."

Roth scowled. He'd been avoiding the meleini, but apparently Derek didn't care.

Leilani, however, laughed and bobbed her head. "I bet they were."

Derek strolled up to her, and the two slapped their hands together in greeting.

"Coffee?" Lei made a shooing gesture with her hands, and the crodoc happily moved away from the counter.

When she turned with the pot, she found Derek holding a large cup toward her. "Yes, please."

"You sure your parents know you're having caffeine?" she teased.

He grinned, showing a missing tooth on the side of his mouth. "I am certain," he paused dramatically, "they do not."

They both laughed.

"How about your end, Derek? How are things going?"

The small creature climbed up to sit next to her on the counter. He took a sip of his coffee and dipped his head once. "We had a few snags, but we dealt with them. Everyone will be where they need to be when the time comes."

She smirked behind her own cup as she took a drink. "From the sound of it, you have some dissenters?"

The warm brown eyes of the cute, little boy shifted to solid black, and a twinge of danger crawled up her spine.

"Nothing I can't handle." The voice came out low, with a strange echoing sound that made her shiver.

Across the small break room, a chair crashed to the floor, but by the time she looked up, Rothar was gone, and the break room door was closing with a soft hiss.

Lei arched a single eyebrow and returned her attention to the small humanoid next to her. His eyes returned to normal, and a thin smile crept across his face.

"Hold a grudge much?"

He snickered, then shrugged his small shoulders. "Perhaps."

"I thought he was a part of the Nasha Na'da?" she mused into her cup.

The boy winked at her and pointed to the door. "That wasn't fear."

Just as she looked up, the door blew inward with a loud pop. As the metal sheered from the wall and blew toward them, the young-looking creature next to her lifted a small hand. The doors bounced off an invisible barrier and crashed into the nearby tables.

A team of a dozen, heavily armored soldiers poured into the room. Each of them carried a different type of weapon, but they were all charged to fully lethal levels and ready to fire.

"Ah." Lei tilted her head back and took a deep breath before taking another sip of coffee.

The sensation of danger was crawling across her body painfully as every nerve cried out. However, reacting to the obvious danger was only going to get her shot.

A large crodoc, in the same armor, marched through the group into the room. He, however, was not wearing a helmet.

"General Horrison, I think this might be a tad bit of an over-reaction," Lei said calmly.

The crodoc shook his head. "No, Leilani. You don't seem to understand that you can't pal around with that thing."

The boy hopped off the counter and handed her his empty cup. "She's knows exactly what I am. It's you who doesn't know what he's dealing with."

Leilani took the cup just as the boy disappeared. He didn't vanish or teleport—he simply ceased to be there. Even the sensation of power that was in the air when he was around was gone.

Narrowing her eyes, she turned her attention to the crodoc. "I wasn't done debriefing him."

He met her glare with one of his own and growled. "You're playing with fire, and you're going to get us all killed."

Sighing, she set her cup on the counter next to Derek's and strode forward to stand less than a foot from the angry general. "I know that when you're dealing with a demon, you need a demon."

They glared at each other for several seconds.

Suddenly, she lifted an arm and waved her hand back and forth in front of his face. "Well, not literally, but you know what I mean!"

She grinned at the look of confusion on his face as she marched through the Nasha Na'da.

"Oh, and Rothar, we're guests here. You need to fix this door."

31

UNDERCOVER GAMES

"I've reinforced the bindings here and here, and the infrastructure of the ribs here." Wendel tapped a section of bulkhead in several places as he strode ahead of her through the shuttle.

Leilani reached up with both hands and rubbed her face. "Wendel."

"And if you have . . ." The delonian paused mid-sentence.

When he locked eyes with her, she smiled warmly. "Will it work?"

"Nothing in life is a guarantee." He shrugged as he brought his hands up to display empty palms. "But in theory, yes."

She turned slowly as she examined the inside of the hastily built shuttle. It was likely a cargo shuttle before being shredded and dumped into a debris field. That left plenty of room for a twelve-person team of heavily armored specialists, a young dracolli, and two ex-agents to maneuver.

Wendel had welded several seats to the deck to make it appear as if it were a transport shuttle. There was even a cockpit, but the pilot couldn't actually fly the vessel. There wasn't a working engine to be found anywhere in the system. So they opted to put Sergeant Mauro, the young Officers Training Cadet, or OTC, kid from the station and the dracolli's bonded partner, in the cockpit to keep him out of the actual altercation.

"Well, I suppose it looks good enough." She returned her attention to Wendel and found him staring intently. "What?"

"Are you sure you're Leilani?"

Looking down at her body, Leilani smirked. The shape-shift disguise made her an exact duplicate of the president—a trick of the trade that would fool almost anyone who wasn't a master enchanter or aether engineer. She was taller than usual and wearing a rather comfortable silk pantsuit. When she'd put it on, she'd remarked how easy it would be to fight in the outfit. Dana chuckled and told her that was the point.

"Kind of creepy, right?" she met Wendel's gaze and watched as he bobbed his head up and down emphatically.

A stocky female in lavender armor stomped onboard the vessel, each footstep echoing throughout the shuttle. "These rickety metal things are absurd."

"No, they aren't. The engineers just didn't account for the weight of a bonded Ngwenyan miner," Leilani retorted with a broad grin.

The dwarf rolled her eyes.

"You ready, Uncle Wendel? Pa says the crazy one is getting trigger-happy." She shook her head and grimaced, scrunching her nose as she did so. "He's been muttering under his breath. It's making us all nervous."

Wendel took a deep breath and let it out slowly. "Yeah, I can see that. He'll be alright so long as no one threatens the president."

At the mention of the elari president, Lavender pointed an armored finger at Leilani. "We sure we have the right one? Because I can't tell them apart."

"I think so." Wendel frowned. "That you, Lei?"

Leilani tried to think of something that would ease their concern. As a thought occurred to her, a coy smirk crept into the corners of her mouth. "I can always tell Lavender how I found you."

The delonian swallowed and shook his head. "No, that's okay. It's Leilani. Come on, Lavey."

"Wait. I want to hear this! How did you find him?"

Wendel pushed on the dwarf, but her heavy, power-assisted armor didn't budge. "Aw, come on! It has to be good if you're avoiding it this hard!"

Leilani chuckled and strolled past the dwarf, out into the courtyard of the presidential estate. "Don't worry, Lavender. If I survive this, I'll tell you all about it over a bottle of cognac."

Wendel's shoulders sagged before he took a deep breath and stormed off into the building.

The dwarf laughed and winked at her. "Good luck."

"You too." Leilani glanced across the courtyard, where a bunch of heavily armored individuals were trying to teach a young male crodoc how to move more effectively with the weapon in his hand. "And Lavender?"

The dwarf looked up at her.

"You and Deloris stay alive. Don't get too cocky. Those ships may seem weak to you, but if they get a hit in, it'll hurt a lot more than that explosion."

The dwarf laughed and smacked her arm into Leilani's, causing the taller but more lightly built elar to take an involuntary step to the side.

"Trust me, we can handle a few tin cans. We'll be fine." She stomped off.

Leilani watched her go and sighed. It didn't matter what she did or said—they were going to see them all as pirates.

"*They're going to learn the hard way that there's a dramatic difference between military and pirates.*"

"*Sadly, yes.*" Rocking her head to the side, she grimaced. "*We all learn certain lessons the hard way. Hopefully, they won't lose too many in the process.*" Leilani glanced at the chronometer in her HuD. "*Where to next?*"

"*The digital command center. You wanted to meet with BB,*" Sarah replied.

"*Roger that.*"

A faint shimmer slipped through the air behind the soldiers as Genna, the young crodoc's bonded, circled the team of leviathan hunters. The agitated dracolli was stalking the Nasha Na'da but choosing not to get involved in the training. For now.

"Roth?"

An armored individual, standing toward the rear of the group, turned to look her direction.

"Four hours. Have him in the shuttle before this starts." Her voice carried beautifully across the courtyard, and she briefly envied the president. She wasn't sure if she was typical of all Tre'dalmor, but if she was, Lei could see why they were drawn to positions of power.

As she marched through the doorway into the presidential palace, the guards snapped to attention and saluted. She nodded to them as she passed. She'd spent the last week questioning the president and poring over video footage of the elar as she learned her mannerisms and thought processes. This wasn't Leilani's first time as a body double. In fact, she was damn good at it. The team had already moved Dana to a secure location far away from the danger. The only people privy to that information, however, were Leilani, the Nasha Na'da, and the people currently guarding her.

It took several days to convince the young dragon to go into hiding. They ended up impressing on her that their combined experience at infiltration was far more rational than her blind faith in her own people.

"Madam President?" A mousy-looking human slid up next to her and held out a pad. "We need your signature on this."

"What is it?" Leilani skimmed the pad without touching it.

The male frowned. He clearly had hoped she wouldn't ask.

Politicians were the same everywhere, and Severious was no different. Everyone that had access to the president, even her supposedly loyal staff, had been trying to sneak totalitarian changes past her since she took Severious system to a level two alert, which basically meant that all nonmilitary or emergency services needed to stop traveling and shelter in place.

"Senator Korlin is requesting permission to temporarily increase his militia numbers for the upcoming threat." There was a brief pause before the mousy man continued quickly. "In order to protect his constituents, of course."

Lei glared down at the man next to her. "Declined." A name flashed into her HuD. "And you should be ashamed of yourself, Norbert."

The man bowed deeply and stopped moving, allowing her to continue down the hall without him.

Another set of guards snapped to attention as she turned into the massive room filled with digital displays. Unlike before, the place was abuzz with over a dozen races all working to prepare the solar system for the inevitable invasion. It was almost deafening, and she grimaced as her ears adjusted to the volume.

In the center, at the large holo-table that displayed the solar system in real time, several military commanders were arguing over troop placement. Leilani, however, turned to her right and took the pad that was held out to her.

The woman next to her was a human with sandy-blond hair and sparkling green eyes—green eyes that never missed a thing.

"Norbert found you." Ginger narrowed her eyes before shifting back to her typical neutral expression.

"Yes." Leilani smirked as the young woman cursed softly under her breath. "Don't worry, I sent him on his way. I even chastised him for trying to use the emergency for political gain."

The woman's shoulders relaxed. "These are the reports you need to sign. I've already gone over and checked them."

Leilani continued walking as she skimmed the pad. She flicked her finger along it, scrolling the data faster than most people could read. Leilani wasn't most people. She was an undercover agent that didn't always have the luxury of time. As she switched to the third report, she paused about three quarters of the way down. Looking up, she scanned the crowd for the greduna standing a head taller than almost everyone else in the room.

As she marched toward her, another unusually tall individual drew her attention. Her stride shifted and she faltered slightly. At the far end of the room, in the darker area that occupied the internal intelligence group that Derek managed, was a massive eighteen-foot-tall bull, watching her intently.

Like many illotaur, he wore ribbons and beads in his thick, black hair and beard. Traditionally, a bull had unique patterns to their horns that depicted the tribe they came from. The last illotaur bulls she'd seen had horns that were over two feet long. But for whatever reason, this bull's horns were missing and capped with intricately carved, golden covers. Between the end caps and the skull, dozens of metal bands and tassels hung as trophies of his past. His face and fur were a dark reddish brown while his eyes were a soft golden color. He wore a large, billowing, red, silk shirt, with his thick arms folded across his chest.

"Ma'am?"

Leilani blinked and drew her attention back to the woman next to her.

"Are you okay?"

Taking a deep breath, she nodded and gave a brief flash of a smile. "I need to talk to the specialists."

"The reports, ma'am?"

The woman reached for the pad, but Leilani held on to it, using it to point to BB and Meeshani. "I'll sign them in a minute, but I need to have them look at this report before I do."

Ginger's composure faltered slightly, her pupils dilating and her heartrate climbing. She smiled, trying to hide her surprise, and bobbed her head. "Yes, ma'am. I'll come back for it when you're done then."

The young woman turned and headed for the door, but before she could get too far, two individuals in solid black armor stepped up to either side of her. They each took an arm as they led her out of the data center.

Turning her attention back to Derek's section of the command center, Lei found the bull still watching her. A faint smile curled into his cheeks as he subtly bowed his head in her direction.

Leilani bowed her head respectfully before returning her attention to the greduna and human less than ten feet from her.

"Ms. Eagleton, would you mind looking at this for me?" She held the pad out to the woman as she stepped up next to her older brother.

BB tapped his forehead respectfully. "Madam President."

"That report came in over twelve hours ago, and it looks like someone buried it as a line item. They waited till now to have me sign it."

"Someone knows?" BB asked quietly.

Leilani nodded but said nothing.

"Who gave this to you?" Meeshani Eagleton handed the pad back to Leilani.

"My personal aide." Leilani bounced the pad absently several times. It was a small behavior, or tell, that the president did when something agitated her. Leilani copied it perfectly.

The greduna woman grimaced then lifted her head to scan the crowded room. "Where is she?"

"Internal Intelligence picked her up a few seconds ago."

The human male next to her wrinkled his nose. "You mean that big cow guy?"

Leilani's arm twitched as she stopped herself from smacking him in the back of the head. "You mean the bull that can hear you? Even through all this noise?"

BB shot the bull a glance, then quickly stepped behind her, trying to put the president between himself and the illotaur.

"Dude, he looks pissed!"

"You were never really a big fan of being called a woman yourself," Lei teased. She turned her attention to the bull and found him still grinning. But then, a bull illotaur never really looked happy, unless one was familiar with their body language. This particular bull clearly found all the chaos entertaining, especially her and BB.

"What's he doing here, anyway?" Leilani asked. "I don't seem to have him in my staff database."

The greduna glanced over her shoulder at the bull, then back to Leilani. Jerking her head toward the illotaur, she asked, "You mean Maca?"

"If that's his name, then yes."

The tall woman looked down at them as she opened her mouth. Then suddenly, as if someone told her to remain silent, she closed it with the soft clack of teeth striking teeth. "No idea."

Leilani snorted, then covered her mouth and faked a cough. "You're a terrible liar. But fine, so long as it's not relevant to the mission."

"It's not." Meeshani bounced the pad in her hand and passed it back to Leilani.

"Fine. BB, I need you to find out who else knows. I'm not going through all of this just to have the entire plan fail at launch."

The human grabbed the imp currently using the console and set it on the ground. "Sorry, Yurt. I have my orders."

The green-skinned imp glared up at him and placed its fists on its hips. "Rude!"

"Blame her." BB waved his hand over his shoulder.

Resisting the urge to slap him again, Leilani instead returned her attention to the two-foot-tall imp as his curriculum vitae appeared in her HuD. "I'm sorry, Yurt. It appears our guest has a serious lack of manners."

"It's fine, Madam President. Is there anything else I can do then?" His high-pitched voice seemed to trigger an idea.

A coy smirk crept into the corners of her mouth. "In fact, there is."

32

THE TRAP IS SET

After the system-wide alert changed the threat level to maximum, command-and-control transferred to a designated emergency bunker. Leilani sat in the now utterly empty command center, gingerly sipping on a steaming cup of coffee. The holo image hovering over the table hadn't changed since last night.

Glancing up at the four Kassian destroyers parked at the gate, which led from the kuldain system of Bendaru to Severious, she sighed. They'd cracked the code to the gate eight hours ago, but they still had yet to move.

She was tired, and she wanted to put her feet up on the table, but resisted the urge. Movement at the edge of her vision drew her thoughts away from the Kassian vessels.

The tiny, green imp in a dark blue jumpsuit hopped up into the chair next to her, then up to the edge of the table. Imps didn't really fly, per se, but they could jump and glide with impressive skill.

Yurt grinned broadly, showing a row of needle-sharp teeth. He handed a smaller-than-typical pad to her. "You were right!"

She leaned forward, set her coffee on the table, and skimmed the imp's report. "I didn't really want to be right."

"Mmm, coffee. I really could use a cup, but I promised the wife. No more drugs while on the job." His voice sounded tired, and Lei could see why.

He'd clearly been at this all night, but an imp on coffee was akin to feeding a child an entire bag of candy. It really wasn't a pretty sight.

As she read on, the same name kept popping up in the report repeatedly. Xandel Corporation was a cyberware company that built technological implants for biological entities. They were the principal supplier for the draconis teams, system-wide. Every person born in Severious system had their tech imbedded within them. And 937 years ago, the head of security was a crodoc named Gordon Hendal.

"*Bring up Wendel's recording,*" Leilani asked her internal oracle.

An image flashed into her HuD of the crodoc with bloody hands. The image shifted in her view to overlay the pad, and Leilani grimaced. It was an exact match.

Lei closed the recording and returned her attention to the report. A year after Krelor erected the barrier, the board of directors made Gordon Hendal acting CEO of Xandel Corporation less than twenty-four hours after a rather nasty shuttle crash killed the old CEO and several members of the board. Six months after that, Xandel Corp slid into bed with Dracko-Tech and began producing cyberware to control the first round of *draconis drackova.*

A tiny, clawed hand appeared in her view. An extended finger pointed to a link at the bottom. "That's not the best part."

Clicking on the link directed Leilani to a second report about a communications company. GTI, or Galactic Telecom Incorporated, launched a year before the eldri-net went live, with a Gordon Hendal as the founder.

"Look at the board of directors."

She skimmed down the incorporation document until she found the list of the board members. The first name on the list was Brently Winston Fathrin, and the second was Delia Glemantha'tel—the yel'adari woman that shot Wendel's partner and stole the AI code. The rest of the names she didn't know personally, but the fourth name had a suffix that concerned her.

Suffixes were common in older elari lines. Originally, they denoted sex and caste of the elar. As history progressed, the castes interbred, and the tradition faded. Delia Glemantha'tel was a good example. The 'tel meant she was a female yel'adari.

But elari weren't the only ones to use the suffixes in this manner. In this case, the suffix was 'fa, which told her that the person was a male igranu. To say an igranu was rare in this arm of the galaxy was a serious understatement, but to find an igranu keeping the company of individuals such as Fathrin and Delia was disturbing. It would warrant investigation if she survived playing the body double.

She continued to read the second report as the doors behind her slid open, then closed.

"Good reading?" Dorthy sounded oddly cheerful.

Shaking her head, she glanced up at him, and her stomach growled angrily as she noticed the plate of food he was carrying.

"You haven't eaten in a while. So, I brought you something Derek made. I may not trust the little monster, but he's an amazing chef."

Trading him the pad for the plate, she stuffed a large portion of beef into her mouth. "Looks like Fathrin was here before us."

Dorthy frowned. "What?"

As he skimmed the reports, Leilani continued to stuff her face much faster than she should have if the shocked look on the imp's face was any sign. She flashed him an apologetic smile and slowed her inhalation.

"Do you need me for anything else, Madam President?" he asked.

She swallowed her food. "Were they communicating with the outside?"

He shook his tiny head, which caused his ears to flap. "Oddly, no. After the barrier, they seemed to forget the link was there." The imp shrugged his shoulders, flapping his wings. "But then most of us forgot that there was anything outside. Some people pieced things together later, but the masses seemed content to forget."

"Yurt, right?" Dorthy drew the imp's attention to him.

"Yes, sir."

The delonian beamed a charming smile at the creature. "This has been very helpful. You should probably get to the shelter before they seal the doors."

The imp bowed and leapt off the table. With almost no effort at all, he floated out the door and down the hall.

"I hate that smile," Leilani grumbled and stood as she set her now-empty plate on the table. "Don't get me wrong. It's sexy, but it's always fake."

He turned to face her and winked as the smile shifted to a coy grin.

"Now see, that's the one I love. What did you find?" Looking over his shoulder, she chuckled and pointed to the pad.

"The insider!" they said simultaneously.

On the pad was a report written for the GTI Board of Directors. It read: "Installation of the Autonomous Oracle into the Mobius Gate was a complete success." At the bottom of the screen, the words Artificially Intelligent Multi-Efficacy Latency Instrument spelled out the acronym AIMELI.

Mobius was Wendel's company with which he built homeomorphic ships capable of traversing both aether and kuldain space without need of switching power or drive systems.

"At least we now know where the AI code went." Leilani elbowed her partner.

"Okay, we now have to assume that Fathrin knows everything." His gaze traveled the length of her, then back up to lock on to her eyes. "You may be more of a body double than we thought."

She smiled and took a deep breath. "Awesome! It's not a case unless I'm on the verge of death at least once."

He threw back his head and let out a loud laugh, and before she realized what he was doing, he leaned in and kissed her. "Just in case I don't get to say it later, it's been both awe-inspiring and utterly infuriating knowing you."

"Maybe so, but I'm not dead yet." She smiled as they stared deep into each other's eyes.

"Oh, I know. I just wanted to kiss the president without getting slapped."

He leapt backward and ducked her swing.

"You jerk!" the Tre'dalmori president snapped at him as she stepped up to a panel next to the door and placed her hand on the pad. The computer system scanned the president's DNA, then flashed green.

It was too late to change the plan now, even if Fathrin knew everything. Luckily, neither of them had discussed the plan in its entirety outside of the secure IIS silcomms. Her playing body double for the president had been their backup. They both knew better than to expect the plan to go off without a hitch. They had too much experience. They knew there was an insider; they just hadn't found them. Until now.

Behind them, a soft chime echoed throughout the empty chamber as the lighting transitioned to blood-red. Above the table, the hologram of the massive ring flashed to life. The ships huddled around it shuffled their positions as they prepared to enter into Severious system. The halo around the ships shifted from yellow to red, but the two agents didn't need to watch the scene play out on the holo-table. They already knew what would happen next.

During the last couple of weeks of training, the constant clash of ranks and titles triggered several arguments among the teams. Finally, they all agreed to flatten the ranks and switch to last names instead. Since Leilani was the person managing the overall tactical plan, they'd all decided she was in positional authority.

She paused at the door and straightened her outfit.

Next to her, the drackova named Genna twisted her head. "Really? Now is a good time to check your clothing?"

"It's the perfect time." Lei grinned and passed her hand over her outfit one last time.

Genna was a beautiful creature with soft amber eyes, golden scales, and ivory horns and claws. She also had the pristine white teeth often found in the young. She was approximately fifteen feet long from the tip of her nose to the tip of her tail. Even at her young age, she was disturbingly lethal and insatiably curious.

"Why?"

Leilani patted the creature affectionately on its thick neck. "Billions of people all across the solar system are about to watch their president speak. Most of those people are afraid, and the rest are going to risk their lives to defend us. The responsibility of all leaders is to inspire confidence. We can do that by looking our best and by being strong and self-assured."

"But you are not our leader," the drackova retorted bluntly.

Lei chuckled and bobbed her head in agreement. "Yes, but they don't know that."

"Oh."

She patted the young drackova one more time and lifted her other hand to tell Rothar to begin the procession to the shuttle. Because of the possible information leak, Dorthy and Lei had made some last-minute changes to the evacuation. The door opened, and three guards in fully sealed armor strode out into the courtyard to secure it for her. "And now you understand the duty of an agent to the government."

Genna puffed out her chest and grinned broadly, baring a row of terrifyingly sharp teeth. "I *am* an agent of the government!"

"Yes, you are, Genna. Remember that as we go out there. Play your part, and remember that everything hinges on you and me. We have to convince our enemy that we're who he's looking for." Leilani reached out and touched a thin, golden chain around the young drackova's neck.

All powerful entities had a power signature. If Leilani wanted the young drackova to appear as a dragon, she'd need help. The president made the necklace to mimick her own signature before she left and then keyed it to Leilani. The necklace flashed briefly, sending a ripple of eldrich away from them. The creature's scales changed to smaller and more supple versions, rippling in the light. She grew a crown of scales and sharp horns on her head, which made her look like a *draconis imperious* hatchling, rather than an adolescent *draconis drackova*.

Lei knew the young drackova wouldn't trick a leviathan, especially not this one. Fathrin spent the last several hundred years living the life of a politician. She knew how his mind worked. She had to convince him that *she* was the actual hatchling—otherwise, everyone in Severious would be in serious trouble. The military wings of draconis might hold their own against the Kassian fleet, but there was no way they could handle an angry whathalis.

She'd stacked the deck by offering to act as the president's double. Now, she was near an active dragon enchantment, which was keyed to her. It would at least stand up to a casual examination. And if that didn't work, Leilani had, unbeknownst to anyone, secured a single scale shed by the young hatchling. It was now mounted on a silk harness next to her skin, just below her breasts.

So long as Fathrin stayed in his senator persona, which was an overconfident, elderly human male, she'd be okay. Well, maybe not okay, but at least the plan should work.

Behind her, a man in fully enclosed armor stepped up and said quietly, "Admiral Jedari'dei just entered Bendaru with three full fleets. We're a go."

Leilani took a deep breath and strode out into the courtyard, the fifteen-foot dragon hatchling trotting alongside her. It ran a circle around her as it checked the area, then fell back into place.

The guards behind them fanned out and watched the doors and windows as they tried to usher her quickly into the shuttle. Leilani, however, refused to be rushed. She continued her long, confident strides toward the ship. When she was about halfway there, she looked up toward the gaggle of drones hovering off to one side and triggered the microphone built into her outfit.

"To the invaders, my name is president Dana Gath'Dalithi. I am the duly elected president of the closed solar system of Severious. I will only issue this warning once. Entering into our sovereign space, without permission, is an act of war. Return now to your own space, and we will not pursue. We do not recognize the Kassian tradition of prisoner trade. If you enter Severious space, you will never return home. You *will* die here." Leilani recited the president's words exactly as she was instructed, careful not to change even a single pause for effect.

The two women had argued for hours over the action of killing naval sailors who were just following orders. In the end, Leilani conceded that this was not Kassian space and that the president had the legal right to proceed according to their laws—laws that were written for pirates, not trained soldiers.

She turned back to the shuttle and saw a massive, blue dracolli on the rooftop nearby. It shifted its weight from side to side as it stretched its wings, readying for flight. As she boarded the vessel, several icons in her HuD shifted from yellow to green as the last of the team boarded the vessel. The doors sealed just before the shuttle rocked as the dracolli team landed on top of them.

"Dorn is in place and awaiting orders, ma'am," a young male crodoc called from the front of the shuttle.

"Let's get this over with," she replied.

The shuttle rocked harder as the bonded team lifted it into the air and began the slow climb out of Severious Prime's atmosphere.

33

DARKNESS

Leilani sat in a seat near the front of the shuttle. The calm before the storm was always a welcome respite for the soldier. It gave her a chance to center herself and collect her thoughts. She went over the plan one more time in her head.

She was about to go toe-to-toe with a creature so old and so powerful that she really couldn't process the threat. All she knew was that her likelihood of survival was extremely low. But even then, the bait on the end of the hook rarely survived.

A friend once told her there were no ends. No matter what happened today, it was simply the beginning of something new.

"*That is a lovely sentiment,*" Sarah chimed into her thoughts.

Her internal oracle had been quiet ever since the outburst in the president's private home. Leilani knew it was partially her fault.

"*But it's not the end or the beginning you need to dread. It's the monotony that exists forever,*" Sarah added solemnly.

Leilani frowned, then remembered that others could see her face. She took a deep breath and relaxed her body and expression.

"You know, ever since Dorthy faked his death, you've been a little off. Is everything okay?" Lei was genuinely concerned about Sarah, even if now wasn't the best timing.

"Define 'okay'."

The brooding tone caused her to take a deep breath. If the oracle got too moody, it would affect her, as she'd recently learned, and she couldn't risk losing control of her emotions right now.

"Look, Sarah. It's been a rough couple of years, but that doesn't mean you aren't still my partner."

"Would I be if you had the choice?"

Leilani walled off her thoughts from the oracle and immediately answered, *"Of course."*

The truth was not what Sarah or Leilani needed right now. Getting the unstable AI out of her head was a problem for another day.

"Try telling me the truth." Sarah's anger fed into the communication, but it didn't threaten to overwhelm Leilani.

"Fine. You want the truth? Something is wrong. I don't know what it is, and yes, I think we should get you looked at for both our sakes, but now is not the time to be brooding over this shit! You are damn good at what you do! And no matter what happens, you are my partner and my best friend. You have been for as long as I can remember." Leilani balled her fists in her lap as her own anger welled up. *"Stop acting like a temperamental child and get your head in the fucking game!"*

There was silence for what seemed like an eternity. Then, as if it were in the distance, Leilani could hear the faint sound of laughter.

She took a deep breath and shook her head. *"Obnoxious bitch."*

"Agreed, ma'am." The laughter faded. *"But you are, of course, correct. This isn't something you should take lightly. I apologize."*

"You can do that?"

"Don't start. I'm making a gesture here."

"Yeah, that's part of the problem. Wait, did you say something I *shouldn't take lightly?"*

"Yes."

"We're about to start a fight with a leviathan. The odds of survival are pretty damn low, and that doesn't have you at least a little concerned?"

"You have an excellent plan. I know leviathans all too well. They're all the same. They always underestimate mortals. Trust me. You'll be fine."

Before Leilani could respond, she heard Dorthy's voice across the shuttle.

"Nine ships just entered system. Two of them peeled off and are heading toward GTI's orbital arcology, and seven are heading straight for us."

"Understood." Leilani opened her eyes and stood. She strolled to the cockpit and rested her hand on the young crodoc pilot's shoulder. "Open the encrypted channel."

The young soldier chuckled. "Yes, ma'am."

Leilani smirked and patted his shoulder. "We have to give them at least something they understand, or they'll be suspicious."

A green light flashed on the panel.

"Go ahead, Madam President."

"Alpha and gamma, you are clear to proceed with phase one."

"Roger, Madam President," the female commander of wing alpha replied across the antiquated communication channel.

No one in Severious used actual radio communications. They used a heavily modified and encrypted form of psionic multiphase field communication. It was a system that could handle the sheer power of the hundreds of thousands of draconis in system. As well as manage the near instant, planet-to-planet and station-to-planet communications.

Kassian vessels didn't have sensors for that frequency, and the utter silence could spook their prey, so Wendel and Jorna had built a few regular communication units and equipped some of the team leads with them. They'd even added an antiquated encryption from nine hundred years ago to make it look realistic while giving the Kassian Naval personnel a sense of overconfidence.

"And, Yadere, be careful. These aren't pirates."

Commander Ysandre Yadere didn't need to project emotion with her response. Her confidence was obvious to anyone listening. "Don't worry about us, ma'am. We'll be fine. Yadere, out."

"Permission to ask a question, ma'am?" The young crodoc looked up over his shoulder at her.

"Of course, Mauro."

The sensor panel in front of them showed two V-shaped wings of green dots closing in on either side of the seven red dots.

He pointed to the sensor panel in front of him. "Why are we doing fly-bys? That's not standard protocol."

Leilani smiled and squeezed his shoulder. She loved the curiosity of children. Up to a point. "You're in officer training, right?"

"Yes, ma'am."

"Have you learned about operational security?"

"Yes, ma'am."

"Sometimes, when you're fighting an enemy, it's useful to only show them what they expect to see. That way, you can keep your strengths close to your chest. Then, if—or when—things go wrong, you still have a leg up."

"Because you can switch to the superior tactic." The young crodoc rubbed his hands together in excitement. "We're basically playing dead, or at least a form of it."

"Something like that, yes. We're showing weakness on purpose. If we seem overwhelmingly dangerous, they might run. And we need them to board us, not run."

"We aren't taught these kinds of deception tactics." He frowned up at her and folded his arms. "I believe that might be a flaw in our training."

On the sensor display, the two wings of red drackova tore past the vessels, ripping sections of the Kassian ships open to space, then continuing on. Their orders were to inflict just enough damage to open specific sections of the ships to space and enact Kassian damage control protocols. By strafing the ships, then making large, slow loops back toward the vessels, the drackova and their riders displayed a clumsy lack of maneuverability—a bald-faced deception which wouldn't last long—but for now, they were still trying to lay the trap for the much larger prey.

When Dorthy originally suggested the tactic at the strategy meeting with the wing commanders, both ex-agents had expected more of an argument. But the commanders saw it for what it was, a ruse. Unexpectedly, they loved the idea.

When their engine compartments tore open to space, the Kassian ships followed protocol 212-Bravo. They spread out, ensuring that if one of the hydrogen bottles went, it didn't take the rest of the ships with them. As they scattered, only one ship continued on course. The other six focused their attention on the Ruby Flight and began weaving a tactical pattern as a wall of missiles launched.

Leilani reached down to the panel next to the main scanner and tapped on the lone red dot. As the image magnified, it switched to a live feed of the Kassian Destroyer IKS Hoganmeyer.

"See, we cut the prey from the herd." Turning her head so that her voice carried into the main compartment, Leilani added, "ETA fifteen. Looks like he's keeping his cover. They're prepping a boarding collar."

"Thank you, ma'am."

She squeezed the young crodoc's shoulder, then strode back into the main compartment.

Thirteen individuals in highly advanced armor, unlike anything she'd ever seen, were standing in a small cluster near the rear of the shuttle, chatting quietly while Dorthy leaned back against the bulkhead to her left.

"It's the Hoganmeyer." She grinned as she spoke.

Both Dorthy and Rothar turned wide eyes on her.

"Are you kidding?" A coy grin crept across Dorthy's face.

Roth shook his head. He was wearing his helmet, but she could still hear him laugh. "Do you think it's a coincidence?"

"Possibly, but I doubt it." She stepped up next to a seat and slid her elbow onto the back of it.

Dorthy strolled up to stand next to her. "I really wish we were putting you in armor right now."

"You and me both, but that's not how this needs to work, and you know it." She tapped her index finger on the delonian chest plate Fendrick had given Dorthy to wear. "Besides, it's not me he's mad at. It's Fendrick. He needs Dana alive."

Leilani stood there quietly as the team completed one last check of their gear, then spread out through the shuttle to their assigned locations. Rothar had explained to Leilani how the Nasha Na'da team worked. They each carried highly unique weaponry. When the time came, they would create a web of energy with the weapons. The goal was to keep the target constantly overwhelmed with the various bands of energy. Some energy types were diametric opposites, and if crossed, could cause an explosion that destroyed everything for a parsec, which was why they had a specific deployment pattern.

When Leilani asked about the power levels of the weapons, he couldn't answer, explaining that it was classified. But he gave her an example: the eldrich weapon he deployed was the same as stepping into a major eldrilin.

"Two minutes," the young crodoc called from the cockpit.

"Mauro, close the door and seal it until this is over."

His reply was higher pitched than typical. "Ma'am?"

"You heard me," she snapped. "I know you want to help, so help by being one less thing I need to worry about."

One of the heavily armored Nasha Na'da paused alongside her and whispered, "Easy, ma'am. He's just a kid. He feels helpless. Even though he's trained his whole life to fight, he's in over his head, and he knows it."

"All the more reason not to argue and shut the damn door." She glared up at the dark faceplate.

The helmet shook slowly, but he said nothing as he strode to his position.

The familiar clang of a docking ring deploying against the shuttle's hull rang through the small shuttle. Leilani closed her eyes and took a deep breath. A loud pop rang through the shuttle as the lock pressurized. She strolled to the middle of the compartment and settled herself with her feet shoulder-width apart and her hands clasped behind her back.

Dorthy stepped up next to her and sealed the helmet on his armor. Sliding the delonian rifle around to the front of him, he clicked off the safety. It wouldn't hurt the senator, but they still weren't entirely sure what to expect from the Kassians.

As the door slid open, several Kassian marines in powered armor flooded aboard. At the rear of them stood a man in a naval commodore's uniform. His hair was a little greyer than the last time she'd seen him, but the stern look on his face hadn't changed.

A single marine kept his weapons trained on Leilani and Dorthy, while the rest covered the others.

Without a word, Commodore Greggory Bain strolled onto the large shuttle.

"Greetings, Madam President. I'm looking for Agent Leilani Falconi."

Leilani arched a single eyebrow, mimicking the president's mannerisms. "There is no one here by that name."

The man scanned the armored soldiers then returned his attention to her. "No, I suppose not. Thank you for your time." He turned back toward the lock before pausing and adding over his shoulder. "If you do happen to see her, please tell her the Kassian emperor would like a private word, if she can find the time."

Leilani resisted the urge to look up at the delonian next to her as the naval officer strolled off the shuttle.

"They're all yours, Senator," he called from just inside his side of the docking collar.

An elderly man with grey hair at his temples stepped into view and smiled warmly. "Thank you, Commodore Bain."

Leilani kept her attention on the senator as he approached the lock.

"That will be all, marines." Senator Brently Winston Fathrin stepped onto the shuttle and scanned the space.

A marine nearest to the lock spoke up. "That is not a good idea, Senator."

"I said get out!" Power rolled from the whathalis pretending to be human.

As it reached the marines, they turned and bolted through the lock. Commodore Bain, however, stood his ground and narrowed his eyes angrily as his marines tore past him. Ignoring the fear effect, he tapped his forehead with his fingertips before bowing toward Leilani and her guard. With a smooth gesture, he reached to the side of the docking ring and slapped the console that controlled the docking collar. The hatches on both vessels sealed with a loud hiss followed by a *ka thung* as the docking collar released her vessel.

The sound of the lock closing behind him caused the senator to raise his eyebrows in surprise. Leilani kept her face neutral, refusing to give him any reason to be suspicious.

She'd never actually met the senator in person. He was good at masking his power signature, but it was still there, even if it was oddly underwhelming. But then, the only other whathalis she'd ever met was sitting in the middle of a mega nexus. Perhaps this was how they usually felt?

"Looks like your ride is leaving." She lifted her chin.

Waving his hand over his shoulder toward the lock, the Senator returned his attention to her. "It is of no matter. I no longer need them. I have what I came for."

"Do you?" She finally allowed herself a coy grin.

His eyes narrowed, and in a blinding flash, he closed the space between them and wrapped his fingers around Dorthy's neck. Before she could even react, he ripped the helmet from his head and narrowed his eyes angrily at Dorthy's grinning face.

That brief pause was all Dorthy needed. His hand snapped up and slapped the sealbands onto the senator's wrist.

With a superhuman toss, the senator launched him into the bulkhead with a loud crash. The delonian slumped to the ground, unmoving, but Leilani didn't have time to worry about her partner.

Dropping to the deck, she spun, attempting to kick Fathrin's feet out from under him, but her heel met only air.

Above her, she heard a deep, menacing laugh.

"Do you honestly think your meager IIS toys will hold me?"

He reached for the spreading band with his free hand. As he tried to rip it off, it expanded to the empty hand. His eyes widened until she could clearly see the whites. He struggled against the slowly expanding cuffs with an increased sense of panic.

Around the shuttle, a soft whine began as the Nasha Na'da soldiers pointed their weapons at him.

Leilani, however, rolled backward away from him as his panic swiftly shifted to rage.

He'd finally realized the trap for what it was. Then, suddenly, he fell to the deck and stopped struggling. His jaw tilted upward as he angled his head to the side. A grin crept across his face, and his eyes locked on to Leilani. "I see you now."

Her skin crawled, warning her of the danger.

"Well played, Leilani. I should have recognized your signature earlier." His voice was calm and collected.

She arched an eyebrow. There was no way he was giving up this easily.

"You were useful to me, but I'm done playing with you." He jutted his chin toward the stirring delonian. "I'm surprised you're working with him again. After everything he's done to you."

Ah, that made more sense. He was going to try turning them against each other.

"After all, he framed you for his own murder. I'm not sure I would be so tolerant."

"He had his reasons."

Fathrin rolled to a seated position on the deck. "Perhaps, but what about Dalori Eight? Did you ever figure out who gave that Ka'va to Senator Hawthorn? Or why your own commander would fight so hard to pin it on you?"

Before Leilani could respond, an explosion rocked the shuttle. The gravity compensators fluttered. The senator and Leilani floated briefly before the compensators kicked back on and they fell to the deck.

Leilani landed in a crouched position, her eyes still locked on the target.

Another explosion rocked the shuttle, and the lights shifted to a soft orange color. Kassian ships didn't use orange, but Fathrin didn't seem concerned with the change.

Leilani and the other occupants of the shuttle, however, knew the orange hue meant they'd lost their dracolli. They were floating free in space. Not a good thing, even without being in the middle of a firefight.

Leilani kept her attention on the man in front of her. He was stalling, and she wasn't sure why. Then, finally, she felt a sensation crawl across her skin. He was drawing in power. Wendel built the bands to block all energy, which was why she didn't notice it right away.

She flattened herself on the deck and rolled away from the senator. "Now!"

A golden dracolli shimmered into view. Twisting into a tight ball, she spun, uncoiling her tail, and knocked the senator across the shuttle so hard that he left a humanoid shape in the hull. If Fathrin had been human, he would've been paste.

The air in the space charged painfully as a dozen highly specialized weapons fired various streams of energy into Fathrin. Around her, the IIS armor deployed briefly, but the technology instantly failed.

"*So much for that idea,*" Lei thought to her internal system.

"*Ma'am, his power is continuing to climb.*"

The number sixty appeared in her HuD and flipped to sixty-one.

"At this rate, he will reach sufficient power to not only destroy his bands, but he will blow the ship and everything within a thousand miles." Sarah remained calm.

The lack of emotion threw Leilani, and she wondered just how much control the oracle had over her emotional state. *"If he blows the ship, we lose. Period. Suggestions?"*

"You will have to contain it."

"Me?"

"Yes, you."

"Alright, and how do you suggest I do that?"

"Remember the Ka'va?" Sarah seemed pleased.

Leilani rolled her eyes. *"You're kidding, right? That almost killed me."*

"That is always a possibility when dealing with leviathans." She could almost feel the oracle shrug its nonexistent shoulders.

"So much for being 'just fine'."

Leilani pushed herself to her feet. Ducking under the electrical beam closest to her, she ignored the arc of lightning as it slammed into her arm, causing it to go numb temporarily.

In the briefing, the Nasha Na'da explained that the mix of energies would destabilize a leviathan, making it hard for him to use his own power. The leviathan-grade sealbands were slow-acting. They wouldn't reach full power until the metal encased his entire body, which meant they had to keep him off-balance until the process was complete.

It didn't matter what Leilani did at this point. Everyone's survival depended on their ability to keep him destabilized. The soldiers wouldn't stop their continuous assault until the sealbands completed their binding.

The last time Leilani attempted to stop an out-of-control leviathan, it hadn't gone well for her. Not only did she end up in a regrow tank for several weeks, but Dorthy and the IIS banished her from Kassian space for it. But this time, she had an idea. It might kill her, but it might not. Either way, if she did nothing, they were all dead, so it wouldn't matter.

Lei didn't even look toward Rothar as she stepped in front of his weapon. The eldrich slammed into her back and arced across her body, causing her arms to flail wildly. She screamed.

Just like when she'd talked to Krelor, the surrounding shuttle froze. She took a step forward, keeping her body in the stream as she half floated, half walked, toward the leviathan. He was so focused on drawing energy that he didn't notice her until she was standing directly in front of him.

She didn't need her HuD to know he was almost ready to break free from the confines. She could easily feel his power now. His eyes snapped up to meet hers as she reached forward to place her hand on his head.

His face contorted into a horrific visage of a humanoid with red skin, solid black eyes, and thousands of spiked horns in place of hair. He hissed at her, baring several rows of needle-sharp teeth, but she ignored his threat.

As she pulled his power from him, she uttered a single word. "No."

The power exploded outward from him like a catastrophic bomb. As the energy impacted her, she allowed her body to absorb it in a brilliant flash of blinding white light.

The blast knocked Leilani away from him, slamming her back into her own body. The screams suddenly began again as her body slumped to the ground and the universe faded to black.

34

VOICE IN THE SHADOW

Leilani sat up and rubbed her arms and legs as she tried to force her overly charged nerves to calm down. She took a deep breath and furrowed her brow. Everything was still black, but she appeared to be fine . . . minus the overly agitated nerves.

"Hello?" She pushed herself onto her feet and turned in a circle. She could see herself but nothing else.

"Hello, Leilani." Sarah's voice echoed around her instead of inside her head.

"Are we dead?"

From the darkness, a tall, elegant creature with translucent wings, that appeared to be covered in stars, strode forward. Her eyes were black, and where the iris should be was a slowly spiraling galaxy. Her pale skin was a stark contrast to the dark eyes and black translucent material she wore, which fluttered around her as if in a nonexistent breeze. She had long ears that tapered to a fine point, protruding from pure white hair that cascaded down her back. Her bare feet and arms gave her an almost innocent appearance.

She sauntered up to Leilani and smiled warmly, clasping her hands in front of her. "No, my dear. We are fine. I just felt it was time we meet."

The voice was clearly Sarah's, but this was not the image Leilani imagined when she envisioned her oracle.

"Sarah?"

The creature bowed her head. "Yes."

"You're not an oracle."

Sarah cocked her head to the side, and the galaxies in her eyes flashed slightly. "No, I am not."

"What are you?"

"That is a discussion for another day. I just felt it was time to be honest with you. You have stepped into the next stage of your evolution and they will soon force me to leave you. But I wanted you to know that no matter what happens, you and I will always be a part of each other. And for that, I can never thank you enough."

The darkness waned as light flooded in from the edges of her vision. As the darkness faded, so did the image of the beautiful creature.

"*Sarah, wait—*"

"She's waking up," Rothar's voice called out.

The sound of heavily booted feet told her she was still aboard the shuttle.

As she turned her head to look around, she found the senator lying on the ground a few feet away among three of the Nasha Na'da, each of them focused on the unconscious leviathan in case he roused. On the other side of her, a drackova stood next to her bond-mate with her tail wrapped protectively around the young crodoc. They both watched her, their brows etched with deep concern—an odd look on the young drackova.

Looking directly over her, she found Rothar and Dorthy smiling proudly.

She couldn't help but chuckle as the crodoc winked and held out his hand to help her up. The lights in the shuttle were flashing red, but the people seemed to be intact.

A cheer erupted throughout the small shuttle as she stood, and her cheeks flushed as she shook her head in disbelief.

Apparently, her insane plan had worked after all.

Dorthy slapped her on the back. "Come on, you insane bitch. We have a prisoner to process."

EPILOGUE

Leilani leaned back in the overstuffed chair and crossed her legs at the knee. She wasn't pretending to be the Severious president anymore, but oddly, she had no desire to prop her feet up on the table in front of her. As she turned her attention to the people walking by outside, she smiled at a man carrying his daughter on his shoulders. The girl pointed to various sights from her new vantage point. Each time, she would squeal happily and smack her father on the top of his head until he looked where she pointed.

A woman in a tight, black skirt and green blouse stepped into view. As she lowered herself into the chair next to Leilani, she took a sip of her steaming hot beverage.

"Hello, Dana." Lei lifted her hand in greeting, then rested it back on the arm of the chair.

"Lei." The woman nodded but didn't look in her direction. "He sends his thanks for saving the fleet. And minimizing casualties where you could."

"Mmhm." Leilani folded her hands neatly in her lap.

The woman finally looked at the ex-agent. "Dorthy?"

"He's moved on."

"That's a shame. He won't be happy about that. But I suppose Dorthy's served the crown long enough. He's earned the right to move on. And you?"

"I'm surprised you had to ask. If I had moved on, we wouldn't be talking."

"Understood, but I had to ask. Protocol after all. Very well, continue on mission." The woman stood and stepped up alongside Leilani's chair. "Oh, and he wants to see you at your earliest convenience."

"I'm aware. I'll get there when I can."

"Understood. Good luck, Agent Falconi."

The woman strode away, and Leilani returned her attention to the people passing by outside.

"I like the new look." A comforting voice broke into her thoughts, and Leilani craned her head to look up at Dorthy as he stepped into view.

He held a large ceramic cup out to her, and she took it gingerly. Lowering it till it was under her nose, she breathed in the warm scent of her favorite brew. The pure white foam on top had an artistic pattern poured into it. It was such a beautiful piece of art; she almost didn't want to drink it.

"I've been wanting to ask you something, but we've been so busy with the hearings and the miles of paperwork." He settled into the seat next to her, effectively blocking her view of the sidewalk.

"Hmm?" she replied through her nose as she took a gentle sip of the amazing cappuccino.

"I was wondering if you'd be interested in being my partner long term?"

She looked over the top of the coffee cup. His posture was relaxed, as was his expression, but she could see the tension in his eyes as he waited for her reply.

"*What do you think?*" she asked Sarah.

An image of a head with black eyes and white hair appeared in her Heads up Display. "*I kind of like him. Not as much as you do, of course, but enough to keep working with him.*"

Leilani grinned and took another sip to hide the expression. "*Working with someone that you're also sleeping with will have dangerous consequences.*"

"*Agreed.*" The strange image of Sarah laughed. "*You already knew your answer before you asked me. Why make him wait?*"

"*I enjoy seeing him squirm.*"

His eyes narrowed as he realized what she was doing, and he took a sip of his tea, watching her patiently.

Sarah laughed. "*Wow, that's vicious.*"

Lowering her cup into her lap, Leilani smiled at him. "You never explained exactly what it is you do."

"Yes, I did. You're just stalling. But I suppose we should discuss how it would work. I've never really taken a partner. I propose we split the fees fifty-fifty. That is after expenses, of course." He tilted his hand toward himself. "I would be the lead investigator just because of my years of experience."

"Older doesn't always mean wiser," Leilani teased.

He took a deep breath through his nose and shook his head. "Always the consummate smart-ass."

"Nah, that was a fact, not snark." She lifted her cup and took another sip.

The two of them were quiet as they both stared at their cups, lost in their own thoughts.

"You realize that if we partner, anything between us is gone, right?" Leilani asked the question they were both contemplating.

Dorthy looked up and met her gaze. "I'm not—"

"There you two are!" an excited male voice called from across the coffee house. "Meeshani, they're over here!"

BB walked between the two of them and flopped into a chair to Leilani's left. He had a doughnut in his hand and happily stuffed it into his mouth all in one bite.

Leilani licked her lips and pulled her gaze from Dorthy to focus on her brother.

"Did I miss anything?" Bits of doughnut flew from his overly stuffed mouth.

Lei smiled and shook her head. "No. We were just discussing the future."

"Awesome!" BB reached up to take his large soda from the greduna woman who'd stepped up next to him. "What's next, boss?"

Leilani's smile grew into a knowing grin, and she turned to face the delonian. "Yes. What's next, fearless leader?"

Dorthy laughed and craned his neck to look up at the greduna. "Please have a seat, Ms. Eagleton. Our new clients asked for all of us to be here."

"Why me?" Meeshani frowned as she pulled over a larger chair and sunk into it.

Dorthy shrugged. "I have no idea. They said you'd understand when you saw them."

"Are we seriously not talking about the elephant in the room?" BB threw his hands in the air. "Tell me that trial wasn't the weirdest thing you've ever seen!"

"It was . . ." Leilani paused as she looked for a good adjective.

"I can honestly say that feeling small was a new sensation for me." Meeshani shook her head and wrinkled her nose. "If you people feel that way all the time, I can see why you're so aggressive."

Leilani and Dorthy laughed.

"Did the greduna just call *us* aggressive?" Dorthy slapped his knee.

Meeshani shrugged.

"I'm just glad they found him guilty. Man, can you imagine that whale thing free to hunt us down? I've never seen anything that furious!" BB shuddered and rubbed his arms.

"You would know about angry people," Lei teased. "And he was a whathalis, not a whale. I, however, didn't find the Grand Draconis

Tribunal surprising. What threw me was that second trial with the Leviathan Conglomeration. That one I didn't expect."

Dorthy shook his head. "No one did. Not even the dragons, as evidenced by the sudden show of force from their war council. But everyone answers to someone, I suppose. Apparently even the Grand Council of Dragons. Did you see the look on the grand chancellor's face when the Galactic Fellowship of Greater Races charged him and his daughter for crimes against sentient species?"

BB and Leilani turned to stare at Dorthy, but it was Leilani who spoke up first.

"There was a look on his face?"

"That thing was male?" BB asked right after her.

Meeshani chuckled.

Dorthy ignored their questions. "All I'm saying is that none of that was what I expected."

"Well, at least we weren't the ones on trial for once." Leilani waved a hand in front of her.

The three ex-IIS agents laughed as they all nodded in agreement.

Behind Dorthy, the people on the sidewalk froze mid-stride as a well of dark power built up behind them.

Dorthy reached for his weapons while BB threw himself to the floor and rolled up behind Dorthy, his own weapon pointed over the delonian's shoulder. Across from Leilani, the greduna turned her attention toward the welling of power and pulled her hands to rest casually in her lap.

Leilani lifted her cup to her lips and took another sip. She recognized the energy's signature and was surprised it took him this long to come find her.

When the inevitable pop echoed through the room, Meeshani's posture relaxed, and she reached for her own drink.

"Impressive entrance," Leilani tossed over her shoulder without looking.

The boyish figure strode around the chair and hopped up into the seat that BB had vacated. Derek shrugged his shoulders and allowed his hands to go even with his ears before letting them fall into his lap. "When dealing with trigger-happy assassins, I find it helps to announce myself."

A female voice behind her chided the meleini. "Derek. The people?"

"Oh, yeah." He lifted a hand and snapped his fingers. The sound in the coffeehouse started back up as the people outside continued on their journey, utterly unaware of the interruption.

The female behind her moved into view, and Leilani took a slow, deep breath. It was the same small greduna she'd seen at Professor Eagleton's when all of this began. Her arms were visible now, showing off some rather spectacular blueish-silver tattoos that held so much power it made Leilani's skin itch to be near them. Her long, dark braid made the white streaks stand out as they wove back and forth. Her eyes were a similar silvery-blue color to the tattoos and also held power. She stood only eight feet tall, which made her very short for a greduna, but very tall for a human.

Leilani wondered again if perhaps she was some sort of cross between a human and a greduna. If so, that was not a comforting thought.

The woman moved around behind Derek and stood with her hands resting on the back of his chair.

"Thank you for coming, Leilani. This is Rainfeather of Clan Blue Mountain, though she prefers Rain."

The greduna woman's hand snaked out and slapped the boy on the side of his head. "I can speak for myself."

He grimaced and rubbed his head. "Ow. Fine. You talk, then."

"The Weavers Council is hoping to hire you four for a minor problem," Rain stated firmly.

"You're finally going to listen to me?" Meeshani spat.

The tattooed woman ignored the angry greduna and continued to talk to Leilani and Dorthy. "The very fabric of reality is at stake."

Leilani blinked several times at the woman.

"Dramatic much?" BB quipped from where he now stood behind Dorthy.

"I find the fabric of reality unraveling dramatic, if that's what you're asking." Rain didn't divert her attention from Dorthy and Lei.

"That doesn't really sound like a minor problem." BB's shoulders sagged.

Leilani turned her attention to the meleini. "Derek?"

The boyish creature chuckled and lifted his hand toward the woman behind him. "She's the boss, not me. If she wants to be ridiculously melodramatic, that's her choice." He ducked, even though the woman didn't move.

He relaxed and sat back upright before continuing. "But she is correct. We do have a problem. We need your help to fix the loom."

Leilani arched both eyebrows high on her forehead. "The loom is broken?"

Both greduna women and the meleini nodded.

She and BB turned to look at Dorthy expectantly.

"*Well, you never answered my question.*" Dorthy's voice resounded in her head through the silcomm.

Her face softened, and she smiled. "*I'm surprised you had to ask. It would be my honor to keep working with you. It's an even bigger honor to do so as an equal partner.*"

Dorthy smiled back at her, the tension in his eyes relaxing into pure relief. He turned his attention back to the tattooed woman, lifting his jaw proudly. "My team and I will take the job."

ACKNOWLEDGMENTS

I'd like to thank Brown Books for their constant support. They love the Eldrilin Chronicles, and each time I come to them with a new adventure they can't wait to read them. These books would not be possible without their inspiring confidence.

Thank you to Erynn Newman, my editor, for keeping me on track and constantly pushing me to write more vivid scenes.

A special thank you to my family, who always allowed me to be the crazy kid with hundreds of invisible friends. Even though that family has grown, they all still support my storytelling by listening.

And lastly, thank you, my reader. Without you, there would be no story. You motivate me each day to try harder and to write more. So, stay tuned, we have a long roadmap laid out ahead of us.

WENDI COFFMAN-PORTER

Wendi Coffman-Porter grew up an only child in a military family. She spent a lot of time as a child inventing new friends and sharing them with others. She began writing her stories down at the age of ten, and by the time her first child was born, she'd written her first novel. Her passion has always been the colorful canvas and creative freedom of fantasy and sci-fi.

Wendi is always developing something new and colorful to share with others, whether she is role-playing or writing in her office at home in Texas in the middle of her pack of furry friends. Her fervor for incredibly rich realities that are as authentic as the ones outside your own window is what drives her to constantly find out what's happening around the next corner. She strives for a deep, new understanding of the nature of life, no matter what form that life might take.

Wendi lives with her family in Copper Canyon, Texas.